FRIENDS

LIARS

A NOVEL

KAELA COBLE

sourcebooks
landmark

Published by Sourcebooks Landmark, an imprint of Sourcebooks, Inc.
P.O. Box 4410, Naperville, Illinois 60567-4410
(630) 961-3900
Fax: (630) 961-2168
sourcebooks.com

Library of Congress Cataloging-in-Publication Data

Names: Coble, Kaela, author.
Title: Friends and other liars : a novel / Kaela Coble.
Description: Naperville, Illinois : Sourcebooks Landmark, [2018]
Identifiers: LCCN 2017014799 | (softcover)
Subjects: LCSH: Homecoming--Fiction. | Friendship--Fiction.
Classification: LCC PS3603.O255 F75 2018 | DDC 813/.6--dc23 LC record available at https://lccn.loc.gov/2017014799

Printed and bound in Canada.
MBP 10 9 8 7 6 5 4 3 2

To my crew, for the family kind of friendship that endures through all the drama, that feels the same no matter the time or distance between meetings, and that loves even when it doesn't like.

PROLOGUE

DANNY
NOW

LOOK AT THEM. I'M DEAD AND THEY'RE STILL PISSING ME OFF.

They're disgusting. Sitting in their pew, huddled together like a pack of wolves. Each playing their part in mourning—the bereaved, the wilted, the guilty. They clutch at one another, leaning on each other physically and emotionally for support. Shaking heads, balled fists, crocodile tears. Asking why, how. Dabbing their swollen eyes with crumpled tissues. Declaring their loyalty and love for one another. For me.

Really, they hate each other, and they hate themselves, and they hate me for making them face their own mortality. And they love me because it fuels their sick sense of pride in their little clan. The crew, they call themselves, even though they haven't been whole for a decade. "Still supporting each other after all these years," they declare, even though they wouldn't know true support if it helped them climb out of a grave.

There's Ally, the great beauty of Chatwick, sitting tall and stoic, practically cradling a weeping, whimpering Steph in her arms. Ally's expression as she comforts Steph says everything about her that you need to know. In this most horrifying moment, she is proud to be the crew's leader, to be the default person in whom to find solace. But the tightness around her lips and the slight narrowing of her eyes shows a bit of the self-righteousness she feels. Steph is a girlfriend of the crew, not an original member. What right does she have to this display? Ally shoots glances at her perfect husband, Aaron. High school sweethearts; couldn't you just puke? Talk about not being an original member... Aaron the dreamboat isn't one either. He didn't swoop in until our sophomore year of high school. And if you ask me, we would have been just fine without him.

Emmett and Aaron sit together instead of with their respective significant others, no doubt upon Emmett's insistence. He has always orchestrated the seating arrangements to split between genders. He's the youngest of three brothers, and therefore the noise, the gossip, and the full range of feminine feelings have always made him uncomfortable. The heightened emotional state caused by my death is no doubt more unbearable for him than my death itself. That he is allowing Ally to tend to his sobbing girlfriend, offering no comfort of his own, comes as no surprise.

He and Aaron mimic the same posture—leaned forward, their elbows resting on the thighs of their cheap woolen pants. They face the front of the church, careful not to make eye contact with each other, so they won't have to utter one of the lame platitudes they've heard too many times over the past days. "He's in a better place." "He's finally at peace." And my personal favorite: "He's with Roger now."

While they should be focusing on the tragedy that is (was) my life, instead my casket is a big, fat, polished-cedar reminder that one day this will be them. They ponder all the predictable questions that even people of the mildest intellect contemplate when faced with untimely death: *Where do we go when we die? What will they say about me when I'm gone? What does it all mean?* Tomorrow they will look into low-premium life insurance plans to take care of their burgeoning families, should something happen to them. It will make them feel like men in control of their lives. But they're not. They're boys, and they're not in control of shit.

Speaking of boys, Murphy isn't here, the coward. He always picks the easiest option, and in this case (and many cases), that means hiding. I'm dead, lying here about to be carried off and buried, but all he cares about is winning the argument. Murphy showing up would mean I got the last word, or that he had forgiven me, and either of those would mean he's weak. He doesn't realize he's the weakest one of the bunch anyway.

That brings me to Ruby. She sits in the pew between the girls and the boys, the space between her and them so slight you would only notice if you were looking for it, like I am. She watches Ally comforting Steph, occasionally reaching out a hand to squeeze one of Ally's. I know Ruby feels genuine grief, but mostly discomfort. She doesn't know her place anymore, her role. I'm only now realizing that she never really knew it. She's been an official outsider ever since she dared leave Chatwick at eighteen, but even before that, she and

I were always the ones straddling the curvature of the crew's closed circle. One foot in, one foot out. The dark ones.

I know it's terrible how much enjoyment I get from watching her squirm, but it's just too entertaining. Besides, with the fate of my soul no longer a question mark, I'm enjoying what I can. My death will be hardest on Ruby, for sure, but she'll never admit it, and our crew won't acknowledge it. She left. She abandoned us, so she can't possibly feel it as deeply as they do. It's amazing how grief turns so quickly from a group activity to a competitive sport.

It seems all of Chatwick turned up in their patent-leather shoes and cheap polyester blends. "To show their support," they'd say. For who? Me? Four days ago, they wouldn't have pissed on me if I were on fire. Most of them are only here to satisfy their morbid curiosity, whispering behind hands and rolling eyes, gathering tidbits to relay later to their neighbors who were unable to make it. But some are here for my mother, Charlene, whose deli (formerly my stepfather's) is where they happily spend their food stamps. Either way, I wish they wouldn't have come. It makes them feel too damn good about themselves, and they don't deserve it. And I don't deserve the show either, even if it is fake.

Mom stares blankly ahead of her as the priest eulogizes yet another man who has let her down. I look—well, *looked*—just like her. If you shaved off her two curtains of waist-length blond curls and straightened out her chest and hips, we would look like twins.

Nancy, Ruby's mother, sits next to Mom, holding her limp hand. Nancy is the one who made all these arrangements, and despite the overabundance of flowers, I still appreciate her efforts. She saved my mother from having to coordinate another funeral, and I think one is enough for a lifetime. Ruby's never forgiven Nancy for the way she handled her own illness back in the day, but as dicey as things got in the St. James household, they didn't hold a candle to my family. Besides, Nancy's one of the only assholes in this town who has any compassion, and I'm grateful she's decided to bestow it upon Mom when she needs it most.

That's all I ever needed. Compassion. If I'd ever gotten a shred of it from any of the people in this room, maybe I wouldn't be in this fucking box.

My "friends" all think they will finally be rid of me once they've fulfilled this obligation. They will go back to the "happy," normal, vanilla lives they lead, and their guilt will subside eventually.

Dumbasses. They have no idea Mom found the letters this morning.

1

RUBY
NOW

I'm the first to arrive at Charlene's house, so I opt for street parking in case I need to make a hasty escape. I've never much cared for being caged in. Especially not in Chatwick.

Staring at the house, the last place my friend Danny was alive, I remember when he moved in here the summer after his stepfather died. Charlene used the moderate payout from Roger's life insurance policy to buy it, and with what was left over, she fixed up the apartment over the deli where the three of them had lived so she could rent it out. She and her son needed a fresh start, she explained to neighbors who raised their eyebrows at the sudden move, so soon after Roger's death.

Charlene's first (and only) house project was to coat the outside with the hideous teal paint that remains today, enlisting the crew to do the bulk of the work. She paid us in subs that she brought over every day after the lunchtime rush. At the end of the day, she served us iced tea she mixed in a large glass pitcher as we melted onto the front porch steps and teased one another about who smelled the worst after a hard day's labor. I can practically smell the iced tea, the paint fumes, and the sweat. It had been a happy time, mostly, but not as innocent as it should have been. At least for those of us who already knew that nothing was as it seemed.

The paint is now chipped and faded, but it still glows with the spark of Charlene's quiet defiance. She never said as much, but she had chosen it as a message: she no longer had to answer to anyone. She no longer had to rely on anyone else to keep her and her son alive. Her choices were hers and hers alone, and if she wanted a teal house, then by God, she would have one.

I turn away from the house and look down the street. This is the "bad" part of Chatwick, below the railroad tracks. Danny didn't mind it so much. He felt he belonged here, but he always hated how his street wasn't lined with maple trees like the neighborhood where I grew up. He liked trees—climbing them, sitting under them, and reading or writing or (later) smoking under their shade—so I was happy to see a gorgeous old maple just a few steps from his plot in the cemetery. I hadn't noticed it until a single red leaf fell right into his open grave, silently landing on his coffin like a flower would have, had we been allowed to lay the traditional roses on top of it. It surprised me to see the red leaf this early in September. It will be many weeks until the foliage in Vermont explodes into color so vibrant you can actually see how it taints the green landscape in photos taken from space, until Vermonters welcome but silently curse the leaf peepers who clog the roads and slow down traffic. So I tried to imagine that this lone early-turned leaf was some kind of message from Danny. He would have scoffed at that idea when he was alive.

My hands are wrapped so tightly around the steering wheel that my palms begin to sweat. I consider driving away, straight out of Chatwick to Burlington, where the plane I am supposed to be blissfully seated on is currently being prepared for its flight back to JFK. In just over ninety minutes, I could be out of Vermont and back to my apartment in Manhattan with the blinds shut. But in my mind, I see Charlene's pleading eyes, asking me to please come to the private service Danny requested. This was no public reception where my absence would hardly be noted; it was just the crew, so they sure as hell would notice if I wasn't there. Although I doubt they would be all that surprised at my absence.

Charlene's words—"That's what Danny wanted"—didn't make sense at first. How could Charlene possibly know what Danny had wanted? Then it sank in.

He must have left a note.

Last week, the governor held a press conference, declaring the epidemic of opiate addiction in Vermont to be so severe that she felt justified in declaring it a state of emergency. She announced that she would be forming a task force—including state senators and representatives, officials from the Department of Corrections, and mental health clinicians—whose sole purpose is to stamp out the drugs coming into our state from New York and Boston and Montreal and address the sharp spike in demand for mental health and rehabilitative services.

In the last few months alone, the hospital in Chatwick has reported fourteen heroin overdoses—four of which resulted in death, one of which was Danny. The tox screens showed they had all used a strain of heroin laced with fentanyl. So we all assumed his overdose was accidental. At least, we all wanted to assume that. Imagine your last shred of hope being that your friend had only *accidentally* died of a heroin overdose. And with one request from Charlene, that hope was taken away. "There's letters for all of you," she had said, once she could see the realization settling over us. "Please come."

Damn it. I wouldn't even be here if it weren't for Ally. I was the first person she called when she heard Danny was dead. My first instinct was not to take the call, but when someone you haven't spoken to in ten years tracks you down at work at eleven o'clock in the morning, you answer the phone. If it had been anyone other than Ally, I would have had the receptionist take a message. Then I would have sent a nice card to Charlene (because Danny hated flowers), and I would have returned to pretending that nothing beyond the borders of Manhattan ever existed. It was Ally's voice, the shock and the pain and the...*Allyness* of it. The way she hadn't asked but demanded my return. "I've never asked you why, Ruby, and I still won't. But you'll come for the funeral. You have to." What she meant, without saying it directly, was that I owe her. And I do. For leaving Chatwick and never looking back. For leaving her behind and never telling her why.

If only I hadn't picked up the phone, I would be at my desk in New York, feeling guilty but safe. Not plagued by the ceaseless nerves bubbling under my skin. Not overcome by an urge to smoke that I haven't had in ten years. There are so many things in Chatwick that aren't good for me, and if I go in that house, I'll be sucked back into them all. I'll spin right back down the drain of this town.

Just as I make up my mind to get the hell out of here before anyone else arrives, Charlene swings open the screen door and stands on the porch with one hand on her hip, the other over her eyes so she can see who's lingering outside her house like a private detective. She recognizes me and waves. Shit. You can't drive away from a grieving mother.

The door of the Sentra squeaks as I swing it open. I took a cab from the airport this morning because Nancy was busy helping Charlene get ready for the funeral, but since I had an hour between my arrival and the funeral I went...*home*, I guess, is its rightful name. I no longer have a key to the house, but the code to the garage hasn't changed (my sister Coral's birthday, followed by my own). In addition to the spare house key that hangs behind my old ice skates, I found, to my surprise, my high school car, Blue, still a piece of junk with its four-gear standard transmission, power nothing, and heat that runs full blast all year long whether you want it to or not.

My father purchased it secondhand for me the year he moved back in with us, a consolation prize for his absence. Despite my insistence that I wouldn't need it after I left for college, Nancy has kept it here for me. The key was sitting in the ignition, and instead of going into the house full of memories I was not ready to face, I sat in the car and listened to a cassette tape—a cassette tape!—of songs I had recorded from the radio when I was twelve years old. Blue didn't have a CD player like my friends' cars did.

I climb the rotting steps toward Charlene, who stands on her tiptoes to hug me. I am not tall: five foot seven in my tallest pair of heels, which I left at home—my *real* home, that is, in New York—but Charlene is a teeny size two, and the top of her head barely clears my shoulders. I feel like a beast descending on her.

"Oh, Ruby," she says, her hands on my face, her puffy eyes beseeching mine. "Thanks for comin'. It's so good to see you." She looks me all over and declares me as beautiful as ever. "Now come have some iced tea with your long-lost mother-in-law." She includes this self-assigned title in the cards she sends every Christmas, despite the fact that I haven't spoken to her son in ten years. She always hoped Danny and I would fall in love, as if I had the power to set his life on the right course. Now more than ever, perhaps unintentionally, it serves as a reminder that I could have saved her son.

As if reading my mind, she stops in her path to look at me warily. "I guess I should stop doing that," she says. "Pushin'. You know, now that there's nothin' to push."

I don't know what to say, so I just shake my head with a sad smile and follow her into the kitchen. Charlene deposits me on one of the red-leather-and-chrome chairs she tells me she picked up at the Margie's Pub remodeling sale for five bucks a pop. I thought they looked familiar, although technically I shouldn't know what they look like, since I was well under the drinking age before I left town. She pulls out the same pitcher from her fridge that she served us from fifteen summers ago and pours the iced tea into a glass I distinctly remember Danny serving us vodka and orange sodas in a few years later. Next, she offers me vegetables from a platter she produces from the fridge, and I wonder how she's still standing, let alone serving me like I'm on a social call and her son will be home to join us any minute.

In keeping with this charade, Charlene insists I tell her about my "life in the big city." There isn't much to tell, so I talk about work. On the plane, I contemplated telling people who asked that I work at the *New York Times* and leaving it at that, letting them assume I've been away from Vermont for so long because I was busy achieving the ambition I listed in my high school yearbook: to be a journalist. But now, at my first opportunity, I hasten to add that it's in the advertising department, because I don't want her to think I'm putting on airs. Who was I kidding, anyway? For one, I'm sure she and my mother have talked about me and my career at least once since I've been gone. And even if by some miracle *Nancy* has let me fade into the sordid history of this town, it *is* Chatwick. Despite the fact that I shy away from social media, I bet you could walk out on this street and ask anyone what Ruby St. James is up to, and they would reply, "Oh, the St. James girl? Reddish hair? Oh yeah, she's living in New York, working at that big paper of theirs. I hear she's single as always and pays more in rent than this whole neighborhood spends on mortgages combined!"

My friends and I always called it "the Chat," this rapid-fire circulation of the unprinted news of Chatwick. The Chat is an intangible presence that cloaks the town in intrigue and fear. The houses are so close together that every argument even one notch above normal speaking level is overheard by the little old ladies rocking the afternoon away on their screened-in porches. Their gossip filters down through whispered conversations at post–church service receptions to parents who repeat it at home in earshot of their kids, who bring it to the playground. The other (and significantly more powerful) origin is Margie's Pub, which trickles news down to the Quik Stop clientele the next day, who bring it back to the below-the-tracks families. Subjects run the gamut from legal troubles to marital stress and right on down to who's dating whom at Chatwick High. No one is immune. I remember Ally once having to defend herself to a neighbor who heard that Ally had broken up with her friend's grandson over the phone. We were in fifth grade.

Danny's family and mine were like gas pumps, fueling the Chat for years on end. From our home, the neighbors would occasionally hear Nancy crashing around the house trying to get from room to room and, shortly after, a shouting match between my parents. At the Deusos' they heard much worse.

The doorbell rings, and Charlene escorts Ally and Aaron in. Ally carries a freshly baked pie, and the gap in time between now and the last time I saw her feels wide as a canyon. Her face—voted Prettiest in junior high and high school—is the face of the girl I stole my mother's car with before I even had a license, driving it all over town smoking cigarettes. It's the face of the girl who told the crew what sex was, her giddy face lit by flashlight in the field behind her house, using the same hand motions she had seen her brother use when he explained it to his friend earlier that day.

In that same field, the night before we started high school, she would gather us together—me, Emmett, Danny, and Murphy, the original crew—to tell us her father had left. After a summer of her parents arguing over the rubbers her mom had found in her dad's pockets while doing the laundry, this came as a shock to no one but Ally, whose fierce belief in true love left her unprepared. That was the night, on the brink of becoming high school students, that she made us promise to always be friends. To be loyal to one another above all else. To never lie to each other. She needed something to cling to, and I could understand that, so I promised, like Ally promised and Emmett promised. Like Danny and Murphy promised, even though the three of us were already breaking it. Even though we've done nothing but break it since that night.

And now Ally's a grown woman. From the clippings my mother periodically sends me from the *Chatwick Gazette*, I know Ally has recently been promoted to manager at the Cutting Edge, the salon where she's worked since she graduated from cosmetology school. I picture her ruling the roost from her position behind her chair, affectionately clucking directions to her junior hairdressers without taking her eyes off the clump of hair she's expertly snipping away at, gathering bits of gossip from her clients like bits of feed.

As we listened to the memorialization of our friend, I noticed Ally scanning my hair, and I know she was contemplating whether she wants to give me highlights or lowlights. She won't get the opportunity. I don't care how much practice she's had; I remember all too well the time in eighth grade when she convinced me to darken my strawberry-blond hair to a deeper auburn hue. She dyed it out of a box we got at Brooks Pharmacy, and I cried for a week until the black streaks came out.

Since we've last seen each other, she's married the man beside her, the man we all knew she would marry since the moment he rescued her from a scum-of-the-earth date at Dunphy's field after homecoming. I've become the girl who didn't even attend their wedding, and she's become a person I don't know. A person who knows that you're expected to bring food to a bereaved person. I imagine this knowledge was passed down to her in some handbook women receive on their wedding day that tells them how to handle uncomfortable life events.

Next in the door are Emmett and Steph, Emmett looking

impossibly mature in a suit and tie that he moves in as comfortably as if he wears it every day. I get a flash of our eighth-grade formal dance and me straightening his tie for him every ten minutes. He was so obsessed with keeping it straight, but so uncomfortable in it that he couldn't stop tugging at it, ruining my efforts. He blamed me for tying it wrong so I told him to screw off, which set off the usual splitting of alliances between the girls and the boys of the crew.

Oh, the drama of those days, over a tie and a few harsh words. Over absolutely nothing at all. How I long for that now.

Nancy tells me Emmett works in finance, in the loans department. Apparently, he golfs with my father on the Sundays Dad's in town. The WASPiness of it all turns my stomach. I half expected him to walk in with a cable-knit sweater tied around his shoulders. There is something different about the way Emmett moves now, and it takes me a minute to pinpoint it. He used to bound into a room, filling every molecule of air with nervous energy, constantly in motion. Now he moves slowly, cautiously, and only his eyes dart around the room anxiously. I attribute it to the situation; it must be difficult to attend the funeral of the boy you once treated like a fly to be swatted.

Steph—whom Ally had pointedly introduced to me at the funeral as Emmett's girlfriend *of three years* (in case I didn't already understand how ludicrous it was that I hadn't even known she existed)—is tiny in comparison to Emmett but just as smartly dressed. She has warm brown eyes, and when I hugged her at the service, I felt instant comfort with her. Perhaps this is because our embrace wasn't impregnated with ten years of absence, resentment, and disappointment. She carries a fruit basket, thus debunking my wedding-day uncomfortable-situation-handbook theory. I am feeling more and more inadequate with the arrival of each guest.

Everyone takes turns hugging, even though we already went through this at the church and then again before leaving the cemetery. But it's something to do, I guess. When the ritual is over, there is nothing but uncomfortable shifting until Charlene decides to dole out the letters she mentioned at the cemetery.

"Must be weird for you to be back here," Emmett says, his talent for adding more tension to a room already humid with it still unfortunately intact. I feel my face instantly begin to burn as I search for an appropriate response. Am I to apologize for being gone so long? I know that's what they're all expecting. At the very least, it's what they deserve.

"At least she *is* here," Ally cuts in. "More than I can say for Murphy."

Even as it softens to Ally's defense of me, my heart jumps at the name. After all the anxiety at just the thought of seeing him, he wasn't at the funeral. When Charlene told us about the closed reception, she had asked me where Murphy was, as if no time had passed and I was still his best friend, the keeper of his whereabouts. Ally had jumped in and offered to make sure he came. I had overheard her on her cell phone before I closed the door to my car: "Murphy Leblanc, if you don't put aside your stupid pride and get your ass over to Charlene's house…" In that moment, despite my leftover resentment, I felt sorry for him. He and I were in the same boat, helpless against Ally's authority, even if we were rowing in opposite directions.

We hear a vehicle pull up in the driveway, but when minutes pass without a knock on the door, Ally goes over to the window and peers through the curtains. "Speak of the devil," she says.

My stomach drops. He's here. Like a ghost conjured by speaking its name, the person I've been simultaneously dreading and looking forward to seeing since I returned to Chatwick is now parked not fifty feet from where I stand, separated only by a rotting porch and a bright-teal wall.

———

I can't help but join Ally at the window. There Murphy is, sitting in a truck I've never seen before. The side is emblazoned with the logo for Leblanc Johnson Construction, the contracting company Nancy tells me he has owned with Aaron for some time. His arms are stretched out straight with the same death grip on his steering wheel as I had moments earlier. "What's he doing?" I ask.

Ally rolls her eyes and snaps her tongue. "Who knows? Aaron, can you go see if he's coming in for a landing anytime soon?"

"What am I supposed to say?" Aaron asks, a deer caught in the headlights. Business partner or no, he wants as little to do with the emotional turmoil today is bringing up. He's a dude. The old-school kind. The Chatwick kind.

Everyone is quiet. I lock eyes with Emmett, each silently battling to relinquish this task to the other. I surrender more easily than I should. "I'll go," I say, and I head through the door before there can be any more discussion. The first time Murphy and I see each other should be just the two of us anyway, even if Ally has her nose pressed up against the windowpane the whole time.

I step out onto the porch, my breath catching in my throat as our eyes meet. I feel the pull. I'm circling the drain. Even though his window is rolled down, I can't hear the four-letter word his mouth forms as he breaks eye contact, but it puts an abrupt halt to the centrifugal force anyway. Thank God.

"That happy to see me, huh?" I ask as I approach the driver's side. Up close, I see that his jet-black hair is now peppered with gray that's too mature for his twenty-eight years, and his rolled-up shirt-sleeve reveals a tattoo encircling his forearm, which is thicker, tanner, and more muscular than I remember. Otherwise, he looks exactly the same.

He exhales an unsmiling laugh but doesn't make eye contact. "Didn't think I'd see you here." His voice makes it more real. The voice I talked to every night on the phone until one of us fell asleep.

"Ally didn't tell you I was coming home for the funeral?" Funny, Ally tells everyone everything, especially if she has a part in making it happen.

He ignores me. "Kinda forgot you even existed," he says, staring straight ahead.

Even though I know he can't possibly mean it, hearing the words and the icy tone of his voice feels like a bullet to the chest. A bullet I quite possibly deserve, although perhaps not fired by Murphy.

"Why weren't you there?" My voice falters, and I realize that I had wanted him to be there more than I wanted him *not* to be there. In fact, I had *needed* him to be there. Suddenly I wish he would jerk his head in the direction of the passenger side, indicating he wants me to get in. To ride around the back roads of Chatwick, head down to the bay. As dirty as *this* section of town is, if you stick with the road for another mile, the below-the-tracks section where Danny grew up suddenly breaks open to beautiful green, rolling pastures of farmland. I can smell the cow manure from here; it's a sweeter smell than I remember. Past the farmland is Chatwick Bay, where we used to escape on the boiling-hot summer nights—skipping rocks, talking about life, skinny-dipping. I suddenly ache to be sitting in Murphy's passenger seat, my legs stretched out, my toes cold in the wind, headed away from the center of town and into our own little world.

Murphy still stares straight ahead, so I risk putting my hand on his arm. "Hey. Look at me."

When he finally does, I see the anger and hurt burning in his eyes. I wonder if he can see the same in mine. "You're not the only one I haven't seen in a while," he says, breaking our gaze almost immediately. "Dan and I…"

"You fought?" I ask, knowing the answer is yes before he nods, but not wanting him to *know* I know. It works in my favor that Murphy and Danny stopped being friends just two weeks before Danny and I did. If they had continued to be as close as brothers, Murphy and I would be having a very different conversation right now. "What was it about?" And this I have truly never known, have tried not to want to know.

His face finally twists into a smile, although not the warm, easy one I remember. "It wasn't about *you*, if that's what you're thinking."

My mouth drops open in feigned shock, because that's exactly what I was thinking. "That's not what I was thinking!"

He snorts out an infuriating laugh.

"Excuse me for trying to figure out what could make the best of friends completely cut off communication for ten—" I stop, realizing what I'm saying. I am a huge pile of hypocritical crap.

Murphy doesn't say anything. He just continues to smile that scary, un-Murphy-like smile.

I raise my hands against the gun I imagine he's about to reload. "Okay. You're right. I'm no master communicator myself. It's just…I *know* what happened between the two of us"—I wave my finger between him and myself—"and I know what happened between me and Danny. What I *don't* know is what happened between the two of you."

"Ruby, not everything is some dramatic thing. I told you it wasn't about you. So just mind your own damn business!" he says.

I spin to go back inside, anger and hurt stinging my eyes. I hear him curse and then the door of his truck opening and closing. He grabs at my elbow and I shrug him off, turning back to face him with my arms crossed.

"Tuesday."

The nickname makes me stiffen. Only he and Danny call me that. Now, I guess, it's only Murphy. It used to drive me crazy, the way they would walk behind me in the halls in elementary school, singing that song over and over again until I shouted at them to stop. Now, I would give anything to hear Danny sing just one horribly out-of-tune chorus of "Goodbye, Ruby Tuesday."

"Listen, I'm sorry," Murphy says. "I'm a little shook up. It was a long time ago, and neither of us got over it…in time. I don't want to talk about it because it seems stupid now. Everything seems kinda stupid."

I know this is as much as I'm going to get from him. "Well, I tell you what's stupid—us standing out here fighting while everyone else is inside ready to hear what Danny has to say for himself. No one is looking *forward* to it, Murphy, but maybe…it will…help." When the tears come to my eyes, his face finally softens. He takes a step forward, opening his arms to hug me, and I get a whiff of his cologne, the same stuff he's always worn. I step back, shaking my head. I can't be hugged by him. It will kill me; I'm sure of it. When I turn to climb the steps, I feel him hesitating, but eventually he follows.

Charlene makes even more of a fuss over Murphy than she did over me. He looks sheepish, undoubtedly feeling the full weight of the rift between him and Danny now that he's in Charlene's house with Danny's school pictures lining the walls. Neither Murphy nor I will resolve our final fight with Danny, and both of us should have been fighting to keep him with us.

Charlene leads us into the basement, which is different from the last time I saw it. There's a futon, a bed, and a mini fridge. Danny must have adapted this room into an apartment of sorts, giving him the illusion of independence and the privacy to numb himself against the world. The hairs on the back of my neck stand up, and suddenly I know—Danny *died* in this room. I picture Charlene coming down with a basket of laundry, calling out in forced cheeriness, "Get up, lazybones!" only to find...

I shudder. I can't even go there. God help me from ever going there.

Aaron hands out the folding chairs we used to use for poker nights. He offers Charlene a chair, but she shakes her head. She stands in front of the old television we once screened porn on—the girls curious to see what all the fuss was about, the boys simply horny teenagers. We arrange ourselves in a semicircle to face her, reluctant pupils in a class we never elected to take. The couples sit together, holding hands, while Murphy and I are lumped together off to the side. As always, the single ones.

I close my eyes, just for a second, and picture the crew as it used to be. Aaron and Ally remain unchanged except for the wedding bands on their fingers, but suddenly it's Emmett's high school girlfriend, Nicki, by his side instead of Steph. Danny is in the corner, making out with whatever below-the-tracks girl he's found to entertain himself this month. And I, without anyone thinking anything of it, am able to lean into Murphy for support. In this world, at the end of the night, it's quite possible I'll return home to find Nancy either high or low—or one of those plus drunk—but it still feels lighter and simpler than the reality I return to when I open my eyes.

Charlene holds a stack of envelopes and two sheets of loose-leaf paper. I can see Danny's scribble through the white-lined sheet, and I remember the first time I looked over Danny's shoulder at this same handwriting. He was showing me a poem he had written, which was better than I expected, much better than my own drippy attempts anyway. After that, he and I started the Dark Children of Chatwick Poetry Society. There were only two members: him and me. We didn't always read poetry; sometimes it was personal essays or journal entries or little stories we made up. We met in secret in this very basement and never breathed a word of it to anyone, inside *or* outside the crew.

It was such a long time ago, and yet not so long. And whatever Charlene is about to read is the last prose of Danny's I will ever hear.

Charlene flaps the piece of paper. "I found it when I finally made myself strip his bed this morning."

My eyes dart over to the bed I had been avoiding until this moment. The little twin mattress is made up with sheets so crisp and tightly tucked in that even Nancy at her most manic would approve. Then I remember that Nancy was helping Charlene with the arrangements, and I realize the hospital corners were probably her handiwork.

Charlene reads:

Dear Mom,

I'm sorry I have to leave you this way. With all we have been through together, I always hoped I could someday make you proud. But life is hard, and sad. It has been for a very long time. At first, pot made it better, and then it didn't so I moved on to other things. They all helped at first, but then they didn't anymore. And now I'm nothing but a junkie.

Charlene's voice falters here, and it takes her several minutes to get through the rest of the letter.

I'm a disappointment as a son and a human being. Nothing I do now can change that. I hate myself for what I've done. For what I am. I don't even deserve the grief I know you must be feeling. Please don't hate me. Try to be happy I'm finally at peace. I want you to know there is nothing you could have done to prevent this. You tried to help me as best you could.

I can tell when she breaks down at this part that no matter what Danny says, she will *always* wonder what she should have done differently. As will we all.

The trouble is, if a person has no hope things can get better, there's not a whole lot anyone else can say to change that.

I love you very much.

DANNY

P.S. There's another letter I'd like you to read to Ruby, Murphy, Emmett, and Ally if you can get them all together. Please read it to them before you give them their envelopes, or else they won't understand.

I barely hear the last part of the letter, I'm so furious with Danny. *I'm sorry I have to leave you this way.* As if he had no say in the matter. I could kill him if he hadn't already done such a thorough job of it.

The weight of Danny's words hangs in the air, already dense with emotion. Ally's hand springs to her mouth, and Aaron wraps his arm around her. Murphy leans forward and hides his face in his hands. My hand shoots out instinctively to rub his back, freezing about an inch above his shirt when I realize the intimacy of what I'm about to do. I pat him awkwardly a few times and then return the disobedient hand to my lap. I look over at Emmett. Steph is looking at him too, but he stares straight ahead, white as a sheet. No one knows what to say. I mean, what do you *say?*

Finally, Emmett seems to return to himself. He clears his throat. "The note says there's letters for us?"

I shoot him a sharp look. He's trying to get this over with, and I understand the urge but don't think rushing Charlene is very kind. He doesn't notice my glare.

"Yeah," she says. She puts the first sheet behind the second. "I haven't read this one yet, since it ain't addressed to me." Oh, Charlene. Even with her bastard ex-husband and her troubled son in the ground, she's still waiting for someone's temper to explode. She sniffs deeply and reads:

To my old friends,

So here you all are. Nice to see you can show up for a person once he's dead.

Charlene stops, her mouth open, her eyes horrified at the abrupt change in tone. Her expression almost exactly matches Ally's, Aaron's, Emmett's, and Steph's. My face and Murphy's have not changed; he and I were expecting this. Probably because we know we deserve it. ·

Charlene's eyes scan the rest of the page, and then she looks at me, as if she's asking permission to continue. I nod my head to grant it.

She looks down at the page again, her hands shaking visibly. She looks back up at me and shakes her head. The first note was bad enough. She doesn't want the last memory of her son to be *this*.

I stand up, grab the box of tissues from the top of the TV, and guide her back to my seat with them. Murphy takes one of her hands. With the other, she dabs at her eyes with a tissue. I take Charlene's place at the head of the class and continue reading:

I haven't heard from any of you in a while. Some of you I see down at Margie's Pub every weekend, so I don't know what makes you think you're so much better than me. I doubt Ruby and Murphy are even here. They're both really good at ignoring problems.

I look at Murphy, who glances at me and then returns to staring straight ahead.

If any of you actually showed up at my funeral, don't feel like you deserve some medal. None of you bothered to try to help me when I was alive, when it counted.

Ally is audibly crying now, her head in her hands, slumped into Aaron's chest.

Charlene's eyes dart between each of our faces guiltily, as if she were the one who wrote the hateful words. "I'm sorry," she says to us. "I didn't know. I thought it would be like mine, not..." She waves her hand at the letter I hold. "Maybe we shouldn't—"

But something in me tells me that Danny's last words deserve to be read. Maybe the part of me that feels I contributed to his demise by abandoning him all those years ago. I turn my eyes back to the page.

You always talked about "the crew, the crew, the crew," like we were some untouchable entity. But when it comes to things that really matter, you guys barely even know each other. I think it's about time you did, if you're going to continue to pride yourselves on being friends since the womb. I know things about most of you that you didn't trust the rest of the crew to know.

Here, I pause, a hot spring of acid burning my throat. If I choose not to continue reading, someone else will snatch this piece of paper away from me. If *I* read it, I can edit the information if it reveals too much.

There is one envelope for each of my dear friends who once pledged to always be honest with each other, and each envelope contains evidence of your betrayal of that pact. I'll leave it up to you. You can either share them with each other, or keep them to yourselves. Just remember that all things done in the dark have a way of coming to light. If you don't tell each other your secrets, you never know how, or when, I might have arranged for them to come out.

He didn't sign the letter *Love, Danny*, which is no surprise after the content. He simply dashed off a large, loopy *D*.

I'm not sure what to do with the piece of paper. I don't want to give it back to Charlene, so I just place it on top of the television, next to the pile of envelopes, which I pick up. Each has a name on it. There is one for me, one for Ally, one for Emmett, one for Murphy, and, oddly enough, one for Danny. I hold them in my hands, little grenades of paper. If I tear them up now, will it stop them from detonating? Judging by the ferocity of Danny's letter, I'm guessing not.

I hand out the envelopes, and as I do, each person looks at me, looking for answers to the questions on all of our minds. I drop the envelope with my name on it back on the TV set, now left only with Danny's envelope in my hands, which has a note next to his name.

I'll go first.

I know what it will say, and I wish I could somehow shrink down and disappear inside the envelope so I don't have to deal with any of what's about to happen. But I don't debate with myself if I should open it, or if I should give it to Charlene for her to sort out instead. I just rip open the seal and pull out a small piece of paper. It says what I thought it might say.

I read aloud the truth that changed everything for him:

I killed my stepfather.

2

RUBY
BACK THEN—(ALMOST) EIGHTH GRADE

I'm used to waking up in the middle of the night. Danny throws rocks at my window every couple of weeks. So tonight, when I bolt upright in bed, I wait to hear the next pebble before I bother getting up. I hold my breath, waiting for the *ping!* against the glass to slice through the thick summer air, but I don't hear it. I draw the curtain to look out to the street, but no one's there.

I lie down and try to fall back to sleep. Sometimes my ceiling fan, tired from the effort of keeping my room cool in the humidity of the Vermont summer, starts to creak in the middle of the night, and in the past, I've mistaken the noise for Danny's SOS. But my fan hasn't been on since the storm knocked the power out hours ago. My phone call with Ally had cut off midsentence after a flash of light, which I'm sure made her more worried. The first night I had a sleepover at her house—we were maybe five or six—there was a thunderstorm so big

I couldn't help but tell her I was scared, and she stayed up with me all night playing Go Fish, giving my hand a squeeze with every boom of thunder. Ever since then, she calls me to make sure I'm okay when it storms. Even though I'm over the fear, I love that she still checks on me.

After we lost power, I tossed and turned, replaying a much more powerful storm that swept through earlier: Hurricane Nancy. She's off her meds again.

"You don't understand how they make me feel, sweetheart," she said, her words racing as she paced my room, gathering discarded clothes from the floor and hanging them in my closet, picking up items from every surface to wipe imaginary dust away with her hands. "I just can't live underwater anymore. You know what they say, water is for fish and seaweed and coral, and speaking of Coral, that sister of yours just keeps antagonizing me, she's so ready to get out of this house; well, she's in for a surprise when she gets out into the real world and realizes there are people in this world a whole lot crazier than me, and…" On and on she went, climbing further up the mania ladder without taking a breath.

The power must have come back on just before I fell asleep, because I could hear her banging pans and cabinet doors in the kitchen, preparing to bake. When I was little, I used to sneak into the pantry and watch her as she kneaded and rolled out the dough in perfect, flat circles. Her baking was magic to me. Now that I'm almost a teenager and have been through this enough times, I know I will wake up in the morning to fresh scones, a mother who has crashed so hard she can't get out of bed, and a father nowhere to be found after conveniently remembering some work that has to be done at the office.

I am so sure I feel trouble that I keep sitting back up to check the window. Finally, I get out of bed and tiptoe downstairs. Sure enough, a tray of baked goods cools on the counter, although the kitchen is dark except for the blinking digital clocks on the stove and the microwave. I open the back door—slowly, so the creaks in the old hinges will be quieter. I don't turn the back porch light on. I never turn it on, even though the dark scares me, because I can't risk waking anyone up.

The earth smells damp and clean, but the storm didn't break the humidity. Steam rises from the driveway. Wind chimes collide on the Bronsons' porch, but there is no breeze. A chill runs down me anyway. The only other sounds come from the pool. I listen to the low hum of water being pumped into the pool and the sucking sound of the filter trying to pull out bugs and leaves from the surface.

Danny is not on the glider, where he usually waits for me. I suppose it's possible I woke out of habit, or just heard the clinking of Nancy washing her dishes before turning in for the night. Still, I can't shake the feeling that something's out of place. I'm about to chalk it up to paranoia and go back to bed when I hear a rustling coming from the lilac bush in the farthest corner of the backyard. I stand on the rough wood of the deck, staring at the bush and telling myself I'll be thirteen next week—too old to believe in monsters in the bushes. But I hug my arms to my body anyway, goose bumps popping up on my arms despite the heat, too scared to move.

Feeling stupid, I whisper "Hello?" into the darkness.

I hear the noise again, and right when I'm about to wet my nightgown, I hear "Don't be scared, it's me." A few seconds later, I make out Danny's figure coming from behind the bush.

"Jesus, Danny, what are you doing?" I whisper yell at him. I want to punch him, but by the look of the bruises on his cheek, he's gotten it bad enough tonight.

"I just needed a place to hide out for a while," Danny says. "I didn't want to drag you into this."

This is weird of him to say, considering he's been "dragging me into" every beating his stepfather has handed him since we were in second grade. When Charlene started dating Roger Deuso, our parents told us how lucky Danny was to finally be getting a father. His real dad left when Danny was just a baby. And Roger, who owns the famous (in Chatwick, anyway) Deuso's Deli, is known for his charity. He's always giving free subs to neighbors in need, and considering the deli is below the tracks, I'm surprised he makes any profit at all.

He became even more of a hero when he married Charlene. "A single mother and her 'troubled' child?" the Chat said. "That Roger Deuso sure is a saint."

So when the neighbors started hearing Danny screaming bloody murder a couple of months after Charlene and Roger got married, they decided Danny was just "a little hell-raiser" and "God bless Roger for putting up with it." Danny's bruises and cuts were waved away. "Must have gotten into a scuffle at school," they'd say. He was called a "sour one" and a "bad egg," and even though he'd never been an angel, it wasn't long before Danny really started living up to his reputation.

Murphy, who's been his best friend since First Communion, still has to pull him off boys at recess more days than not. Danny is not even allowed at Emmett's, and while Ally never comes out and says it, when Danny is with us, we always play in her back field instead of going in the house, so I don't think he's welcome there. It makes me so angry that he gets all the blame, but Danny made me promise not to tell anyone what Roger does to him. I think he's afraid his mom will pick Roger over him. Can you blame him? She's not deaf, dumb, or blind. In a way, it's like she already has.

That's why Danny comes to me. He knew I understood the value of discretion back before that was one of our vocabulary words in fifth grade. I know how to hide stuff because my family's almost as screwed up as his. Almost. I'll take my mother and her tendency to self-medicate her bipolar disorder with alcohol over Roger any day. But still, we're different from our friends. We know what it's like to not just worry that the bottom will drop out from under us, but to be certain that it will, because it always has. We stick close together at Christmastime, afraid to go home, while the rest of our friends are merry and chipper and filled with the Christmas spirit.

On Christmas Eve, Danny and I sneak out of our houses and climb to the very top of one of the bare maple trees on my street to mock the Christmas carolers as they make their rounds. Last year, Danny slipped on an icy branch, fell out of the tree, and broke his arm. It ended up being the best Christmas he'd had in years, because he was in a cast for a normal-kid reason, and because Charlene actually stood up to Roger and made him leave Danny alone since he was already hurt. Of course, come New Year's, she couldn't leave the house because even sunglasses wouldn't cover the black eye Roger gave *her*.

We sit on the glider, and Danny winces when I reach out to examine his face. Because I wasn't sure he was here, I am not prepared with the first-aid items I usually meet him with—a towel of ice,

Neosporin, and some Band-Aids. His eye is swollen shut. If I hadn't seen him from the other side, I would barely be able to tell it's Danny. I get up to go inside and retrieve my supplies, but he grabs my hand.

"Don't go." He whispers it so quietly I'm not sure he really said it. He starts to shake, so I sit down and wrap my arms around him sideways to warm him up, to steady him, whatever he needs. But he jumps away from me. He usually flinches when people get too close to him—in fact, that's what most of his recess fights are about—but he's not usually like that with me.

"What set the asshole off this time?" I whisper, savoring the feeling of the swear word on my tongue.

"Don't call him that," he snaps.

This is also new. Usually Danny doesn't start defending Roger until he's already called him every name in the book and is trying to prepare himself to return home. He'll say stuff like "I shouldn't have left my skateboard in front of the shop. He says it looks trashy" or "I shouldn't have left the laundry basket open. He's told me a million times to keep it shut." I mean, my house has a lot of dumb rules like that too, but if I break one of them, I get yelled at. I don't get *hit*.

"What happened?" I demand. I don't usually push like this, I wait until Danny's ready to talk, but tonight something is off. (1) He didn't wake me up. (2) He was hiding in my backyard, not sitting on the glider like usual. (3) He said he "didn't want to bring me into it," but he's been bringing me into it for years, so why is tonight any different?

The eye that can still open looks around wildly before settling on my face. "I think you should call Murphy."

We don't always call Murphy when Danny gets a beating. It's only when Roger is so fired up that he screams at Danny to "never show your rotten face here again" as he (literally) kicks him out on the street that we call Murphy, because those are the times that Danny needs a place to stay. Danny always comes to my house first, because he knows I'll tend to his wounds and let him cry if he wants to. After that, we assess whether it's worth waiting it out, giving Roger some time to cool off before Danny sneaks back in, or if we need to give Murphy the warning call that Danny's on his way and he'll need to be snuck into the basement again.

The first time we called Murphy for help, his terrifying mother screamed at us in French and hung up before even asking who was calling. Since then, Murphy has learned to keep the portable next to his bed. So I'm not surprised when he answers on the first ring.

"Yeah, I'll wait for him on the side porch," Murphy says groggily before I even speak.

"No, Murph," I say. "He wants you to come here this time."

"What? Why?"

"I don't know. He's acting really weird. Just get the hell over here!" I whisper yell into the phone.

While we wait for Murphy to arrive, I hold Danny's hand and use my feet to keep the glider rocking back and forth. I hope the motion will soothe him, but I get no sign either way. He is silent, staring down at the pool like he's thinking of jumping in and never resurfacing. It seems like hours we wait for Murphy, but it can't be that long because he only lives three blocks away. None of us lives more than three blocks away from at least one other member of our crew except for Danny, who is ten blocks.

Finally, Murphy climbs the back steps and joins us on the deck, wearing the same shorts and T-shirt he wears to swim in to cover up the baby fat he hasn't shed yet. He looks at our clasped hands, confused. I realize he probably thinks he's been called here so Danny and I can announce we've become a couple. Or maybe ask permission, since Murphy and I were boyfriend and girlfriend for like a week last year before we realized we can't stand each other when no one else is around. He *would* think that's what this was about, despite all the times Danny has been our mutual crisis. What an idiot.

Then, without looking at Murphy or me, Danny just starts talking. "It was just like always," he says. "I was sleeping, and then suddenly Roger busted open my door and yanked me out of bed. He lifted me by my shirt"—he grabs the top of his shirt at this, twisting it into a knot—"so I was looking right in his eyes, and he had that look, and I knew I was in for it. He asked me what the hell was wrong with me, and when I didn't say anything, he dragged me into the living room and pointed at the Sega. I forgot to put the controller away. I said I was sorry and went to wrap the cord up and put it in the drawer under the TV, but he smacked it out of my hand and picked it up and started hitting me over the head with it. Hard.

"My mom woke up from the noise. I always try to be quiet, to keep her out of it, but when he hit me this time, it felt like my skull was cracked open. When she yelled at him to stop, Roger turned on her and started shaking her. 'This little bastard has no discipline! I take you into my home, and this is the thanks I get? I gotta live in this fucking pigsty?' Same stuff as usual. When she begged him to leave me alone, he slammed her head into the wall.

"He went to do it again, and then suddenly he stopped. Roger *never* stops hitting until someone's on the floor crying, so right away I knew something was wrong. I couldn't see his face, but his back kinda stiffened up, and then he bent over, grabbing his arm. When he dropped to the floor, I could finally see his face, and it was redder than I've ever seen it. Including the time I called him a dickhead and he broke two of my fingers.

"My mom called out his name and kneeled next to him, crying. She told me to call 911, that Roger was having a heart attack, but I didn't move. She asked me again, but I just stood there and waited for her to look at me. Roger was rolling around on the floor, begging us to help him, but I just looked at my mother and told her to go back to bed. She shook her head at first, saying we had to do something, and I yelled at her to get back in her room and to not come out until I told her to. I sounded just like Roger does when he yells at her to stay out of our fights."

Danny stops talking for a minute, seeming to be surprised at what he's just said.

"Anyway, she listened," he continues. "She got up, went back to her room, and closed the door."

My hand is over my mouth now. I know how the story is going to end, but Murphy either doesn't know, or just needs to hear Danny say the words, because he asks, "Dan, what happened to Roger?"

Danny looks at Murphy like it's the first time he's really seeing him, and then he answers. "After a few minutes, he stopped rolling around. He just looked at me, mad as hell but scared too. And I sat down on the couch and just looked right back at him. Until he stopped moving."

I wait a beat before I ask, "And then you left?"

Danny nods. "I knocked on my mom's bedroom door and told her she should call 911. I knew it would…look funny if she didn't."

Murphy and I look at each other. We both know this is way over our heads. My hand is still on top of Danny's, and the squeeze I give him is like the flip of a switch. His face crumples, and he starts to cry. He cries so hard I'm worried he's going to choke.

"Breathe, Danny, breathe," I say, rubbing his back.

"I just wanted it to stop," he says between moans. He repeats it over and over, and I pull him to me. Finally, he lets me. He feels so small. He sounds like he did in kindergarten, when Emmett used to steal his lunch, and I realize the part of Danny that is still in any way a child is making its final appearance tonight. And the parts of Murphy and I that are supposed to be children—supposed to be worrying about whether we're going to make the baseball team or who we're going to take to the dance—they're gone now too. We can't ever unknow what we know.

We're not paying attention to how loud Danny is being, so we all jump when the back porch light flicks on. My mom is standing in the doorway. "What on earth is going on out here?" she screeches.

Murphy and I look at each other again. He shrugs. It's up to me to decide how this all moves forward.

"Mr. Deuso had a heart attack," I say, looking not at my mom but at Murphy. "Danny's mom found him, and Danny was upset so he came here."

I look at Murphy again. I've learned from watching Danny make excuses for his cuts and bruises that the trick is to stay as close to the truth as possible, and that's as much as I can say without cracking.

Murphy nods and takes over. "Danny's really worried," he

says. "Can you call Mrs. Deuso and see if Mr. Deuso is okay? They're probably at the hospital."

3

STEPH
NOW

WELL, THIS IS AWKWARD. FIRST TIME I MEET CHARLENE, I'M sitting here listening to her dead son's murder confession. First day I meet Ruby, she's reading it. Her words—well, Danny's—hang in the air like when church bells stop ringing but you swear you can still hear them. The echo survives Ally's gasp, and Charlene's too. I suppress mine so I won't get another lecture from Ally about how I can't possibly understand the pain of losing Danny like she and the rest of the crew who've "been there since the beginning." Honestly, if she knew the real reason I lost it at the funeral, I bet she wouldn't have given me such crap. I won't have time to bet, though; they're all about to find out. They have to. It's the only thing I can say to distract them from what's really inside Emmett's envelope.

Charlene shakes her head, saying no over and over again. Of course she doesn't want to believe it. That her son killed her husband?

That's like something straight out of a Greek play. And hasn't Charlene been through enough? She shouldn't beat herself up. I hate to think this about anybody, but the more I learn about Danny, the more I think maybe he really was beyond help.

Charlene stands up, and Ruby puts her hands on Charlene's shoulders and tells her it's okay, that it's going to be okay. I've only met Ruby today, but I already like her way more than I thought I would. Way more than I planned to, anyway. Emmett has always put her on such a pedestal, and from what Ally tells me about her, I was expecting her to be a little stuck-up. I mean, she's lived in New York and London and God knows where else, and she hasn't talked to any of them since high school.

And then there's poor Krystal. Ally straight up told her that she could forget about Murphy paying any attention to her once Ruby St. James blew into town, that whether or not Murphy went to the funeral, he would wind up spending as much time with Ruby as he could before she blows back out. I don't think Ally *meant* to make Krystal jealous, but she could have been a little more sensitive in her phrasing. Krystal's been sleeping with Murphy for *months*, and even though she follows Murphy's lead in pretending there's nothing official going on between them, I know she's hoping he'll change his mind. I've known the girl since we were babies; I can read her mind like it's my own. I bet if I check my phone, I'll already have at least two text messages from her asking if I've met Ruby and what I think of her.

I was hoping I could report back to Krystal that Ruby acted like she was better than everyone, or that she looked anorexic and had no boobs, or at least that she weighed like four hundred pounds. Imagine my surprise when at the funeral Ally introduced me to a pretty but not over-groomed or over-perfumed, average-sized girl in unlabeled clothing, who smiled and hugged me as if I were one of her long-lost friends. She seems...down to earth. Sweet even.

Ruby is the one from the stories—All. The. Stories.—who is decidedly fearless: the first girl to leap from the fifty-foot jump at the quarry (since Danny was always the *first* first), the girl who stole her parents' car when she was thirteen, the one who's traveled and moved to big cities on her own. And yet when she entered the church, she looked like every step was a difficult decision to move herself toward us.

When she got closer, I could see the quiver in her smile, and something told me it wasn't just the anxiety of grief. She was nervous to be among people she's known since preschool. And yet now, in the tensest of moments, she is in complete control. Maybe Ally was wrong when she said Ruby thinks she's better than all of us, but she *might* have been right in her description of her as an *odd cluck*, if what she really meant was *odd duck*. (Ally has a tendency to mess up all those old sayings. I don't have the heart to tell her.)

Perhaps that's how I can summarize this girl to Krystal, who was dumped by her high school sweetheart not six months ago and whose ego is fragile as a fresh egg. "She's okay," I'll say, even though I think she's kind of wonderful. "She's a bit odd," I'll add.

"Guys, it ain't what you think," Charlene pleads, as if we were walking out the door in disgust. But none of us has moved. We're frozen to our seats. I look over at Ally. Her face has been white as a sheet ever since the envelopes were handed out, which, of course, makes me wonder what hers says. I know what Emmett's says.

Or at least, nothing in that envelope could be *worse* than what I already know.

Charlene tells the story of the night Danny's stepfather died. Apparently, Roger was abusive, and one night when he was hitting both of them, he had a heart attack. Instead of calling an ambulance right away, they waited until...well, you know. So Danny didn't exactly *kill* Roger, but he didn't exactly *not* kill him either.

"It sounds like maybe he was just scared," Ally says quietly. "Like he was just in shock and didn't know what to do."

Aaron shoots her a look, which makes Ally cry out, "What?" Aaron just shakes his head and shrugs.

"Ally, don't be so simple," Emmett says. "He meant for Roger to die. It's pretty obvious."

Geez, Em, don't hold back or anything.

"Watch how you're talking to my wife, Emmett," Aaron says.

"Well, come on," Emmett says. "Why *confess* in a suicide note if it isn't true?"

"Maybe he just feels guilty because he couldn't save him," Ally says. I notice everyone is still talking about Danny in the present tense.

"Stop being such a Pollyanna, Ally. You know that's not what he means." Emmett's ears are getting red now, which always happens when he's about to blow his top and storm out. This isn't the place for that, and it's really important Emmett doesn't get too stressed, especially now. So I hook my arm through his, our little sign he needs to calm down. I feel his muscles relax a bit. He nods at Charlene. "Not that I'm saying what happened was right or wrong," he says to her.

Charlene dissolves into tears. "Excuse me," she says, and flees up the stairs.

"Jesus, Emmett," Ruby says when she hears the door to the basement close. "Why don't you just punch her in the face?"

Emmett shoots her a look.

Ally says, "Well, I don't care what happened that night. If Danny let Roger die, then Roger deserved it. As far as I'm concerned, Danny acted in self-defense. I didn't want to say it when Charlene was here"—she lowers her voice to a hiss—"but if Roger was hitting them, *someone* had to stop him, and it obviously wasn't going to be her."

Aaron chimes in. "Now that I think about it, as long as I've known him, Danny's always been pretty protective of the people he cares about. Remember when he got in a fight with that carny at the Maple Festival for grabbing Ally's ass? I bet the whole thing with Roger was more about protecting his mom than himself." Aaron has hereby redeemed himself to Ally for the skeptical look he gave her earlier, no doubt avoiding a blowup at home later.

Meanwhile, I'm silent. It's not my place to speak. Maybe it's the Catholic guilt in me, but I can't help but think being responsible for someone's death, in whatever way and for whatever reason, is still called murder. I didn't know Roger, and it sounds like he was an awful man, but it wasn't up to Danny to decide whether he lived or died. Besides, only half of me is keeping up with the conversation. The other half is trying to find my opening.

I think Emmett is speaking to me when he says, "You've been awfully quiet," but when I look at him, he's glaring back and forth between Ruby and Murphy. "What do you two think about all of this?"

They look at each other, like they're trying to decide something. Murphy nods, then Ruby says, "We knew."

Another round of gasps ensues. "Since when?" Ally says.

Ruby is quiet, making more decisions about how much truth to tell. Her shoulders fall, and she says, "Since the night it happened."

"You've known since we were twelve years old that Roger was beating Danny and his mom, and you didn't *tell* anyone?" Ally cries.

The first crack in Ruby's poise is in her voice when she says, "Actually, I've known about the *abuse* pretty much from when it started, and that wasn't long after Roger and Charlene got married."

All eyes grow wide.

"We were in *second grade* when they got married!" Ally is all but screeching now. "That's *four years* before Roger died!" Aaron folds his hand over hers. Their little sign.

Ruby looks at each of us. The tears forming in her eyes make them seem bluer. They have the same deep sadness as Charlene's when she looked at us, pleading for understanding. For forgiveness.

"Unbelievable," Emmett says, and I know he's about to put words to the accusation formulating in all our minds. I squeeze his arm hard now, hoping he will back off. "Ruby, do you realize if someone had stopped Roger, maybe Danny wouldn't have been put in that situation in the first place? That maybe he wouldn't have tried to drown his guilt in drugs? That maybe—"

"Okay that's *enough!*" Murphy roars as he jumps out of his seat. "I get it. We're all upset. Keep in mind when all this started, we were *eight years old*. In case you don't remember, Emmett, when you were eight, you were playing with Hot Wheels and collecting Pogs. Not exactly old enough to know what to do when your friend is getting beat up by an adult. You do *not* get to pin this all on Ruby. No. Way."

Ruby looks at Murphy with gratitude and a little hint of

something else that piques my interest. I probably shouldn't tell Krystal about it. Or should I?

"Who should I pin it on, then? You? What did you have to do with this?" Emmett and Murphy are now practically toe-to-toe.

"It wasn't always safe for him to go back home right away, so Danny would crash on my couch for the night to give Roger time to cool off. He never wanted to talk about it, but I knew anyway. It doesn't take a fucking rocket scientist," he says and looks pointedly at Emmett, then at Ally. "The night Roger died, Ruby told me to come over instead, and he told us what happened."

"And you didn't think to tell the rest of us? So we didn't look so stupid when we were all telling Danny how *sorry* we were that Roger died?"

I want to smack my forehead. We're talking about some of the heaviest stuff you *can* talk about—child abuse, murder, suicide—and Ally is concerned she reacted inappropriately to a situation that happened over sixteen years ago.

Ruby gracefully ignores Ally's point of focus. "We talked about it afterward and decided the fewer people who knew the truth, the better. We didn't want Danny getting in trouble, when all he was doing was protecting himself."

"You should have gone to the police," Emmett says. Ally whips her head around, her mouth hanging open.

"Emmett. Come on," Ruby says.

"What? He was a minor! A little *boy*, for Christ's sake! They wouldn't have thrown him in jail. But at least the truth would have been out, and Danny wouldn't have to live with this giant secret his whole life! He could have gotten help. *We* could have helped him through it."

We hear the basement door open, and Charlene descends the stairs, her eyes red but dry. She reclaims the seat next to Murphy, her posture stiff. She looks strange, calm, as if nothing had happened, as if she hadn't just run out of the room in tears. She says, "I'm sorry about that. It's been a really hard day," and her voice sounds different too. Resolved.

But who am I to judge what looks and sounds normal for a mother on the day she buries her son? Charlene's reentrance changes the atmosphere in the room, everyone calming slightly so as not to say something else to upset her. The silence provides the moment I needed to figure out how to handle this whole secret business.

"Emmett," I say. "I don't think you should be so hard on Ruby and Murphy. After all, you're not exactly the poster boy for being honest." Emmett spins around and looks at me, a look of betrayal on his face. I widen my eyes, trying to beam a telepathic message that it's okay, that I have a plan.

"Steph, you keep your mouth shut," he says.

Clearly, he didn't get the message.

Whatever, him being a jerk just makes it that much more believable, and it makes it easier for me to throw him under the bus. "Emmett," I say, trying to keep my voice calm even though I want to shout and swear like Ally does so effortlessly. "I've kept this secret for you because I love you and it's what you wanted. But they should know." This part is true, at least for what I'm about to tell them.

Talk about secrets turning you into something dark… Emmett's temper has been out of control these last few months, and I've had about enough. I snatch the envelope from his hand and stand up, holding it over my head. This next move is risky, but I need to do it in order for them to believe me. I pull out the piece of paper, nod like it's only confirming what I'm about to say, and slip it back in the envelope before I speak.

"Emmett has a heart condition."

"Steph—" Emmett starts, and then stops, realizing that's all I said. He's not happy this is getting out, but this is not what he was expecting me to say. It's certainly not what I just read on that slip of paper.

I notice Charlene twitches ever so slightly, her head tilting to the side. I hope I haven't upset her. Today should be about her son, and we've already heard quite enough without adding Emmett's health problems to the mix. But after all, this *was* her son's intention, even if I'm not telling the whole truth.

"What does *that* mean?" Ally asks. She stares at me accusingly. I know what the look means. *How dare you keep me out of the loop? You're just the girlfriend, but I've been here since the beginning.*

"He's got a condition called hypertrophic cardiomyopathy."

"Hyper *what?*" Ally asks.

"It's HCM for short. It means the walls of his heart are thicker than they should be, which causes problems in the heart's electrical functions."

"That sounds… Is it serious?" Murphy asks.

"No, it's really not that big—" Emmett starts.

"It is serious," I interrupt. "In most cases, people don't know they have HCM until their heart stops. Especially in young athletes… Often it's not discovered until after they've dropped dead in the middle of a game or something."

"Oh my God!" Ally gasps. "Now I remember! Wasn't that what Lucas had on *One Tree Hill?*"

Everyone looks at Ally in disbelief.

"What?" she asks. "It was really serious…"

"So how did you find out?" Ruby asks, ignoring Ally. She directs her question at Emmett, probably hoping he will look up from the spot on the floor he's currently drilling a hole into with his eyes. He is red to the tips of his hair follicles.

"He was lucky," I continue. "For him, it started with what's called A-fib, which is like a rapid fluttering in your chest. About nine months ago, he was playing basketball with his work buddies at lunch and had to stop because he couldn't catch his breath. He started to say something about his heart before he passed out for a minute. They thought he had a heart attack, but at the hospital they ran all kinds of tests and diagnosed him with HCM." A chill runs through the group. There are a lot of heart problems in the air. First Roger's, now Emmett's.

"How do they treat it?" Ruby asks.

"Well, the danger of HCM is that your heart will stop, so if no one is around to start it again… Well, you can imagine." I can't say the words. "So they…*installed*…a defibrillator. You've see doctors on TV rubbing those big paddles together and yelling 'Clear!' until all the nurses get out of the way? It's a miniature version of that. It will start his heart again if it ever stops beating."

"So then, you're fine!" Ally says, brightening. "As long as you have that, you're fine, right?"

Emmett nods slowly, not removing his eyes from the spot on the ground.

"Not really," I interject. Might as well give them the whole ball of facts, as Ally would say. At least about this part of it. "He has to be on medication that makes him dizzy and sometimes nauseous and drowsy, and he has to be a lot more careful about his heart rate. Which means no strenuous exercise."

The crew is silent at this, and I know what they're thinking. Emmett, the Chatwick High basketball star, who used to be as active as they come—even when he wasn't playing basketball or hockey, he was running or swimming, always in motion. It's not that he can't do any of those things anymore, it's just that he has physical limits he can no longer push, and pushing limits is what Emmett has always prided himself on.

We thought getting the defibrillator put in and the recovery would be the worst part, but it wasn't. The hard part has been the aftermath. The changes in his lifestyle. The struggle to regain a sense of normalcy, the loss of the confidence that made me fall in love with him in the first place. His temper has never been so short, and it's so important that he stay calm and not put more stress on his already overburdened heart.

"Steph," Murphy pipes up. "When you say *installed*, do you mean…"

I nod. "Surgically."

He rounds on Emmett now. "You had your *chest cracked open*, and you didn't tell anyone about it?" Murphy asks. I breathe a silent sigh of relief. Just as I had hoped, this part of Emmett's secret is big enough for them to believe.

I interject, "He didn't exactly have his chest cracked open. They did an incision here." I point to the spot on Emmett's chest, just under his collarbone on the left side. Emmett jerks away from me, but I continue anyway. "And they ran the leads—the wires—down into his heart laparoscopically."

"Still," Murphy says, "how is it even possible to pull something like that off without any of us knowing? In this town?"

"I don't know, Murphy. How is it possible to cover up a murder?" Emmett shoots back. They glare at each other.

"We went down to Brigham and Women's Hospital in Boston," I explain before this all turns nasty again. I catch Emmett's eye and look pointedly at Charlene, who's shut her eyes against us. Emmett softens and mumbles a "sorry" in her direction. "They have one of the world's leading experts on HCM, and it worked out for Emmett that she's in Boston because he didn't want anyone to know. He didn't even let me call his parents until after he was out of the hospital." I had strongly objected to this, but I was so concentrated on him staying alive that I would have done anything he asked me to.

"But *why?*" Ally asks, her voice more full of hurt now than anger. And I understand it. Why wouldn't he want his friends to be there for him?

"I didn't want people treating me differently," Emmett says. "Ally, you would have made a big fuss and started bossing me around. Don't"—he holds up one hand as Ally opens her mouth to protest—"act like you wouldn't. We all know you can't help yourself."

The crew smiles at this. Well, all except Ally, who goes into a reflexive pout before she shrugs and nods in agreement.

"And you guys"—he looks at Aaron and Murphy—"you'd start taking it easy on me on the court, looking at me funny. I just couldn't take it. I still can't. That's why I'm always 'too busy' to play."

Everyone nods in agreement. They are promising to themselves, to each other, that they won't treat him any differently. That they won't pity him. But they will. I know, because I made those promises too.

"We thought you were just whipped," Aaron says, lightening the mood. One sweet moment of relief after all the awful news.

Ally looks at me, a twinkle of honest-to-God understanding in her eye. "Is that why you were so upset at the funeral? Were you thinking about what it would have been like to…"

I look at Charlene, hoping Ally will understand that I don't want to insult her son's memory by affirming that my tears had nothing to do with him. Ally is mostly right, but I just shrug. It's more complicated than that. Danny said it himself: *None of you bothered to try to help me when I was alive, when it counted.* Just like everyone else here, Emmett and I could have helped Danny, but we didn't.

After a moment, Ruby asks, "The thing I don't understand is, if you kept this under such tight wraps, how did Danny know? I mean, you guys were never exactly close."

Emmett turns to me, trying to hide the panic in his eyes.

"He didn't exactly choose Danny," I pipe in, looking straight at Emmett. "After the diagnosis, Em didn't have much of an appetite, and I had trouble sleeping. We needed something to…ease the anxiety."

I watch as they struggle to connect the dots. Then Ruby claps her hand to her mouth, stifling a bark of a laugh. "You went to Dan to get *pot*?"

Emmett's face flushes, and he shoots me a glare that says I'm in for it when we get home. But who cares? His reaction still perfectly confirms Ruby's theory. It's close enough to the truth that no one will question it and far enough away to keep us safe.

The crew howls with laughter, but Charlene's expression remains grim. I'm guessing she doesn't find drug use particularly funny these days, even the herbal kind.

"What is so fucking funny about that?" Emmett demands, losing his already miniscule amount of patience.

"I'm sorry," Ruby chokes out between giggles. "It's just…the guy who gave us a Nancy Reagan lecture every time we lit up a joint becomes a pothead at twenty-eight years old!" Fresh waves of laughter ripple through us.

"Just say no," Murphy says, wagging his finger and deepening his voice to imitate Emmett's serious voice. More laughter.

"Ruby, you're destroying your brain cells," Ruby says, doing the same.

"Well, you were," Emmett says. Even I have to giggle at the way he stands with his arms crossed, in perfect Stern Dad posture.

"And now *you* are!" Ruby says through her giggles. It's not really all that funny, but the laughter is needed after the day we've had. After the *year* Emmett and I have had.

"*Anyway,*" Emmett says over the din. "Dan, of course, had to give me the same hard time you're giving me—"

"Or he was concerned about you because twenty-eight is a little old to start experimenting with drugs," Ruby interrupts.

"—and I lost my temper—"

"Shocker."

"—and I ended up telling him. Honestly, I didn't think he would remember. Toward the end he was, you know, pretty out of it."

That sucks the mirth right out of the room.

"All right. Your turn," Emmett says, his arms still crossed. He looks straight at Murphy.

"My turn for what?"

"Your secret. I went. Your turn."

Murphy breathes a laugh out of his nose. "You didn't exactly *go*. Your girlfriend went for you."

Again, three years with these people, and I'm still just the girlfriend.

"Whatever. I don't care. Out with it."

"We just talked about it, dude. Ruby and I knew about Danny and…the thing…with Roger." He shoots a look to Charlene, who looks surprised. I doubt Danny shared with her the fact that he confessed to Ruby and Murphy that night.

Ruby, meanwhile, says nothing.

Emmett narrows his eyes at them, but he must decide it's better not to press, considering he's lying too. He turns on Ally. "And you?"

Ally hesitates, looking at Murphy and Ruby as if she's hoping they will take their turn again. "Mine is…" She looks at Aaron, who looks just as interested as Emmett. She's on her own. Her face suddenly brightens, her posture straightening. "It's nothing bad. It's good actually, and I'll tell you guys… I just don't want to tell it today. Not after the day we've had. Okay?"

Charlene crosses her arms, seemingly dissatisfied. I'm sure she doesn't want to be left out after being involved up until this point. I mean, wouldn't you rather be distracted by our drama than mourn your only child? Ally looks at the rest of us, waiting for us all to nod, which we do.

When it comes to things that really matter, you guys barely even know each other.

Ally's, Murphy's, and Ruby's envelopes all remain unopened, their hands clutched around them like their lives depend on keeping them closed.

4

RUBY
NOW

"Remember when Emmett mixed up mayo and ketchup and hot sauce and Kool-Aid and dirt and all that shit and then paid Danny a dollar to eat it, and when he didn't pay up, Dan threw up on his shoes?"

"Remember when Ruby drove us home from the homecoming party during that freak snowstorm, and when she started to skid, Murphy panicked and pulled the e-brake, and we ended up in that ditch facing the other way? And the cops brought us home?"

"Remember when Ally's bikini top popped off when she jumped into the quarry, and she was so shocked by the cold water she didn't realize it for, like, five minutes?"

The stories from fifteen years of friendship flow like a faucet that won't turn off. Despite Aaron's signature method of peer pressure (one hand clasped on my shoulder in what the crew lovingly calls "the claw," the other hand holding a shot of well liquor under my nose), I have stood strong, shaking my head at each one-ounce parcel of liquid courage. The crew, who do not have my self-imposed three-drink limit, have partaken enough to get us to this point: the proverbial walk down memory lane.

Adhering to our old customs, I have already gotten complete histories on two high school classmates I only vaguely remember; I've debated the upcoming election with Emmett while the crew rolled their eyes in the background; and when he realized he was losing, he resorted to picking apart my outfit. (Ally's black top and dark-wash jeans passed inspection, but since I couldn't squeeze my big feet into Ally's dainty shoes, we searched through my high school wardrobe and fished out my old cowboy boots from my high school closet, which Ally had declared "classic.")

But not everything is the same. A welcome addition to the night's proceedings has been getting to know Steph. In addition to siding with me while Emmett and I debated equal pay (Emmett refuses to acknowledge it's a problem), Steph works at the Chatwick Community Library, which explains the instantaneous ease I felt with her earlier. She carries the scent of old books. It makes me think of the days when I used to sneak the ancient editions of classic novels from my father's bookshelf and read them by flashlight in my closet. He didn't want me reading them until I was older and more "responsible with the bindings."

Sometimes I would fall asleep reading them, and Nancy would find me in the closet the next morning, nestled among a heap of pillows I'd assembled for comfort. She never told my dad, just smuggled the book back into its place before he could notice.

Reading—and everything about it—provided the escape I needed from whatever turmoil was going on in the house, and I think she knew that.

An unwelcome change I can't shake is the way Murphy and I sit on opposite ends of the row of stools the crew occupies, although the scent he carries isn't having any trouble infiltrating my nose from there.

I try to remain present, but every few minutes I find my eyes wandering to the Exit sign. It hurts to be here. In Chatwick, for one, but especially in Margie's Pub, otherwise known as the congregation of Chatwick's finest. The town is made up of rednecks, who farm on the outskirts of "the City" (which is really a bunch of neighborhoods, a few blocks of shops, and the high school); white trash, who live below the tracks and off the government; and *richies*, a relative term the other two camps invented to make people like me and my friends feel like snobs for living in the hill section of the city and having parents who own local businesses or commute to more affluent communities, like Burlington, to work. All three groups are fairly represented tonight, and they've all spent the evening staring at me, trying to decide exactly how to describe me to the Chat tomorrow.

But the biggest reason I am so uncomfortable at Margie's is the memories. Memories I shouldn't have, considering I left Chatwick when I was eighteen years old, well before I was legally allowed to gain entrance. The last time, I was responding to a courtesy call from Monty, the four-hundred-pound bouncer, to warn me Nancy was approaching her cutoff point and I'd best get down here before she pitched a fit and then hopped in the driver's seat. This was a fairly regular occurrence my freshman and sophomore year of high school, to the point that Monty knew he could reach me at Danny's if I wasn't at home, and any one of my friends would call out "It's Nancy time" when they answered the phone.

They all took turns coming with me to help carry Nancy's deadweight into the house after she inevitably passed out on the short drive back from the bar. Danny was with me the last time, when we had to leave my sixteenth birthday celebration to pick her up. That was the very special day Nancy drunkenly told me she wished I'd never been born so she could actually have a little fun. Happy Sweet Sixteen, right? That was the last time I tried to save her, and the day I stopped calling her Mom. She didn't remember it the next day, or at least she acted like she didn't remember.

I was surprised when Monty slapped my hand away as I tried to show him my driver's license and pulled me into a hug instead, although we did have quite the special relationship back then. Besides the warning calls, there was the time a beer-bellied redneck got handsy with me as I pulled him off my mother. Monty dragged him into the alley and beat the shit out of him. So I guess Margie's has produced one happy memory for me. Of course, that was followed by two months of harassment at Chatwick High from the redneck's kids, who were forced to pick up the slack around the farm for a week because their father was out of commission. So, a bittersweet memory, I guess.

Before I could even ask Monty how he was, he assured me Nancy wasn't here tonight, that she hadn't been in over ten years. Ally, who had her hand clamped on my elbow (I imagine more in an effort to prevent my escape than to stay linked as we navigated the crowd of smokers outside the bar), explained to him that I am here to be with friends tonight, not to drag my mother out by her hair.

By the time the crew was exhausted from the day's drama, it had grown dark outside Charlene's basement windows. Charlene once again retreated to her room and wouldn't come out despite Ally's and my attempts, so we joined the crew in the driveway where they were already making plans to meet up here. I had nodded with my fingers crossed behind my back. My plan was to shut myself in my childhood bedroom, pretending to answer client emails but really refreshing my computer screen every thirty seconds to see if a flight back to New York became available. Because Vermont's main airport in Burlington is so small, the seat I vacated today to attend Danny's "private reception" was the last seat back to New York until Sunday night—three days away.

But Ally was one step ahead of me. I had just barely settled in and booted up my laptop, suddenly unsure if I could even connect to the internet in this house, when she showed up. She waved Aaron off in his LJ Construction truck as soon as her foot was in the door.

"He has to go save our seats," she said. "It gets rough down there."

As if I didn't know that.

"Plus, I thought it would be fun to ride down just us girls. I know Nancy hasn't gotten rid of Blue. She brings it into Borbeau's every six months or so. Danny worked on it himself."

The thought of Danny working on my car in the shop he's worked at since high school makes me suddenly sick. All these years, Danny had worked on the car we spent hours tooling around in. We were still connected, and I didn't even know it. It's as if my car is haunted or something. Ally must have felt this too, because it silenced her for a full ten seconds. Then she brightened decidedly and dumped out the bag of clothes she brought for me, assuming—correctly, since I hadn't planned on staying past the funeral—that I hadn't packed an appropriate outfit for a night at a bar.

We really didn't need to drive. Margie's is only about four blocks from my parents' house—an absurdly lucky walking distance in New York but unheard of to walk here. Everyone drives everywhere in Chatwick. If you're walking, you're trash who can't afford a car. The neighborhood about had a conniption when Nancy quit drinking and started taking daily walks to keep herself "centered."

The short ride down to the bar was quiet, and not in the comfortable, peaceful way our rides around the back roads of Chatwick used to be. The air was thick with questions we were both too afraid to ask, for fear of them being turned back around to ourselves. Now, at the bar, that doesn't seem to be a problem. It only took a dead friend, a threatening letter, and three hours at Margie's to catapult us from awkward estrangement to our new sense of normalcy. The one where we are all together without Danny.

In an effort to fit in, I pipe up with my favorite story from our high school years. "Remember when Emmett ate the mushroom pizza?" I ask, eyeing him.

"Oh. My. God. The mushroom pizza!" Ally cries. Murphy and Aaron throw their heads back in laughter.

"What pizza?" Steph asks.

I cock my head, not taking my eyes off Emmett while I ask, "Oh, you mean he *never told you that story?*"

"Ruby…" he warns.

"So we're all at Danny's about to try mushrooms for the first time," I start, ignoring Emmett to the rest of the crew's utter delight. "Emmett, of course, is all bent out of shape about it because he was all 'Just say no' about everything but booze. Back then, anyway."

We giggle, thinking about his recent dalliance with marijuana a good half-life after the rest of us.

"So when Danny goes to dole them out, Emmett *slaps* the bottom of Danny's hand, and the mushrooms go flying everywhere. Now, we're out in the woods behind Danny's house, and it's dark out so we can't see where they land. So Danny goes to get the flashlight Charlene always kept in the kitchen junk drawer, but it's not there, so we have no choice but to give up the search until the next morning."

The others are hanging on my every word, Ally and Murphy and Aaron clutching at each other, knowing where the story is going but in suspense for the punch line nonetheless. Emmett crosses his arms and purses his lips, shaking his head, his face the color of Pepto-Bismol.

"So we're all pissed at Emmett, even though he *swears* up and down he didn't mean to lose the 'shrooms, that he was even thinking about trying some…like we believed that! So we spend the night drinking instead, but what Emmett doesn't know is before we went into the woods, Danny had cut up a couple of the 'shroom stems and spread them over the leftover pizza in his fridge. Charlene *always* had leftover pizza, and Emmett *always* ate it late night when things started winding down. You could almost set your watch to it. When Emmett started eating pizza, it was twenty minutes before everyone went to bed."

"He still does that," Steph says, glancing lovingly at her boyfriend before seeing his now-fuchsia face and darting her eyes back to me, tucking her lips in to stifle a laugh.

"So we all go to bed…Danny in his room with Jenny or Heather or whoever he was dating at the time, Aaron and Ally in the spare, Emmett in the basement, *or so we thought*."

I leave Emmett's old girlfriend, Nicki, out of the sleeping arrangement discussion, because Emmett's pissed enough at me already, and I don't know yet whether Steph is the jealous type.

"And Murphy and I are on the trampoline in the backyard, where we always slept in the summer because the couples always claimed all the beds. Well, the next thing I know, I feel like someone's staring at me, and when I roll over, there's Emmett, standing by the trampoline, his eyes so alert and wide open they practically glow in the dark, and he just says 'Hi' with this big dopey grin on his face." I pause, giggling at the image of how cheerful he was, blissfully unaware of what was happening to him.

"Then he starts babbling at the speed of light about how drugs are bad and we don't need them and didn't we have a great time just drinking and hanging out"—Ally points out here how ironic this is—"and then he gets distracted by something and starts running around the yard mumbling something about 'the goddamn fairies.'" This gets big laughs, although I remember being completely freaked out about it at the time.

"I wake up Murphy to help me get him under control, but he of course makes it worse, pointing out things in the woods that aren't really there and then pretending like he never said it." I give Murphy, who's moved closer to me now, a playful punch on the arm, and Emmett does the same.

"Dude, I was sixteen!" Murphy says, laughing. "I was an asshole." At least he admits it.

"So Emmett takes off into the woods, and Murphy the hero passes right back out, and I can't wake him up again, so I have to go inside and wake Danny and Aaron to go out and find Emmett—with no flashlights, mind you—while Ally and I argue over how long to wait before we wake up Charlene or call the police."

"I still feel like we should have woken her up right away," Ally says. She also doesn't mention Nicki's role in the story, which was to cry and wail, convinced her boyfriend had been abducted.

"I didn't want to get Danny in trouble!" I say. I'm momentarily knocked off course when I hear myself say the words I've said too many times before.

"So what happened?" Steph asks, prompting me back on track after a minute of staring into space.

"Right. So right as we're about to go wake Charlene up, Danny and Aaron drag Emmett in, dirt *all over* his face, and he's holding"—I pause here for dramatic effect, and Steph leans in, her eyes wide—"the missing flashlight!"

We all laugh at this, including Steph, but not Emmett. When I come up for air, I add, "He purposely hid it under the porch before we went out in the woods. He planned to ruin our night all along. Serves him right!"

As the laughter dies down, Emmett starts nodding his head slowly and with a sadistic smile on his face. I know I'm in for it.

"I could tell some stories about Ruby too," he says, not taking his eyes off me.

I ignore the tingling in my gut and put a challenging look into my eye. "Oh yeah? Try me." I take a sip of my last allotted beer for the evening and wait. Emmett and I go way back, but we've never been the type of friends to confide in each other. I'm reasonably confident my "Danny secret" is safe.

"Remember the time when Ruby *finally* got drunk, and she gave up her virg—"

"Emmett!" Steph cries. The sound of his girlfriend's voice wipes the snarl from his face. His eyes open wide, seeming to understand that he went too far, too fast. "I'm sorry," Steph says. "His temper since the surgery…" And she leads him away from us like he's her child who just misbehaved in front of company.

I'm left behind, my face burning.

"Hey, let's dance!" Murphy cuts through the awkward silence. Before I can protest, he practically yanks me from my stool and shoves me out to the dance floor. The band plays "Folsom Prison Blues," to which everyone roars approval, and they start stomping around, clapping their hands. I stand stock-still, too stunned at what Emmett was about to say to move my body in any kind of rhythmic fashion. It's been so long since I've thought of any of that.

I open my mouth to ask what the hell just happened, but Murphy holds his finger to his lips and takes my hand, spinning me under his raised arm. Soon Ally and Aaron join us, and I feel the sensation return to my feet. I look over to the bar, where it looks like Emmett is getting a dressing-down from Steph before she leaves him there to join us on the dance floor.

Damn, I *really* like this girl.

After a few minutes, Emmett makes his way over to us. He clasps my arm—to prevent me from leaving or socking him one, I'm not sure—and mouths *I'm sorry*. It's so surprising he's apologizing that I instantly forgive him. I remember now. This is what it's like, what it was always like, the constant ebbs and flows of being with the crew. Drink. Gossip. Fight. Make up. Repeat.

The song changes to "I Love This Bar," which my friends seem to know every word to. They couple off and, as always, leave Murphy and me standing alone. He pulls me to him, and when I instinctively stiffen and try to pull back, he clutches me so tightly I can't help but laugh.

"No running away," he says into my ear. "No more running away."

I keep the smile plastered on my face, but my eyes water, and I'm grateful we're dancing the grade school way—my arms around his neck, his encircling my waist, my head safely looking over his shoulder. If we were dancing the traditional way, he would be able to see my tears and feel my sweaty palms. As it is, I have to reach up to get my arms around his shoulders, and it's much more of a reach than it was the last time we danced.

We turn slowly around the dance floor, every muscle in my body on high alert. His smell overwhelms me. Since I can't seem to get away physically, I try to detach myself from this moment mentally by scanning the room as we spin. I notice at least four beams of hatred trained on me, and I wonder if the last dance at Margie's with Murphy Leblanc is a coveted privilege. I think about asking him, but I find myself breathless, and not just because he's holding me so tight. We've danced together like this a million times, always the ones left out together. The last time was senior prom. Jesus, I cannot think about senior prom.

"You're welcome," he says into my hair.

"Oh," I say. "Thanks for the save. Emmett's such an assh—"

"I'm not talking about Emmett."

I look at him now. His eyes shine with the familiar spark of something only we know, a spark we've shared ever since the night Roger died. But this has nothing to do with Roger, just like our secrets don't. I wasn't sure before whether he was covering for us or not, but now I know.

When finally, blessedly, the song ends, the bright overhead lights turn on and bathe the bar with a shocking reminder there is life outside Margie's. I hug everyone goodbye, thinking as I do that I've actually made it through this roller coaster of a day. More importantly, I've made it through without my secret being outed. Now all I have to do is hide in my room for the rest of the weekend.

But as the girls and I collect our purses from behind the bar, where Murphy had "his buddy" the bartender keep an eye on them, someone from the other side of the bar catches my eye. It takes me a second to place her, and by the time I do, she's already made a beeline for me.

"Ruby. *Saint*. James." she says, sneering her emphasis on the "Saint." She is thinner than I remember her, almost sickly thin, and her hair frames her face in two limp, greasy curtains. Her eyes are bloodshot; her nostrils, pink-rimmed. The years have not been kind to her. I try to appear as if this girl's presence is a happy surprise, but my breath is caught in my throat.

"Brandy…"

"McCallister," she scoffs, mistaking my panic for forgetfulness. If only she knew I have never forgotten her full name. That sometimes I wake up in the middle of the night with it on the tip of my tongue.

"McCallister, right. How are you?" I smile weakly. The fluorescent lights grow brighter, doing nothing to hide the harsh reality of Brandy's appearance.

"It's actually not McCallister anymore," she says, flashing a diamond the size of a flea.

"Oh?"

"It's Crane. Mrs. *Hardy* Crane." The name causes an instantaneous flutter of anxiety in my stomach, but she says it with a flourish, like she's been rehearsing this moment for a decade.

Suddenly it feels like I'm trying to swallow sand. "Oh!" I say. "How wonderful." I risk a glance around to see if Hardy himself is here to haunt me.

"He's not here," she says, following my gaze smugly, mistaking my fear for interest.

"He's at home with *the kids*. Girls' night out." She points to a posse of girls who are watching us carefully. Like Brandy, they are dressed in age-inappropriate clothing fished out of the clearance bin at the Fashion Bug off I-89. If their outfits weren't so tight, I would have been worried about concealed weapons, the way they're looking at me.

"Doesn't look like you've changed much," Brandy says. "Still running around after other girls' men." She looks at Murphy. "Where's Krystal tonight, Murphy?"

I look at Murphy, who rolls his eyes. My instinct, my inner Chatwickian, wants to ask him who the hell Krystal is, wants to defend myself to Brandy that I have no idea who she's talking about, that I'm a different person now. But I don't. I'm not going to allow myself to go back down this road, back to high school. "Well, best of luck to you, Brandy," I say and turn to leave.

She grabs my elbow, clamping down with all her might. She leans in and snarls into my ear, "If you think you can just saunter back into town and—"

"Back off, Brandy." Ally steps in between us.

Brandy instantly drops her grip, but she doesn't step back. "I'm just telling her—"

"I know what you're telling her. You're the only person in this town who thinks Hardy Crane is some prize to compete over, but you're embarrassing yourself. I think it's time for you to head on home."

Brandy looks at Ally through narrowed eyes, drunkenly trying to decide whether to press the issue. She opens her mouth again, but then Murphy steps in.

"You heard her, Brandy. Go on home to your family." It's so strange to hear such grown-up words coming out of Murphy Leblanc's mouth. Here we are rehashing drama straight out of Chatwick High as if I'd never left, but he's talking like a grown man to a grown woman who has a *husband* and *children* at home. The surrealism makes me queasy.

Shaken, I thank Ally, giving her and the rest of my friends a farewell hug. How sad it is for the evening to end this way, after the already tragic day we've had. Who knows when I will see my old friends again, and the last thing they will remember of me is the old business with Hardy Crane.

Murphy hovers nearby as I shrug off Ally's attempt to further engage about what just happened. He puts his hand in the small of my back and starts to guide me through the crowd. When I look at him questioningly, he smiles sadly and says, "I'll walk you to your car." In that look, I know he knows I'm not planning on attending any more reunion events. And he's not letting me leave without a private goodbye.

Once we're outside, I point to the farthest corner of the lot where I'm parked. The lot is not large, but the walk seems endless. I haven't been alone with Murphy since the summer before I left for college. I cringe, thinking about that summer. "So, Ally tells me your business is doing well," I say. I'm trying to rebalance from the drama that just occurred, but my voice shakes. My mind is still trapped in a time I have fought so hard to put behind me.

When he doesn't answer me, I risk a glance at him. His hands are in the pockets of his jeans, making him look like he's mid-shrug. I try not to notice the muscles showing through his formfitting T-shirt. The tattoo is still throwing me, as is the gray peppering the thick head of hair that used to be black as night. I never dreamed he would be any different than he was the last time I saw him, as if he was just going to freeze in place when I left.

But he didn't. There's no sign of the extra layer of fat he grew up with, and his posture is straighter, more confident. I had just started to look at him as handsome before I left for college, but it's still a shock to see him like this. It's like I blinked, and the boy who used to wear a T-shirt to go swimming disappeared in favor of this…*man*. A beautiful man at that. A head-turning kind of man.

I tear my eyes away, wondering if I should bring up the confrontation with Brandy. Wondering, most of all, if I should ask who the hell this *Krystal* is. When I look at him, though, he is smiling a bemused smile and staring off into nowhere. When he finally speaks, it's not to talk about any of that.

"Where you been, Tuesday?" It's the question I didn't think he'd ask. We walk in silence the last few feet to my car.

I sigh. "You know where I've been, Murphy. New York. London. New York again."

"No phones in New York or London? I mean, I can understand why you didn't call *me*, but Ally? Emmett? Danny?"

"I…got busy." The excuse is pathetic and untrue. I look down, my hands trembling as I search for the right key through the tears that fill my eyes again. He takes both of my hands in his and pulls me to face him. His brown eyes are like magnets, and I don't know how long we look at each other before he reaches into my clasped hands, fishes out my keys, and swiftly inserts the one with the Nissan emblem on it into the keyhole. Our gaze breaks along with the tension.

"Still drivin' this thing around, huh? Old Blue?" he teases, his tone suddenly jovial again.

"It's been in my parents' garage all these years. You know Nancy," I say as I open the door and climb into the driver's seat. It's the middle of September and just cold enough for an open window to be unnecessary. I crank it down anyway to get another few minutes with him.

"It's a perfectly good car!" Murphy says, in a spot-on imitation of Nancy. "No use getting rid of something that works just fine!"

I laugh, and he crouches down and rests his arms on the windowsill. "Nice to hear that sound again," he says. I'm starting up the car, so I don't know if he's talking about Blue's sad little engine or my laugh. Again, our eyes lock. Suddenly the smile is gone, and his face is moving toward me. *No*, I think, but my head moves toward him despite it.

"Hey, Murphy! Wanna get a move on? The bar's closed, and I need to take a piss!" Emmett. Sweet, eloquent Emmett.

"Yeah, I'm comin'," Murphy says. He looks at me one last time, smiling, and gives his shaggy head a shake.

"Drive safe," he says. He stands up, but seems to change his mind and leans in again. "You know, you've come a long way since Hardy Crane, Tuesday."

I watch as he walks away with a sad smile on his face. As soon as I pull around the corner and am out of sight, I cry the whole way home.

5

ALLY
BACK THEN—(ALMOST) JUNIOR YEAR

I don't like what I'm seeing with Ruby and Hardy Crane. Hardy has that look in his eye, the same look my dad used to get before he went out hunting with Uncle Charlie. And he's refilling Ruby's shot glass like he's looking for a tip, and I don't mean a dollar bill. His antenna is up for sure—the one that tells him when there's a vulnerable girl around.

Meanwhile, Danny and Emmett just sit there, laughing as Ruby gets wasted. I can understand Danny—he does, after all, have a skewed version of what *wasted* means, and he doesn't want to offend his best customer—but Emmett, Mr. Sobriety, is trying to be Mr. Cool just because we're sophomores and Hardy is a senior. Who cares? It's his second time being one; that doesn't exactly make him Top Shit.

I figured Hardy would leave Danny's house after Danny sold him whatever it was he wanted, but he's still here and for no good reason. I mean, he's on the hockey team with Aaron, but they are *not* friends. Aaron *knows* what happened when Hardy and I dated. It's actually how Aaron and I met. When I was a freshman, I was too dumb to know better, and I fell for Hardy's bad boy act too. But only for a week or so.

On our third "date" (if you count mud bogging in his truck and him pawing me on Lester Gabrioult's couch as dates one and two), Hardy took me to the homecoming after-party at Dunphy's field, got so drunk he pissed his pants, and slapped me across the face when I tried to quietly point it out. Hardy's friends hauled him away, and I was too shocked to move. Then Aaron came out of nowhere, this handsome guy I'd seen around the halls at Chatwick High who came from the Town School. He offered me a ride home in his brother's car, and we've been together ever since.

I don't know why Ruby is even *talking* to Hardy, let alone going shot for shot with a guy who uses his liver like a toilet. She's never really been a big drinker, at least not compared to the rest of us. I'm guessing because she doesn't want to end up like her mother. I mean, she'll have a beer or two and take a poke of whatever's being passed around, but I've never seen her *drunk*. That would mean she'd have to lose some control, and we all know she can't do that. But suddenly she's Miss Free Spirit, sniffing after my sloppy seconds.

I think I've been pretty good about giving her space since she's been staying at my house (as much space as you can give when you're sharing a bed), but *clearly* she isn't dealing with her family drama as well as she'd like us all to believe. Wouldn't you think if your mother landed in rehab and your father told you he's not coming back until she's sober for a year, you would want to talk about it? Especially with someone who knows what it's like for your dad to quit on you?

Not Ruby though. When she's going through stuff, she wants to be left alone. And if you push her, she'll just clam up more. So I let her be, and try not to be too mad when she sneaks out of bed and brings the cordless into the bathroom to call Murphy. Ruby is usually pretty serious, especially these days, but you'd think she was at a comedy show from the sounds I hear coming from that bathroom. Murphy's not even that funny.

It makes no sense to me. When we were really little, Ruby and Murphy weren't very close. In fact, they sort of "went out" for like a week in sixth grade just because everyone else was going out with people and they didn't want to be left out. But after they went to the movies, Ruby came back and complained that Murphy's hand was sweaty when he tried to hold hers, and Murphy complained that Ruby wouldn't let him kiss her, and that was that.

And then suddenly, right around the time Danny's stepfather died, Ruby, Murphy, and Danny seemed to spin off into their own little crew within the crew. I get Ruby and Danny—their families are the most messed up, even considering my parents are divorced—but Murphy? I'm guessing he started hanging around her so much because she got boobs.

Anyway, when Ruby's dad checked Nancy into rehab and then decided to take his own little vacation from parenthood, he made arrangements for Ruby to stay with us. He left her plenty of money, but she still insists on working at that secondhand store. I used to think she just liked having clothes different from the rest of the kids at school—although I *personally* don't see what's wrong with shopping at the Burlington Mall at the Gap or American Eagle for brand-new clothes that haven't been sweated in and who knows what else by some stranger.

But now I think it has something to do with the old ladies she works for. They're like forty and fifty. I don't know what they could *possibly* have to talk about, but every time I walk in there to visit her, they're just chattering away. Maybe it's because she's like an old lady herself. No one knows that about her, because she's been through so much and talks tough and smokes cigarettes like a chimney. But underneath that, all she cares about is getting good grades. I swear, when we used to ride the bus together, she would pull out a *book* and just sit there and *read*. What a nerd! I mean, I'm sitting *right there* for her to talk to, and she's got her nose stuck in a book. How rude!

And *speaking* of rude, the boys are getting less helpful by the minute. Jenny shows up, Danny's girlfriend (or whatever she is to him these days; I can't keep track), so he disappears into his room with her. Nicki's parents are out of town again, so Emmett leaves to take advantage of her empty house, and Aaron and *Murphy*, Ruby's so-called best friend, haven't gotten back from their munchie run to the Quik Stop, leaving me all alone as Hardy moves in on Ruby. I have to do everything around here. When Hardy goes to refill Ruby's glass again, I finally say, "Ruby, I think you've had enough."

Ruby just glares at me—like I'm the bad guy here!—and Hardy says, "Ooh-hoo, looks like someone's jealous she's not getting all the attention anymore."

"Oh fuck off, Hardy, that has nothing to do with it." Yeah, right, *I'm* jealous. I'm sure that's exactly what he wants with this whole show he's putting on. I'm just not sure why Ruby is going along with it. It's like she's trying to hurt me and herself at the same time. "Look at her!" I say. "She can't hardly stand up!"

"Ally, I take care of m'self," Ruby slurs.

"Clearly," I say. She nods her head self-righteously, not picking up on my sarcasm.

Hardy mutters something about being "over this business" and makes like he's going to leave. Good riddance to white trash. This town is crawling with it, and Hardy is just one example of white trash who happens to be good at something (okay two things—hockey and funneling beer), so he's actually popular in spite of it. Just when I'm about to breathe a sigh of relief, he turns to Ruby. "Wanna get out of here?" he asks, like he couldn't give a shit whether she said yes or no.

Ruby just nods. I stand in front of her as she goes to follow him. "Ruby St. James, you are not getting in a car with someone who's been taking shots all night."

She pushes past me, says again she can take care of herself. "You're not my mother!" she yells as she struggles to slip on her shoes.

"Yeah, I know. Because if I were, I would be in *rehab!*" I yell back. It stops her in her tracks, and the hurt in her eyes makes me immediately regret saying it. But in my defense, for one, it's the truth; for two, she's treating me like shit just because I'm trying to protect her from being killed; and for three, I'm hoping it will make her mad enough that she'll stay here and fight with me.

It doesn't work. She slams the door behind her, and I hear the tires screech out of the driveway a minute later.

———

I sit up all night waiting for Ruby to come back, pacing and worrying like her goddamn mother should be doing. I switch between being pissed as all hell and sorry about what I said.

The thing you should know about Nancy St. James, in case this all comes back around to me, is that she's not *always* a useless, crazy drunk. Most of the time, she's like June frickin' Cleaver. Like bake sale director, food drive organizer, Halloween costume seamstress for Ruby *and* for me (because my mother has a job and zero sewing skills), cheerleader at Ruby's debate club *and* my tennis matches *and* Murphy's baseball games *and* Emmett's basketball games *and* Danny's... Well, Danny isn't heavy into extracurriculars that don't involve getting high, but you get the point.

I mean, sure, once every few months she's been asked to leave one of those events because the encouraging words she shouts are a little slurred and there's booze on her breath, but at least she makes the effort, right? She even has this slight southern accent that for some reason always makes me want to strap on an apron and make a cobbler or something. And the St. Jameses' house is so neat, with every last thing always in its proper place. Sometimes we rearrange her tchotchkes just to see if she'll notice. She *always* notices.

Then every once in a while, she'll get in this mood. Ruby calls them black periods, and it has something to do with being manic-depressive. Nancy stops coming to our games, and she stays in her room when we come over, and she stops doing all the stuff that makes her Top Shit Mom. After a week or so of that, she starts drinking. I don't know if she's trying to cheer herself up or what, but she drinks at home for a few days before she runs out of booze at the time of night when it's too late to restock at the gas station.

When that happens, she heads down to Margie's and doesn't leave until she's forced to.

Mr. St. James used to fish her out of there, but if the rumors are true, one night he found Nancy making out with some 'necker and said he was done rescuing her. So since before either of us even had permits, Ruby's been taking her dad's BMW to drive the four blocks down to Margie's and back. The whole town knows she does it, but they don't say anything because she can't be expected to drag Nancy kicking and screaming up that hill all by herself, and it's better than Nancy's drunk ass driving home. The advantage for the rest of us was that Ruby learned to sneak out and to drive so well that she could easily steal the car other times, just to tool around with us, and she taught all of us to drive.

When Aaron and Murphy finally get back, they've already devoured the entire food supply on the walk. Aaron is so stuffed he's "too tired" to stay up with me, so he goes to bed in the basement. I love him, but sometimes I could just pop him one. Murphy asks where Ruby is and I tell him *exactly*. He looks all worried for a second, but then he just goes to the spare room to sleep. Now it's frickin' three in the morning, and I'm sitting here on the love seat all by myself, flipping between the "Are You My Daddy?" talk show and an infomercial for this vibrating belt you strap to your stomach to lose weight.

"I can think of something else you can use that belt for," comes Danny's voice from the doorway.

I snap my tongue. "Ew, Danny, don't be gross," I say, but I lift up the afghan that's covering me so he knows he's welcome to sit with me. My legs are swung out, so I lift them too, and when he sits down,

I rest them on his lap. I wouldn't do it if Aaron were here, but that little bastard went to bed, and Danny and I have been friends since we were little, so I don't really care what Aaron thinks.

"Where's *Jenny*?" I ask.

"Sleeping," he says, grinning like a Cheshire cat. "She's very worn out."

I sock him on the arm. "What is the deal with you two? I thought you broke up."

He shrugs. "We did."

I do *not* understand their relationship, or really any of his relationships. Danny's one of those guys who doesn't like labels. He says putting a label on the interactions of two people suddenly shackles them to "a matrix of appropriate behaviors that correspond with that label." I don't understand what the hell he's talking about half the time.

"What are you doing awake?" Danny asks, giving my feet a squeeze over the afghan.

"Waiting for Ruby to come back."

He looks at me, confused. "She's not with Murphy in the spare room?"

"No. She's out with Hardy."

He looks at me like I just told him Ruby left with Marilyn Manson or something. "Oh shit," he says. He leans away from me against the arm of the couch, rubbing his forehead with his hand.

"Yeah."

"This is my fault."

"No it's not," I say, laying one hand on his shoulder.

"He was here because of me. I know what kind of guy he is. But I just thought Ruby was finally blowing off some steam. I never would have expected…"

"Hey," I say. "None of us would. Danny, look at me." I grab the hand that's still on my feet and hold it in mine. "You know how Ruby is once she gets something in her head. Remember that time she made us climb Hardrock Trail at midnight on New Year's Eve? Even if none of us followed her, she still would have done it."

But his face doesn't change. I can see he won't forgive himself. "I should have stuck around until Hardy left. I should have protected her. She's always done that for me."

"What do you mean?" I ask.

He looks into my eyes then, and I see a sadness I've seen before. I saw it the day I first brought Aaron to his house. I saw it for a long time after Roger died, and sometimes even before. He opens and closes his mouth, and I know whatever he's going to tell me is big, but then Ruby waltzes in.

She's not drunk anymore. At least, she's not stumbling all over the place. But she does look like hell. Her hair's all messed up, her eyes are puffy, and her shorts and tank top are wrinkled to shit. It doesn't take a genius, but I still can't believe it. Ruby St. James, Miss Top Shit Honor Roll, losing her virginity to some dumbass second-year senior? One that I dated, at that? I mean, it's not like I'm proud of it or still like him, but shit, chick rules, you know?

Danny stands up, and by the way he can hardly look at her, I know he knows what she's been doing. "You okay?" he asks.

For a second I think her face is going to crumple, but she changes her mind and gives him a bright smile. "I'm fine, Dan.

Go on to bed." He kisses her on the cheek before he follows her orders, leaving the room. And then it's just the two of us.

"Have fun?" I ask in a way that should tell her I'm pissed. I worried all night, and here she just strolls in without a word.

She pretends she's real into the talk show as she flops onto Charlene's La-Z-Boy, even though she always teases me for watching this shit. "Yeah," she says, casual as anything. "Hardy is actually pretty cool. We talked about our parents. His are even more fucked up than mine, if you can believe it." She says it like she rehearsed it. "Hey, are there any smokes left?"

Oh, and now she's going to *lie* to me and act like nothing happened? I've been walking on horseshoes for two weeks while she just pretends everything is fine, and now she's going to treat me like I'm *stupid?* "Really?" I say. "In all this time you spent 'talking,' did he tell you all about his girlfriend?"

That gets her attention. She narrows her eyes at me and shakes her head. "He said he wasn't seeing anyone. That he just broke up with—"

"Brandy McCallister?" I say. Ruby nods. "Well, that's funny, because Brandy McCallister called here about two hours ago. She said she was waiting for her *boyfriend* to get back with the weed. Wanted to make sure he was okay."

Ruby's face gets even whiter than usual. She swallows. "What did you tell her?"

"I told her he got you drunk and fucked you, Ruby," I say sarcastically. "What do you think? I lied! I told her he left hours ago, and I didn't know where he went. She was probably worried out of her mind he was in a ditch somewhere. Too bad she was right."

"Ally, cut it out," I hear from the doorway behind me. Oh, perfect. This is when Murphy decides to make an entrance, swooping in just as Ruby starts crying so I look like the bad guy and he gets to be the big hero.

Ruby crosses the room to Murphy, and he hugs her. Without a word, he leads her into the spare room where he's been sleeping while I've been up worrying. I'm about to sneak over to the door to see if I can hear them talking when Murphy comes back.

"Ally, what the hell is wrong with you?" he whisper yells at me.

"With *me*?" I whisper yell back. "What's wrong with *me*? I'm the one who's actually looking out for her, Murphy. What the hell did you do to help?"

"I wasn't even *here*!" he says.

"Exactly. You're supposed to be Ruby's 'best friend,' and you didn't think it was important to stay close and protect her when she's obviously going through a rough time?"

"Protect her from what? As far as I knew, *our friends* were supposed to be here shootin' the shit in Danny's basement, like always. Was I somehow supposed to know some predator would be here, just waiting to get Ruby drunk so he could—" He swallows. He doesn't want to say it. He doesn't want to think of Ruby acting so... Well, I don't need to say it out loud. You know what I'm thinking.

"Whatever, Murphy. All I'm saying is don't yell at me for not being able to stop Ruby from leaving with him. I *tried*. But you know Ruby. She doesn't listen to anyone. If you had been here, maybe you could have stopped her. God knows, you're the only one she listens to."

Murphy just looks at me. We're both pissed—at each other, at ourselves, at Hardy, but really at Ruby. And I think we both realize it, because we stop yelling. "I'm gonna go check on her," he says. I follow him, thinking I could probably comfort her better than Let's Have a Farting Contest Leblanc, but he closes the door on me before I can set foot in the room.

As the door is shutting, I see Ruby sitting on the bed with her head in her hands, and something is strange. I realize after the door shuts what's bugging me—the bed was made and the curtains were wide open on the window that faces the street. It looks like I'm not the only one who was waiting for her to come home.

I rest my ear against the door. I mean, it's only right to listen and make sure she's okay. I guess I *was* kinda harsh, but that's tough love. What was I supposed to do? Congratulate her on her first time being with a lowlife like Hardy? Pat her on the back for throwing out her virginity with the bathwater? She didn't confirm it, but I know what happened, because I know Hardy. And I *thought* I knew Ruby, but I guess not. She's supposed to be the smart one. Even if she didn't already know what Hardy did at Dunphy's field, she's still lived in this town all her life. She's pulled older versions of Hardy off her mother long enough that she can smell a bullshitter coming from a mile away.

All I hear for a few minutes are muffled sobs, and every once in a while Murphy shushing her and saying it's okay. Another relationship I will never understand.

The sobbing seems to be slowing down now, a good sign. I hear a sniffle and then "Oh God, I didn't know, Murph."

"I know," I hear him say.

"How could I be so stupid?"

"You're not stupid, Tuesday. You just made a mistake."

"Yeah, a really fucking stupid mistake." *Amen, sister,* I think.

"I already catch shit for Nancy being a slut. I can only imagine what's going to happen when people find out *I*—"

"Ruby, stop it. You are not a slut."

"I am! What else do you call losing it to someone else's *boyfriend* in the back of a *truck* on the side of the *road*? I'm a slut and a terrible person. Oh my God, I think I'm going to throw up, I'm so disgusted with myself."

"You are not a terrible person. You're one of the best people I know. If you're going to puke, I'm guessing that has more to do with the vodka. Ally told me you were hitting it pretty hard."

I hear a small laugh, a sniffle, and then silence. Then Ruby says, so quietly I have to really press my ear against the door to hear, "School starts next week. Everyone's going to be talking about it. Nice way to kick off junior year."

"No one's going to find out. I don't think Hardy will exactly advertise it and risk Brandy finding out."

"Murph, she knows. There's no *way* it's going to keep quiet."

"I'll talk to her, and she won't say anything."

Who the hell are they talking about? Brandy? How would Brandy know? *Hardy* certainly isn't going to tell her. And if she does figure it out, how is Murphy going to stop her from spreading it all over school? Hell is not as furious as a woman…who's furious, or whatever.

"Yeah but she's definitely going to tell Aaron. And Nicki. And Nicki will tell Emmett, and then all of a sudden the whole hockey team knows—"

Bitch! She's talking about *me*? After all I've done for her, here she is acting like I'm some enemy? I would never ever tell anyone this. I mean, Aaron was *there*. He already knows. And I would *never* talk to Nicki about it. I love her and all, but she's Emmett's girlfriend, not an original crew member. She's in the circle, but not the *inner* circle.

Am I the only one who remembers the night before we started ninth grade? Everything was changing so fast—my dad leaving, my brother already away at college, starting high school with kids from all over the county upsetting our place on the social ladder. I just wanted to pump the brakes before we crashed into all that. What did we say to each other?

"I promise to be loyal to the crew above all else, to always be honest and true through good times and bad." And it worked, I thought! If it weren't for those promises we made, the promise to stay close, to trust each other, would we even still be friends? How are we supposed to take care of each other if we have secrets from each other?

And now Ruby is talking like I'm some monster who just wants to ruin her reputation. Well, I'm washing my hands of this whole mess. If Ruby thinks staying out of each other's business is what friendship is, then I will. And I will keep her out of mine. From now on, we're just roommates. She can have all the time she wants to talk on the phone with *Murphy*. She's his problem now.

6

RUBY
NOW

THE SMELL OF THE LINENS TELLS ME I'M HOME BEFORE I EVEN open my eyes. They smell like the cedar chest at the end of the bed where they're stored between uses. I slept on these pale-blue sheets (alternating with their fraternal-twin set of pale green) for over fifteen years, ever since I graduated from a crib to a big-girl bed. Coral used to tease our mother—back when she still spoke to her, that is—about never updating or replacing any of the furniture or decor, but Nancy would always reply, "They're perfectly good sheets! There's no use spending the money on something we don't need!" which is where Murphy's impression of her comes from. Swap out the word *sheets* with dresser, couch, throw pillows, shoes, car, or anything with the potential but not necessity for updating, and you could pretty much script any conversation from my childhood that included a request for material goods.

Nancy was raised by a poor, single mother in North Carolina, back when they were called unwed mothers (a.k.a. whores), and therefore balks at the idea of buying something just because you want it. They moved up here when Nancy was in high school because my grandmother wanted her to have a better education than she could in the south, thus providing her with the opportunity for a better life. But Nancy's bipolar disorder made school a struggle, and holding down a job even more so.

Her last job was as my father's secretary at his office in Burlington when he was just starting out as an investment advisor. Instead of firing her, he married her. (He jokes he proposed to avoid having to pay severance.) After that, Nancy devoted her time to being the perfect wife and mother, and caretaker for my aging, ailing grand-mother, and as a result, she drove us all insane.

When I was entering high school and Coral had already left for college, Dad started splitting his time between the Vermont office and company headquarters in New York City. But even though this upped our income considerably, and my grandmother had passed away, Nancy didn't want to leave Chatwick. She says she didn't want to uproot us, but I think she couldn't handle the lifestyle change of moving to a community where she didn't feel she belonged. She never settled in to the idea that she no longer had to struggle for every little thing; being too comfortable made her nervous because she was always waiting for the other shoe to drop.

It used to drive Coral up the wall, having old things and used clothes when we could have afforded the latest and greatest. But then again, what didn't drive Coral up the wall about our mother? It's lucky for Nancy that I was the one home when my dad was gone and not

Coral; Nancy would have ended up wrapped around a tree or in a ditch somewhere.

This morning, I'm grateful for Nancy's frugality. Despite my best efforts to deny my homesickness, I can't help but smile as I run my palms over the worn-out cotton that is somehow always cool to the touch even after eight hours of sleeping on it. Perhaps my childhood was less than ideal (whose wasn't?), but in this bed, in this room, I was always safe. Just like last night, surveying my unchanged room makes me feel like Kathleen Turner in that movie where she is suddenly transported from middle age back to her high school years. As I sit up in bed, I half expect the mirror above my dresser to reflect a girl in a poodle skirt and a letter sweater.

Along with the yellowing white desk where I used to write atrocious poetry and maudlin short stories, the closet and dressers still stuffed with clothes that haven't fit me since high school, and the Eminem poster on my wall (which makes me cringe), my bed is just where I left it, flush against the wall with the double windows that face the street. This was the only true surprise about the state of my room, as Nancy always threatened to move the bed away from the radiator the second I left the house. She claimed to worry about it being a fire hazard, but really, she just has a thing about everything in the room being perfectly centered. I've always had a thing about looking out the window from my nice, toasty bed. It was a never-ending battle that I seem to have won.

It's a beautiful, sunny morning, and when I peel back the lacy white curtain, the view is exactly the same as I remember, except perhaps for everything being a little smaller. The maple trees that line the street, the ones we used to feel so brave for climbing to the top of, seem to have shrunk. The one in front of the Menkins' house, the one Danny fell out of and broke his arm, has a couple branches hanging that need to be removed. The yellow paint of the Flemings' house is peeling off in large chunks. These are facts Nancy no doubt laments every day on the phone to her sponsor, who reminds her she must "accept the things she cannot change." I have to crane my head to look down at our front porch, where the half-size whiskey barrels spill over with the impatiens Nancy plants every spring. It's fall now, and soon they will be dead.

Dead. Like Danny.

The thought enters my mind and sucks all the nostalgic air right out of the room. Suddenly, the charming view outside my window changes. Now it's nighttime. Little eight-year-old Danny is bathed in the light from the streetlamp, his fist full of rocks minus the few he's expertly aimed at my window to wake me up. He holds his finger up to his mouth and points to the back of the house. This image has haunted my dreams for years, but especially frequently in the last couple months. It was a sign that I ignored. Danny needed me, but I didn't answer the taps at my window.

I would give anything to rewind a few months. To pick up the phone and reach out to him. Maybe it would have made a difference to hear from me, to know that I had never stopped caring about him. Probably not. The time I really could have made a difference is when we were young. Thinking about it now, what I can't believe is how little we were. I shouldn't have known yet how to take care of someone's wounds. How to keep secrets that big. But I did, because I had already kept my mother's illness hidden for years.

"Hi, sweetheart." My mom's voice jars me away from the window, where Danny's wounded face still stares up at me. I feel wetness on my cheeks and realize I'm crying. I try to wipe away the evidence, but Nancy doesn't miss a thing when she's sober, which she's been for eleven years next May as far as I know.

"Oh," she says. The sound seems to escape her mouth by accident. Her tall, slim figure makes a few jerky movements back and forth, as if she is arguing with herself whether to bolt or to comfort a daughter who has called her by her first name since she was sixteen years old. In the end, I think she realizes she has no choice but to try. She sits on my bed and rests her hand on mine. My knees are tucked into my chest with my arms clutched tightly around me, my default position when I'm upset. She squeezes, hoping it will trigger me to unwrap and fall into her like I did when I was a child. It won't work this time.

"How are you doin'?" she asks. Despite living in Vermont since she was fifteen, Nancy retains a hint of her southern drawl. I used to get embarrassed when she would ask my friends "How are y'all?"

"I'm fine," I say.

"Sweetheart, you are not fine. How could you be fine?"

"Where were you last night?" I ask, my tone coming off more accusatory than I intended in my haste to change the subject. In truth, I was mostly relieved when she wasn't home when I returned from the nightmare at Danny's house. It gave me a chance to wander through the rooms on my own, examining old photographs and trying to determine from the poses who had just fought with whom before the flash went off. But I had also felt the familiar surge of panic of Nancy being out at night, which I tried to suppress by reassuring myself she's not my problem anymore.

She sighs, withdrawing her hand. "I wasn't at Margie's, if that's what you're askin' me."

"I know. I was there."

Her face falls. "Oh, Ruby, did you go lookin' for me? I think after more than ten years of sobriety, I at least deserve the benefit of the doubt. I may be behind the times but I *do* have a cell phone you could've called."

"I wasn't looking for you. I was with the crew."

She nods at this, but I see the slightest hint of a furrowed brow. Does she think I'm dumb enough to follow in her footsteps? "I was at Charlene's," she explains. "She called me after y'all left and asked me to come over. I saw you in Blue and I waved, but you didn't see me."

"No, I was a little out of it. In shock, I guess. It's…a lot."

"Do you want to talk about it?" I shake my head. And what I mean by that headshake is *I don't want to talk about it with* you. *You couldn't handle it. I can't even handle it.* But she presses on. "What did yours say? Your letter, I mean. Charlene told me you each got one, but she didn't tell me what was in 'em."

I work hard to make my face weary instead of angry, my default reaction to Nancy's pushing. "Nancy, I *really* don't want to—"

She raises her hands. "Fine. Fine. Sorry, you don't want to talk about it." She sighs, staring out the window. "It just so hard to believe he's gone. That someone could be here one day and gone the next."

"It's not too hard to believe, considering he spent his time shooting up in his basement and writing hate mail."

Whoa.

I don't know *where* that came from. A minute ago, I was feeling guilty, making excuses for him, and now I feel like screaming. It might be that old default reaction wriggling its way back in. At least I hold back my comment on being familiar with the concept of here one day and gone the next, due in no small part to her and my father.

Nancy's sympathetic face falls into a frown. She is disappointed I am reacting in anger rather than sadness. Sadness she can hug. Anger she must be cautious of, because she knows what it's really aimed at. Or rather, who. "Ruby St. James, I am disappointed in you. I raised you better than to judge people on their weaknesses."

This is true, although it was less a conscious instillation of values than a by-product of growing up constantly navigating the tumultuous waters of *her* weaknesses.

"I guess I'm just a little tapped out on empathy. I know you've told me a million times that addiction is a disease, just like bipolar disorder or heart disease"—suddenly I feel nauseated, thinking that I now know people who have all of these conditions—"but people can make a choice to get better. Look at you! You've managed to control yourself."

"Well, I couldn't for many years, baby girl, and you know that more than anyone."

I cringe at the term *baby girl*, which she calls me only when she wants to put me in my place. What right does she have to remind me of those years? Of course I know better than anyone. Dad gave up trying to save her from herself when I was too young to realize I couldn't. And when he got really fed up, he left for a year while Nancy proved to him she could maintain sobriety after treatment.

After the three months she was in rehab and I was boarding at Ally's, that left nine months on my own with Nancy, nine months of sheer terror that she would go back to her old ways. Nine months of lying awake at night with my bedroom door cracked so I could better discern if the clinking of a hidden vodka bottle was real or imagined. Was that the cap of a pill bottle I just heard, or was it just a tube of Chap Stick?

The answer was consistently benign, hence my father's eventual return, but I didn't relax until the very morning my father pulled his BMW into the driveway and casually lifted his small leather Samsonite out of the backseat, as if he had only been gone for one of his business trips. *Welcome home, Daddy. Here's your perfect family. All fixed, without any help from you.*

"So when is Dad back from New York?" I ask.

Nancy sighs. "I think on Friday."

"Hmm, well, I'll just see him back in the city, then," I say.

Her lips tense, but she doesn't say anything. I know she's annoyed that my father sees more of me than she does, although not by much. Twice a year she comes to the city with him. While he works, she goes to museums and wanders around window-shopping (never buying anything, because she has perfectly good clothes at home). She and I have lunch together in the same restaurant every time, and she always orders the exact same thing. Routine keeps her sane, she says, when I encourage her to try some other delicious-sounding item on the menu. Time has provided just enough healing for the two of us to sustain hour-long chunks of civil if not personal conversations over tea and sandwiches, but being back in my childhood home makes it much harder to ignore the ghosts of the past.

"Have you heard from Jamie lately?" Nancy asks, soft as an under-hand pitch. I sigh. Jamie was my boyfriend when I lived in London.

My mother is a treasure trove of topics I do not wish to discuss this morning. "Ruby, I'm just *asking* a *question*," she continues. "I'm trying to have a conversation with my daughter. Is that such a crime?"

I guess not. "I got an email from him last week, actually. His first book is selling really well, and he's working on the final draft of his second one, so that will come out next year. And," I say, pretending to inspect and flick off a speck of lint off my knee, "he sent flowers when he heard about Danny." Despite me waking him up with my call, not an hour later a dozen pink roses were delivered to my desk with a note. *Love always, J.*

"Is he seeing anyone?" Nancy leans in closer as she says this in a conspiratorial tone, as if we are girlfriends out getting pedicures or something.

I can't resist a smile so I turn my head and look out the window again. Danny's face is replaced by a young couple who must be new to the neighborhood, walking their dog and pushing a stroller. A brand-new baby Chatwickian, not yet affected by the oppressive small-mindedness of this town.

"Oh fine, I give up," Nancy says when she realizes I won't say any more. "Get in the shower, and I'll start breakfast. I picked up some fresh blueberries for your pancakes." Blueberry pancakes were my favorite when I was five. I'm told for six months, that's all I would eat. When my mother wasn't in a black period, she was the type of mother who would actually cook breakfast for us every morning—eggs, bacon, pancakes—as opposed to my friends' moms who worked and barely had time to shove a cereal box and a carton of milk at their kids as they ran around the house with one leg in a pair of pantyhose and one hand applying deodorant. I guess I would rather have eaten cold breakfast if

I could have had a mother who wasn't completely mental about a third of the time. My friends were jealous that mine was always around, at least when they were too young to realize there was something wrong with her. We always want the *other* kind of mother.

"Anything else I can get you?" Nancy chirps, her hands poised in the air like a waitress about to write down my order.

"Coffee, please."

She perks up, glad to be doing something for me. "How do you take it?"

"Black." She raises her eyebrows before she stands and leaves the room. I know she's thinking I'm too much like my father. Living in New York, working too much, not bothering to sweeten my coffee. Next thing you know, I'll be married to someone with bipolar who uses martinis as medication instead of lithium.

As I let the water bounce off my outstretched palm, my hope quickly dashed that she's replaced the water heater that takes a full five minutes to kick in, I think about Jamie. Unlike with my connections here, even after Jamie and I broke up and I moved back to the States, we've managed to remain friends. He sort of insisted on it. I smile as I picture him sitting in his overstuffed armchair, his yellow-lined legal pad in hand, scratching out some prose before committing the words to his computer. It feels good to think about anything unrelated to Chatwick.

The smell of pancakes drifts up from the stairwell, and my stomach (that I realize has been empty for the better part of twenty-four hours) growls with anticipation. I hurry through my shower and shimmy into a pair of jeans and a T-shirt from the bag of clothes Ally brought me, tying my hair in a knot at the base of my neck and racing downstairs. Nancy clucks her tongue at me. "Sweetheart, I wish you would keep your hair down. You know how pulling it back makes your ears stick out."

Blueberry pancakes and criticism. A fine way to start the morning.

"Coffee?" I remind her, not responding to the feedback.

She pours me a cup from the pot she was given as a wedding gift thirty years ago and plops down a bottle of Mrs. Butterworth's next to my plate. I'm surprised she can even *find* the stuff in this town. It's blasphemy that she stocks this in the house when there are dozens of maple sugaring farms within a ten-mile radius, and gallons of Vermont pure in all varieties are available at any store in downtown Chatwick. My southern mother actually *prefers* this crap to the sweet nectar of the real thing. I used to hide it when my friends came over just so I wouldn't have to hear about how weird we were as a family. I had plenty of other stuff that I couldn't hide from them.

Nancy prattles on in her usual fashion, quickly graduating from the weather, her flowers, and this summer's disappointing yield from the vegetable garden (too humid) to her sponsor (Harriett), her therapist (Louise), and my father's workaholism. She works a few of my father's worst qualities into every conversation we have. She's so used to her family pointing out her flaws that it's her passive-aggressive way of maintaining the balance. She needn't bother; my anger is pretty fairly distributed between the two of them already.

Nancy's in the middle of explaining why she thinks Louise is secretly working for Dad, and I am in the middle of mentally constructing my to-do list to make up some of the work I've missed, when the phone rings.

Nancy picks up the receiver, not bothering to pause her

diatribe. "…and if he thinks I'm going to edit myself so I don't hurt his feelings, he is crazier than I am. Hello, St. James residence." Her voice goes from bitter and indignant to syrupy sweet in 0.3 seconds. "Why, Murphy Leblanc, is that you? How nice to hear your voice! How are you doing with, you know, this whole Danny business? What stage of grief would you say you're in? I think it's safe to say our Ruby is nestled stubbornly in anger. Surprise, surprise, right?"

She lets out a peal of laughter, and I can hear him do the same on the other end of the line. I wonder if there's ever an age when you cease to feel embarrassed by your parents. I try to pluck the receiver from Nancy's hand, but she blocks me as she tells Murphy it can take months or even years to get to acceptance.

"Hi," I say when I finally win the wrestling match.

"Want to come over?"

"I…" *What?* Come over? I thought we had an understanding that last night was goodbye! "I can't. I have to work. I've got at least eight hours to make up from yesterday." It's not just an excuse; I have a mental picture of my inbox, overflowing with estimate requests and billing issues. If the accounting people ever developed solid people skills, I would most certainly be out of a job. But admittedly, I don't think being around Murphy is a very good idea.

"Okay. Later then. I live in the biggest of my parent's rental properties, top floor. You know the one?"

He hangs up before I can nod a confused assent.

7

RUBY
BACK THEN—SENIOR YEAR

I scan the cafeteria, deciding against the freshmen and moving on to the sophomores. A fifteen- or sixteen-year-old would be a good fit for Murphy. Young and innocent enough to find him cool and charming, but not so young and innocent it would be gross. After all, Murphy just lost his virginity, so the ship has sailed on having a PG relationship.

Ally sneaks up on me. "What's with you?" she asks as she plops her tray down beside me. Even though I'm the only one at the table, she sits beside me instead of across from me because that's where she always sits. Emmett and Danny sit across from us, with an empty seat in the middle reserved for whoever's girlfriend gets there first. Aaron sits on Ally's other side. Ally is always in the middle; that way she can have one ear in any conversation. Murphy doesn't have lunch this period, despite his valiant efforts to arrange his schedule to align with

the rest of ours. For the last couple days, I've been endlessly grateful to Mrs. Clasky, the guidance counselor, for being one of the few
people immune to Murphy's charms. I used to be one of them too.

"Nothing is up with me," I tell Ally.

"Why are you squinting over at the sophomores? Did one of
them piss you off?" Her eyes gleam. She's ready to slay anyone who's
done me wrong. To be fair, she also wants a good story. I have one too.
Boy, do I. I just can't tell it to her.

"No. I'm just trying to pick out a girl for Murphy." I shouldn't have
even told her this much—if I open the door, she'll kick it in—but I'm
distracted. I don't know any of these girls' names, but I've seen them
at parties sipping on peach schnapps and wine coolers and giggling
like idiots. Murphy would do well with an idiot. Not that you'd have
to be an idiot to like Murphy. That's not what I'm saying. He just
needs someone fun. Light.

Ally shakes her head. "You guys are so weird."

"Weird how?" I ask.

Ally sidesteps the question with another question. "Can't
Murphy find his own girls?"

"Of course," I say. "He's just not as good at it as me."

She smiles, but her lips are pursed. She doesn't like it when I'm
cocky, but when it's at Murphy's expense she allows it.

Nicki and Emmett sit down and immediately start making out,
which puts me off my Tater Tots. Danny joins the table and asks
what's going on.

"Ruby is taking it upon herself to find Murphy a girlfriend,"
Ally informs him, reaching across the table to swipe a chicken nugget
from his tray. Usually Ally steals nuggets from Aaron's tray, but he's

not here today. Lucky for her that Danny decided to stray from his regular cheeseburger.

"Hey, no fair. What about me?" Danny asks. "Murphy's not the only one who could use some action."

We all look at him. "What happened to Jenny?" Ally asks. Danny and Jenny have been on their longest stretch—a whole six months. I try to be supportive, but she doesn't seem to make him especially happy. When Danny actually brings her around, she hardly even talks. Actually, she kind of just hovers and stares. Actually, she kind of scares the shit out of me. Those hawk eyes and all those piercings.

"I haven't seen her much since she dropped out of school," Danny mumbles.

"Hmm," we all murmur. We're all thinking the same thing— that Danny will be the next to drop out. Yesterday, since everyone else was at practice or at work, Danny and I had a Dark Children of Chatwick reading. He showed me a poem he wrote about yearning for freedom from dreams he can never realize. At first, I only heard what I wanted to hear. I hoped it meant that he was realizing that Jenny was never going to be the girl he wanted her to be. He and I have had our expectations set for us at a pretty low bar, but the more he read, the more it felt like he was giving up on the idea that he could be happy with anyone, doing anything. It felt like he was saying it wasn't worth trying.

I wonder why anyone would drop out of high school, especially in Chatwick. I mean, what else is there to do in this town besides go to school? Hang out in Barnard Park? Work at the Quik Stop? If you're *lucky*, I guess you could get a job at the Endless Power battery factory at the north edge of town and hang on long enough to collect your pension after forty years of standing on an assembly line.

Personally, I'm getting as far away from here as possible, as *soon* as possible. I want to experience things—art, music, culture, stores and restaurants that are open past 9:00 p.m. Closest thing you get to any of that in Chatwick is our high school's Miss and Mister Bobcat talent competition, which I will *not* be taking part in, no matter how much Ally begs me to do a duet with her. She's even got Nancy in on it, ganging up on me to discuss costumes. Since my dad's been back, Nancy has been on her best behavior, and tailoring is her distraction of choice. Lucky me. The woman wants to sew my prom dress even though I've told her a million times I'm sticking with the one I ordered.

"So you got dumped?" Emmett says, coming up for air to tease poor Dan.

"Shut up, Emmett," I say. I never miss a chance to tell him to shut up, but especially when he's shitting on Danny. He sticks his tongue out at me. Danny reaches around Nicki to punch Emmett in the arm. Emmett tries to kick back under the table, but from the sound Nicki makes, I'm guessing he missed. "Cut the shit, guys!" she whines.

"So what's this about you finding a chick for Murphy?" Emmett asks as if nothing had happened.

"It's been like four months since he dated that last one," I say. "What was her name?"

"Misty," Ally says.

"Exactly. *Misty*," I say, rolling my eyes. The girl who told me she liked my earrings but that the only accessory a girl really needed was cleavage. "*That* winner. And she only lasted a few weeks. He's over it.

It's time he gets back on the bike. Or the horse, or whatever stupid expression that is."

"It's 'back in the saddle,'" Ally says. We all look at her in amazement. Somehow, Ally and I have momentarily switched brains. I'm sticking my nose in someone else's business, and Ally is correcting me on figures of speech.

"Are you sure he's not already in the saddle, Tuesday?" Danny asks. One eyebrow is raised. My heart drops. Oh crap. He's looking at me like he knows something. Does he know something? Did Murphy tell him something?

"I'm sure, Danny," I say, raising my eyebrow back at him. His expression clears immediately. Maybe I was just imagining it.

Emmett looks back and forth between Danny and me. I hold my breath when he turns to me, but instead of pressing the issue, he says, "So can you believe this governor? How does she plan on paying for this jobs program of hers when we've got a fifty-million-dollar deficit?"

The crew groans and rolls their eyes.

———

I pull into my usual spot in the alley behind the Exchange, which shares a parking lot with Margie's Pub, and open Blue's rusty door. It's late April, and the rain falling on my skin is still cold as ice, but I've abandoned my winter gear. A person can only wear puffy coats and hats and mittens for so long without going insane. The rain magnifies the smell of cigarette butts and day-old beer from the bar side of the lot. It turns my stomach, making me think of the nights I've been forced to inhale that smell as I wait for Nancy to finish her last drink. It's not like the smell isn't also associated with my friends, but somehow it's different when I'm with them. Maybe it's because we're at the age where you're *supposed* to be stupid and messing around with that stuff. And maybe it's because I know when to put the drink down. Well, except for those few times...

I lift my backpack and see the envelope. Inside contains my entire future, a.k.a. my deposit and commitment letter to New York University. I haven't mailed it in yet. I don't know what's stopping me, considering it's the key to all I've ever wanted.

None of my friends know I was accepted. I try to pinpoint why I haven't told them as I slam closed the metal gate and pull down the wooden doors of the ancient elevator that takes me up to the shop. I've talked before about going out of state for college, but I don't think any of them have taken me seriously. People who grow up in Chatwick generally don't stray too far. For example, Ally is going to cosmetology school about ten minutes outside of town; Aaron will go to Vermont Technical College a few hours south; Emmett's going to the University of Vermont in Burlington to study business; and Nicki will enroll in the nursing program at Norwich University in north-central Vermont.

They all have plans to come back to Chatwick on weekends. Danny is going to work at Borbeau's, the mechanic shop where he already works/sells pot most days after school. The most disappointing is that Murphy will work for his dad. With his talent, he probably could have gotten at least a partial baseball scholarship *somewhere*. It's amazing to watch him at bat. He could get out of here, but he won't.

That's why I have to find him a girlfriend. If he doesn't have anything else to focus on, we're going to end up sleeping together again, and then who knows what mess will be made of my plans.

It was enough of a mistake the first time. I *knew* accepting those last screwdrivers Ally made was a bad idea. Once everyone had scattered off to bed, Murphy and I found ourselves alone, as we always find ourselves. Normally, we just play cards or, better yet, go to sleep, but the extra drink was what pushed us into that dangerous territory between reminiscing about the past and worrying about a future where everything will be different. The next thing I knew, we were kissing. And then we were more than kissing.

He claims not to understand why it can't be an ongoing thing. Of course he doesn't understand—he's a guy! And before that night, he was a virgin! Of course he's going to want to keep having sex, the poor boy. But it cannot happen again. Not with me. Murphy is my best friend, nothing more.

Granted, before last weekend, we *did* kiss on two occasions. One was on a particularly rough night, about three months after I lost my virginity to Hardy Crane, when I realized Hardy was never going to leave Brandy for me. Trust me, I *know* how disgusting that is, on all levels. Hardy is the most grotesque being on the face of this planet, and I'm convinced the only reason I was into him was because of what was going on with my parents. Plus, the therapist my parents forced me to go to when they got back together told me about this bonding chemical that gets released in girls' brains when they have sex. It's the same one that gets released when you breastfeed. For a girl who's never experienced it before, the shrink says, it can be particularly overwhelming. So I blame that. Plus, I was drinking a little more in those days. Ironic, huh? While my mom was finally drying out?

Anyway, one night after Hardy canceled plans on me for, like, the *tenth* time, Murphy literally shook me by my shoulders and told me Hardy loved Brandy, not me, and I needed to get over it because I deserved better than that scumbag anyway. I was in such pain, but so grateful for someone finally shaking me out of my trance that I kissed him. But it stopped there.

The other was after Murphy got dumped by Charlotte Bicknell. She is a year older than us, and all the boys were completely infatuated with her (or rather, with her enormous boobs). I didn't think Murphy even *liked* her all that much (at least above her chest), but he sat on my glider, crying. Actually crying tears. I had never seen him cry before. I'd *heard* him cry, over the phone, those first few months after what happened with Danny's stepfather when we started talking to each other because we couldn't talk to anyone else. But I'd never seen him do it in person, and I thought maybe he would want me to pretend like it wasn't happening. But when I stood up and said I was going to go get him a glass of water, he caught my hand and pulled me onto his lap. He kissed me long enough that I forgot about the water. By the time he went home, he wasn't crying anymore.

Both times, we agreed it was a huge mistake, brought on by loneliness rather than any desire to be together. We didn't want to ruin our friendship. So when we woke up the morning after we had sex, I assumed we would be on the same page. Instead, when I said we couldn't do it again, Murphy seemed disappointed. He said he was thinking it should happen *more*. Well, *of course* he thought that. I mean, he *is* a guy.

It's not that the sex was bad. Not like I'm some expert, but it was miles better than the handful of times I was with Hardy. It turns out Ally's right about sex being better when it's with someone you care about. But that's just it. Murphy and I care about each other, and bringing sex into the mix will just confuse things. I don't want to lose my best friend just because we had a hormonal teenage moment after a couple drinks and a hit of Danny's new supply.

The worst part is, even though the exact details are kind of hazy, I can't shake something Murphy said when we were lying together after it happened. I was trying to make light of the situation, so I said, "You see? It's not such a big deal. I don't know why you waited so long."

And then he said it. "I think I was waiting for you."

Shit.

Well, maybe not. He could have just meant he was waiting for me because we're friends, and he knew I would be nice even if he sucked at it. That's probably what he meant.

Right?

As I walk into the shop I'm greeted by Shawna and Donna (yes, they rhyme), who are waltzing to Garth Brooks. The sight is funny all on its own, considering Shawna is five ten and robustly framed and Donna, the owner, barely clears Shawna's elbow and would weigh about a hundred pounds soaking wet after a hot dog–eating contest. But the oddity is compounded by the fact that Donna is wearing a purple velvet monstrosity of a hat on her head, complete with rhinestones and fringe. I will excuse that the day's Ugliest Drop-Off winner has been chosen without our normal voting ritual, because I can't imagine anything could top this hideous thing.

I lean against the doorframe, happy to be out of my head and overtaken by something silly. Donna tips her head back and, finally able to see, spots me. She breaks away from Shawna and shuffles toward me, her hand outstretched. I smile and take it, and she shuffles me back to Shawna and positions our hands together.

"You need the practice, Ruby," Donna says. "Prom will be here before you know it!" She steps back and waves her arms in the air like the conductor of a symphony as Shawna and I begin to sway, me stepping on Shawna's toes every five or six counts.

Crap. Prom! Of course Donna would remember. I think she and Shawna are more excited about it than I am. For months, every time I came to work, one of them thrust a formal wear magazine at me with the corners turned down on pages of dresses, hairstyles, and makeup they liked. Shawna ordered the dress I finally selected at cost from some retail connection she has, and she even spoke directly with Cecile, Murphy's mom, to tell her what to order me for a corsage that would match it. I think Nancy is feeling a little resentful that she's been boxed out of the process, which makes me feel guilty, and that leads to me feeling angry. Shawna stepped in last minute last year when she realized Nancy was out of commission and it was getting down to the wire. Excuse me for betting on a more reliable horse this time around.

The radio changes to a more fast-paced Dixie Chicks song, and Shawna and I break apart. The three of us jump and shake our hips and twirl each other around. As always at work, I feel my burden lighten. With these ladies, Shawna in her early thirties and Donna well into her fifties, I feel my age, instead of the hundred years I feel compared to my friends.

Halfway through a mock pirouette, I spot a customer standing in the doorway, looking hesitant to fully enter the shop.

"Come, come, dear!" Donna says, and leads her into the store. "You don't have to dance, but you must sing a tune for us!"

The girl indulges Donna with a smile and laugh, but is clearly uncomfortable, and rightfully so. I recognize her as one of the giggling sophomores.

"She's kidding," I say to her. "How can we help you?"

"My mom sent me in to check if she has any money on her account." At this, the dance party is over. Donna heads into the window to model her headgear, and Shawna starts straightening the rack of jeans nearby, still bopping and humming along with the music.

"No problem, what's her code?" We're a consignment store, so people bring us their old clothes and we sell them, splitting the profit with the consigner. It's up to the client to come in and check if we owe them any money, and we assign each an account code so we know the person checking the account is allowed to collect it. We've had a few cases where kids have tried to collect on their parents' accounts in order to buy drugs. I know because I see them at Danny's later.

"77621," she says.

I circle around the cash-out counter to punch the code into the prehistoric Mac computer and get the hourglass symbol on the screen. "It's just going to take a couple minutes to pull up."

She smiles. She has a nice smile. Kind eyes too. "No problem," she says. "I've never been in here before, so I'll look around. You guys have some cool stuff!"

"Absolutely. We actually just started taking summer stuff, and there's a bunch of cute sundresses right over there if you want to check them out."

"Thanks, I will!"

Shawna sidles up and plops down in the chair next to the computer. Just as Ally did earlier, Shawna notices me squinting toward the back of the store, lost in thought. She whistles and waves her hand in front of my face. "What's with you?" she asks.

"I think I might have found Murphy's next girlfriend."

"Oh! You caught your reflection in the mirror, then?"

"Oh, Shawna, give it up!" She's been convinced Murphy and I are destined for each other since… Well, I've worked here for two years, and Murphy came in to take my lunch break with me my second week, so…one year, eleven months, and two weeks? When I mistakenly told her he and I had made a pact to go to senior prom together, our "fate was sealed," according to her. I *told* her the only reason we decided to go together was because of our respective *junior* prom experiences.

I went with Eddie Rodowski, who grabbed my ass about forty times before puking all over my dress. He went with Ramona Sturgess, who Emmett set him up with because she was rumored to be easy. She spent so much time complaining about her recent breakup with Jed Donaldson that Murphy deposited her at Jed's feet and told them to work it out because he didn't drop a hundred dollars on a tux to be a couples' counselor. After that, we thought it would be best to go with each other so we could be ourselves and not have the huge romantic pressure that comes with prom. We have the best time with each other anyway.

Even knowing all this, Shawna thinks we're secretly in love. Just because she's older than me, she thinks she knows everything.

"You listen to me, Miss Ruby. Your generation might buy into the whole 'men and women can be friends' thing, but it's a load of bull. Sooner or later, something is going to happen between the two of you, and when it does, you're going to feel like a total idiot for waiting so long to see it."

I feel myself start to blush and get up to busy myself straightening the rack of yet-to-be-tagged clothes behind the computer. Once the sophomore girl leaves, I will stand on a stool and read the brand, size, and category of each garment to Shawna as she types them into the computer, and based on the condition and popularity of similar items in the store, we price it. Then we print the labels and tag the clothes before we put them out on the floor. I look forward to the repetitiveness of this process. It will help me focus on something other than what I'm focusing on right now, which is the memory of Murphy's mouth on my neck.

"You little hooker!" Shawna cries out. My eyes shoot over to the sophomore, who whips around to see the commotion, smiles, and then returns to browsing.

"Shhh, Shawna, Jesus!" I whisper yell at her.

She lowers to a whisper, but gestures emphatically at me to follow her to the dressing rooms on the other end of the store. I do, but only to avoid a louder scene. "Something already happened between you two, didn't it?" she asks.

"No," I say, but I struggle to suppress a smile.

"Hooker!" she whispers at me, swatting my arm.

"Okay, okay! We...*accidentally*...had sex."

She shrieks and claps her hands, moving into a happy dance.

"Stop it. Stop it!" I say, grabbing her arm to get her attention in the midst of what appears to be some kind of fit. "Listen, it didn't mean anything, and it's never going to happen again. So there goes your little theory right out the window." I go to march back to the computer, and she stands in my way. I try to go around her, and she blocks me with one hand on my shoulder.

"Ruby, you're eighteen, and you've had a pretty fucked-up couple of years. I'm sorry if I'm the first to tell you this, but sex *always* means something. You and Murphy have something special, and you know it."

I think for a second, my eyes stinging. "Murphy and I *do* have something special. It's called friendship. It's one of the few things I've ever been able to count on, and *that* means more to me than any stupid sexual encounter. Now please, drop it."

She lets me pass this time, and when I get back to the counter, the sophomore girl is waiting. "Sorry for the wait," I say, plastering a smile on my face as I circle back to the computer. "It looks like your mom has $43.31 on her account. Do you want to take those off that amount?" I point at the short stack of sundresses she's laid on the counter.

"No, I'll pay for those myself. I wouldn't want to do that without asking her," she says.

I smile. So she's cute, she's smiley, she's a sophomore, she's *not* a spoiled brat, and she's cool with shopping for secondhand clothes. I like this girl.

"You go to Chatwick High, right?" I ask as I open the cash register and count out her mother's money. It's a dumb question. Of course she goes to Chatwick High—it's the only high school for twenty miles. She nods. "What's your name?"

"Taylor. Taylor Bishop." She smiles and extends her hand to me. Bonus points for using her last name and shaking hands, unlike most people our age.

"Taylor, I'm Ruby St. James. Tell me, do you happen to have a boyfriend?"

8

RUBY
NOW

I CLIMB THE STAIRS TO MURPHY'S APARTMENT, ALL FIVE FLIGHTS of splintering wood attached haphazardly to the back of the apartment complex. The staircase has the appearance of a fire escape, but it is actually the main entrance to the apartments, one on each floor. From the street, the building gives the appearance of a single-family Victorian mini-mansion. Chatwick's Main Street is lined with buildings like this—enormous, old, and audacious in color, with chipped paint and sunken front porches piled high with items to be included in next summer's yard sale.

I remember when I was little, imagining cavernous hallways and rooms filled to the brim with antique items little girls were normally not allowed to touch. It wasn't until Murphy started taking me with him on his maintenance trips that I realized most of these buildings were sectioned off into depressing two-bedroom units his parents rented out. This one is the largest one.

I hesitate on the landing before the final flight of stairs. What the hell am I doing here? This was not the plan. All day I threw myself into work, assuring myself I would *not* be coming here. Not only does Murphy's arrogant summoning deserve to be rebuffed, but the more I interact with my old friends, Murphy in particular, the more likely it is that the secret I've worked so hard to bury will be resurrected. And yet here I am.

What is wrong with me? This is ridiculous.

I turn to go back down the stairs.

"Someone there?" Murphy asks. I remain frozen midstep. Maybe if I don't move, he'll think he imagined the noise and just go back into his apartment. "Ruby, I can see the top of your head, dummy." I look up and see him looking down at me through the wooden slats of the stairwell, waving. "Hi. Would you get up here already?"

I concede, trapped.

"What were you doing?" he asks as I get to the top of the stairs.

"I wasn't sure this was your place."

He nods slowly, his lips pursed. He's not buying it.

I stand on my tiptoes, peeking over his shoulder. He remains still, sizing me up. "So are you going to invite me in or not?" I finally ask.

"I guess," he says sarcastically, stepping back and waving me inside.

"Jesus, Murphy, do you have to make everything so goddamn awkward?" I say as I move past him.

"Me?" he says innocently. "I'm not the one creeping around on the stairwell!"

"I told you, I—"

"Wasn't sure it was my place?" he mocks.

"*Yes.*" I feel my face flush, so I don't meet his eyes. Instead, I survey the place he calls home. It's small by Chatwick standards but large for New York City's, a typical bachelor pad complete with leather furniture and a neon beer sign over the kitchen sink. I'm surprised how tidy it is, remembering the state of his childhood bedroom. There is a distinct smell of Pine-Sol, and imagining him spending the day cleaning in preparation for my arrival is no small consolation for the vulnerable position I find myself in.

Murphy shuts the door, and my heart races as if he's slid closed the bars of a jail cell. It's the first time I've been alone in a room with him since I was eighteen years old. Despite the flush of heat from my aerobic climb, I shudder, thinking of the last time I saw him before I left Chatwick.

"Nice print," I say, pointing my chin at the canvas hanging on the wall that's farthest away from him. It's not actually that nice; I just want an excuse to put some distance between us. It's a generic painting of a little bistro with café tables and barrels of flowers in front. Two people face each other, their silhouettes blurry, sipping coffee. The colors are muted; the texture is flat. It looks like it was mass-produced for customers of Bed Bath & Beyond who need something to hang that goes with everything.

"Thanks. Mom picked it out." I glance at him, and he is half grinning. Is he smiling because he's embarrassed his mother decorated his apartment, or because some other woman chose this for him? This Krystal person, perhaps? How ridiculous that I'm even putting this much thought into it. It shouldn't matter to me. And it doesn't.

It doesn't!

"So," I say, running my hand over a plush blue blanket flung on the back of his black leather couch and adding it to my mental evidence locker. "Now what?" Oh God. Did that sound like what I think it sounded like? I still can't manage to meet his eye. If I do, it will be so much harder to pretend he's just any other person.

"I don't know. You wanna go for a ride?"

"Sure," I say, thankful he didn't respond in the pervy way he would have when I last knew him.

Murphy grabs his keys, and we make our way back down the stairs. "So I guess climbing these is the drawback to living in 'the penthouse' rent free?" I ask.

He laughs, but he wears an offended expression. "Have you *met* Cecile? Not only do I pay rent, I don't even get a discount for being the super."

When we get to his truck, I think back to yesterday and how I wanted nothing more than this ride. Part of me wishes I had just hopped in then and demanded he take off. We would never have heard Danny's suicide note, dripping with disdain. We would never have been handed our secrets in little envelopes like remotely operated bombs. The others could read them, but who cared? We would be long gone.

As soon as I buckle up, I kick off my flip-flops and fold one leg underneath me. I reflexively reach for my purse before I realize rooting around in it will not produce a pack of Camel Lights and a lighter. I quit before I went to college, just one of the many bad habits I decided to leave in Chatwick.

Murphy is eyeing me. "Feel free to make yourself comfortable," he says, laughing.

I flash him a sheepish smile. "Force of habit."

"Your feet stink," he says.

"They do not!" I protest, whacking his arm with the back of my hand.

"Some things never change."

We look at each other, and I see that damn twinkle in his eye. I look away. "And some things do," I mutter.

We're both silent for a few minutes after that. Murphy takes me through town, and it's so surreal I feel almost sick. With its row of brick buildings from the 1800s, hand-painted signs hung in front of each shop; with Barnard Park and its Saturday farmers' market and its twelve-foot oxidized-copper fountain that hasn't worked since the early nineties, downtown Chatwick is so charming that passersby might assume the people in this town live sleepy, uncomplicated little lives. They don't see what happens behind closed doors; they don't guess at how the boredom and the lack of lucrative jobs and the six months of postcard-perfect snowy winters create the ideal breeding ground for depression and addiction.

As I drove through it myself yesterday, it was easier to keep my eyes safely trained on the car in front of me without seeing what I now see. The Burger King the crew would hang out at after Emmett and Aaron's hockey games. Margie's Pub, and the retail space where the Exchange used to be—it closed about five years ago, Murphy tells me as we pass. After I left, at their insistence, I used to send Shawna and Donna letters care of the store, actual handwritten letters on fancy stationery I purchased at the NYU bookstore.

I told them the same pack of lies I told my parents during my rare calls home. That I was healthy. Happy. Thriving in my new life.

After a while, it got to be too hard, so I stopped. Had I kept up my correspondence, I probably would have known they went out of business. Suddenly, the image of them closing up shop for the last time, without me, wrenches my heart almost as badly as Ally's call about Danny's death. Everywhere I turn, more grief.

We pass the high school, that pile of ivy-covered bricks that used to look so gigantic and frightening. There's my pediatrician's office, where I used to love going because at the visit's conclusion they would give me this weird kind of bubble gum with a cold, liquid center. Nancy tells me Dr. Bates is still practicing, despite the fact that he was approaching retirement age when I was his patient twenty years ago. Murphy turns onto Lake Road, and we go over the tracks and pass Charlene's Deli, formerly Deuso's Deli.

I stiffen, and Murphy squeezes my shoulder, only for one second, before returning his hand to the wheel. I close my eyes against the words repeating in my head: *None of you bothered to try to help me when I was alive, when it counted.* When I open them, I see we're passing Hardy Crane's old house. Neither Murphy nor I comment on this particular landmark.

Not far after the deli, the homes and shops become farther apart, and Murphy picks up speed as we head into farmland. We pass the old white church I used to feel a tug toward. I was not raised religiously, like Murphy and Danny. Instead, I grew up worshipping Santa Claus and Bob Barker, so the source of the tug was more a sense of mystery and magic than of any type of real faith. The people spilling out the church doors on Sunday mornings always seemed so bright and happy, and I longed to belong with them.

After the church come the farms and the manure. I take a deep inhale and instantly feel more relaxed. This is the part of Vermont I truly miss. The country. "Nothing like a little cow shit to remind you you're home," I say. I glance at Murphy and instantly realize my mistake.

"There's more to Chatwick than cow shit, Ruby."

I forgot the number one guiding principle of this town. You can only talk smack about it if you're an insider. The crew and I used to bitch about this place all the time, but that was when we were in it together. The second I packed my bags and left, it became forbidden for me to utter so much as a syllable against it. It's like how you can criticize your mother, but no one else had better except your sister. Even *then*, it's only okay if your sister still *talks* to your mother. (I know, because mine doesn't.) Murphy, like Ally, like everyone I know here, is poised to attack anyone—including, or maybe especially, me—who talks shit about their proverbial mother.

"I'm actually serious, Murph," I say. "I really have missed this." It's the truth. The sensations I'm experiencing from riding around with him are exactly what give me anxiety every time I think about coming home. They're exactly what I was afraid of feeling: Youthful. Yearning. Alive.

As we drive farther, I can see the sun starting to set over the lake. This used to be my favorite time of day to ride around, the light filtering through the leaves and branches of the hundred-year-old maple trees. The promise this time of day has always held, the night stretched ahead so full of opportunity for mischief or excitement or even disappointment. Anything to make you feel...something. Now, just like back then, the moment is so romantic it feels sad. That beautiful, lonely kind of sad.

We pull into the parking lot of Chatwick Bay Park. We're not supposed to be here past dusk, but that's never stopped us before. I look out over the lake and remember all the times I came here with Murphy or Danny or Ally, or by myself to let the placid waters smooth out the clutter in my mind from the latest blowout at home. Murphy swings the truck around in the parking lot so the bed of the truck faces the water. We get out, and Murphy opens the tailgate. He holds out his hand to help me into the bed of the truck. I pretend I don't see it and haul myself up on my own. He laughs. "Still a toughie," he says.

"I don't know what you mean."

"It just kills you to ask for help. Or even accept it when it's right in front of your face."

"I didn't need it." I shrug my shoulders. He nods, looking at a spot on the lake way in the distance and smiling to himself.

We sit in silence for a while before he says, "So...should we talk about—"

"Emmett. We should talk about Emmett," I interrupt. I know he's going to want to talk about our secrets, and I can't lie to him. And I *definitely* can't tell him the truth.

"Right," he says, his face becoming grim. He turns to face the water. After a moment, he whispers, "He could die. He could have already died."

As overwhelmed as I feel, I can only imagine what Murphy must be feeling. Emmett could have died during that basketball game, or on a morning run, or just sitting at his desk at the bank, and they wouldn't have known what happened until after he was gone. Like Danny. This could be the second funeral I've come home for, instead of the first. Murphy could have lost them both in one fell swoop.

These people are part of my past—hell, they *are* my past—but to Murphy they are his present and future too. And they all seem to be disappearing. Even though Emmett assures us he's fine, that could change at any minute, according to Steph.

"Are you okay?" I ask. He nods, staring off into the distance. "It's okay if you're not, you know," I say. I put my hand on his knee, and he covers it with his. I get a flash of us in this same position, Murphy's hand over mine on Blue's gearshift, on the way to dropping him off at baseball practice. I remove my hand and tuck both of them underneath me.

"Why was it always so hard for them?" Murphy asks softly.

"Hard for who?"

"Em and Dan."

I look at him in shock. "You're kidding, right?"

He shakes his head.

"Oh, Murph. You really don't know?"

"What?" he asks, his voice edged with irritation. "What the hell else don't I know?"

I ponder how to word this thing that has always been so obvious to everyone but him. "It was a competition."

"For what? They never dated any of the same girls."

"Not over a girl. Over you."

It's true. Murphy's mother, who was no great fan of Danny Deuso, once confided in me while we watched Murphy pitch a no-hitter that she blamed herself for Danny's presence in Murphy's life. She and Emmett's mother were in the same birthing class—so Emmett and Murphy really were, as Danny so bitterly articulated, "friends since the womb." Their moms decided to separate them in kindergarten to allow them to develop more on their own. This didn't faze the affable Murphy, but Emmett, who was painfully shy at the time, was miserable.

At the end of their first day of school, Emmett's mother called Cecile to report Emmett coming home in tears. Apparently, at recess time, he looked all over for Murphy and found him up the highest branch of the tallest tree, Danny by his side, both boys hanging from their knees and grinning like they didn't have a care in the world. I don't think Emmett ever recovered from Danny's abrupt and unwelcome entrance into his life. He spent the remainder of Danny's life competing for Murphy's love.

"The thought never even occurred to you?" I ask.

"I guess I never really thought about it like that. I just thought they rubbed each other the wrong way."

"They are very different," I agree. "Were." Truth is, the two couldn't have been *more* different. Where Emmett was well behaved and liked to be in control, Danny was a troublemaker who went with the flow. Where Emmett was smart and liked by the teachers (despite his occasional smart mouth), Danny battled with paying attention and was constantly lectured by even the nicest of our instructors. What neither of them realized was that they balanced each other out perfectly, and that Murphy needed them both. They were like the angel and the devil, one on each shoulder. The good and the bad, the stable and the adventurous.

"We should probably talk about the other thing. You know, the secrets," Murphy says.

Surprised by the change of subject, I don't have enough warning to stop myself from tensing slightly, which I'm sure Murphy notices.

He leans forward to reach into his back pocket and pulls out his envelope, already creased at the midpoint, the ink spelling his name already faded as if he's been carrying it around with him for years.

Just remember that all things done in the dark have a way of coming to light.

"All right. What's your secret?" I dare.

"What's yours?" he asks.

Simultaneously we shout over each other, "I asked you first!" which makes us laugh.

When it gets quiet again, I feel the panic tighten my gut once more. How reckless of me to play chicken with something this serious. If he *does* tell me his secret, it's only fair I tell him mine, and as I mentioned, that is not an option. If my suspicion is correct, Murphy thinks my envelope matches his. He thinks all he covered up yesterday with the crew was a simple indiscretion between two consenting, horny teenagers, and I want to keep it that way without having to lie to his face.

"We don't have to talk about it, Murph. I mean, let's not."

He seems relieved, and I wonder briefly if I'm wrong. Does the paper in that envelope say what I think it says? Or is Murphy's secret some other twisted, dark thing? Maybe it's something that doesn't have anything to do with me. It's been ten years. It could be anything. He could have lied, stolen, killed, or all three in that amount of time. But no. It's about me. It has to be. Why else would he be pressing the point now that we're alone?

"What about what Danny said?" he asks. "If we don't tell each other—"

"Oh, Murph," I say, smiling in that pitying way I know he hates. "Do you really think Danny Deuso—the guy who wanted to climb Mount Kilimanjaro but wouldn't even go for a short hike up Hardrock Hill, the one who was going to find the cure for AIDS but failed chemistry, the *King* of Big Ideas with no follow-through... Do you really think he would have actually taken the initiative, as his last act, to *prearrange* some big, public reveal of all our deepest, darkest secrets?"

"Danny was a lot smarter than people gave him credit for," he says.

I purse my lips against the frosty mood that is suddenly in the air. "I *know* Danny was smart. Don't talk to me like I didn't know him." Murphy looks away. "I'm just saying," I continue, realizing I'm using one of Nancy's famous introductory clauses Coral and I always mocked, "he wasn't much of a *doer*. He was smart about people and, I hate to say it, about how to get them to do what he wanted. He was pissed at us and blaming us for everything that went wrong with his life, and in some drug-induced haze, he wanted to get back at us. He's just *saying* he arranged for everything to come out because he wants to force our hands."

"Then why wouldn't he just put them all in his letter?" Murphy asks.

I sigh. "I'm guessing he liked the idea of us all squirming to figure out how to cover up whatever we didn't want the rest of the crew to know. I mean, how would it even work? Say he picked someone to reveal our secrets out in public, announce them at Margie's or wherever he felt appropriate. What's the trigger button? How would that person know whether we already told each other or not?"

"You've given this a lot of thought," Murphy says. "And you sound a little panicked."

He's right; I *have* given this a lot of thought, and I've decided to buy into my own theories. I have to believe that Danny's threat was empty, that in this town where everyone knows everybody's everything, somehow the five of us will be allowed to keep our secrets. The alternative would be disastrous. Still, I know I sound like Nancy when she's manic, so I take a deep breath and count to ten before continuing. "I just think I knew Danny pretty well."

"And I didn't?"

"I didn't say that."

"But that's what you meant. You always mean what I think you mean, but you *say* 'I didn't say that' because you think I'm stupid and can't read between the lines." His words snap like a whip, and I look at him in shock. As much as he and I have bickered in the course of our friendship, I don't remember ever feeling such blatant hostility from him. There was a hint of it in Charlene's driveway, but last night with the crew, he was… That's it. He's fine when we're in a group, but when we're alone, the real feelings come out.

"You're angry with me," I say.

He snorts and folds his arms. "I see the great New York education has paid off."

"*You're* angry with *me?*" I launch myself off the tailgate, spinning around on him.

"Well, I know that's just impossible to believe, isn't it? That *I*, the asshole, the villain of every story, could be mad at the Almighty Ruby St. James, who is so high above everyone else she thinks she knows *everything* about them. Even though she hasn't bothered to so much as pick up a phone in ten goddamn years!"

Well, that shuts me up.

I march around to the passenger side of the truck, slamming the door after hopping inside. I glance in the side-view mirror and see Murphy kick at a clump of dirt and storm off toward the water. I sit with my arms crossed, fingers tapping on opposite elbows, lips pursed. I know I look like Nancy when I do this, but I'm angry, and I can't help it.

A few minutes later, he wordlessly opens the driver's side door and climbs in, slamming it closed behind him. He looks over at me, and I look out the window. He sighs, starts the truck, and we rumble out of the parking lot. I remain in the defensive position, cursing Danny for dying and Emmett for having a heart condition and Ally for looking at me at the funeral as if we were strangers for a millisecond before she hugged me. Most of all, I curse Murphy. It's because of him that this is all so much harder.

When we pull into his apartment parking lot, I jump out of the truck practically before he comes to a complete stop. We both slam the doors after we get out, and as he bounds up the flights of stairs to his apartment, I rummage through my purse for my keys, coming up empty. "Shit," I whisper as I increase the intensity of my search. "Shit, shit, shit." I go back to the truck, whose door is mercifully unlocked, hoping my keys fell out in one of Murphy's angry sharp turns on the drive back from the bay. Nothing on the floor, in the glove box, in the cup holders. Not between the cushions, or under the seat, or in the side panel.

I get out and dump the contents of my purse onto Blue's hood, but my search is futile. When I look up, Murphy is at the top of the stairs, dangling my keys over the banister. "Missing something?" he shouts.

"All right, Murphy, drop 'em." He raises his arm, and for one horrifying moment I'm sure he is about to throw them with his pitcher's arm into the woods beyond the parking lot. I get a mental image of how demeaning it would be to crawl on my hands and knees through the bushes to find them, especially as the sun sinks below the horizon and I, like many years ago in Danny's backyard, do not have a flashlight. Perhaps he gets the same image, because he lowers his arm and turns around to go back inside.

"Come get 'em," he calls over his shoulder.

I stand at the bottom for a minute, contemplating alternative solutions that don't involve spending one more second in this man's—scratch that, this boy's—company. I could walk home, but there's no spare key for Blue, so I'd have to come back anyway. I could call Nancy to pick me up and send *her* up the stairs to his apartment. She'd probably love it; when has *she* gotten to rescue *me*? For a second, I actually consider having Nancy call Cecile. That would serve him right—a phone call from his mother telling him to cut the crap. But I can't bring myself to sink to the same tactics I used when we were ten and he wouldn't stop yelling "Mushroom!" every time I walked in the room for six weeks after I cut my hair short.

Finally, I give up. I take a deep breath and bang my way up the five flights again. By the time I reach the top, I'm huffing and puffing from the effort and the anger. Murphy has disappeared into his apartment, leaving the door open for me to storm through. I grab my keys from the counter where he's tossed them. I should just leave. I know that. I should leave right now, and that would be the end of it. But I can't help myself.

"You know," I say. "You all think I'm some pretentious city snob, that I think I'm better than you. But it's not true." I'm so angry my voice breaks, and hot tears sting the corners of my eyes. "I miss this place. I miss the crew." It's true. I didn't realize it until I came back, but I've spent the last ten years walking around with a hole in my heart, shaped like four little punk kids from Chatwick City.

"Well, you can really tell from this end," he says, his voice rising even as it drips with sarcasm.

"What do you expect from me, Murphy? What do you want?"

"I want to know why it took Danny fucking killing himself to get you to set foot back in this town. I want to know why..."

"God, Murphy, are you really that stupid? Why do you think?"

He says nothing, continuing to glare at me.

"You want me to say it? Fine. The reason I haven't been home, haven't kept in touch, haven't been here for friends who have needed me? It's too hard, Murphy! It's too hard because everything is associated with *you*." His face changes then, understanding dawning on him. The thought actually hasn't occurred to him before, the idiot, and it's only in this emotionally collapsed state that I could ever admit it. He charges toward me, arms outstretched, and I know what he's going to do, and I know I should stop him, but instead, I move to meet him halfway. We are like two freight trains about to collide. We know it will be messy, but there's not much we can do to stop it now.

He plants his hands firmly on my face and kisses me. A jolt goes all the way through my body and back up again, and everything I've ever felt for or about Murphy Leblanc comes over me like a flash flood. I stop him from kissing me only long enough to lift his shirt off over his head, and he gives me the look I know well; he knows what's going to happen but can't quite believe how lucky he is.

He takes my shirt off, kisses my neck, and cups my breasts, and then he consumes me in a bear hug and lifts me so I can wrap my legs around him. He walks us to his bedroom, our lips never leaving each other, and we fall onto the bed, clumsily fumbling off the rest of our clothes until there's no more to remove. His eyes, pools of black, stare into mine. I nod, and he reaches into his nightstand for a condom.

They're both really good at ignoring problems.

9

RUBY
BACK THEN—SENIOR YEAR

MURPHY FAKE GASPS AND CLUTCHES HIS HEART DRAMATICALLY when I emerge from my kitchen, freshly made up and styled by Shawna, the queen of all things girlie. From all the cheesy teen movies and TV shows in which prom is like the be-all and end-all of life, he knows a big reaction is expected of him. Of course, instead of doing the genuine jaw-dropping thing (that I well deserve, I might add, with three hundred bobby pins, a can of hair spray, a gallon of makeup, and four-inch heels), he makes it into a joke. Would a moment of stunned silence be too much to ask? I guess with Murphy, it would be.

It doesn't matter anyway, because he's somebody else's boyfriend. It's amazing how quickly Murphy and Taylor became a couple. All I did was point her out to him in the cafeteria, initiate a mutual wave, and pass along her number to him. It seemed like a nanosecond after that they were going out. It's not really like Murphy to rush into things, so she must be one hell of a girl. I mean, she seemed to be completely fine with us sticking with our original pact to go to prom together, so she's either awesome or a really good liar.

I gave him an out, told him if it made things awkward, he could take her and I would find someone else. But he insisted that we made plans long before Taylor was in the picture, and he wasn't going to go back on his word. I was secretly relieved, because there's no way I would have found an acceptable replacement on this short notice (even Eddie Rodowski has a date this late in the game), and after all the planning Shawna and Donna did, I would hate to disappoint them.

My parents take about a thousand pictures in the foyer, on the porch, in the driveway. They're smiling and being all cheesy, and I go along with it because I know they so desperately want to forget that my father wasn't here for junior prom, and my mother was sleeping off a depression crash inside and not even aware when Eddie picked me up on the back of his motorcycle. I'm sure neither of them would have approved, had either been present.

To be honest, I didn't really approve either. I had to put a helmet over my updo, and by the time we got there, my hair was flat and I was covered in bugs that had met their death on my skin. To top it all off, Hardy Crane was the first person I saw before I got a chance to straighten myself out, and the way he smirked at me made my bug-splattered skin crawl. Later, he and Brandy McCallister were crowned prom king and queen, which Ally complained shouldn't be allowed since Hardy was a second-year senior at the time.

Murphy opens the door of his truck for me, which is a welcome change. Normally if he's driving, he'll roll the car forward a little bit as

I try to get in, laugh hysterically, promise he isn't going to do it again, and then he does it again. One time he did it so many times that I went back in the house and refused to go anywhere with him. He's as stubborn as I am, so instead of apologizing, he just left. When he called me later that night, we didn't discuss it.

We go to Emmett's house and take *more* pictures with the rest of the crew. It's weird not going to Danny's, where we always meet up, but he can't come to prom because he was suspended for smoking on school grounds. Again. Even if he weren't suspended, he probably wouldn't have come. He and Jenny have been over since he caught her making out with Brad Lewis down by the tracks.

After the dance, we'll all go to Nicki's house, because her parents are in Michigan taking care of her stepfather's mother who just broke her hip. We're not allowed at Danny's because Charlene is in one of her rare "putting my foot down" modes and is disgusted with Danny's smoking—even though she herself smokes and half the time buys extra because she knows Danny will steal them. Charlene must have attended the same School of Sporadic and Hypocritical Parenting Nancy went to.

Emmett and I get in a fight over who gets to ride shotgun. Emmett thinks "the boys" should ride up front together and I should sit in the back with Nicki. I say it's prom, and we should sit with our dates. Emmett says it's not like Murphy and I are on a real date, and I blush as much with anger as embarrassment. To my surprise, Murphy tells Emmett to get his ass in the back or he's going to have to beg a ride from Aaron and Ally, who have made it clear they want to have dinner alone for once.

We go to a restaurant in Burlington, for no other reason than it's thirty minutes outside Chatwick and it gives us more time in the car, more distance and independence. It gives us a one up on the rest of our class, who are all congregating at one of the two restaurants in town, both of which have newsprint as place mats and coloring crayons as utensils. *Our* crew isn't afraid to leave Chatwick. At least not for one meal.

While we're waiting to be seated, an older woman on her husband's arm leans in to Murphy and says, "Your girlfriend is stunning." He doesn't correct her about my title. He just nods, says "I know," and then loops his arm around my waist. I can't help but smile.

When we arrive at the school gym, we mingle a little, the girls all comparing dresses. Mine is royal blue, with little silver sparkles woven in the fabric. It looks like the sky just after the sun sets, and not to sound cocky, but I like it the best. I *should*, considering the length and intensity of the vetting process.

Murphy drifts over to Taylor and starts dancing with her not long after we arrive. We talked before about this, and I told him I didn't mind, but he's gone for so long that everyone else starts to couple off and I'm left standing alone. I try to appear totally comfortable standing in the corner and watching, but I'm not. I feel lonely and stupid. I should have just gotten another date or stayed home. *He* was the one who insisted we still go together. Now he's probably going to be with her all night, and I'm just going to be the loser in the corner. Suddenly I have to get out of here. I rush into the bathroom and breathe deeply once I'm inside the stall. I'm careful to not let the tears in my eyes actually fall and ruin Shawna's hard work in the process.

I wait in there a few minutes, but Ally doesn't enter the bathroom, which means she didn't see me getting upset. Good. She was supportive of the idea of Murphy and me keeping our date, but a little too supportive: "Ruby, who cares about Taylor? She's a *sophomore*. She doesn't even belong at prom."

Ally is not so keen on Taylor yet. She doesn't trust she'll be around for the long haul. The idea that the goal of most high school relationships is not, in fact, to end up married is unfathomable to Ally. You wouldn't sense the distrust based on how she and Taylor gossip together when Murphy actually brings her around. But if Ally saw me upset, it would lead to drama. She would give Murphy a talking-to, and then everyone would be talking about it.

As it is, I feel like a horrific cliché, the girl crying in the bathroom at the school dance. How pathetic. I leave the stall and stare myself down in the mirror, mentally giving myself a no-nonsense pep talk. I look pretty, and I should go out and find some other loser who doesn't have a real date and dance with him. I wish Danny were here. He might not have danced with me, but he would have stood in the corner and mocked everyone with me, which is even better. *And* he would have snuck in a flask. *That* would make this whole thing more bearable.

When I finally come out of the bathroom, Taylor is lingering outside. I force myself to brighten, like nothing is bothering me, and ask her if she's having a good time. She smiles, either faking her warmth or genuinely tolerant of her boyfriend being at prom with another girl. (For some reason I don't understand, I really feel like it's the latter.)

She says, "Murphy's waiting for you by the stage. Sorry I've been hogging him!"

I immediately feel guilty and cover it by saying, "Of course not!" I am amazed at how good I've become at this fakey girl shit I've always hated, but if I don't play along, I end up looking even more pathetic than I already do. "Hey, he's your boyfriend," I add, feeling a little kick in the gut as I say it.

I find Murphy waiting where Taylor said he would be. Wordlessly, we start dancing to a fast song, Murphy spinning me around and shaking his hips goofily. We dance to three fast songs in a row without stopping, laughing the whole time. I'm the one who taught him to dance, if that's what you call this. It was back in eighth grade, the first time he was the only one to show up at my house after school. He confessed he didn't know how to dance and that's why he always sat on the bleachers at school dances. I turned on music and made him show me. It turned out he wasn't a bad dancer, just a silly one, which made it all the more fun. When a slow song came on, I showed him where to put his hands for a slow dance. "No, not *there*, you perv," I had said.

Like then, the music slows, and I shuffle backward to make my exit so he can dance with Taylor, but he grabs my elbow and pulls me close to him. His cologne, which he always wears just a touch too much of, fills my nose. He's been wearing the same kind since we were freshmen—some uncle brought it down for him from Montreal. I got him a new bottle for Christmas this year, noticing the one in his bathroom was running low. His mouth right up against my ear, making me shiver, he says, "I'm sorry if I've been dancing with Taylor too much."

"Oh, stop it," I say to cover, pulling back slightly. "Don't worry about it. She's your girlfriend. You can't just ignore her! I'm the one who should be sorry. I'm feeling a little stupid now that we're here. It's like you're my big brother and our mom forced you to take me."

Murphy slows his swaying almost to a halt. "That's not what it's like," he says. "I brought you because I wanted to." When our eyes lock, I feel something shift inside me.

Before I can put a name to it, the fire alarm goes off.

Our look lingers for another second before a couple bumps into us on their way to the exit. I glance around to see if anyone noticed our little moment, but all I see is the blur of my classmates making their way out of the gym. Murphy puts his hand on the small of my back and guides me through the crowd.

It's raining when we get outside. Of course. I suppose I should be grateful it isn't snowing; it wouldn't be the first May snow shower in Vermont. The rain has warmed up in the last couple of weeks, officially launching Mud Season (which, Vermonters joke, is a more accurate name for the two weeks between winter and summer).

Mrs. Parizo, my AP English teacher, tells us the alarm was triggered by the fog machine, and we can't go back inside until the air has cleared. I look around for our friends but don't see anyone, even in the stilts I'm wearing for shoes. They must have gone out one of the other exits. All the girls around me are freaking out because their hair and makeup is getting ruined. I look at Murphy and say in a mocking tone, "Do I still look pretty?" knowing full well my updo is now both flat and frizzy and my makeup is smudged.

He shakes his head and pulls me in so his lips touch my ear again. "Beautiful," he says. I shiver again, and he thinks it's because of the rain, so he covers me in his tuxedo jacket.

When we're given the all clear to go back in, we decide to go have our official prom picture taken before we forget. The photographer positions us in the classic cheesy couple pose—Murphy standing behind me with his arms around me, both of us facing the camera. I try to explain we're not a couple, but he says this is the best way to show off the dress, so I comply. Murphy holds me a little tighter than is really necessary and cracks a joke about the photographer's coffee breath, making me laugh just as the camera goes off.

After the king and queen are crowned and it's not Ally and Aaron (which Ally refuses to admit she's been expecting and waiting for), we all disperse. Danny picks up Emmett and Nicki, who are in charge of getting one of Emmett's brothers to buy us beer for the night. Aaron and Ally go to pick up snacks for later. Murphy says good night to Taylor, who has curfew and isn't allowed to come to Nicki's for the after-party because she let it slip there wouldn't be parents there. I wait patiently, but feel a weird twinge when he kisses her goodbye.

It's just me and Murph as we walk down the sloping hill to the parking lot. The rain stopped at some point when we were inside, so the air smells like fresh, damp earth, and the clouds are clearing to show the stars. The moment is too quiet, something I'm not used to when I'm around my best friend, so I complain about my feet hurting. He scoops me up without a word and carries me in his arms until we get to the car. I force myself not to ask what's gotten into him. The answer might ruin everything.

We're the first ones to get to Nicki's, so we use the Hide-A-Key under the frog statue as Nicki instructed. We head to separate rooms to change into the casual clothes we packed into overnight bags earlier. I feel sad changing out of my dress. It's the prettiest I've ever felt, and I'm not ready for that to be over. I sit at Nicki's vanity and stare at myself, then I lift a piece of the skirt to my nose. It still smells like Murphy's cologne.

After a minute, I hear a soft knock on the door. I open it, and it's Murphy. He's in jeans and a T-shirt, and has two beers in his hand he must have stolen from Nicki's fridge. I make a mental note to replace them when our beer gets here so Nicki's parents are none the wiser.

"Just wanted to see what's taking you so long," he said, raising his eyebrows that my appearance hasn't changed at all.

"I couldn't reach the zipper." I'm too embarrassed to admit I'm already feeling nostalgic for this night, for senior year, for our crew as we know it, and it's not even over yet. He crosses behind me and starts unzipping my dress. I close my eyes and feel his breath on my shoulder blades. Suddenly, I'm transported back to a few months ago at Danny's house. With the rest of the crew in bed, Murphy and I had reminisced and even cried a little about the future, about separating and leading different lives.

We stared at each other for a minute, and I felt a different kind of connection than we'd ever felt. It wasn't about getting over someone else; it was just about the two of us. When I pulled away, said it was time to get ready for bed, I thought the connection was broken, but then he snuck up behind me and whispered in my ear. I don't even remember what he said; my brain was too fuzzy from Ally's screwdrivers. Before I knew it, we were kissing, and we just barely closed the door to the spare room before we started stripping off each other's clothes.

"What are you guys doing?"

Murphy and I spin around to find Danny in the doorway, and the strap of my dress falls down, revealing my strapless bra.

"Whoa!" Danny says.

"Get out!" I yell, hastening to cover back up.

"Why doesn't *he* have to get out?" Danny protests as Murphy clamps a hand around the back of Danny's neck and hustles him out of the room.

"Her zipper was stuck, you asshole," I hear Murphy say through the door after he slams it shut behind them.

Danny's voice trails down the stairs as Murphy continues to guide him away from me. "Oh, well, maybe I should hang around up there, in case any of the other girls need help out of their dresses."

A minute later, I hear one of Aaron's signature burps, signifying the rest of the crew's arrival. I never thought I'd be so grateful for Aaron's gas. The girls come into Nicki's room—Danny not daring to make the same joke that he did to Murphy in front of Aaron or Emmett, who wouldn't find it funny—and we change into jeans and sweatshirts but leave our hair up and makeup on. There isn't much choice in the matter. Removing the clips and bobby pins now would leave a Bride of Frankenstein mess of our hair, and none of us feels like completely showering off our fancy looks yet.

We drink and get a little high and smoke Nicki's mother's secret cigarette stash. We play Asshole and continue to dance, staying up most of the night. People start trickling off to various bedrooms, but Murphy and I stay up, continuing to play cards as if we have some unspoken agreement that we need more time for just the two of us. Finally, I declare I'm ready for my last cigarette. Even though Murphy *never* smokes and normally complains when I do, he comes outside to the porch with me. It's cold, so Murphy takes off his coat—this time his trusty blue flannel in place of the tuxedo jacket—and drapes it over my shoulders.

Once again, the moment is too quiet, the crickets and my

sporadic exhalations the only sounds. So I say, "What's with all the chivalry tonight, Murph?" I mean it to be funny, and I expect him to overcompensate by giving me a brotherly cuff on the arm, breaking the tension. But he's quiet. He opens his mouth, closes it. Opens it again. Closes it.

My heart starts to beat harder, because I think he's trying to figure out a way to kiss me, and I don't know what to do if he tries. I thought we were past this. No matter what I've been feeling tonight, Murphy has a girlfriend. After Hardy, I swore I would never be the other woman again, and I won't let Murphy become a cheater either. Just because it's too soon for Taylor to give it up, doesn't mean I'm his automatic sexual consolation prize. Besides, all those feelings before, I was just swept up in the whole prom mania. Twinkly lights, overplayed love songs, all that chiffon. Murphy's my best friend, and that's all. Right now, he's just trying to get into my pants. It's bound to happen; he's a dumb, horny boy.

Then he says, clearly but softly, "I love you, Ruby."

Oh.

10

RUBY
NOW

I LIE IN MURPHY'S BED, COMFORTABLE ENOUGH CONSIDERING I'M
naked and slipping around on satin sheets. Murphy Leblanc—little
Murphy, who was chunky until the eleventh grade, whose proverbial
cherry I am personally responsible for popping—now has satin sheets.
It's nauseating and hilarious at the same time. They positively *reek* of
his cologne, or maybe my nose is just hyperaware. They say smell is
the most powerful of the senses, the one most tightly connected to
memory. I catch a whiff of this scent or something similar in the city
from time to time—getting off the subway, in a crowded theater, at
the bodega across the street from the office. It never ceases to make
me simultaneously anxious, aroused, and headachy.

We both lie on our backs, staring at the ceiling, catching our
breath and our thoughts. Outside, it has started to rain, as if nature
itself is displeased with our reunion. Neither of us knows what to say.

At least, I don't know what to say, and I'm not sure if he cares enough to say anything. It's silly that I'm surprised when he breaks the silence with a joke. "So…how you been for the last ten years?" he asks.

I laugh, clutching the smooth sheet in my hands. He laughs too, which sends me off into a fit of giggles, like we're fourteen and on the phone until way too late.

He asks me about my life now, and I tell him about New York, how my job is fine but unfulfilling. I tell him I spend time in bookstores and cafés, hoping to be inspired by all the pretentious hipsters jabbing away at their MacBooks, but instead of inspiring me to write, the trips usually end with a return to my couch to eat potato chips in front of bad reality TV shows. I tell him something I haven't yet said out loud, that I'm thinking of going back to school to get my MFA, if for no other reason than to force myself to write something other than apologetic emails to clients.

He likes the idea, he says, because then the countless hours I spent reading my short stories to him over the phone will have been worth it. I tell him about how much I love the city—the MOMA, Central Park, the shops with fresh flowers on every corner. How I pass a million strangers, and none of them know anything about me. I tell him about the monthly (more like quarterly) dinners I have with my father. Away from my mother's penny-pinching, he has his assistant book us at exclusive restaurants where I wouldn't otherwise even be able to get a reservation, let alone afford half the check.

He asks me about my friends, and I tell him about some of my coworkers that I occasionally have drinks with. He tells me they don't count. I tell him I see my sister when she blows through New York, but I admit that happens only three or four times a year since she's a freelance nature photographer and I can hardly keep track of which continent she's on at any given moment. I tell him about Greta, my roommate from the London years, who moves freely about the world as if things like working visas and health insurance are of no importance. I've gotten a free place to stay in Brazil, Vietnam, and (my favorite) Turkey as a result.

When I mention that my favorite thing about Greta was how she didn't care what anyone else thought, that she slept with any and everyone and had no qualms about discussing the gory details, his interest is piqued. I tell him what I especially loved was when she talked about her conquests in front of Jamie. His princely manners disallowed him from any comment, so the best part was watching him squirm.

He doesn't ask who Jamie is, and when I realize my story probably doesn't make sense and start to explain, he tells me it's not the first time he's heard the name. Apparently, Nancy and Cecile swap stories when they run into each other at Martin's, the grocery store. Nevertheless, he asks me more about him. Later, I will need to examine my reasoning for dropping Jamie's name so casually into a conversation with a man I've just slept with. Nancy's therapist would have a field day with that one.

"Is he good-looking?" Murphy prompts.

I purse my lips at him. "No, he's a troll. Yes, of course he's good-looking."

He squints his eyes. "As good-looking as me?"

I laugh. "Yes. In a different way though."

I know he wants me to say more, but how can I possibly explain that while Murphy is more rugged and brutish, Jamie's appeal is more subtle, more intellectual, hidden behind glasses and amplified by the sexy English accent?

"He's more nerdy cute," I settle on, feeling guilty that I'm downplaying Jamie's looks to boost Murphy's ego.

It works though; Murphy looks pleased with my answer. For a foolish moment I hope that's the end of it, but he wants to know more. "How did you meet him?"

I tell him the story: Jamie was the professor's assistant in my Gothic literature class when I studied abroad. He resigned halfway through the semester, and as the dozens of other lovestruck girls fawned over him after his announcement, I suddenly had a surge of panic that I might never see him again. So I asked him out. We went to a coffee shop and talked about books for hours; he teased me when I tried to impress him by "casually" dropping in references to Chaucer and Hawthorne.

He told me he had resigned because he wanted to "give writing a go." I found out later he comes from a pretty well-to-do family, which is how he could afford this luxury. I hasten to tell Murphy that, beyond Jamie's impeccable table manners, you wouldn't have suspected he came from money. Especially with that sloppy hair and the corduroy blazer with the elbow patches, frayed at the edges, straight from the clearance bin at Professors R Us. It feels important Murphy doesn't think I spent three years in a relationship with a snob.

"Sounds like the kind of guy we all thought you'd end up with," he says, and I wonder if it hurts him to say it as much as it hurts me to hear. "Did you love him?"

I think a minute before responding and decide to tell him the truth. There's enough that I'm hiding from him without adding to it. "I did. It took a while, but I did. Very much." I glance at Murphy but don't look into his eyes. I didn't say this to hurt him, but at the same time, I'm terrified that I will see his indifference to it.

It did take a while for me to love Jamie, or at least to realize that I loved him. Instead of coming home and attending NYU graduation, I skipped the ceremony (much to Nancy's dismay), signed another lease with Greta, and took a job at the *Sun* in their sales department. I swore it wasn't about Jamie, that I just loved London and my job and Greta and loathed commencement ceremonies (based solely on my high school experience), but of course it was about him. It wasn't until about a year after that I knew for sure.

It was when I read the pages of his first book. I remember how nervous he was to hand them over. We had been in bed, just like Murphy and I are now, when he carefully placed them on my lap. Instead of watching for my reaction as I read, which would have been vain and obnoxious, he simply got up and left the room. His writing was so beautiful, yet simple, just like we were. With each turn of the page, I knew, finally, that I was in love.

"So why did you break up?" Murphy asks after a silence.

I sigh, my lips reverberating on the exhale. "Timing, I guess?"

"Explain."

"I'd rather not."

He holds up his hand, his fingers clenched like talons. "Tell me, or I'll give you the Aaron claw."

We both laugh. And then, because it's Murphy, and because before we fucked everything up, we used to spend hours dissecting stuff like this, I tell him the truth. The only thing Jamie and I ever argued about was living together. He was approaching his thirties toward the end of our relationship, so all his friends were settling down and he was ready to take steps that I just wasn't ready for in my midtwenties. He wanted me to move into his gorgeous flat, live off his family money, and start writing. (I know. What a prick, right? *Not*.)

I should have *leapt* at the chance, but I couldn't make myself want it. I didn't feel comfortable not paying my fair share (and I *never* could have on my salary, because even if I had kept my job, I could barely afford the crap shack Greta and I stayed in). Besides, I already had a good thing going with Greta. I liked living with her. She was entertaining and fun. She cooked things I still can't pronounce, and I cleaned up after her. I got to hang out with Jamie when I wanted to and be on my own when I wanted to.

It worked for three years. But then Greta, the bitch, decided to follow this guy she'd been seeing for just four months to *Ghana*, of all places, and that decision held a giant magnifying glass up to Jamie's and my relationship. He asked me one more time to move in with him, and when I refused, he ended it.

What I don't tell Murphy is that my reasons for not moving in, although true and valid, were only branches on a whole tree of excuses. The root of the problem was that I was twenty-two, then twenty-three, twenty-four, and twenty-five, and I just wasn't ready to move in with him. With anyone. It wasn't Jamie. Jamie was practically perfect. It was that the closer we got, the more I started to feel like I couldn't breathe. The better he treated me, the more I resented him for being overall better than me—a better writer, a better partner, a better person.

I hate myself for what I've done. For what I am.

Since Jamie, there's been no one of significance. Sometimes I meet someone interesting, or my coworkers play matchmaker and I go on dates. We go see a movie or comedy show, or for dinner somewhere trendy, a walk through Central Park, or to a museum. It rarely goes past the second date. I'm not very interested in third dates, the famous one where you're supposed to have sex with a person you barely know. The guys I've gone out with are attractive enough; it's just that none of them have made me feel as safe and loved and adored as Jamie. And none has made me feel as alive and excited and crazy as the guy lying next to me. I *definitely* don't tell him that. And I don't tell him that, considering Jamie and Greta are still my best friends and neither even lives on this continent, I'm a little lonely.

"How about you?" I ask, purposely leaving the question open-ended. I don't want to ask specifically about this Krystal person who, truth be told, I haven't thought of until this moment. She can't mean all that much to him considering what just happened, or at least I would hope not. He doesn't bring her up though, or any other girl. Instead, he tells me more about his business, how happy he is to be building homes and running his own crews.

"There's always a finished product, a good home for a family to be raised in, and it'll be there at least as long as I'm alive, if not forever." I picture him driving in his truck, a grandson in the passenger seat, pointing out the buildings he's responsible for. It's a nice picture, but it also makes me sad.

I ask about his mother, realizing she is another person once a part of my life and now all but forgotten. "She gets tougher with every sunrise," he says, as he's always said of her. Cecile *is* one of the toughest ladies around, but not many people have seen the soft side I've seen. After I got Blue but before Murphy got his first truck (a gap of about a year that felt like ten for him), I used to shuttle him back and forth from baseball practice, smoking and doing my homework in Blue in between. The first time I came to pick him up, Murphy had read his schedule wrong and we hung out at his house for an hour to kill the time.

Cecile's small but solid frame thundered in after dealing with a rat situation at one of their apartments, and she was in no mood to have *deadweight* hanging around the house. (She actually used that term.) She put me to work chopping onions for the dinner she would heat up when I brought Murphy back from practice. Nancy was going through a black period at the time, which meant a frozen dinner on a TV tray on a *good* day, so the experience of chopping and chatting with Cecile—once I proved I wasn't totally useless in the kitchen— felt blissfully normal and domestic.

After that first day, I started showing up early on purpose, and without any discussion, Cecile would put me to work, instructing me in her gravelly, accented voice and occasionally guiding my hands to show me the proper technique for a stir or a whisk. Her hands were always pleasantly cool, even when working over her enormous gas stove, and I secretly treasured the intimacy of it. Murphy, meanwhile, would pore over his schoolbooks, struggling to complete his homework and biting his tongue in concentration. Perhaps this is why we, and our friends, bought into our insistence we were "like family" for so long. The picture of the boy doing his homework while the womenfolk busy themselves making dinner is like a goddamn Rockwell painting.

I gradually became less and less afraid of Cecile, and she came to display a sort of muted approval of my presence in her son's life, despite her skepticism as to the need for young boys to have female friends. I wonder now if she knew about Nancy's disorder and was doing her part to make me feel like I still had a mother when things at my house were bleak. I was always invited to dine with the Leblancs when I brought Murphy home from practice, and many times, I took her up on it. Except for when I was dating someone—then I would just tell Nancy I was at the Leblancs' and would go off with the guy instead.

Murphy tells me that Cecile was diagnosed with Lyme disease, which I take harder than he seems to think is appropriate. It doesn't bother her much as far as he knows. I point out that she wouldn't tell him if it did. He says he would know anyway, and I know that's true. One of the many things I know about Murphy that most people don't is what a mama's boy he is.

He tells me his father retired around the same time Murphy started his company with Aaron, but he still consults on some of Murphy's larger projects, and Mr. Leblanc and Cecile still run all their properties with the help of Murphy's older brother. His brother had "a few bad years" when he dated Jenny Albrecht, Danny's on-again, off-again girlfriend from high school, but they've been broken up for over a year. The only residual effect from the relationship is his need to smoke pot at the beginning of each day. Considering the stuff Danny was into at the end, both of us agree this is no cause for concern.

"And?" I finally ask. "Are you dating anyone? Has there been anyone special...recently?"

"No," he says. He doesn't elaborate, and I don't press. I don't think I can remain as stoic as Murphy if I have to listen to him talk about his love life.

We listen to the rain against the windowpane for a moment, our eyes drooping in the peaceful postcoital haze. Everything is different, and yet it's as if no time has passed. Later, the hurt will come, but I choose not to think about it.

After a while, a question floats into my head, and I ask it despite the risk of it making us both sad. "Where do you think he is?"

"Who? Dan?"

I nod.

"I don't know. Heaven, I guess."

Try to be happy I'm finally at peace.

"Heaven," I repeat. It's a concept I haven't really contemplated in a long time, even when I first heard Danny was gone.

"You don't think so?" Murphy asks, rolling over to face me, his head propped in his hand. I roll to mirror his posture, which is a mistake, because from this angle I can see the sparkle in his eyes. The thrill of it is like a stab through my heart.

"I don't know," I say, looking away. "It's always seemed like such a nice idea, that we all go to this big, pillowy cloud place after we die. But then what?"

He laughs. "I don't know, I guess I never thought past that part."

"I mean, it seems kinda dull, doesn't it? We just float up there, strap on an unflattering toga, and stroke a harp all day? I mean, that's why we work hard to be good people? That's our big reward?"

He's amused now. This feels just like one of the conversations we used to have at night after our parents had gone to bed (or Nancy had gone out), whispering into the phone so we wouldn't get hollered at to hang up and go to bed. "There's probably more to it than that," he says.

"Like what?" I ask, collapsing my arm and lying back down, my hands pressed together under one cheek. I look expectantly at him like a kid waiting for their parent to tell them a bedtime story. He laughs at this.

"Maybe it's like this movie I saw once. You get to pick if you stay in heaven or if you go back for another life. And if you choose heaven, you kind of create whatever you want it to be like."

"What do you think Danny would choose?"

"Well, given that he just offed himself, I don't think he'd be too psyched about the idea of living life all over again, or taking his chances on a new one. He's probably up in heaven dealing dope to all the angels," he says. The mental image makes us both laugh, but after a minute it hits me what we're *really* talking about, and I start to cry.

"Hey," Murphy says, pulling me into him and speaking softly into my hair. "I'm sorry. I shouldn't have made a joke."

I shake my head. "No, it's not that. It's just…everything. Danny and Emmett and…this."

"Was I that bad?" he asks, mock offended and clearly trying to lighten the mood.

"No," I say, pulling myself together and giving him a little kiss on the forehead. "That's not what I meant."

"Was it better than…you know, before?"

I roll my eyes. "Murphy. The last time we had sex you were a newbie. If you hadn't improved your skills since then, it would be a problem."

He searches my face and must realize this is the highest praise he's going to get from me.

"What would you choose?" I ask him. I'd quite literally prefer death to talking about us back then.

"Heaven for sure," he says as if it's the most obvious thing in the world.

"And what would your heaven look like?"

He thinks for a second, stroking his chin to emphasize his deep contemplation. "It would be like one endless night at Margie's. Cold beer. Good friends. Beautiful, easy women."

I groan. I can't help myself. This is what Murphy has become? A 'necker? Has he always been one, and I just never noticed because I was surrounded by them?

"Oh and what would your heaven be, Miss Priss?" he asks, pushing pretend glasses up his nose with his index finger. "Sitting on the sofa with a glass of wine and a good book?" He says it in a mock British accent, and I wonder if he's taking a dig at Jamie. I should never have talked about him. The two of them are supposed to be completely separate worlds for me. It's like I'm not even the same person when I'm thinking about one or the other.

"Actually, that sounds kinda nice," I say. "But I would pick reincarnation."

He rolls his eyes. "Of course you would, Tuesday."

I'm taken aback. "Why 'of course'?"

"Because you're always in search of something better. Always have been, always will be." He looks into my eyes now, and I turn to lie on my back.

"That's not true," I say defensively to the ceiling. But at the same time, I wonder if it is.

We're quiet for a minute. "You know," he says in what I recognize as his I'm-about-to-poke-a-bear-(you)-with-a-stick tone, "I really think we should just tell people. I mean, I'm guessing your secret is about us. It happened so long ago, and I think people will understand. What's the big deal?"

The words feel like shots to the kneecaps, even considering he thinks we're talking about two totally different things. The time in our lives he's referring to has defined me in ways I still haven't been able to process, and yet for him it's something in the past, something he washed his hands of long ago. I nod slowly, feeling the color drain from my face, my tongue heavy and stuck as if it's glued to the roof of my mouth. I want to cry, but I can't give Murphy the satisfaction. Mr. What's the Big Deal?

"Right," I say finally, throwing off the covers and jumping out of bed.

"Hey. Where you goin'?"

"Sorry, I gotta go. More work to do."

"It's Friday night."

"Yeah, well, you know what they say about New York." I force cheeriness into my voice as I make a beeline for the door. "It never sleeps!"

"Ruby, wait," I hear him say as I let his screen door slam shut behind me and run out into the rain.

11

RUBY
BACK THEN—SENIOR YEAR

I DON'T SAY ANYTHING FOR WHAT PROBABLY SEEMS LIKE A LONG time. But I can't help it. I mean, he *loves* me? *Murphy?*

"You mean as a friend, right?" I ask, glancing in his direction and then returning to stare straight ahead. I'm giving him an out because it's prom, because we've been drinking and smoking, and because this has suddenly gotten way too serious. It's entirely possible that my freak-out radar is just oversensitive. We've always said how great it is to have a best friend of the opposite sex. You get the companionship without the commitment, the perspective without the pressure. What's not to love? I must be misunderstanding. He must have just forgotten to add the "man" and punch me in the arm.

"No," he says. "I've been *in* love with you. For a while."

So much for that theory. "How long?"

"Two years."

I take a puff of my cigarette to trap the gasp in my throat, then offer it to him. I'm not surprised when he actually reaches for it and takes a deep inhale. His confession is changing everything; it might as well change his stance on smoking. "Two years," I repeat when he passes it back. I try to calculate backward. Two years ago would be sophomore year. We had dated dozens of people between the two of us since then. One of them being Hardy Crane. "All this time? Why the hell didn't you say anything?"

"You know why, Ruby. The timing was never right. Either you liked someone, or I liked someone, or neither of us liked anyone and we would kiss and then you would tell me what a mistake it was because it would ruin our friendship."

"I thought we were in agreement about that. I mean, you're my best friend."

"I know."

"That's not something I've ever wanted to risk. Boyfriends and girlfriends break up all the time."

"I know."

I stamp out my cigarette on the side of the staircase and let it drop to the ground. I think briefly how much time we're going to spend combing the lawn for butts in just a few hours. We really should have put a can out.

"I can't believe you've been hiding this for so long," I whisper, letting my head—too heavy now—drop into my hands. Maybe I did see this, *feel* this coming. I guess if I'm completely honest, there have been times when I sensed Murphy might want more, and there were also times I thought my feelings might tiptoe over the friendship line, but we never talked about it, so it always passed like a storm cloud over an otherwise sunny day. To hear it out loud like this? It's too real. I start to sniffle. Then, floating above us for a moment and seeing that my best friend is—for the first time—telling a girl he loves her, and wanting better for him than a tearful reaction, I make myself shiver to pretend the sniffling is from cold rather than emotion.

He puts his arm around me and I lean into him, even though my instinct is telling me to run away. I thought setting him up with Taylor would set us back on the right track. The friendship track, where we get to have fun and be ourselves and never fight. Not about anything real, anyway.

"I'm sorry, Murph. I don't know what to say," because I don't. I can't say for sure I feel the same way, but I can't say for sure I don't.

"You don't have to say anything," he says, and I can tell he's trying really hard to sound fine with it all. But how can he be? The only desired outcome of telling someone you love them is for them to say they love you too, and immediately. Any variation from that is crushing. We wordlessly get up, creep inside and up the stairs, and climb into the twin bed of one of Nicki's brothers' rooms. At first, our backs face each other, but despite my good intentions, I start to cry, and Murphy rolls over to hold me. He strokes my hair, peppering my hairline with tiny kisses, and whispers that it's all right until I fall asleep.

⌒

When we wake up the next morning, Murphy is still holding me, and I find I don't feel as sad as I did the night before. A little anxious, maybe, but not sad. And maybe even a little…happy?

We tiptoe downstairs in an attempt to sneak out before anyone wakes, but Danny grunts and stretches on the couch. "Too early," he mumbles, his voice scratchy with last night's smoke.

"Morning, sunshine!" I say, purposely bright in order to annoy him. Murphy and I both sit on him on the couch and bounce up and down.

"Fuck off! Fuck off!" he says, until finally he threatens to throw up on us and we leap off him.

"Suckers," he says, grinning. He smiles at us for a long time, looking back and forth between the two of us. It must make Murphy uncomfortable, because he begs off to use the bathroom and leaves me and Danny alone in the living room.

"What?" I finally ask.

"Something happen between the two of you last night?"

"No," I say reflexively. It's sort of true. Murphy and I didn't so much as kiss last night. If we had, Danny would be able to tell. He always knew when I'd hooked up with Hardy, before I even opened my mouth. Good thing he stayed asleep when Murphy and I snuck out of his house the day after we *actually* had sex.

"Hmm," he says. "You look…happy." His voice is filled with suspicion.

"Oh yeah?" I shrug. "Just in a good mood, I guess. It's a beautiful day outside," I say, bending to peer out the window, up at the sky. It *is* gorgeous—the sun is shining, not a cloud in sight. True to Vermont's fickle nature, overnight it decided to transition from Mud to Summer.

Danny nods slowly, but I can tell he knows something. Finally, he shrugs, reaching for his cigarettes and shuffling one out of the pack to stick behind his ear. "Enjoy it," he says, standing to leave. "Your 'good mood.' You and I aren't the type to be happy for very long."

After I help the girls clean up all the beer cans and cigarettes (while the boys play with Nicki's little brothers' friggin' Nerf guns), Murphy and I go to his house right around the corner. I know I should go home, and I get a wave of guilt thinking about Taylor, who is sitting at home waiting for Murphy to call. But Murphy is the one who invited me over—hell, he's the one who started all this—and I'm not ready to go home to sift through this mess alone. Suddenly alone doesn't have the appeal it used to have. I feel like there's some kind of spell over us, and as soon as we part ways, it will be broken.

I change into Murphy's T-shirt and nylon athletic shorts, which are now designated as mine after so many post–field party visits when I demanded comfy clothes that didn't reek of bonfire. We grab a blanket and lie in the sun on his back lawn. I spend the time practically, trying to convince Murphy he doesn't really love me. If he cracks, I'll know he doesn't, and then it will all go back to normal before this all gets out of hand.

"You hate the way I say 'orange,'" I remind him.

"Well, Jesus, it's 'oar-inge,' not 'arnge,'" he says.

"And you hate that I smoke."

"You'll quit. Someday. Right?"

"I've whored around for two years."

"Tuesday, you've slept with two guys, and one of them was me."

"Yeah, and neither of them were my boyfriend. What do you call that?"

"You're independent. Unconventional. And awesome."

"I don't even know how to have boyfriends, Murph. I don't even know if I want one."

"Okay."

"And we've been best friends since eighth grade. Who would you talk to when I piss you off?"

"Good point," he says, smiling. "Probably the same person I talk to about it now. You. I'd say that gives us one up on most of the couples we know."

I don't bring up the biggest question on my mind: *What about the crew?* These friendships, however flawed, are the only thing I've been able to count on through the whole mess with my parents. I don't want to risk losing them. Even when I didn't know what Nancy's mood would be like from one day to the next, when I didn't know if my parents were together or divorced or something in between, I've always *known* I can go to Ally and feel mothered, or at the very least to dance around in my underwear; I can go to Danny and feel like I'm taking care of someone who really needs it; I can go to Emmett and fight if I need to blow off steam. And I can go to Murphy and laugh and know everything will be okay.

But if they all know about Murphy and me, it will be weird and awkward. Suddenly we'll be a *couple*, and every bonehead comment Murphy makes will be a reflection of me. We'll be responsible for each other's actions in a way we haven't ever had to be. We've always just been able to enjoy each other, and now we'll have to defend each other. Our disagreements will affect the crew. They will be *owned* by them. Every touch and look and sentence uttered will be up for analysis. And I don't want to be a contestant in the relationship contest that Ally and Nicki seem to be in. They alternate between competing over who has the best boyfriend and who has the worst, depending on the drama of the day.

I bring up the question that *should* be the biggest on my mind—if I were a better person, anyway. "What about Taylor?"

His face clouds over, and he takes a moment to respond. "She'll survive." He doesn't explicitly promise to break up with her, and I don't ask him to.

After several hours of alternately dozing and indulging my neuroses, Murphy sits up straight, suddenly hard-faced. "Look, Ruby. I said what I said last night, and I meant it. If you don't feel the same way, that's fine. I'm not going to die. But I thought you should know the truth. Now let's just drop it. And maybe you should go home and shower, because you kinda stink." I give him a playful sock on the arm, and he pulls me close and gives me a quick peck on the lips. Uh-oh. I push him off and glance around frantically. What if Cecile sees?

"Okay, I'm going home." I stand up abruptly. "Listen, I don't think we should tell anyone—"

"Anyone about this, especially the crew, because it's none of their business and we don't want it to become 'a thing,'" he recites. It was the same thing I said to him the night I took his virginity.

<hr />

The next few weeks are a blur of confusion, excitement, and despair. Murphy and I continue to hang out, but just as I worried, everything is different. It's good and bad. The bad comes when we see each other in the halls or greet each other in front of our friends. We're both trying to make it seem normal, but suddenly we can't remember how we used to act around each other. The more casual we try to be, the more awkward it is. One time, we even shake hands before heading into homeroom. I'm really glad nobody saw that.

The good, and I mean *really good* part happens when we manage to be alone. At first, tension crackles like there's an electric fence between us. It's the same spark and playful sense of humor that's always been there, but now I'm hyperaware of it, and it's obvious to me that what we have—what we've always had—is more than friend-ship. Everything is amplified.

I drive Murphy to get his hair cut at Le Beaux Cheveux (whose name implies a higher level of sophistication than Chatwick is capable of). Since I got my car, I've taken any excuse to leave my house, even if it's chauffeuring my friends to appointments like a soccer mom. It's a chance to sit in my car and smoke and read and not worry about a tense conversation coming around the corner at home. But lately, it's more about getting to spend any amount of alone time with Murphy that doesn't appear suspect. This time, I don't sit in my car; I go in with him and sit in the waiting area. I pretend to flip through a magazine, but every few seconds we exchange flirty eyes in the mirror. The stylist makes a comment about what a cute couple we are, and we immediately stiffen. I go back to my magazine, and Murphy tells the stylist, "We're just friends." I'm not looking at him, but I can tell he's smirking when he says it.

Afterward, we walk down the gravel driveway and I risk contact by running my hand through his still impossibly thick hair. I tell him the cut looks great, and he looks at me with that gleam in his eye that I now realize is there for a reason. He bends down quickly and scoops me up in his arms, just like he did on prom night. I let him carry me a few feet, but squiggle out of his arms as we approach my car, which is parked on Main Street.

Not ten seconds later, we hear a honk. A maroon SUV drives by, Taylor waving from the passenger seat of her mother's car. Murphy and I wave back enthusiastically, then avoid looking at each other on the ride home.

That's the other bad part. He still hasn't broken up with Taylor. I don't want to ask him to do it while I'm still unsure about taking her place. It occurs to me that *he* hasn't made up his mind either. He told me he loved me, not that he wanted to be with me, and that's not always the same thing.

A few days later, I drive over to his house to give him a ride to baseball practice. I haven't done it recently because he got his truck right before the season started, and since Dad came back, Nancy makes a big show of having dinner on the table every night. But his truck is at Borbeau's getting an oil change. It's another cover we don't discuss. Murphy knows how to change his own oil, and even if he didn't, an oil change doesn't require an overnight stay in the garage. I pretend it's out of habit that I'm here early, ready for my cooking lesson with Cecile, but when I find out she's showing an apartment, I'm not exactly crushed.

I pull up a stool and look over Murphy's shoulder at his homework. Murphy is *not* stupid, but school doesn't come as easily to him as it does to me, and besides homeroom, we aren't in any of the same classes. The work he's doing now is precalc, which I took last year. I point out a couple errors in his work and give him a few tips on remembering the formulas. I can tell he's a little embarrassed, and I internally scold myself for being such a know-it-all. After a few minutes though, we're laughing about it and he's asking me more questions. My hand brushes his as I point something out in a textbook, and he looks at me. I feel myself blush, so I get up with the excuse that I'm thirsty.

There is so much tension in the room that it feels like I'm trying to run through water as I cross over to the fridge. I can feel Murphy wanting to ask me if I've given *us* any more thought, and I'm sure he knows I want to ask him what's going on with him and Taylor. It's been so many days since his big confession that I'm starting to wonder if it was even real. And neither of us wants to bring up anything that might break the spell. Just being in each other's presence lately has been intoxicating. Our feelings for each other are forbidden, and wrong, and therefore incredibly hot.

After rooting around in the refrigerator for an impolite amount of time, I grab a Diet Coke and pop the tab. When I turn around, Murphy is there. He grabs my face and kisses me with all his might, pushing me up against the fridge. His kiss is so full of passion that I lose complete control, dropping my soda on the floor and wrapping my arms around his neck. The already infinitesimal gap between us closes, every cell in our bodies charged with heat. In one movement, he pushes up my skirt and slides me further up the fridge so I can wrap my legs around him, and I feel like I'm going to explode if I can't have him, right here and now.

But just as suddenly as it begins, we hear the rattle of keys from the side porch signaling Cecile's return, and Murphy drops me like a sack of potatoes. I hastily grab the towel from the fridge's door handle and act like I've been on the floor all along, diligently mopping up the spilled soda. Murphy darts over to the sink to retrieve the paper towels.

"What happened here?" Cecile demands.

"He did it," I say, pointing at Murphy, while he simultaneously says, "She did it," and points to me. We laugh. We continue sopping up the mess until Cecile taps her watch and tells us we're going to be late, that she'll finish cleaning up. Murphy and I stand and hurriedly dispose of our towels, each getting a gruff kiss on the cheek from Cecile, and rush out the door to my car.

We resume laughing once safely in Blue, and when I rest my hand on the gear shift, Murphy reaches over and covers it with his. In this moment, my questions about whether or not he really has feelings for me or is just a horny teenage boy disappear. This isn't just about sex. Not for him. Not for me either. It's love. First love.

⌒

When Murphy's done with practice and a warm bowl of his mother's tomato soup fills his belly, he calls me. I'm still so shocked by the realization that I'm in love with my best friend that I can hardly speak.

"What's with you?" he demands, after a silence longer and more awkward than we've ever sustained.

"I." It's all that can come out at first.

"Yeah?"

"I wish things were different."

"Meaning?"

"You and Taylor."

"That's all I needed to know," he says, and he hangs up the phone.

12

RUBY
NOW

56 MAIN IS PACKED, PROVING THAT SUNDAY BRUNCH IS NOT JUST hellish in the elitist bistros of New York. I fight through the crowd, trying to spot my friends while simultaneously trying not to make eye contact with the people around me. The last thing I want is to run into my third-grade teacher or one of the families I used to babysit for before I realized my general dislike of children under ten. I very much want to avoid a conversation with a kid who doesn't remember me changing their diapers and is now all awkward and pimply and gives off the sticky scent of puberty. "I remember when you were this big" is a platitude I would very much like to keep out of my vernacular.

I spot the crew at a long table at the back of the restaurant. I take a deep breath, telling myself this is the last thing I have to do before my mother drives me to Burlington, where I will board a plane and put everything that's happened here back into the little Chatwick box I keep buried deep, deep inside my emotional closet. Yesterday was the only day I was able to successfully hide in my room, feeling guilty that I wasn't visiting Charlene or trying to get together with Ally, or even talking to my own mother. I tried to work but spent most of the day reading my old diaries, rehashing mistake after mistake after mistake. So when Steph called to invite me to this last-minute gathering, sweet as can be, both my guilt and my need to get the hell out of my childhood bedroom made it hard for me to say no.

Now that I'm here, I wish I had said my flight left much earlier than it does. The table my friends occupy is huge and peppered with outsiders I wasn't expecting. Steph is seated at the middle of the table next to Emmett. They are turned away from each other, speaking to people on either side of them—Emmett to Murphy, who sits next to a girl I don't recognize, Steph next to two older people I also don't recognize, whom I assume are her parents because Emmett's parents sit across from him.

I'm a little taken aback by the parental presence. Is it customary to invite parents to brunch with friends if you all live in the same town? Should I have invited Nancy? Emmett and Murphy shoot me a wave in greeting but quickly go back to their conversation, Emmett smirking and laughing. My inner twelve-year-old wonders if they are laughing at me, like the day Emmett pointed out to the cafeteria that I was wearing a bra for the first time. Jesus, I really need to get out of this town.

I stop to hug Mrs. McDowell, who tells me all about myself based on what she's heard from Nancy and the Chat. "Our big-city girl." She winks. Next to the McDowells are Aaron and Ally. They are both frowning, but Ally brightens when she sees me, waving me over.

"I saved you a seat," she says. I smile and sit in the empty chair. Something about Ally has always made me seek her approval, probably explaining why even when we were kids I struggled to share things with her. Looking back, it was less because she was a gossip than the fact that I always wanted her to like me, and telling her all the awful things I thought or felt or did risked her thinking poorly of me. But times like now, when she saves me a seat, when she goes out of her way to make me feel included in a situation where *I* am now clearly the outsider, make me feel the same way I did when I was in fourth grade and she wanted me to sit next to her at lunch. Cool. Special. In.

I survey the room. This is a new restaurant, at least since I've been gone. When I lived here, it was called McAlister's, and the room we now sit in was an ice cream parlor where I worked illegally the summer I was fourteen, earning $3.50 an hour under the table plus half the tip jar (anywhere from twenty-five cents to a whopping two dollars). I made sundaes and ice cream cakes and covered everything edible in hot fudge, sneaking it into my mouth between customers. The brass bars I used to polish every night and the garish rubber-rimmed maroon area rugs have been removed, but copper fans still hang from the beveled, multicolored ceilings.

Ally reads my mind. "Remember when I used to come in, and you would charge me for a small but give me an extra-large?" she asks. I smile in the conspiratorial way we always smile. I do remember. Often Danny was trailing after her, pretending like ice cream was too babyish for him to be excited about, but his eyes flickering for just a moment when I placed a banana split he didn't order in front of him.

Steph finishes talking to her mother and notices that I'm here. She introduces me to her parents, whose hands I shake, and to the girl sitting on the other side of Murphy. "And this is my best friend, Krystal," she says.

My stomach drops as I reach out to shake the girl's hand. She has acrylic nails, an orangy hue to her skin that can only be attributed to self-tanner, and hair highlighted to within an inch of its life.

Or am I perhaps judging her a little too harshly because she's sitting next to the man I slept with two days ago, in a seat that would historically be mine?

"Krys and I grew up together in Branton." Steph pronounces the name of our rival town like most Vermonters do: *Breh-in*, harsh emphasis on the first syllable, the *n* and *t* in the middle skipped over like a waste of time.

Krystal smiles and says it's nice to meet me, but the warmth does not reach her eyes. I try extra hard to project friendliness and nonchalance to make up for my internal dressing-down, but her expression doesn't change.

We all hold our menus without reading them, distracted by our individual pockets of conversation. My end of the table is oddly quiet, especially considering I'm next to Ally, so I follow Emmett's and Steph's parents' discussion, laughing politely in the pauses of well-polished childhood stories, most of which I was present for. Every so often, I risk a glance down the table at Krystal and Murphy. I notice whenever she speaks, she puts one hand on Murphy's arm. Whether she's claiming him as her own or just trying to make sure he realizes she's there, I'm not sure. I also notice as she does it that Murphy tenses or shoots her a confused look.

"That girl, Krystal?" I ask behind my menu to Ally. "What's the deal with her?" I am as casual as I can possibly be, considering I'm starting to get a sinking feeling about the relationship status of the man I just had sex with.

When it comes to things that really matter, you guys barely even know each other.

"They're 'special friends,'" she says with air quotes, rolling her eyes.

I knit my eyebrows, plastering an artificial smile on my face to keep up the pretense for any onlookers. "What does that mean?"

"Well, everyone knows they're sleeping together, but Murphy insists they aren't a couple. I can't blame him. She's really obnoxious."

"Hmm." I can feel the patches of furious red hives start to spread on my chest, and I adjust the cotton scarf I borrowed from Nancy to cover them more completely. Girlfriend or not, Murphy's been sleeping with this girl, and he didn't even see fit to mention her to me? Preferably *before* we had sex?

Krystal looks down the table then and catches Ally's eye. I worry she overheard us, but she just calls down. (A little more loudly than necessary for the size of the table, I might add. Whoops, sorry. Did it again!) "Hey, Al! Are we on for Zumba tonight?"

"Of course!" Ally says as if they are best friends. When Krystal looks away, I raise my eyebrows at Ally.

She whispers, "Well, she asked me to go with her. What was I supposed to say?" I can't help but laugh. Ally will never change. You're never quite sure where you *really* stand with her.

After we put in our orders, everyone resumes their conversations. Ally pretends to examine the dessert menu but lifts it to her face to indicate she has another private thing to say. I lean in to listen, noticing that Aaron is eyeing us.

"Hey," she says. "You haven't gotten another note, have you?"

"A note?"

"From Danny."

I look at her quizzically, but before she can say more, Emmett clinks the side of his mimosa glass to get our attention. I wonder briefly if he should be mixing alcohol with the blood thinners he told me he has to be on. In the old days, I would never have questioned his stringent following of doctor's orders, but in light of his self-prescribed antianxiety treatment, I can't be sure.

"I have an announcement to make," he says and looks at Steph, who blushes and shrugs her shoulders up, ducking her head slightly. I suddenly know what he's about to say, the reason we are all here, the reason their parents are here. I feel dumb for not figuring it out the second I walked in.

"Steph and I are getting married," he says. "Soon. New Year's Eve." Krystal and all the parents immediately exclaim in delight, leaping from their chairs and surrounding Emmett and Steph. The rest of us are on a five-second delay. In those five seconds, my mouth goes dry and I forget how furious I am with Murphy as my eyes automatically search for his. I know we are thinking the same thing. Emmett used to say he planned to hold out on marriage as long as possible. Has he just grown up and fallen in love? I mean, I can't imagine anyone more worthy of the change than Steph. But is this his 'as long as possible'? Why so soon? New Year's Eve is less than four months away. Is he not telling us something?

I feel Ally's hand squeeze mine under the table. It's both a reassurance she's just as scared as me, and a reminder we're supposed to be enthusiastic too. I feel us mentally put our hands in the center and break with a "Go, team" as we jump up in unison to congratulate the happy couple. I'm either noticeably stiff as I hug Emmett, or he was just as much a part of our psychic huddle as the rest of us, because he whispers in my ear, "It's not what you're thinking. I said I'm going to be fine, and I am. I promise." I relax, sending out vibes to Ally and Murphy to do the same. After the week we've had, our reaction isn't out of doubt that Steph is the one; it's out of fear that another of our friends will disappear.

The food arrives and we all take our seats. Steph and Krystal start chattering with Steph's mother about the logistics of planning a wedding for this winter with a family as large as Steph's. I hear Krystal faux whisper, "How are you going to pay for a wedding? I thought you had all that debt from the operation?"

"Krys," Steph says sharply, giving a sharp shake of her head. Emmett shoots daggers at Krystal and then his fiancée. He may have been successful in keeping his situation from the crew and from his own parents, but I'm not sure how much of it was *ever* a secret from Steph's people. And good for her. Why should she have to bear that burden on her own? I look at Ally to see if she overheard this too, but she is pouting at Aaron, trying to get him to loosen up.

Krystal straightens her posture as if she hadn't asked the last question. She asks in a singsongy voice I'm instantly annoyed by, "So, Stephie, who's going to be your maid of honor?"

"You, of course!" Steph says, elbowing Krystal. "That is, of course, if you're up for it."

Krystal feigns surprise, and her eyes well up as the pair exchange a warm look. "I'm just so happy for you guys," she says, dabbing the tears. I can tell that they are genuine, and it really is a nice moment.

Until Krystal puts her damn hand over Murphy's.

I shoot a pointed look from him to his hand. *Not seeing anyone, huh?*

"And Murphy will be my best man," Emmett says, grinning and Murphy rips away the big old innocent eyes he's giving me.

"What? No courting process? You're not even going to ask me if I want the job?" Murphy cries in mock offense. The rest of the table laughs.

"No," Emmett says to more laughter.

"What about your brothers?" Ally asks.

"They'll be groomsmen, but they live too far away." He shrugs. I know that's not the real reason; it's just a convenient excuse. Murphy would be Emmett's best man even if his brothers lived next door to him. He asks Aaron to be a groomsman as well.

"We're going to ask Charlene to do a reading," Steph says. "One of Danny's poems." A quick glance at Ally reveals I'm not the only one touched by this. "We had to find some way to honor him. He was so helpful to us before he died."

Emmett puts his hand over Steph's, and her eyes widen as she realizes she's said something she isn't supposed to say. I don't look at Ally, but I know her radar must be up along with mine. Danny? Helpful? To Emmett? How—by selling him weed?

"Of course we're not sure we'll find one that's appropriate." Emmett laughs, glossing over it.

"You will," I assure him. Danny had notebooks and notebooks full of poems, and while most of them were dark and haunting, I remember a few that radiated love from every drop of ink. He would never tell me who they were about, but I can't imagine Jenny Albrecht inspiring that kind of prose.

"Ally, would you be one of my bridesmaids?" Steph asks.

"I would be honored." The way she says it is practiced, and I wonder how many brides she has stood up next to over the years. She was probably maid of honor at Nicki's wedding, who (Ally had informed me at Margie's) married a soldier in college and had a baby six months later. Ally is little Wyatt's godmother, and when she showed me pictures on her phone, I nearly choked. Nicki and I weren't exactly close, but I considered her a friend, and it's surreal to think of her as a mother to an eight-year-old boy.

Emmett refuses to acknowledge the boy's existence, even though they broke up years before Nicki and Wyatt's father got together. Ally doesn't understand his inability to let it go, but she's *married* to the first person she fell in love with. She doesn't understand that the rest of us still feel like our first love is ours forever, far beyond the point they're no longer in our lives. Or so I'm learning.

"And, Ruby," Steph says, "Emmett and I have talked about this, and I know you live in New York so if you want to say no, we totally understand, but I would love for you to be one of my bridesmaids too."

I'm stunned. "Me?" I can't imagine she's serious. I met her less than a week ago, and she wants me to be a bridesmaid? A moment ago, I was wondering if I'd even be *invited*. If it weren't for Danny dying, I doubt I would have been.

"Yes," she says, linking her arm with Emmett's and exchanging the kind of smile that makes single girls feel all the more single. "Emmett has always said he thinks of you as a sister, and family is the most important thing in the world."

My eyes sting, and I take a second to swallow back my emotion before I say, "Yes, of course. I would love to be a part of your wedding."

And just like that, my graceful exit from Chatwick disappears, and I am a member of the crew again. Full-fledged.

———

We remain stubbornly at our table long after our plates are cleared and both sets of parents drift off. We stir the dregs of our coffee, order another round of mimosas, and toast to Emmett and Steph. We talk about where to have the events leading up to the wedding. Without thinking, I offer to host everyone in New York for the bachelorette party. After it comes out of my mouth, I worry it will sound like I don't think Chatwick is suitable or that I don't want to be bothered traveling back, but Steph squeals in delight, and even Krystal says something about a *Sex and the City* tour, and the deal is sealed.

We toast to Danny. We reminisce about high school, the last time we were all together. They reminisce about other things that happened while I was in New York or London. I suddenly ache to be a part of those stories somehow, or at the very least for my absence to have been felt. It's selfish, I know, given I was the one who left, and it would have been impossible, given what I was carrying around. But I even wish, just a little, that I had never left. That I had made different choices.

It makes no sense. Growing up, all I ever wanted to do was get out of here, and now that I'm back and surrounded by my friends, I'm wondering what was so wrong with it in the first place. I knew this would happen when I came home, and perhaps, more than anything, this is why I've stayed away so long. This place, these people, these feelings. They're intoxicating. I'm as much an addict for Chatwick and the pain and the drama as Danny was for anything that numbed him. I've relapsed after a ten-year run at abstinence from Chatwick.

And now I'm nothing but a junkie.

"Well, I really don't want to steal you guys' thunder, but there's something I'd like to say before Ruby disappears again," Ally says, looking pointedly at me before squeezing Aaron's arm and smiling. Aaron's eyes widen, and I'm surprised to find him shaking his head at her. She doesn't see; she's already turned back to the group. My eyes connect with Aaron's, and I narrow mine in concentration. It's no use. Aaron grew up in Chatwick Town and didn't join our Chatwick City group until high school. The telepathy doesn't extend to Townies.

After a pause allowing for sufficient anticipation to build up, she says, "We're pregnant!"

Everyone stands, and another round of excited hugs is exchanged. The boys clap Aaron on the back, making lewd comments about sperm and masculinity, but Aaron remains grim. A feeling of panic courses through me, just as it had when Emmett made his announcement. Why isn't he more excited? Why didn't he want Ally to tell us? Did he just feel like it wasn't the right time, or is there something wrong with the baby? I think back to Charlene's house; it felt like Ally was lying when she said her secret was nothing bad. So is there impending doom accompanying this happy news?

Ally reveals nothing as she is questioned about when the baby is due (in the middle of March) and if they are going to find out the sex of the baby (no). Every inch of her is a proud mama. She takes a sip from her glass, and I realize she's been drinking water while everyone else has been sucking down breakfast cocktails. Thinking back to the night of Margie's Pub, I remember Ally holding a clear fizzy drink with a lime and a straw. I had assumed it was a vodka soda, but it must have just been soda.

"Wow, so, Ally, was that what Danny had on you? Was that your secret?" Steph asks.

"Steph, please, let's not bring all that up again," Emmett says, more polite in his request than he had been the day of the reading at Danny's house. He must have learned his lesson about what happens when you tell Steph to shut up.

"Secret?" Krystal asks.

"Oh, it was the strangest thing," Steph says, turning toward Krystal. "Danny had an envelope for each of them with secrets he knew about them. He told them they had to reveal them to each other 'or else,'" she says. I am disappointed in my new friend, the way her eyes glisten with the power of information. She is not above the Chat. None of us is.

"Ooh, what a fun little game," Krystal says. "Well, let's hear 'em!" She looks at me as she says it. The feeling she has it out for me strengthens. Whether Murphy told her about our little rendezvous, or she's just the type of person who is distrustful of new women, I don't know. Either way, I don't feel the need to deal with her attitude any longer.

"I think the key words you missed are 'reveal them to *each other*,'" I say, forcing a smile that matches Krystal's in that it is completely fake. I want to say more, like "It's none of your fucking business and keep your orange nose out of it," but I don't want to ruin the happy mood. Krystal and I remain smile-snarling at each other, neither of us looking away until Ally speaks.

"Yes, to answer your question," she says, breaking the dense air. "That was my secret. I ran into Danny at the pharmacy when I was picking up my prenatal vitamins, and he noticed. I was just too excited to lie, so I just blurted it out, and—"

"That's fucking bullshit," Aaron cuts in, shaking off Ally's hand. Despite the usual low tone of his voice, I can see people at the next table shoot inquisitive glances over at ours.

"Aaron!" Ally starts, looking stricken by her husband's sudden rebuff.

"That's not your secret, and you know it," he growls.

The disgust in his eyes scares me more than whatever Ally's secret could be. I've never seen Aaron look at Ally like this. Ever since high school, even when the two of them had their stereotypical adolescent squabbles, his eyes always held nothing but patience and admiration when they were trained on her. It was something I was always jealous of, something I *thought* I saw in Murphy's eyes, something I definitely saw in Jamie's. I wonder for a second what Jamie would think of this little crew, and of me suddenly reclaiming my place in it, but the combination of the champagne and my two worlds mentally colliding makes my head hurt.

"I read your secret," he says. "You wouldn't open it in front of me, and then you just told me it was about the baby and wouldn't show it to me. I found it in that compartment in your purse you think I don't know about, the one with the cigarettes in it." He stops at this point and gives an aside to the group. "She hasn't had any in there since we found out she was pregnant."

I'm relieved, not because Ally has finally given up her occasional secret smoke, but because despite Aaron's fury, he is still clarifying his own anger in order to defend his wife. It's a good sign.

"Oh, Aaron, you don't understand," she says, visibly deflating.

"I can't believe you would do that," he says. "I can't believe you would have—"

Ally gasps, and it seems to pull Aaron out of whatever rage trance he was in that made him start this scene in the middle of a Chatwick restaurant. He looks at her for another moment, her eyes pleading for understanding, his filled with disappointment and hurt. Then he tosses his napkin on the table and walks out of the restaurant without another word.

"Aaron!" Ally calls again, knocking over her chair in her haste to chase after him. The rest of us remain frozen, stunned by the abrupt change in tone.

After a few moments I say, "Um…should we… Should I?" I want to make sure Ally's okay, but I don't want to be intrusive.

Emmett and Murphy shrug their shoulders. Like they have a clue. I look to Steph, the newbie, to tell me what to do.

"I can go check on her, if you want," Krystal says.

I shake my head. I know she is trying to be helpful, but the thought of sending this girl in my place makes me feel sick. I wonder why? "I'll go," I say.

Ally is easy to locate. As soon as I open the door to the restaurant, I hear her voice. I remain on the sidewalk, watching across the street where she stands at the window of Aaron's truck, pleading with him to listen to her. The engine is running, and his hand is firmly on the steering wheel. "Aaron, I'm your wife. You can't just leave me on the street! We have to talk about this," she says.

"You had an abortion and didn't tell me about it, Ally. There's nothing for us to talk about." He all but peels out as he pulls away from the curb.

I stand there, wishing I hadn't heard what I just heard, my mind whirling. With the truck gone, there is nothing blocking Ally's view of me. Our eyes connect, and then she sags, her hands covering her eyes. I cross the street to go to her.

"You heard?" she asks when I reach her and wrap an arm around her.

I think about lying to make her feel better, but she saw the look on my face when Aaron pulled away. "Yeah," I say.

She snaps her hands away from her face. "It's not true! That's why I hid it. I didn't have an…" She puts one hand on her stomach, reassuring her fetus of its safety. "I don't know why Danny wrote that." Tears spill onto her cheeks, and I put one hand on her back, rubbing gently.

"Come on, I'll bring you home," I say.

"I left my purse in the restaurant," she moans. "I can't go back in there right now."

"No one heard anything," I say. Although it's unlikely that the patrons of the restaurant could make out what Aaron said (even from their positions pressed up against the picture window), it's just as unlikely that not *one* soul took notice of Chatwick's most darling couple hollering at each other on Main Street. I suspect the Chat will be abuzz tonight. "It doesn't matter," she says. "That was so *embarrassing*. I look like such a *liar*."

I give her my car key and tell her to go wait in the car; I'll get her purse for her. Once I'm inside the restaurant, they all look at me inquisitively. "She's fine," I say. "I mean, she will be. I'm going to give her a ride home."

I hug and say goodbye to Emmett and Steph. Murphy opens

his arms to give me a hug, but I pull away. "See you at the wedding, *buddy,*" I say, instead giving him an aggressive slap on the back.

He looks at me, hurt and confusion in his eyes.

"See you both there," I add, looking at Krystal. "Nice to meet you," I say to her, and she says the same with a thin smile, looking back and forth between him and me, searching for signs of a threat.

"Ruby," he starts, but I'm already on my way out of the restaurant, the same kind of exit I made from his apartment two days ago. The same kind of exit we made from each other's lives ten years ago. Unfinished. I wish with my whole body that Murphy would come after me to stop me from leaving. To tell me there is an explanation for the girl who can't stop touching him. To tell me I mean more to him than she ever could. That he wasn't just using me for sex. It seems I've been waiting for him to do that for a decade.

Just like before, he doesn't.

13

RUBY
BACK THEN—SENIOR YEAR

"So, Murphy, have you talked to Taylor since...?" Ally asks Murphy.

My ears perk up in the middle of my conversation with Danny about how much he thinks he'll make scalping his tickets to the Tragically Hip show in Burlington tomorrow night. It was less than twenty-four hours ago that I told Murphy I wished things could be different. He had hung up pretty quickly, and I had spent the night lying awake trying to interpret whether he was mad or just decisive about his next course of action.

I shoot Murphy a look, but he stares straight ahead and keeps walking. We're on our way to the gym for the stupid end-of-year assembly, the one where they hand out awards for things none of us have—perfect attendance, school spirit, best hair... (Well, Ally's in the running for that last one, but rumor is it's going to Gwyneth Grant and her white-girl dreadlocks.)

"Hello? Murphy! Answer me!" Ally says, grabbing his elbow to slow him down.

"No, I haven't," he says.

"Well, is she doing okay?" Ally persists.

"I don't know, Al. I just said I haven't talked to her," he says through his teeth. "It was just last night. I don't even know how you know already."

"What are you guys talking about?" I burst in. I don't want to have this conversation here in the hallway outside the gym, with the entire student body milling around us, but I have to know. And more importantly, I need to know what *Ally* knows.

Ally just looks at me, then looks at Murphy, her entire face a question mark. "Murphy broke up with Taylor. Last night." She looks back and forth between us again, searching. "How did *you* not know this? Emmett told me this morning."

I feel my face turning bright red, and I know Ally is already starting to be suspicious, so I tell them I forgot something in my locker and make a break for it. It only takes about five seconds to get lost in the crowd. From time to time, I shoot a look over my shoulder to see if Murphy is following me. I hope he isn't, because then Ally would *definitely* know something was up. But when I look back and don't see him, I'm disappointed, because I want to pull him into a deserted classroom and talk. Or not talk.

———

For the second night in a row, I can't sleep. Murphy is free. There's nothing standing between us now. Well, there's *no one* standing between us. Which means, of course, that I need to figure out what the hell to do. Murphy is still my best friend. I'm still feeling a little guilty Taylor got hurt. I'm still going to NYU, and Murphy is still staying here.

But suddenly all these barriers don't mean as much as they did before. Now, all I can think about is being with him. Laughing with him, kissing him, making love to him. My heart is racing. I am so happy just at the thought of being with him that I feel like I'm going to burst. I can't contain it for one more second. I have to go to him. I have to tell him.

I glance at the clock. It's after midnight on a Thursday. I pick up the phone, but almost immediately put it back in its cradle. There's no way I can call him. First of all, the last time Cecile slept through a ringing phone in her house was the night Roger died.

Still, I can't wait to talk to him. I can't sleep, or stop thinking, or even breathe until I get the words out. I launch out of bed and dress as quietly as possible in sweatpants and a hoodie. Then I change my mind and put on jeans. I'm about to go tell Murphy Leblanc, my best friend since eighth grade, my buddy since kindergarten, that I love him. The moment calls for more than sweats. Although, we *are* talking about the guy who once held me down and farted on my head until I threatened to throw up on him. So I keep the hoodie.

I creep past Coral's room. She's home for the summer only because her recent breakup left her without a place to stay. I'm more worried about her waking up than my mom. My dad is in New York this week, and my mom's lithium makes her sleep like the dead. I know Coral won't stop me, but seeing her will be my reality check. I don't want to think about reality right now. I just want to be happy.

I decide not to drive. I don't want the sound of the engine starting to alarm Coral, and Blue rolling into the driveway would *definitely* wake Cecile. Plus, the walk will give me a chance to work out exactly what I'm going to say. Unfortunately, it also gives all the doubts I've been pondering for a week a chance to creep in. I stop in the middle of the road. I have an academic scholarship to NYU. Murphy's not going to come to New York. But he could, right? Or, if he wants some time to think about it, we can do long distance for a while. It's not like we don't have plenty of experience talking on the phone. We live in the same town, see each other almost every day, and we still manage to fill up hours every night with phone chatter. It could work. I mean, we *love* each other. What's more important than that? I keep walking.

I stop again. What if I wake up the Leblancs? Or what if they discover me trying to sneak into the house? What if I can't wake Murphy? It's a risk I have to take. I have to try to see him right now, before I chicken out. I keep walking.

Right before I get to Murphy's driveway, I stop again. What if I misunderstood? Prom night is kind of hazy, and maybe Murphy was just drunk and trying to get laid. I mean, he didn't *tell* me he broke up with Taylor. Why wouldn't he tell me that? But I remember the look in his eye when he danced with me at prom, when he whispered in my ear that I was beautiful out in the rain, when he picked me up outside the barbershop, when he put his hand over mine on the way to baseball practice. I keep walking, and this time I don't stop until I get to Murphy's house.

I tiptoe down the gravel driveway, sending up a thank-you that his bedroom is on the ground floor of the big brick house. His window is slightly open, and I press my ear against the screen. It occurs to me, somewhat irrationally, that Taylor could be in there with him. Maybe she just *had* to see him in the middle of the night too, to try to get him back. Maybe it even worked. But I don't hear anything except the fan Murphy needs to have on in order to sleep.

"Murph," I whisper, barely audible. I try again, a little louder. "Murphy." Nothing. I wonder if I should throw stones or something, like Danny used to. Like he still does sometimes, when he has nightmares and can't sleep. I think of Danny. What is *he* going to think of all this? Will he approve of his friends getting naked and falling in love? Or will he think it a disaster, like I did up until tonight?

I decide against throwing stones, mostly because I would feel like an asshole throwing stones when Murphy's window is within arm's reach. I give a light knock on the sill and hear an immediate rustling of sheets. My heart is pounding so hard I temporarily can't hear or speak as Murphy's face appears in the window. On the way over, I imagined the conversation would go something like this:

"*Ruby. What the fuck?*" *he would say.* (*He's very grumpy when he gets woken up.*)

"*I need to talk to you,*" *I would whisper.*

"*Now? Are you insane, woman?*" *he would demand.*

"*No, tomorrow. I just thought I would deliver an in-person twenty-four-hour notice,*" *I would start to yell.*

Then, he would meet me at the side porch entrance and we would have a very awkward conversation about our feelings for each other. Instead, without saying a word, Murphy lifts his screen, reaches down, grabs me under my armpits, and pulls. He knows why I'm here in the middle of the night, and it's certainly not to deliver *bad* news. I use his force to help me scale the short climb and topple into his room. Thankfully, his bed is pushed up against the window like mine is, or my leg or arm or face would be broken.

He kisses me, and before I know it, my shirt is off, and then his shorts are off, and then everything is off. His mouth moves all over my skin, and I bite my fist to keep from moaning too loudly. I kiss him everywhere too, and he lets a groan escape. He fumbles through his nightstand for a condom, and I realize this is the first time we'll have had sex completely sober. But I don't feel sober. I feel high, like I'm flying. He enters me, his arms framing my head, his hands in my hair. We lock eyes as we make love. Making love. I'm not a virgin, but this is a first.

When we're finished, we lie next to each other on our sides, looking into each other's eyes, not able to stop touching one another. I know I haven't yet said what I came here to say, and I know I have to in order to make this real. In order for us to move forward, and stop the game playing and the secret keeping. The words spread inside my chest, looking for an escape. It's painful. I can't say them. Saying them will kill me for sure.

"Murphy," I finally say tentatively.

He doesn't say "What?" or "Yeah?" He just waits. He waits for several agonizing seconds.

"I love you."

"Duh, Ruby," he says, and he gathers me up and rolls me on top of him, my heart feeling like it's going to explode.

14

RUBY
NOW

I sit at the marble-topped bar at Ardesia—the wine bar in Hell's Kitchen that my coworkers and I refer to as our "bitching grounds"—waiting for them to arrive. This is our spot, chosen deliberately because it's just outside the detestable tourist area that is Times Square. Hell's Kitchen is too gritty, too harshly industrial, too close to the view of New Jersey across the Hudson to be an attraction for anyone but actual New Yorkers. And we'd rather push through crowds of suits than I Heart New York sweatshirts and fanny packs any day. There was no question we would end up here tonight. We knew as soon as we came in to inboxes flooded with angry, red exclamation points that today would be "that kind of day"—the kind that either ends with an oversize glass of wine or a gun to the head.

Yesterday there was a last-minute breaking story about the mayor "misappropriating" city funds to pad his reelection campaign, and Layout had to get "a little creative" to make everything fit. As a result, ads were moved or shrunk and, in some cases, cut off in the middle of a sentence, and that was the nightmare of the sales department today. Miraculously, only a few of my clients were affected, so my list of kiss-ass phone calls to them offering discounts and better placement if they didn't pull their advertising was complete long before Larry's, Saleisha's, and Micah's were. But as I threw on my coat and messenger bag, I put my thumb up to my lips, my pinkie tipped up in the universal signal for drinking, and they had all nodded with wide eyes that told me they would be here as soon as humanly possible.

True to form, at 8:00 p.m. the place is filling up fast for the after-work rush, and I'm getting the side-eye from all the women in heels and men in suits anxious to snag the one bar stool next to me that I've managed to save. Above the bar is a second level, a platform where waiters in tight vests and skinny jeans go to retrieve bourgeois bottles of wine from a glass display, and all around me people are discussing politics, plays they've seen, books and articles they've read. This is exactly the type of place I always thought I belonged in, and exactly the type of place I could never picture Murphy stepping foot in. *Maybe* Emmett, although he would be immediately annoyed that they don't take reservations and that no one knew who he was—*the* Emmett McDowell, Chatwick High's all-time scoring leader in basketball.

Just the thought of either of them being here—in this bar, in New York—makes me smile. I'm missing them. Missing Chatwick. I've been going up to the roof of my apartment building a lot lately. From there, I can see the East River, and I look down on it hoping to get the sense of peace I used to get from sitting in front of Chatwick

Bay. It doesn't compare. Here, there are thousands of people between me and the water, people walking on the streets or moving around in their apartments, but somehow the sight of them makes me feel more isolated. So many people in this city, and I have no real history, no real connection, with any of them.

The only one of my Chatwick friends I've spoken with since my September visit has been Ally, all via text message, to coordinate Steph's bachelorette party in a few weeks. I'm highly anxious about it, not only because I don't know Steph that well and I'm worried about her having a good time, not only because Krystal is coming, but because I'm scared to tell Ally what I know I have to tell her.

"Anyone sitting here?" a man in a crisp navy-blue suit asks, his hands resting possessively on the back of the chair where my bag lies.

"Yes, sorry," I say. "I'm saving it for someone." I shoot him a polite smile, but I don't fully look at him until I notice that he hasn't moved away yet. When I look back, I notice that he's handsome in that overly groomed way I've never been particularly fond of. You know the kind: a two-hundred-dollar haircut, flawlessly clean-shaven, eyebrows and nails a bit too perfectly formed for you to believe they aren't "professionally handled." He's grinning as if we've just exchanged an inside joke, and there is a glint of overblown self-assurance in his eyes that tells me this is about to be unbearable.

"Saving it for me, right?" he says.

Why, oh *why* did I have to smile at him? Why couldn't I have replied to his request for my chair in the New York way, with a sarcastic barb like "No, I just like my bag to have its own seat because I'm an asshole like that." It's the damn Vermonter in me that defaults to politeness.

"No," I say, this smile more curt than the first. "For my boyfriend."

He scoffs. "You don't have a boyfriend. No girl comes to a place like *this*, looking like *that*, to meet her boyfriend."

I look down at my clothes, and while the slacks and button-down shirt are certainly fitted, they don't even approach the realm of sexiness this man is implying, which makes me think this is a line he uses liberally, that it has nothing to do with me.

"Can I get you a drink?" he continues. "They make a phenomenal Bourbon Apple Sangria here."

I actually cringe, lifting my still half-full glass of 2006 Chappellet merlot. "All set," I say.

He snorts now. "Wine in a wine bar, how original. You know—"

"I should really find out where he is…" I interrupt, pulling out my cell phone and dialing a number I've used in many a situation like this.

"Hi, love," comes Jamie's most welcome voice, a little hoarse and groggy. I feel a pang of guilt for calling at 4:00 a.m. London time, but I'm guessing he was already up. He is the kind of writer who works "when the fever strikes," as he says, which is often from midnight to five or six in the morning.

"Hi, baby. Where are you? I don't know how much longer I'm going to be able to hold on to this chair."

Jamie is familiar with this game, so he plays along. "I'm in bed, thinking of you," he says.

"Oh, you're ten minutes away?" I say. "Should I order you a drink?"

"Yes, do, and while you're at it, tell the tosser who's chatting you up to bugger off."

I smile and look at the pristinely manicured man, who is still clutching the chair. "My boyfriend has asked me to tell you to bugger off."

The arrogant smile fades from the man's face, and he does as he's told.

"Ha! It worked," I say to Jamie.

"You could do that on your own, you know. You don't need to call me at all hours." He is just pretending to be grumpy, so I don't bother to apologize.

"I know, but this way I get to talk to you. Did I wake you?"

He laughs in that sexy, sleepy way that always gets me. "It's all right. You can make it up to me by telling me what you're wearing."

It's my turn to laugh. "A collared shirt and gray slacks."

"Sounds fetching," he says. "But I much prefer that black little number. Remember that one you wore for Christmas that time?"

I feel myself blush. "I remember."

"That was the night I decided you would be my wife. How's that coming, by the way? You ready to move back to London and have a farmer's share of babies?"

My body tightens as it does whenever he talks like this, which is probably the reason he broke up with me. But I can't help it; he drops it into the conversation so *casually*, as if he's asking me to get a cup of coffee. "Tell me what you did tonight," I say, trying to steer us into safer territory.

He sighs. "Well, after an extraordinarily dull dinner with my parents and my dreadful brother and his dreadful wife…" (They're not actually dreadful; they're lovely people, and Jamie adores them.) "I met some mates at the pub."

"I couldn't at *all* tell you'd been drinking," I say. Hey! There's that New York sarcasm.

He tells me the pub celebration was for his friend Johnathan, who just got engaged. I remember the *weeks* of tension that would follow an engagement announcement when we were together—that big flashing reminder that I couldn't commit to him. Sitting here listening to his accent, a smile spread on my face as we banter and flirt, I can't for the life of me remember why.

"And how goes the plans for the hen night?" he asks, refusing to submit to the American term *bachelorette party*.

I groan. "I don't know what I'm doing," I say.

"Don't overthink it, love. Just get a bunch of objects shaped like tallywackers, and call it a day."

"It's more than that."

"Oh," he says. "Nervous about your big secret coming out?"

"Maybe," I say. After I returned from my weekend in Chatwick, Jamie was the first person I called to fill in about Danny and his envelopes. He's heard a lot about Chatwick over the course of our relationship. He knows about the crew and what they've always meant to me. Each time I spoke of one of them, he encouraged me to reach out and reconnect. I've even gone so far as to tell him that Murphy was my first love.

"Don't you think you'll feel better if you simply tell me what your secret is?" he says, a hint of mischief in his voice that reminds me that love of gossip is not limited to the people of Chatwick, Vermont. When I don't respond, the mirth disappears from his voice. "Seriously, Ruby. It can't be that bad, and I can help you sort out how to tell your mates."

"I don't want it to change…things. The way you look at me."

Jamie scoffs. "Well, in my eyes, you're already a troll. How can it be much worse?"

I laugh.

"Oh, I've got it. You were born a man, weren't you?"

"Yes, that's it. How did you guess?" I ask.

"I knew you were too good to be true."

"Speaking of too good to be true…" Again, I skillfully change the subject, this time to his next book, which is due by the end of the year. He starts to tell me about it when my phone buzzes in my hand. Thinking it's one of my coworkers giving me a status update on their whereabouts, I ask Jamie to hold on so I can check. I find it's not a text message but a notification from my work email. I'm about to ignore it—I can deal with work tomorrow—but the *From* field reads *AnonChat@yahoo.com*.

My heart quickens as I click to open the message, which says only: All things done in the dark have a way of coming to light.

I return the phone to my ear to hear Jamie telling a story about the "shit meeting" he had with his editor this week. Apparently, he didn't hear my request for a pause in the conversation. "Jamie," I interrupt him. "Do you think this is funny?"

There's a pause. "Think what's funny?"

"This email."

"What email?"

I repeat the message.

"Cryptic," he says. "Where have I heard that? It's from the Bible, right?"

"I'm not laughing."

"Ruby! I didn't send it. Why would I?"

"Well, it's just interesting timing, don't you think? We were just talking about the Danny secrets, and I get an email with the threat from Danny's letter, word for word? I know you think this is some hilarious game, but for me—"

"Ruby," he interrupts, his voice stern. "I didn't know Danny said that in his letter. You never told me that."

My hands and feet go numb as I realize he's right.

15

RUBY
BACK THEN—SENIOR YEAR

The next day at school, Murphy and I keep our distance until our friends are out of sight. Last night, we didn't really talk about what comes next. (We didn't really talk about much of anything, come to think of it, although I did manage to squeeze out of him that he didn't tell me he broke up with Taylor because he didn't want to put pressure on me.) We can't exactly start making out in the hallways without sitting our friends down for one of those after-school-special-style talks.

He manages to sneak my books into his pile on the way to homeroom, prompting me to ask him if we're going to split a milk shake before the sock hop later. Then once in homeroom he passes me a note. "Do like I did," it says. "Tell the crew you can't hang out this weekend."

"Okay," I scribble back, giddy as…well, as a girl in love.

———

We spend most of the weekend at my house, since Dad decided to stay in New York for the weekend and Nancy is in a black period, which means she stays in her room and watches TV until the storm passes instead of going out drinking. Coral is off hanging out with high school friends and keeps out of our hair on the rare occasion she is home. She was not a bit surprised when I filled her in on Murphy and my Big Feelings. (I had to tell *someone*.) "I wondered when you were going to figure that out, dummy," was all I got from her.

Murphy and I snuggle and kiss on the couch, jumping away from each other when we hear Nancy's footsteps on the creaky staircase. When she descends, she suggests we all watch a movie together, and I make up an excuse to leave the house—that I'm teaching Murphy to drive standard. We decide it's not the worst idea for him to learn anyway, so we go down to the parking lot of Chatwick Elementary to give it a try. Murphy is hopeless, and we end up laughing too hard to drive and instead have sex in the backseat. Famished afterward, we pick up fast food and bring it back to his house, snuggling and kissing on *his* couch now, the one in the basement, away from his parents, until late into the night. We fall asleep watching a stupid movie where all the actors are dressed up like apes, and wake up in the middle of the night to make love again before I sneak out to go home.

Since the warm weather has held out but my parents aren't physically or emotionally present enough to do it, Murphy spends most of Sunday morning giving our pool a final cleaning so we can take a swim. The water is still freezing, but we splash around for most of the afternoon. I ride around on Murphy's back like I've done a million times, enjoying the weightless feeling and the close contact with another human that doesn't feel threatening. Only now, I occasionally spin around to face him, and he carries me to the part of the pool that's blocked from the house's windows by the deck to press me up against the side and kiss me.

As the sun starts to go down, we wrap ourselves in towels and sit close together on the glider. I am happy and warm.

So naturally, I have to fuck it up.

"Murphy, what are we doing?" I ask, breaking away from a kiss.

His eyes, just a moment before full of desire and love, suddenly look panicked. "What do you mean?" he asks.

"I *mean*," I say, exasperated. "You love me, I love you, now what?"

He frowns and shakes his head. "I don't know."

"Well," I say, resentful at having to pull his teeth, "are we a couple? And if so, what happens next year when I'm at NYU?"

He pulls away from me, his whole energy stiffening. "I don't know," he says again.

Now I panic. This is not the answer I've been expecting. As fun and wonderful as Murphy is, he's not the type to do something without thinking. Case in point, he's been in love with me for two years and hasn't said anything because he couldn't be one hundred percent sure of how it would all turn out. I guess, knowing this, part of me assumed Murphy already had some kind of plan about how to move forward.

"Ruby, we're having a nice day. Do we have to talk about this now?"

My jaw sets in frustration. How is this not an important conversation to have? And why does he seem caught off guard? I mean, did he *forget* I'm going away to school in four months? We sit in silence for several minutes, questions racing through my mind like the news ticker at the bottom of the CNN Money channel my father always has on in the background when he's home.

My frustration turns on a dime to regret. We *were* having a nice day, and now there is frost in the air I'm unsure how to thaw. True, we *do* need to have this conversation, but it doesn't need to be right now. We just began to enjoy each other, and now there is a physical space between us that hasn't existed in over thirty-six hours. I have a fleeting feeling the gap will never again be closed, but I dismiss it as silly.

"No. We don't have to talk about it now," I say, forcing a chipper tone. "Come on, let's go get a snack." But the last thing I feel like doing is eating. Suddenly I feel like I have ten pounds of lead in my stomach.

"Actually, you know what?" Murphy says, standing and vigorously drying off with his towel and pulling his shirt back on. "I forgot I told Emmett I'd help him and his dad finish their deck. I should probably go. I said I would be there an hour ago."

My mouth falls. Murphy's lying. Even if I *didn't* know already he had told the boys he would be out of town until Sunday night, I would know he's lying to me. It's not that he's obvious about it; it's just that I know him. I'm the only one who can beat him at poker, not because I'm such a skilled card player, but because I can always call his bluff. But I want to believe him now, even though I know I shouldn't, because if I don't, it means he's blowing me off. It means that, just as suddenly as I've come to have him, I'm losing him.

"Okay," I say, again with forced nonchalance. "Call me later?" I cringe inwardly as soon as I say it. I'm becoming everything I hate about girls with boyfriends—purposely ignorant, clingy, dependent.

"Yeah," he says, forcing a smile. "Of course." He stoops to give me an awkward kiss on the cheek and then hightails it through the gate.

He doesn't call me later. He barely looks at me the next day at school, and he doesn't return my calls the next day, or the day after that or after that. And even though something in me *knew* from the second he pulled away from me on my deck that it was over, that he had changed his mind, I'm still not prepared for Friday morning when I see him headed down the stairs at school. Just as I'm about to call out his name, to confront him then and there and make him tell me what the hell is going on, I notice he's not alone.

He's holding hands with Taylor.

Over the weekend, I hide from my friends, too shocked and hurt to trust myself around them. Murphy doesn't call to explain what I saw, even though we made direct eye contact for long enough he almost fell down the stairs. He doesn't even call to see how I'm doing. It's not just the guy who said he loved me not caring; it's the guy who's supposed to be my best friend not caring that kills me.

It's not until Monday, when I'm alone at our bank of lockers, that he walks up and says hello, casually as if it were any other day. I don't respond, just hastily swap my paper bag–covered calculus book for my journalism notepad and slam my locker door. He dances around to block me from leaving. "You're just not going to talk to me?" he demands.

He looks hurt. Legitimately hurt, as if *I'm* the one in the wrong. "Why should I?" I shoot back. "You didn't talk to me before getting back together with Taylor."

"Tuesday," he starts.

"Don't call me that. Don't call me anything. I don't want to talk to you."

"You have to let me explain," he says, pleading, his eyes watering.

"It would have been nice if you had 'explained' before I had to see the two of you together like you and I..." My voice falters, and I wave my finger back and forth between the two of us. The lump in my throat prevents me from saying "like you and I never happened."

"Look, I'm sorry, okay? I didn't mean for it to happen like that. I was trying to figure out how to tell you, and then Taylor came to talk to me before I saw you, and it...just sorta happened."

I feel like I'm going to be sick. I'm looking at a boy I've shared everything with, who I love, who I thought loved me, but he's explaining himself as if he had smoked my last cigarette instead of stomping on my heart in the middle of the hallway.

"It's just, when I thought about you going away to school, and being without you, I'd be so miserable when you were gone. And then you would come home for a weekend or for Christmas and I'd be so happy, and then you would just leave again. I don't think I could handle it."

The million questions that have been simmering for days burn in my throat. *Why didn't you tell me you were feeling this way so we could work it out together? Why didn't you think of this before you told me you loved me and ruined everything? Why does that mean you have to get back together with Taylor? Did you just tell me you loved me because you wanted to sleep with me, and you thought you were safe because it was so unlikely I would end up feeling the same way?*

Before I can decide where to start, Ally and Aaron round the corner. I want to scream, to tell them and everyone else in the hallway what is really happening. Ally would be on my side, and at least then I wouldn't be alone in this. He wouldn't just get away with it. But I can't. I don't want everyone knowing that Murphy Leblanc has essentially played me. That I'm a complete idiot. That I'm heart-broken and weak.

I lean close to him and growl, "You're a coward, and you make me sick. Don't talk to me." I hug my notebook to my chest and turn to go to class. Of course I don't really mean it. I want him to know that I'm about to be out of his life forever, and I want that to be enough for him to chase after me and tell me he's made a mistake.

He doesn't.

16

ALLY
NOW

I NEVER UNDERSTOOD WHAT IS SO FRIGGIN' GREAT ABOUT NEW York City, and I still don't get it as our bus pulls into the station. I mean, sure, the buildings are cool. They're super tall and shiny, and there are more windows in one skyscraper than in all the homes in Chatwick put together. Back home (actually in all of Vermont, I'm pretty sure), there's a law against building over a certain number of stories. I think it's like five or six. Not that there's much call in Chatwick for buildings with more than three or four floors.

Don't get me confused with a country bumpkin. I've taken my fair share of trips to Boston with Aaron for Red Sox games and to Montreal for barhopping and shopping. In grade school, Ruby and Emmett and I were part of the band. (Ruby played clarinet, I played trumpet, and Emmett played flute, believe it or not. He had a crush on Addie Helsley, who played the flute, and he thought it would be a good way to get close to her.) Anyway, we took band trips to Washington, DC, and yes, even to New York.

I mean, a city's fun for a visit, but to live? No thanks. All it is, is a billion people crammed into too small of a space, living on top of one another, breathing in the revolting smell rafting up from the sewers. What *is* that smell anyway? It's like sour breath and dirty socks with a hint of urine. I'm not looking forward to it with the increased sense of smell the baby has brought on.

And why are cities always so gray? It's not just smog; it's like the *weather* is always cloudy. It's like the sun can't shine on a place with so many miserable people living in it. Ruby talks about the museums and the theater and the restaurants, dropping their names like I'm supposed to be impressed, but if you ask me, you can get all of that in Vermont; there are just fewer choices. I don't think that's the worst thing in the world. Sometimes too many choices just make people pick nothing at all, and if I'm going to pick nothing and just sit at my house, I can do that in Chatwick for a third of the cost, and I'll be able to find my way around and get a parking spot a hell of a lot easier, thank you very much.

But fine, we're here. Steph is excited to be having her bachelorette party in the Big Apple, and it's all about keeping the bride happy. (I don't know that I was given the same courtesy—it seemed to be more about what everyone else wanted to do—but I didn't know these girls then, so it's not their fault.) I reach across the aisle to shake Steph awake. She is wearing a BACHELORETTE sash I got at the party store and sleeping on Krystal's shoulder, while Krystal snores up against the window. I guess the "supersecret" Nalgene bottles filled with boxed wine Krystal packed might not have been the best idea. They got all rowdy and obnoxious after an hour and then passed out for the rest of the ride. I guess if I weren't pregnant, I would be in the same boat. But I'm a mother now, so I have to be the responsible one.

Who am I kidding? I would have had to be the responsible one anyway. I always have been. Emmett *thinks* he is, because he's all upstanding citizeny, but all he cares about is himself. I'm the one who has to think about everyone else.

The girls and I get up and stretch. We're at the back of the bus at my request (near the bathroom, since I have to pee every ten seconds), so we have to wait until all the other passengers file out. I hear a knock on the side of the bus, and when I look, I see Ruby standing there in a blue peacoat that probably cost more than my first car. Her hair comes down in long waves from a cable-knit hat. The curls have kinks at the bottom, and I know I will have to fix them for her. The girl never did get the hang of a curling iron. It's cute that she tried though.

She waves one mittened hand at us. The other is holding a sign in Ruby's computer-neat handwriting that says *Chatwick Bitches*. I laugh when I see it, glad she is still the same old potty mouth Ruby and not some proper city snob. She laughs too, and when she does, a little puff of fog fills the air. It's early December, and it hasn't snowed yet back home, and it doesn't look like New York has gotten any either. Usually we've gotten at least a dusting by Halloween. The smart parents order their kids' costumes one or two sizes larger so they can fit over a parka. It's funny to watch the neighborhood fill up with puffy little witches and Supermen. Anyway, I wish the snow would just come already. I'd rather it snow than just be cold and dead and gray. God forbid we have a white Christmas and start and end winter on time.

It's been a looong fall. The shitstorm Danny unleashed with his little team-building exercise back in September still hasn't settled down. That little fucker, trying to stir up trouble. The worst thing is, it's working. My own husband is taking the word of a heroin addict over me. I've tried everything to get Aaron to believe me that I didn't have an abortion. And I just want to say, for all of you who are getting ready to line up behind me with those disgusting signs with pictures of aborted fetuses on them, that I don't have anything against women making their own choices. I just don't think I could make that choice myself and, more importantly, I *didn't*.

I've told Aaron that the only reason I can possibly think for Danny making that up is to cause trouble for me and Aaron, because we're happy and he was miserable. Secretly, I know that doesn't make sense, because if Danny really wanted Aaron and me to be miserable, he could have put my *real* secret down on that slip of paper.

It doesn't matter anyway, because Aaron didn't buy it. I even offered to get him a copy of my medical records, but he said I could have gone to Planned Parenthood under another name. He said the only reason he can think of for me to do something like that and not tell him is that I was pregnant with someone else's baby and I didn't want him to find out. The man I married, the man I've loved for half my life, thinks I am capable of that. After that conversation, I gave up on trying to get him to believe the truth and started being angry right back at him. So yeah, my second trimester has been great, thanks for asking.

Sure, it didn't help that I made a big show at that brunch of lying and saying my secret was that I was pregnant. What can I say? I panicked. That morning I found a note in my mailbox, in an envelope sitting right there on top of the morning paper. The note said: *All things done in the dark have a way of coming to light.* Holy shit, right? I don't believe in ghosts, but that shit was *spooky*. Like, how could anyone but Danny know that I hadn't revealed my secret yet? It was even in Danny's handwriting. So yeah, I decided to say something, *anything* to get some heat off my back. I mean, technically I *had* been keeping it secret, and at least that secret was *true*!

Notice that Murphy and Ruby haven't said word one about what's in *their* envelopes. If you buy that load of bull about Danny's secret being theirs too, you are a fool. Well, joke's on them, because their dirty deeds will come out just like everyone else's. At least if whoever's sending those notes has anything to say about it. Maybe I shouldn't judge Ruby and Murphy for lying. I know I lied too. But it was to protect my *relationship*. My *marriage*.

The only thing Murphy is protecting is himself, like always. And Ruby? I expected more from her. I'm not sure why. I mean, she *did* basically chuck our friendship (and all our friendships) the minute she pulled out of her driveway for college. And *perhaps* I'm a little bitter because all she has to do is show up at Danny's funeral and everyone acts like she's some hero just for gracing us with her presence. Meanwhile, she wouldn't have even come if it hadn't been for me.

You should have *heard* how she expressed her condolences when I called to tell her the news, as if it were *my* loss and not hers. Like I was telling her my grandmother or my dog died. In that minute I left open for her while I was crying, she put up the wall that separated herself from me, from the crew. Sure, she'd been away for a while and God knows why. The girl already missed my wedding, and I didn't make a peep. I just wrote her a nice thank-you card for the fancy champagne flutes she sent from London.

But there's no registry for people who have just lost a son or a childhood friend. I wasn't going to let her just send flowers, throw some money at the problem, and bury it like Danny was about to be buried. She needed to be there. She needed to come back to help fill at least a little bit of the space Danny left open. And even though it might not sound like it, I am glad she did.

Now the wedding is only four weeks away, and we're having the bachelorette party now instead of a week before the wedding (like most people do) because of Christmas. It's just too hard to get everyone together. Planning this has been like being a dentist. I feel like giving birth is going to be easier than being a bridesmaid in this wedding.

Every time there's a decision to be made, I make sure to text Krystal and Ruby together because if I make the decision myself, Krystal throws me the "I'm the maid of honor" attitude. And I don't want Ruby to feel left out just because she's in New York, but she always responds with "Whatever you guys think is fine with me!" which is *so* helpful, especially when Krystal refuses to respond because she is offended I've included Ruby, who she considers to be a bridesmaid "in name only," whatever that means.

We get off the bus, and Ruby hugs all of us. Me, because it's me; Steph, because you have to hug the bride even if you've only met her a couple times before; and Krystal probably because Ruby doesn't want to be rude. I'm confused when Krystal makes a big show of hugging back with both arms, like the two of them are the best of friends even though it seems Krystal has decided to hate her just like every girl Murphy dated in high school did.

Ruby takes my luggage, even though it's a rolling suitcase and I'm perfectly capable of handling it. We cross the street after waiting like ten hours for the pedestrian light to give us the go-ahead. We have a couple lights like this in the busier intersections of Chatwick, but no one uses them. When there are two lanes of traffic instead of these six, it's pretty easy to tell for yourself when you have enough time to cross.

Ruby hails a cab without breaking conversation, and I can't help but feel a little proud of her. I remember her being kind of awkward, especially in groups of girls. She was always quiet and let others take the lead, except when she and Emmett would get into it about politics or whatever smarty-pants shit they were talking about. Here she smiles a lot, she leads us around like it's nothing, and she chatters with us excitedly about our trip and our plans for the weekend. Her eyes shine. Her skin glows. I don't know if it's just that she's older and more confident, or if New York brings out the best in her. Maybe there's something about the gray of everything that makes her more colorful. At any rate, I'm starting to rethink my theory that Ruby has stayed away so long just to be stubborn and prove us all wrong.

After a terrifying cab ride to a place she tells the non-English-speaking driver is called Murray Hill (I don't know if that's the name of her building or what. I thought we were in Manhattan?), we are finally at her apartment. She apologizes once for every flight of stairs we have to carry our luggage up, so about seven times. It's amazing that in New York City they haven't heard of elevators. Isn't it a law that you have to have them in buildings with multiple stories? How do handicapped people get around in this city? It's hard enough just being pregnant and having to hike up all these stairs. Now I see why Ruby has designated herself as my bellhop, and I'm grateful for it.

She shows us into her apartment, which is filled with streamers and balloons and a *lot* of penis-shaped decorations. I can tell Steph feels special Ruby went to the effort. It's weird… Ruby's never shown any signs of her mother's homemaking skills before, which I've always thought was a good thing. If she doesn't have Nancy's good qualities, maybe she won't have her bad ones either. But I remember Ruby's birthday parties growing up. There was always a theme, and her mother would make these elaborate cakes and decorations. It was the one thing Nancy could be counted on—to make a big deal of her children on their birthdays. More birthdays than not, anyway.

Some of that must have stuck to Ruby. Not only did she go all out with the party stuff, but underneath all the fluorescent crepe paper and penises, there's a pretty decent apartment, decorated simply and comfortably. Unlike her mother's house, there are no pink flowers or girlie prints of any kind, but it's clean and cozy and softly lit, and there are a couple throw pillows and blankets. There are no dishes in the sink or cockroaches on the floor or rats scurrying through, so right away it's more than I was expecting. (Tidiness was never Ruby's strong suit as a teen. I suspect being messy was her way of rebelling since she didn't drink much. Well, being messy and that affair with Hardy Crane.)

The place isn't huge, but there's a decent living space with a small, modern kitchen and bathroom. I put my things in Ruby's room. We worked out ahead of time that I would sleep in her bed, because she knows me best. Steph and Krystal will sleep on the blow-up mattress in the living room that looks brand new; Ruby must have purchased it for our stay. I get the feeling she hasn't had visitors before, and I wonder for the first time what her New York friends are like. Does she have a tight group of friends here like the crew? Is there a New York version of an Ally, an Emmett, a Danny? Or does she keep to herself without anyone forcing her not to? I can't decide which scenario makes me sadder.

I pick up a picture on her nightstand of her and a man I don't recognize. He's handsome in a Clark Kent kind of way, glasses and all. I show it to her. "Holding out on me?" I ask. It would be just like Ruby to have a boyfriend all this time and not tell anyone about him.

She shakes her head. "That's Jamie."

I remember the name. He's the reason she stayed in London, although she said it was for "a job opportunity." He's the reason she wasn't at my wedding.

"That was actually taken last year. I spent Christmas with his family in Bloomsbury."

"Didn't you guys break up when you moved back to the States? That was at least two years ago."

"Yeah." She shrugs. "We're still friends. He's kinda my best friend, actually."

I look at her like I'm always looking at her, like she's got snakes coming out of her ears. But that answers my question. If Ruby's best friend is an ex-boyfriend who lives on another continent, how happy can she *really* be here?

"Just because Jamie and I didn't work as a couple, it doesn't mean we don't care about each other. Besides, I've cut enough people out of my life just because they've hurt me."

"Or sometimes for no reason at all," I say before I can think. She winces. "I'm sorry," I say, even though I'm not. Not really. It needed to be said.

"It's okay." She starts to say something else, but our conversation is interrupted by the sound of a bottle of piss-warm champagne—transported all the way from Chatwick in Krystal's suitcase—being uncorked in the living room.

—⁓—

"Do you need anything before I turn out the light?" Ruby asks. It wakes me up. We just got back to Ruby's place about twenty minutes ago, but I was asleep before my head hit the pillow. I actually fell asleep in the cab on the ride home, in the midst of Krystal and Steph screaming the lyrics to an old Britney Spears song at the top of their lungs. I must have gone deaf and passed out. Or maybe it's just the weekend that's exhausting me. Cities are tiring enough as it is with all the walking, but being pregnant is a whole other ball of facts.

I hate to say it, but I can't wait to go home tomorrow. Don't get me wrong. It's been fun, and Ruby's been great. She took us to this restaurant last night where you sit on the floor and eat with your hands, which was…different, although the baby didn't seem to enjoy the spicy food. Then we saw *Mamma Mia!* on Broadway, which was really fun.

Ruby says she got the tickets free from a "hookup at work." I don't know if she meant a connection from one of her advertising clients or a coworker she's hooking up with. When I asked, she just giggled like I had told a joke. Either way, it was nice to do something where I could sit down and not feel left out because I can't drink. I think Ruby planned this on purpose because of me, which was nice of her.

Even though I've known her all my life, there have been times this weekend when I feel like I'm getting to know Ruby right along with Steph and Krystal. Who knew she was such a considerate person? I mean, she's always been *nice* and friendly to people, at least until they give her a reason not to be. And I remember she was always good about offering to share. Like if she was using Chap Stick or chewing gum, she would always offer it to me too. And we almost always shared cigs even if we had more than one. There was something about the passing of it back and forth that made us feel connected, I think. Like with each puff we were taking on a bit of the other's pain—the fight she escaped from at home, the worry that Aaron would cheat on me like my dad always did on my mom. Damn, I miss smoking.

Today we went shopping, which was a *huge* ordeal. Krystal insisted on going to stores like Prada and Manolo Blahnik, just to say she'd been there, but we would get into the store and the sales associates would give us the stink eye because we're so obviously not able to afford the stuff, making us all feel like shit. Then Krystal would shout about how expensive everything was, making us all embarrassed to be seen with her. She also insisted on taking pictures in front of the signs of each store and every landmark we went to after, and she would always ask Ruby to take the pictures, like it was a Chatwick girls' trip and Ruby was the tour guide instead of part of our group. Ruby didn't complain, but by the end of the day, I could see the little wrinkles around her lips that mean she's irritated.

I don't know what's gotten into Krystal either. I mean, she's always a bit much, but you'd think she was the *bride* this weekend the way she's carrying on. For example, at lunch Steph asked Ruby to tell the mushroom story again, which was a big hit. Everyone's laughing, even me who's not only heard it before but actually *lived* it, and Krystal cuts in and starts talking about how she knows what we mean about how hard it is to wake Murphy up, and how she has to practically slap him awake "every morning" (as if that was the point of the story). Me and Steph make eyes at each other; we know very well she doesn't live at Murphy's, and as far as we know, she only sleeps over on the nights he can't find anyone else to take home from Margie's.

But for the rest of the day, it was Murphy this and Murphy that. "Oh, Murphy would love that shirt. I have to go in and get it for him," and "Murphy told me he loves it when I wear black, so I really want to find a sexy black dress for the rehearsal dinner." It's like since Murphy's out of earshot, she's given herself free rein to pretend he's her boyfriend. But trust me, she is a girl playing make-believe. Murphy hasn't settled down with anyone since Taylor, and if you ask me, he never really settled down with her either, if you know what I mean. And Krystal? He's just using her for sex. I'm not saying it's right, but it seems to be their understanding.

Poor girl. As annoying as she is, it's obvious that Krystal (like every girl who's ever been dumb enough to like Murphy) is threatened by Ruby, and hearing that they slept on the trampoline together probably triggered her competitive instinct. It's funny because, even though we all wondered if something more was going on between Murph and Ruby, them sleeping on the trampoline together was the one thing that *didn't* raise a red flag. The real couples always took the bedrooms (for privacy), while the two of them slept *outside* where anyone could see them. Plus, they were on a squeaky trampoline. We would have heard if something was going on.

But this is what's always happened between Ruby and Murphy

and their significant others. I can't say I blame people for getting jealous when the person they're dating is on the phone with someone else of the opposite sex for hours on end. Even though Ruby was always overly nice to Murphy's girlfriends, some of them would draw the line with Murphy. It was them or Ruby. Most of the time he dumped them. Sometimes, if the girl had particularly large breasts, things would get chilly between him and Ruby for a few weeks. But that never lasted. Part of the reason he and Taylor lasted so long is because Ruby moved away and stopped talking to all of us.

Ruby's boyfriends didn't stand a chance either, with Murphy being so "protective" of her. He would either get all puffy-chested tough guy about it or freeze the guy out entirely. He used to say if they weren't man enough to stand up to him, they weren't strong enough to handle a girl like Ruby, and it was better she find out sooner so she didn't get hurt. The one guy who Murphy didn't manage to scare off was Hardy, and we all know what good that did her.

So anyway, Ruby did a good job at being superpolite with Krystal, but her lips got more and more wrinkly as the day went on. By the time we got to the male strip club where she had reserved us a table, she was drinking double vodka tonics. She didn't have a lot of them, but as she sipped, I couldn't help but think of Nancy rattling the ice in her glass to scare up every last trace of alcohol after a particularly hard day.

Now I know this might sound bad, but when Ruby went to the bathroom, she left her phone on the table next to mine, and when it vibrated, I picked it up. *For the record*, I thought it was mine at first. But when the notification said *Text Message from Jamie Wells*, I pressed the button to open it before I could stop myself. It said,

Reading Steinbeck and thinking of the time we had a row over his merits. Years later, I'm finally giving him a second chance. You were right, it's gorgeous. Hope you're having a good time at your hen night. Xoxo, J. Best friends, my ass. Like she and Murphy were best friends? It's like she has a permanent blind spot when it comes to the way the men in her life feel about her.

Tonight was less fun for me, not that it matters. Steph had a blast, stuffing singles into G-strings and getting lap dances, and the fact that *she* had fun is what matters. But do you know how *weird* it feels to be *pregnant* in a *strip club?* From the looks I was getting, I felt like a hooker in church. I kept trying to cover my swollen belly with my coat, but it still didn't feel right. So when Ruby asks me if I need anything before she turns the light out, all I can think is that I want to be home. Not the home that exists now, but the one I had before Danny died, when I had a husband who loved and trusted me, who was excited to bring the baby growing inside me into this world. And because I'm exhausted, and because it's Ruby, I tell her that's what I want.

Ruby isn't facing me, but her posture slumps. She hangs her head, and then rests it in her hands. "I'm so sorry, Al," she says.

I roll up to my elbow and reach out to touch her back. She gives a little start. She doesn't like being touched unexpectedly, even now. "Thank you, but it's not your fault," I say.

She nods and turns to me. "Yes it is." I watch her, not understanding, as she opens the drawer to her nightstand and pulls out the envelope labeled *Ruby* in Danny's handwriting. "It's my fault," she says, "because I think Danny mixed up our secrets."

17

RUBY
BACK THEN—SENIOR YEAR

Today is a day I'm supposed to feel happy, accomplished, joyful, hopeful. At the very least, proud.

I feel nothing.

After the ceremony, my friends gather behind the gymnasium for group pictures in our caps and gowns. I smile through gritted teeth at the other end of the row from Murphy, who gets to enjoy this day. Then Taylor, who sat with the Leblancs during the ceremony, jumps into the photo session as if she's been a part of the crew all along. I step out of frame, letting myself get swallowed up in a sea of cheap green polyester. For a moment, I stand in the same spot where Murphy told me only weeks earlier as we stood in the rain in a gown and a tuxedo, that I was beautiful.

Each of us has our own family graduation celebration before we're supposed to meet up at Ally's house later for the big party. Ally's mom agreed to let us have the party at her house without supervision after days and weeks of Ally pouting that we had no place to go since Danny wasn't graduating and he didn't want us at his house. Ally's mom finally gave in on the day Ally's dad informed them he would be bringing his new girlfriend to the ceremony.

My parents and Coral and I are going to Rick's Seafood for dinner, and that leaves a few hours to kill. I can't decide if it's worse to be alone with my thoughts or to endure the exhaustion of pretending I'm happy for my family's sake.

At home, Nancy hands me a card with Murphy's name on it and instructs me to run it over to his house. I hold it up to the light. There's money in it. Nancy is sending me to the boy who broke my heart with a cash reward in hand. Because he's "part of the family." Meaning, he was the one who was there for me when my parents weren't. Also meaning, he would sometimes carry Nancy to bed after she passed out on the kitchen floor and was polite enough to never bring it up.

I could refuse, or even pop it in the mail, but as much as I hate him, I want to see him too. I want him to see me and feel awkward because I'm there. I want him to feel the same discomfort I feel, as if he could even handle it. I want him to have a chance to realize he made a mistake.

I pull up to see Murphy's entire family, including his relatives from Quebec, milling around the yard. Murphy's back is to me, playing volleyball with his cousins, occasionally hollering out a swear word in French to make the younger ones giggle. Before I can take so much as a step toward him, Taylor spots me. She waves enthusiastically and then bounds up to me like she hadn't just seen me hours ago.

"Ruby! I'm so glad you're here. Everyone's speaking French, and I have no idea what they're saying." She lowers her voice. "I think they might be talking about me."

My annoyance at her presence softens. It isn't her fault what Murphy's done, as much as I want to blame it on her. If anything, I'm the one to blame. "I know how you feel. I used to think that too. But it's more likely they're talking about snowmobiling or hunting." I somehow manage the energy to smile.

She exhales, relieved, and then a lightbulb seems to come on. "Hey, Murphy said you couldn't come because you had your own family thing," she says.

"Oh, I can't stay. My mom just wanted me to drop this off to him." I wave the envelope.

"Wow, your mom is giving Murphy a graduation present? And I saw one on the counter for you too. You guys really are like family." It seems she is reassuring herself more than looking for confirmation.

"Speaking of which," she says. "I'm really sorry about, you know, your family situation."

I stare at her blankly. "Excuse me?"

"Well, Murphy told me about your mom and how she's a little"— she circles her temple with her finger—"and how your dad moved out for a while until she stopped"—she simulates glugging a bottle. "That must have been really hard for you. That's why when he told me he worried about breaking your pact to go to prom together, I was like 'Oh my God, I totally understand. The poor girl has been through enough without getting *ditched* right before prom!'"

It's a blow so sudden and so deep I have to stop myself from doubling over. I swallow, knowing the color has disappeared from my face along with the fake smile. Not only did Murphy share the personal details of *my* life with his little tween, but he actually made it seem like he felt *sorry* for me? And now this *toddler* is in on the pity party?

"Hey," Taylor says, noticing the sickly hue of my skin. "I'm sorry... I probably shouldn't have—"

"Yeah," I say, looking her straight in the eye to let her know that she, indeed, shouldn't have. I want so badly to hurt her back, to put her in her place. I contemplate for a moment telling her everything. How she is nothing more than Murphy's consolation prize, for the *second* time now. How he kissed her goodbye on prom night and then told *me* he loved me. How he broke up with her the minute I said I was ready. But then I remember how he pulled away from me that day on my back deck. The look on his face when I saw him holding hands with her in the hallway. He took her back. He chose her. No matter how you dissect it, she wins, and she didn't even know she was competing. What use would it be to hurt her? It's him I should be kicking in the junk.

"So, look, I really have to get going. Can you give this to Murphy for me?" I shove the envelope in Taylor's hands and turn to leave, but not before Cecile catches my eye. It looks as though she's been watching me and Taylor. She points to the side entrance of the house and waves me over. I consider ignoring her, but her movements get more emphatic and less patient, so I obey, following her into the kitchen.

Handing me the envelope with RUBY printed in block letters on the front, she pulls me into a hug and says, "For the daughter I never had." For Cecile, this is an emotional scene of epic proportion. Maintaining her firm grip, she says, "I'm so glad you came into Murphy's life, and mine." Just as the tears start to line my eyelids, she whispers into my hair, "And I'm so, so sorry that things couldn't work out."

I pull away, looking at her eyes. Pity. A less-patronizing pity than what was in Taylor's eyes moments before, but pity all the same. Cecile knows. Of course she knows. Of course Murphy would share our story with his mother. Of course her opinion would carry the most weight with him. Suddenly his words—*You would come back and I would be so happy, and then you would just leave again*—float through my head in the low, gravelly tone of Cecile's voice. It was she who advised against the heartache of a long-distance relationship. She can say she thinks of me as a daughter, but the long and the short of it is, I'm not. Murphy is her son, her baby, and she has to think about what's best for him. No matter who gets hurt.

I can't think of anything to say back to her. When I try, nothing comes out but a pathetic little squeak. I hold the envelope up to her to make sure she sees it before dropping it on her kitchen counter with a *thwack*. Wordlessly, I exit the kitchen and climb into my car. As if sensing my presence, Murphy's eyes connect with mine before I press down hard on the clutch to jam the gearshift into reverse.

I bypass the turn to my street and continue down the hill, past the school where I will never step foot again, past the bars and the railroad tracks. I park so hastily in front of Danny and Charlene's teal house that one of my tires is up on the curb. I ring the doorbell and wait for what seems like an eternity until Danny shuffles to answer the door. His eyes are bloodshot, and he reeks of smoke. Good, he's already in numbing mode.

"Hey, Tues," he says. "Something tells me you're not here to read poetry."

"Let me in. I need to get high."

He smiles, opens the door wide, and steps aside to let me in the house.

———

The ringing phone pierces through the scene playing on the backs of my eyelids. It is an unwelcome sound, at once making the streets of Paris and the harmonica vanish, along with Murphy and me dancing in our prom wear. I wince my eyes open and quickly reach out to pick up the portable from my bedside table.

"Hello?" I croak.

"Ruby St. James, where the hell have you been?" Ally's voice comes barreling through the receiver.

"Um," I start as I rub my eyes, unsure how to explain. I haven't spoken to Ally, or anyone from the crew, since graduation day, two weeks ago. And if it hadn't been for the knee-jerk reaction of being woken from a sound sleep, I wouldn't have answered the phone now.

"And why do you sound like you're sleeping? It's two o'clock in the afternoon!"

Is it? I glance over my shoulder at my clock radio to confirm. It's across the room, strategically placed to force me out of bed to turn off the alarm each morning. The clock is another thing I've neglected since graduation. I've actually rearranged my shifts at the Exchange to afternoons so I can wring every possible second of unconsciousness from the day. I panic for a second, thinking I am late for the second time this week (after assuring Donna I would never let it happen again) before I remember it's Sunday. The Exchange is closed because everyone in town is at church instead of shopping for sweaters priced at $7.95.

"I must have dozed off reading," I lie, trying to force some cheeriness, or at the very least, normalcy, into my voice.

"Oh yeah? Must be one hell of a book to forget about your friends for two weeks."

"I'm sorry, Al. I haven't meant to ignore you. I just have all this summer reading to do." I clench my teeth after I say it. Not only am I lying, but I'm bringing up a sore subject to deflect attention. Ally found out I was going to NYU from Murphy; I didn't tell her myself. She was hurt and confused that I kept it from her, or at least that's what she says. She's really just offended I'm going away at all. To her, it's a comment on her own choice to stay in Vermont.

She is quiet. "I've missed you," I say, placating her. "What's new?"

"Well, Aaron is spending more time playing basketball at Barnard Park than with me. I know we're not going to be *that* far away from each other next year, but it would be nice if he wanted to spend some time with his girlfriend before everything changes."

"That sucks… And how's Murphy?" I try to ask casually. I don't want to know, but I desperately want to know.

A pause, then… "You don't know?"

"Don't know what? What happened?" I ask. Did a tree fall on him? Did Taylor dump him? Is he in New York City, trying to figure out if he could live there with me? I don't have time to contemplate which one would be preferable.

"Nothing," Ally rushes to say. "I don't mean something *happened*. I mean, he's been kind of a prick lately. I think he's bummed that Taylor is away at horse camp or whatever. I just mean, you don't know how Murphy is? I figured you were at least keeping in touch with *him*." Resentment drips from her voice.

"Horse camp?" I say, ignoring her jab.

"Yeah, you know, she's riding horses and shit. Aquarium camp or whatever."

"Equestrian?" I offer, a smile beginning to twitch at my lips.

"Yeah, that's what I said." We both laugh. I bask in the thought of Taylor being away and Murphy being miserable. Then I have a sudden, wonderful thought—maybe Taylor dumped him before she went away, or better, maybe he dumped her, realizing he made a mistake when he chose her over me. Maybe that's what he's been calling to tell me, and I should have picked up the phone when I saw his number appear on the caller ID, just once out of the sixteen times. Suddenly, I have to know. But I can't ask Ally or she'll know something's up, especially considering my hibernation. And I can't just call him. If I'm wrong, what kind of conversation will that be? I can't imagine anything more painful or humiliating.

"So there's a party at Luke's tonight. In his field," Ally says.

"Luke?"

"Yeah. Danny's friend, from the garage?"

I murmur acknowledgment even though I can't find Luke's face in my memory. Danny's name stirs feelings of guilt. I've been ducking his calls along with everyone else's, ever since graduation day when I got way too high in his basement, cried for an hour, and then left without telling him why.

"We're all going. It would be nice if you could take a *study break* long enough to see your oldest and dearest friends. We don't have that much time left together."

Suddenly, it feels like that's exactly what's in order. A nice, big party with lots of people around. I can put in some face time with the crew to alleviate my guilt. Plus, a bonfire is an easy enough setting to pull someone into a cornfield for a chat. Lots of shadows.

———

I ride to the party with Ally and Aaron, deep into the countryside. I'm quiet in the back of Aaron's pickup, the nerves from being out in public again, being around the people I no longer belong with, pulsing under my skin. The sun went down hours ago, leaving only a vague outline of the trees flying past my window. I wish I could jump out and hide up the highest one, so high that no one could find me.

Most of our graduated (or not graduated) class is there. Danny hugs me and Ally and slaps Aaron five, asking him to be his beer pong partner. Aaron is known as King Pong in some circles. Murphy and Emmett haven't arrived yet, but Nicki sees Ally and me and extricates herself from a crowd of rising senior girls. She drags us off for a half hour to strategize about how to act around Emmett now that they have officially broken up. I try to be sympathetic, but I know they'll be wrapped around each other by the time their fifth beer is popped.

When Emmett and Murphy pull in, Emmett unloads the bright-orange cooler, fishes out a cold one, and makes a beeline for the group of basketball players that just so happen to be at the opposite side of the field from me and the girls. I think he's avoiding Ally more than Nicki, since Ally is the one who will call him a dickhead for the way he broke it off. Even though they had agreed to end before they left for college, unceremoniously showing up at Nicki's house with a box full of CDs, books, and clothes she left in his car was not the proper way to end a four-year relationship.

Meanwhile, Murphy struggles to balance the tent bag, tarp, and sleeping bags. He spots me, looking surprised. As if in two weeks he's forgotten I existed. I remind myself of the sixteen phone calls, but it doesn't help. "Tuesday, lend me a hand?" he calls out.

"No," I reply in what I hope is a cool tone. My heart is thudding wildly at the sight of him, and suddenly, the idea of being even semi-alone with him makes me panicky. But when I turn back to Ally, she and Nicki are both looking at me in surprise. I cannot tell them about what happened—not ever—so I sigh inwardly and go.

I grab the sleeping bags and follow him out way past the fire, almost to the corn. We are silent as we try to get the poles to come together through the little loops in the burgeoning darkness.

"You and Em looking for a little alone time tonight?" I ask, noticing how far away we are from the other tents. These are the first words I've spoken to him since that day at our lockers. The day my heart shattered.

He laughs. "I doubt Emmett will be bunking with me tonight," he says, tilting his head to a spot a little way away from the fire, where Nicki and Emmett now stand arguing. "First step, fight. Second step, get drunk. Third step, fuck each other's brains out."

I want so badly to laugh, for everything to be back the way it was just a few months ago. But it isn't, and I can't. "So why do you need so much privacy?" I can practically taste the acid dripping from my words.

He tosses the rain guard over the peak, even though there isn't a cloud in the sky. "I just wanted to talk to you. You haven't answered any of my calls."

"Well, I don't understand why you're calling."

He looks genuinely taken aback.

"Because—"

I interrupt him, knowing this is my chance to ask the question I came here to ask. "Is it because you grew a set and changed your mind? Is it because you and Taylor aren't together anymore?"

He sighs deeply. "No."

Of course not. How is it possible I had hoped for anything else? Has the part of me who's grown up with my parents' fucked-up version of love learned nothing? I know love isn't some fairy tale, that it doesn't transform you into some perfect person. That people fail and don't live up to their end of the bargain, that sometimes they don't even try—and when they do try, it's way too late. "Well then, what's the point? You made your decision. I'm not going to beg you to be with me if that's what you're waiting for."

"That's not what I'm waiting for."

Why not? I want to ask. *Why did you tell me you loved me if you didn't want to be with me?*

"I'm waiting," he continues, "for my best friend to come back."

For a moment, I think I might actually black out. After all this, it's so easy for him to pretend like nothing happened.

"Hold your breath until she does," I say, dropping the edge of the rain guard and spinning to leave. With every step back toward the crowd, I force myself to calm my breathing, to stand up straight, to not let Murphy see the effect he's had on my heart. But despite my best efforts, I believe later they will say I stormed up to where Emmett and Nicki are fighting. I walk directly between them and pull Nicki away with a pointed look at Emmett. "Come on," I say to Nicki. "You don't need this bullshit. Let's fill up before the keg is kicked."

~

After filling a red Solo cup to the brim and losing Nicki again to her drama with Emmett, I spot Danny sitting alone, his legs dangling from the deck of Luke's ranch-style house. The flames from the bonfire barely reach his face, but I can tell he is sulking.

"Aaron's off his game tonight," he says, shaking his head as I hoist myself up next to him. "The one thing that kid's good for..." Danny's drunk. And what's worse, tonight he is Gloomy Drunk Danny instead of Fun Drunk Danny. And I'm fixing to be Stupid Drunk Ruby. This is not a good combination.

"It's just a game, dude," I say, nudging him with my elbow and forcing a casual air to my voice to lighten the mood.

"I know!" he says. "I'm not stupid."

"I never said you were s—"

"Where you been?" He cuts me off. He slugs down the rest of his beer, crushes the empty cup in his hand, and lobs it angrily at a small group of lacrosse players gathered about fifteen feet away from us. They give us the finger and move along when Danny stretches out his arms, challenging them to do something about it.

I take a sip from my cup to buy some time. As usual, the taste makes my stomach turn a little, but I'm determined to push through it. "I've been around," I say.

"Bullshit."

"Seriously! I've been getting ready for school. Driving to Burlington to get stuff I need for my dorm, doing my summer reading." In truth, I haven't done any of those things. I should be more ready than ever to get the hell out of here, but thinking about New

York makes me feel sick now. "Plus, you know, hanging out with the girls before I go." I throw this in for good measure, even though he knows as well as anyone that the girls of the crew haven't ever been my first priority.

He snorts lightly. "The girls," he says. He looks at me, and I see my lie in his eyes. "Did you ever think I might be worried about you?"

I pause. I hadn't actually thought that. I'm so used to worrying about Danny, and to Danny only worrying about partying, that I thought he might forget my grad day breakdown.

"I'm sorry, Dan. I should have explained. I was just…emotional… it being graduation day and all."

He snorts. "It wasn't *everyone's* graduation day."

"I know."

I know why he's angry. I'm supposed to be there for him. Murphy *and* me. We're not supposed to go off the grid and leave him to stew in his basement because he either has to repeat senior year or give up on his high school diploma altogether. We're supposed to tag team him, to take turns being fun and energetic and distracting (Murphy), and supportive and nurturing and take-charge (me). I've been so wrapped up in my own heartbreak that I don't even know if Murphy is holding up his end of the bargain or if he's too busy with his fifth-grade girlfriend.

As if reading my mind, Danny says, "And what the hell is going on with you and Murphy?"

My pulse quickens. "What do you mean?"

"The only time I've seen you in the same area since graduation was right over there"—he points to the cornfield where Murphy's tent is set up—"and you were fighting."

"Oh," I said, waving my hand dismissively. "That. He said something insensitive about Hardy being here tonight. You know Murph."

Danny nods, still looking at me like he knows I'm full of it. I don't know if he knows the truth about what happened between me and Murphy, and I can't ask. I can't hear the disappointment in his voice that I snuck around behind his back. That I kept such a secret from him when he's always told me even the worst of the things he's done. That I'm now choosing to nurse my heartbreak alone rather than share my misery with him as always. As long as these things remain unspoken, maybe I can keep up the illusion that we are all just good friends, and that I am just an excited upcoming college freshman ready to bust out of this wasteland of a town.

So we sit in silence until Ally and Aaron approach us, followed by Emmett, then Murphy. One by one, each of them hoists themselves onto the side of the deck, their legs dangling off the side like mine and Danny's. Just as always, we are sequestered from the outsiders, creating a wall of friendship we're all too afraid to admit is crumbling.

After my second keg stand, Murphy pulls me away from the crowd.

"Ruby, what the hell are you doing?" he demands, as if he has any right.

"What?" I ask, lifting my hands. "I'm having fun." My speech, I notice, is slightly slurred. I didn't sink any of the cups in my three beer-pong games, which means I had to drink all the ones my partner didn't sink himself.

"Yeah, well, the last time you had 'fun' like that with Hardy

Crane"—he lowers his voice, realizing he's treading in dangerous territory—"it didn't end well for you. Remember that night?"

I poke him in the forehead, which, after I do it, seems like quite a silly thing to do. He grabs my finger gently and doesn't let go. I rear back from him. "Actually, I don't really remember. Do you remember...when you told me you loved me?" I hiccup at the end of this, my eyes filling with tears.

"Tuesday—"

"I told you not to call me that anymore. Only my friends can call me that."

"Oh, like your good friend Hardy?"

"He's just my beer-pong partner. What happened with us was a long time ago."

"Yeah, and you worked really hard to put him behind you."

"What do you care, *Murphy?*" I hiss at him. "It's none of your business who I do and do not fuck."

"Please, Ruby. Don't do this. Don't let it be like *this.*" Even in my double vision, I can see the strain in his eyes, the desperation to make everything different. But he can't. There's no turning back now.

"What's going on over here?" a voice says. Hardy appears by my side.

"Stay the hell out of this, Hardy," Murphy warns.

"Ruby, are you okay?" He wraps his arm around my waist and pulls me to him possessively.

"No," I say, looking straight into Murphy's eyes. "I wanna get outta here. Where's your truck?" The look in Murphy's eyes is at least in the same ballpark as what I've been feeling for the last month, but as I walk away with Hardy, I'm nowhere near vindicated. Not yet.

18

RUBY
NOW

I DIDN'T THINK IT WAS POSSIBLE TO BE MORE NERVOUS ABOUT going back to Chatwick than I was for Danny's funeral, but as I maneuver my rental car onto I-89 in Burlington, only thirty minutes away, I hold the steering wheel in a death grip to steady my shaking hands. I rented a car this time so Nancy wouldn't have to drive all the way to and from the airport twice, and because the universe has a fantastic sense of irony when it comes to me, the only car available at Hertz was a Nissan Sentra. This one, about fifteen years newer than the one currently rusting in my parents' garage, has nothing on Blue. Sure, it has power steering, but that only serves to jerk me wildly off course with every surge of nerves. I do have to hand it to the winter tires though. Blue's tires are more suited for a bike ride on a flat, even surface than a drive on Vermont roads with their frost heaves and black ice.

It's a pretty drive, this section of the interstate between Burlington and Chatwick. Yesterday, northern Vermont had its first snowfall of the year (besides the light dusting in October, which, if you ask any Vermonter, doesn't count). Sparkling white snow lines the branches of the pine trees and piles up on each side of the road, not yet collecting the mud and slush resulting from weeks of traffic. But I barely register the snow globe I'm driving through. I'm too busy thinking about Danny's letter. *You never know how, or when, I might have arranged for your secrets to come out.* Right before that, he had said, *All things in the dark have a way of coming to light.* That was what he had said, wasn't it? The same phrasing that was in the message I got at my *work* email address.

I haven't mentioned the message to anyone from the crew, but didn't Ally say something to me that day at brunch—something about getting a second note from Danny? So much happened that day that I didn't even remember it until now. And neither of the times I've talked to her since she was in New York had seemed like the right time to ask. The first time was the day after she left New York. I called to apologize *again* for not claiming the secret earlier. To be fair, I wasn't sure what had happened until Ally told me in earnest the secret wasn't hers. I *suspected* what had happened, and I suppose the reason I never opened my envelope is so I didn't have to know for sure. That, and I didn't want to see Danny's last angry thought about me.

I insisted on getting on the phone with Aaron to tell him as much. It was the least I could do. To Aaron's credit, he accepted my apology graciously. I could hear a hint of curiosity, but he did not, as Ally had, demand details like when exactly it happened and how could I not have told anyone and who was the father, anyway? I remained vague.

I told her it was a really difficult time for me, right before I left for college. I told her the father of the child was not someone I was proud of, and that he never even knew about it, so I didn't feel right telling her either. All that was true. But just like with Danny, I didn't tell Ally the whole story, and she drew her own conclusions.

The only thing Aaron put me on the spot about was Ally's real secret. She still insists Danny outed her pregnancy—her completely planned-for and very much wanted *first* pregnancy. I told him the same thing I told Ally: that I hadn't read it. But based on the way she snatched the envelope out of my hand and inspected the seal for tampering, I'm guessing she's hiding something a little darker. I did not voice this suspicion to Aaron. They've been through enough, and I'm not going to play any further part in straining their marriage than I already have.

Just remember that all things done in the dark have a way of coming to light.

The second time Ally and I have spoken since the bachelorette party was her call to invite me to her annual Christmas party. Could I come home a couple days early in order to make it? Just like when we were young, I was so happy she seemed to have forgiven me that I immediately agreed. I had already taken the days between Christmas and New Year's Eve off for the pre-wedding festivities and, of course, the wedding itself. But I asked my boss if I could have a few extra days with my fingers crossed behind my back for him to refuse. The fact that he agreed to it is just my karma for allowing Ally to take the fall for me, because it means I will be spending Christmas with Nancy and my father.

I've gotten out of coming home for every holiday season since college by scheduling a trip to see Coral or my London flatmate, Greta, wherever in the world they are living or working at the time, and then there were several years I spent with Jamie's family. I cite limited vacation time to Nancy, but she's not stupid. She knows I don't want to come home. Just the thought of spending the holidays in the place I grew up brings on a flood of images—Nancy in a black period, too depressed to get out of bed and prepare the fancy Christmas Eve dinner she planned, a ham spoiling on the counter while Dad hid in his den. Nancy still drunk in the wee hours of Christmas morning while we opened presents and pretended not to listen to the veiled insults she and my father traded. My parents screaming at each other on New Year's Eve after coming home from a party where she drank too much and he flirted with someone else's wife.

But I can't blame my white knuckles *completely* on my family. Some of it lies with Danny, and some with me. Mostly, it's the unknown. When I came home in September, I knew it would be awful—an overwhelming mess of grief, awkwardness, and nostalgia. Not great things, but I could anticipate them. This time, I have no idea what to expect. Ally assured me she wouldn't tell anyone but Aaron the true owner of the secret from her envelope—after all, neither of them ever substantiated the rumors that Aaron was yelling the word *abortion* at her in the middle of Main Street. But how can I trust Ally not to cave at the slightest challenge—the girl who *lives* to gossip and who cares more about what people think than anyone I know?

And then there was that missed call I got last week. It was from an 802 number, Vermont's one and only area code. It could have been anyone, except for Ally, Emmett, Steph, my family, or even the dreaded Krystal, all of whose contact information I have stored in my phone. It could have been Murphy—maybe he got a message as well, although I doubt he even knows how to use email, or maybe (I hesitate to even think it) he missed me like I've been missing him. But I don't think it was Murphy either. When the number flashed on the screen, my mind went instantly to AnonChat@yahoo.com, and I immediately hit Decline. Whoever it was, they didn't leave a voicemail.

Ever since I received that cryptic email, I've been looking over my shoulder, my body a constant, chilling, bubbling of nerves, making me feel like my blood is some mutant form of ice-cold lava. Every unexpected noise launches me out of my skin. Every night's sleep is filled with images of Danny, sometimes memories resurfacing from the past, sometimes things that will never be, conversations I want to have with him that will never take place.

When I'm awake, it's like I feel him watching me. I know the message was warning me that he'll make good on his promise. That somehow, the whole truth will come out. And when it does, despite Ally's assurance she'll always be my friend, I'm not sure if she, or anyone, will ever be able to forgive me. As angry as I am with Murphy for not telling me about *whatever* the hell it is that's going on between him and Krystal, what I'm hiding from him is so much more unforgivable.

Please don't hate me.

I've thought about canceling. Oh, believe me. I've had the phone in my hand a dozen times, poised to dial Emmett's number and tell him I got pulled into a shitstorm of work to wrap up before the end of the year, and I'm not able to come home for the wedding after all.

But then I picture his face. Emmett, my brother. The pain-in-the-ass boy who grew up to be a man with a heart that will kill him before his time. And Steph, sweet Steph, who has welcomed me into her family despite knowing nothing about me. I can't disappoint them.

And even if I could be that horrible, something tells me I'm in this now. That I have to see it through to the end. That it's time.

I pull up to the house, hesitating before I park *this* Sentra in the same spot I used to park Blue, and I sit for a few moments before I get out. Twinkling lights rim the roof and shine through the inches of snow covering the cedar bushes in front of the house. The two white columns that support the front porch roof are wrapped with red ribbon (one ruby red, one coral red, my mother used to say), giving them the appearance of candy canes. Through the sheer curtains of the living room, I see the artificial tree decorated with the same ornaments we've always had.

We always begged for a real tree cut down from one of hundreds of Vermont tree farms, but my mother wouldn't hear of the money wasted each year to kill a plant that would only end up on the curb at the end of the season. As much as we hated it, I realize now there's a certain beauty in this pathetic little tree, which has overseen our Christmas proceedings for as long as I can remember. No matter what phase our family was in, the tree remained unchanged. There was comfort in that.

I walk up the steps and through the back door that leads into the kitchen, inhaling the scent of baking bread, and I remember that not all the days of Christmas were so tense and melancholy. There were days when the lights first went up, when Mom would take our picture in front of the newly decorated house for the annual Christmas card. There was the party at my father's company headquarters in New

York, where all the employees' children got an age-appropriate toy we then played with obsessively on the trip home.

There were the Christmas hams Nancy *did* manage to serve, with all the trimmings, and the sugar cookies we helped her frost as we stood on stools and donned aprons our mother had hand-sewn, our tongues poked out in concentration as we tried to copy her intricate frosting patterns. There were the Christmases when Mom would invite Danny in from our mocking spot in the tree and shove a mug of hot cocoa in his hands, and we would sit by a roaring fire and watch old Christmas specials on TV, forgetting that we were supposed to be too damaged to enjoy this.

I feel suddenly sick with guilt and nostalgia. Nancy has been on her medication and off the hooch since I was seventeen years old, and yet every year I make an excuse to stay away from her on a holiday that is so centered around family. I wonder if this is the first time she's even made the effort to put up the decorations since both her daughters left home. And in punishing her, we're punishing ourselves, because we've missed out on ten years of the best of our mother.

How much it must break her heart for me and Coral to withhold our love year after year, and still she stays sober. Still, she remains committed to treatment for her illness. It occurs to me that Nancy is not the only one I've shut out of my heart rather than forgive, and it's about time I change that. The realization freezes me to the spot in the kitchen. I drop my bag, my body racked with violent sobs. Just like the evening in Murphy's bed, it's too much. Too many memories, too many old feelings. Too much regret.

And then my mother is there, enveloping me in a hug. I fall in to her and cry, telling her how sorry I am, and she is shushing me and stroking my hair and telling me everything is going to be okay. She smells like vanilla without even a hint of wine. It's going to be a sugar-cookies-and-ham kind of Christmas.

But first. "Mom," I say, using her proper title for the first time since I was sixteen, "I have to tell you something."

19

RUBY
BACK THEN—THE SUMMER BEFORE COLLEGE

I SIT WITH MY KNEES HUGGED TO MY CHEST, A BLANKET WRAPPED around me, watching the bursts of light explode over the lake, miles and miles away. It's chilly for the Fourth of July, even by Vermont's standards, but I'm not sure that has anything to do with my shivering. Lately, I feel an almost constant chill.

I think of the crew, arranged in a semicircle in their camp chairs down at the park. At least that was the plan Ally left on my answering machine, since no one's been able to get ahold of me to see if we're watching them from my roof, like we have every other year. I imagine all the details that she didn't dare leave in her message—that they'll be sipping from Burger King fountain soda cups that are secretly filled with liquor, surrounded by hundreds of Chatwickians doing the same. That for the first year, Taylor will be beside Murphy instead of me.

It's been another two weeks of deep hibernation, only leaving the house to do shifts here and there at the Exchange. I've been training Lacey, my replacement, a rising sophomore who is painfully chipper against my canvas of depression. Another person who's shown me how easily replaced I am among the people I love. Shawna and Donna love Lacey, the crew has embraced Taylor since her return from "horse camp," and I have been forgotten.

I'm startled by the whoosh of a screen opening. Before his feet even appear through my parents' bedroom window, I know it's him. The tears that spring to my eyes dissipate the image of him and Taylor holding hands from adjacent nylon chairs. What is he doing here?

"Jesus, Tuesday, it's not *that* cold," he says, craning his head to see me and nodding at my blanket.

"Go away, Murphy." I bat at my eyes with the back of my hand before he can see that his appearance has made tears appear at the edges.

"No." He navigates the slope of the roof carefully and joins me, mimicking my posture. We sit in silence for a moment, watching the fireworks.

"What are you doing here?"

He looks at me in surprise. "It's the Fourth of July. Where else would I be?"

"Down at the bay, with the rest of the crew?"

He shrugs. "I was on my way. Saw you up here alone, thought I'd swing in."

I nod, but I know he's being intentionally casual. My house is not "on the way" down to the bay from his house. Or from Taylor's.

"Where are your parents?" he asks next.

"In Jamaica. Another 'reunion' trip." He nods. Every time my parents fight now, they make up by going on a trip together rather than (metaphorically) traveling apart. Their therapist is very supportive.

"How's the crew?" I ask, the bitterness in my voice not entirely fair. I can blame Murphy all I want, but I've made the choice not to reach out to them, not to explain, not to answer their calls. I'd rather it be my choice to pull away than to watch it happening.

"Good," he says, either missing or choosing to ignore my tone. "Ally and Aaron are fighting all the damn time, and it's annoying. Nicki comes around every once in a while to glare at Emmett. Emmett's boning anyone and everyone like a kid in a whore store."

"Is Danny okay?" I ask, feeling like a divorced parent of a child I no longer have custody of. I still want to know how he's doing, even though he picked the other one when the court asked him who he'd rather live with. I know that's not a fair analogy though. Danny didn't choose Murphy over me. He didn't even know he had to.

"He's doing fine," Murphy says. "I think. I should probably give him a call. I've been busy with…"

"Your new girlfriend?" I ask. "How are things with Miss Teen Vermont, by the way?"

"Don't do that," he says. "She's actually—"

"I don't actually want to know, Murphy."

He sighs. "I miss you. I *really* miss you, Tuesday. I know I'm the bad guy here, but you're not the only one whose heart is broken. And it fucking killed me to watch you walk away with Hardy that night. It fucking killed me."

I don't even know how to express my inability to understand this. How can he be heartbroken and happy in a relationship at the same time? What kind of sociopath can compartmentalize his feelings so ruthlessly? The word that appears in my brain every morning when I wake up flashes like one of the fireworks I'm pretending to watch: *Why?* But I don't ask it.

"I'm sorry, Tues. I don't like the way this all happened. I shouldn't have—"

"Lied to me?"

Murphy looks stricken. "What did I lie about?"

"You should have never told me you loved me. I'm your best friend, and you used the oldest trick in the book to get me back into bed."

"Is that what you think?"

"Of *course* that's what I think, Murphy! How could you love someone and then just cut them loose without any explanation?"

"I gave you an explanation!"

"Yeah, I know, I remember. You didn't want to have to miss me. Genius plan. Clearly it's working wonders."

"It wasn't just that."

Again, I don't ask what else it was. I'm afraid any more weight on my shoulders will topple me right off this roof. But he tells me anyway.

"Ruby, look at me."

It takes me a second to gather the strength, but I do. He's the same old Murphy, but now that I know I love him, it feels like staring into the sun.

"We would have the summer, then you would leave. For New York, where you've always dreamed of living. And you'll change there. You're *supposed* to. And I'll be here, doing what makes me happy, and pretty soon the gap between who we are now and who we become will just be too big."

In his eyes is something I've never seen before. A maturity, but also a sorrow.

I sniff, and my voice cracks with every word. "But we could have tried, Murph. I think with all that we mean to each other, we at least should have tried."

"And what would the best-case scenario have been for us as a couple? That you would miss me so much you would come home, live in Vermont forever? Then what?"

"Then maybe we could have been happy."

He takes my hand. "Maybe for a little while, but how could I do that to you? How could I hold you back from the life you've always wanted? How could I be happy knowing what you gave up to be with me?"

I watch as the words come out of his mouth, but it sounds scripted, like something a boy would say to a girl in a Lifetime movie. Like something a boy would say to a girl because he thought that's what she wanted to hear. And suddenly I'm angry again. "That's a real pretty speech, Murphy. Tell Cecile she should have been a writer."

He looks as if I'd slapped him, and it feels good to see him hurt, to have some of my power back. So I look away, and just let my comment hang there.

"Fine," he says. "All right. You want to know why I didn't go through with this? With us?"

"I do, but I don't think you're really going to tell me."

"It's this! This right here. You make everything so hard! You never let me get away with *anything*. You know every secret and everything I'm thinking and every feeling before I can even put a name to it."

"And that's bad?"

"It's fucking annoying! Maybe I want to have some secrets. Maybe I want to be with someone who doesn't have debates with Emmett that make me feel stupid and small."

"I don't make you—"

"Someone who doesn't tell me how I feel. Someone who wants a simpler life, like me, who isn't going to spend her life being disappointed in me and resenting me for what she could have had. With Taylor, it's…"

"Easy," I say.

"What's wrong with easy?"

At first, I can't think of an answer. What *is* wrong with easy? I don't know. I've never known what easy feels like. And Murphy, aside from keeping Danny's secret, has never known what hard feels like. He's not built for it. He's not strong enough. I look him in the eye, mustering all the fury and all the pain I've felt in the last few months.

"You are such a coward," I say.

His face turns cold, and he stands up and scales the roof to climb back inside.

I follow him, not ready to let him leave without a fight. "That's what they call people who do the easy thing instead of following what's in their hearts. You go ahead and build your simple little life with your adoring little puppy-dog girlfriend following you around and doing whatever you say, but you'll be bored to tears. You'll always have me in the back of your mind. And I won't be there. I'll move on. I'll get over it, because at least *I* tried. But you'll regret this decision for the rest of your life."

He looks at me, the anger fading from his eyes as he sees the tears stream down my face. He knows what I'm saying is true, just as I know what he's saying is true. If we were to be together now, we would destroy each other.

Murphy puts his arm around me and pulls me to him, and with my head buried in his shoulder I hear him sniff, and sniff again. I put my hand up to his face, and then we are clutching onto each other, crying. Then kissing. Kissing, kissing, kissing. We fumble our clothes off, tasting each new revealed fragment of flesh like it's our last meal. We fall onto the bed, naked, desperate for each other.

"Are you sure you want to do this?" he asks me. "I'm still with…"

I nod and pull his face toward me before he can finish so he can't see the doubt in mine.

Afterward, I whisper "I love you" into his ear. He says it back to me. Then, I watch him as he gets dressed and walks out the door. His shoulders are pinched, and I know if he turns around, I will see tears in his eyes. So he doesn't turn and say goodbye, or offer any lame platitudes like "Good luck in New York." He just walks out the door and out my life, forever.

"Goodbye, Murphy," I murmur.

The pain will kill me. I'm sure of it.

⁓

The doorbell rings, startling me enough that I knock over one of the sky-high towers of books that surround me. I've spent the entire morning sorting books into piles: to bring to NYU, to leave at home, to give to Danny, to donate to the Salvation Army. I leave in three days, and I don't think that's enough time for me to get through them all. Nancy occasionally peeks her head in my room and clucks her tongue in disapproval. "Ruby St. James, if you don't stop messing around with your books and start in on your clothes, you are going to be one well-read, naked college freshman."

Things have gotten better in the six weeks since I said goodbye to Murphy. Not great. Not good even. But better. I've remained in hibernation, licking my wounds. After the Fourth of July, Danny started coming over to watch TV with me, not talking about anything important. I don't know if Murphy told Danny the truth or just that I had said I was worried about him, and I don't ask. I don't want to talk about Murphy with Danny. I don't want to talk about Murphy ever again.

I take an occasional phone call from Ally but list any number of excuses why I can't hang out. Work. Family obligation. The trusty "summer reading assignment." Trips to Burlington with Nancy to fight in Bed Bath & Beyond over the price of linens for the extra-long twin mattress NYU insists I need special sheets for. The crippling pain has settled into a dull, constant ache, but Ally will pry it out of me, turning the intensity back up.

"Aaaaally darlin'!" I hear my mother exclaim from the door with that sugary-sweet southern hospitality that makes me cringe. "Ruby! Ally's here!"

I freeze. This was inevitable, I know, but still I'm unprepared.

"I'll just go up and see her, Mrs. St. James," I hear her say. I stand up among the rubble of my books, actually contemplating whether I could hide in my closet without being found. But who am I kidding? It's Ally.

So I go on the offensive. "Hey, Al! I'm sorry I've been so busy. It's been forever," I say brightly when she opens the door, moving toward her with my arms open for a hug. But she's on to me. Instead of returning my embrace, she holds her hands up in front of her.

"Don't," she says. "Don't. You. Dare."

I step back, shocked by the bumpy but measured tone of her voice. I have never seen Ally this mad, and that includes the time Emmett called her the c-word when she wouldn't let Aaron go to a strip club in Montreal for his eighteenth birthday.

"Al—"

She ticks off on her fingers. "You've ignored my calls. You've blown me off every chance you get. You missed my birthday party. Thanks for the *card*, by the way. That was real *swell*."

"Ally, I'm sorry I've been—"

"Busy." She nods, her lips pursed. She looks around at my piles—linens, clothes, toiletries. For such a frugal woman, in the end, Nancy sure has stocked me with a year's supply of literally anything I could possibly need.

"I don't know what the hell is going on with you," she says. "You won't talk to me, and Murphy, for once, doesn't seem to know what's going on either. Not that he would tell me."

I feel a stir at the mention of his name, like a beast roused from sleep.

"And you know what?" she cries, flinging her arms up in surrender. "I don't even care anymore. My oldest friend is leaving, and she doesn't even care enough about me to try to…see me before she goes." She falters and walks over to my nightstand, where a (miraculously full) box of tissues sits, and blows her nose. "Do you even know what I've been dealing with, Ruby? Do you even care? Aaron wants to 'take some time apart' when he goes off to college."

"I-I'm sorry, Al. I didn't know that."

"Of course you didn't! You've been too busy with that *scumbag*."

"What are you talking about?"

"Hardy Crane, Ruby. I excused it the first time—the sneaking around, the lying—because you were going through your parents' separation, and I knew you were hurting. But now... I mean, for God's sake, Ruby, you're going to *college*. Why are you wasting your time on that trash instead of hanging out with the people who love you?"

Oh my God. She thinks... A surge of rage washes through me. She actually thinks... Fine. Let her think it. Let them all think it. It doesn't matter anymore. In fact, I might as well stop pretending things can ever be the same.

"Ally, you really need to grow up."

She reels back as if I've slapped her.

"I'm sorry, but this whole loyalty to the crew crap you spout off... Don't you think we're a little old for it? Maybe it's important to you, since you're sticking around, but I'm going to *New York* next week. I'm getting the hell out of here. And I don't plan on coming back." I hope she doesn't hear the falter in my voice at the end. I feel a wave of nausea, knowing exactly what I am doing to my friend. To our friendship. All because of something that isn't her fault.

She inhales sharply through her nose, finally resigned that this is the way it will be. "Well. Good luck, then."

I want so badly to stop her, to go after her as she leaves the room. But in her haste to escape the venomous bullshit I'm spewing, she knocks into a stack of sundries my mother has piled on my dresser, and a huge box of tampons falls to the ground.

Tampons.

When's the last time I used one of those?

And I'm stopped dead in my tracks.

20

RUBY

NOW

"'Taking heroin intravenously is comparatively more cost effective, at two to five dollars for a high,'" Emmett says, reading directly from the *Times* article that came out a few weeks ago. He has me cornered in Ally's kitchen next to a Crock-Pot full of roasted wieners (a specialty of Aaron's, I've learned, as he's proudly pushed them on me all evening). The article is creased and faded from where Emmett has folded it. I imagine he's been carrying it around since it came out, pulling it out at every lunch break, in every doctor's office waiting room, his lips moving as he reads it, shaking his head every few sentences, crossing and uncrossing his leg, ankle to knee.

"'Dealers from Montreal and New York move their product in the desolate corners of rural communities like Chatwick, Vermont,'" he continues, an angry fleck of spittle flying from his mouth during his sharp enunciation of the word *Chatwick*, "'where boredom and poverty create high demand, and low supply warrants a higher premium. Eighty grams of OxyContin sold on city streets for twenty dollars goes for upward of forty dollars in Chatwick, which adds up quickly once the user is addicted. That's why so many users in the area turn to Oxy's less costly alternative, that is, the injection of heroin intravenously. A few months ago, a batch suspected to have been smuggled in from Canada was laced with lethal doses of fentanyl, causing the deaths of no fewer than four citizens of this sleepy town.'" He finishes and looks at me expectantly.

I nod cautiously. "Yes, Emmett, I read the article." It's possible I read it as many times as Emmett did, spooked as I was that the town I was so desperately trying not to think about was suddenly featured in the newspaper where I work. I was happy that such an alarming problem was getting some attention—the end of the article had the address of the rehabilitative center and the methadone clinic where donations could be made—but I was sad too. Because despite our charming downtown buildings and local color of the Maple Festival, which draws people from all over the state, *this* is how Chatwick will be seen by the world now.

Emmett scoffs at me. "Yeah I'm sure you *read* it. Have to proof-read your own work, don't you?"

I roll my eyes. "Emmett, why don't you just say what you want to say?"

"Well, it can't be a coincidence that the *New York Times* just *happens* to discover this little Podunk town and its rampant substance-abuse issues with a former resident in its employ. One who just returned after a decade away from it. You might as well have just used your real name."

Emmett McDowell, ever the conspiracy theorist. "Emmett." I clasp my hands, both to indicate my sincerity and to give me something to squeeze to keep calm. "I sell ad space. All day long, I talk to clients about rates and pixels and price per column inches. I don't have any input into what the *New York Times* prints in their newspaper beyond three-by-five-inch ads for condoms and Metamucil!"

He doesn't seem entirely convinced.

"The ad staff sits on an entirely different floor from the writers," I continue. "I don't even *know* any of them." Technically, this isn't true, as Jamie has contributed the occasional book review, but that certainly wasn't relevant to the argument, and I didn't want to materialize any opportunity for a dissection of my love life. "Besides," I add, "if I got a *byline* in the *New York Times*, there is *no way* I wouldn't use my real name, and you know that."

"So you admit it! You're nothing but a fame whore."

Yep, that's me in a nutshell. Ruby St. James: Account manager. Anonymous city dweller. Non-practicing writer. Fame whore.

"Hey!" I hear a deep voice boom from the doorway.

I look over to see Murphy in the arch between the kitchen and the living room, slightly hunched, fists clenched, poised to attack. I look back to Emmett, realizing he is about an inch from my face, his tall frame lumbering over me. I furrow my brow. Does Murphy think Emmett's trying to get fresh with me? Just the thought of it makes me giggle.

"Who you callin' a whore?" Murphy says to Emmett.

I scoff, pushing Emmett gently away from me with one finger and opening the fridge to fill my empty wineglass from the box inside. "I don't need your help, Murphy," I say coolly. "It's just Emmett." I stick my tongue out at Emmett before brushing past Murphy into the living room.

I stand there for a moment, looking for Ally or Aaron or Steph so I have someone to talk to. Instead, I find a sea of hairdressers and hairdressers' boyfriends that Ally introduced me to earlier but whose names I can't remember. Murphy comes and stands beside me.

"I know it's just Emmett, Ruby. I was just trying to—"

"What, Murph? Defend my honor? Don't make me laugh."

"Listen, I know why you're pissed, but if you would just let me explain…"

I spot Krystal talking to someone on the couch and giving me the side-eye. "There's nothing to explain, Murphy. You and I don't owe each other any explanations." I walk away from him again, this time into the hallway leading to the bathroom. He follows me again, this time grabbing me by my waist to spin me toward him and backing me up to the wall as he kisses me. Deeply.

I pull away and look at him, eyes wide. "What was *that?*"

"Mistletoe," he breathes into my ear, his hands still on my hips.

I look up. "There's no mistletoe in here!" I exclaim.

He pulls back, but only slightly, and shrugs. "Well, I guess I must have been imagining it," he says. His eyes twinkle with the mischief of days long ago, and I wish I didn't have to push him away.

He sighs and reluctantly moves to the other side of the hall. "Do we always have to fight?" he asks, perfectly faking a puppy-dog expression. "I wish we could just talk, instead of you running in the other direction every time I come within five feet."

"Well, maybe I don't want to deal with your crazy girlfriend out in the living room," I say, copping out. Really, I'm less annoyed that he's sleeping with Krystal than I'm trying to avoid the conversation I know I need to have with him. Especially now that I've told Nancy the truth. I'm just not ready. Not tonight.

He points to himself. "I have a girlfriend in the living room?" With mock interest, he adds, "Is she hot?"

Now I'm working not to smile. Trying to have this much control over my face is exhausting, not the way I ever used to feel around my best friend. "Don't play dumb, Murphy. You know I'm talking about Krystal." I hate myself for adding, "And no, she's not, in my opinion." What is wrong with me? This guy doesn't just make me *feel* like I'm sixteen; he makes me act like it too.

Murphy slaps his palm against the wall, genuinely angry. "Krystal is *not* my girlfriend," he says firmly.

"You might want to tell her that," I say, my arms crossed against both his bullshit and his sexual advances.

He rolls his eyes. "What now?"

I tell him about all the obnoxious conversations I've witnessed over text message and about her behavior when she was in New York. As I talk, a familiar calm settles over me. It starts to feel like before we messed everything up with sex, and he was just the person I complained to about stuff. I'm not talking to a man I'm sleeping with about a woman he's sleeping with. I'm talking to my best friend about a girl who pisses me off. He is listening intently, laughing in places where I add dramatic storytelling flair, his jaw tensing during the parts where my feelings were hurt.

"I'm sorry, Ruby," he says when I finish. "I guess she thinks we're a little more involved than we are. But it's not my fault. I've always been clear with her that I'm not interested in a relationship."

He has either chosen his words carefully or just lucked into them, but I find myself wondering whether he's not interested in a relationship in general, or just not with Krystal. How ridiculous that I even care. "Why not?" I ask, hoping this will encourage him to clarify his point without sounding like I'm fishing for a relationship myself.

He considers this for a few seconds. "She's just not the one."

I arch my eyebrow at him, and his face lights up with recognition. He tries unsuccessfully to arch one back at me, resulting in a look like he's trying to poop. It's an inside joke from ninth-grade homeroom, when I tried to teach him how to control his brows individually, alternating between serious instruction and uncontrollable giggling.

Frustrated, I had used my fingers to help guide his right eyebrow up. It was the first time I had ever touched his face, and I remember the way he looked at me when I did it. Was that when everything started to change? Anyway, after that day, whenever I arched my eyebrow at him (which was quite often), he would do the same little wiggle, and it made me laugh every time, no matter how angry I was at him. Unable to stop myself, I cross the hallway to touch his eyebrow and guide it upward. This time we're not giggling.

They're both really good at ignoring problems.

"What are you guys doing out here?" Krystal's voice pierces through the bubble that surrounds two people with history when they are left alone. I draw my hand back, but not sharply. I don't care if she sees. Murphy will always feel more mine than anyone else's, and in Krystal's presence at least, I'm not going to apologize for it.

"Just trying to teach this old dog a new trick," I say without looking at her, and go into the bathroom to avoid whatever hissy fit Krystal is about to throw. When I come out, the hallway is empty.

"I swear, Rube, I haven't told anyone you had a…you know," Ally says, darting her eyes around, although we're in the same dark hallway where Murphy pressed me up against a wall less than an hour ago, and the music and the chatter from the living room has gotten so loud that no one can hear us. We are the only two not drunk, although I have had two of my allotted three glasses of wine and am secretly wishing Ally wasn't pregnant just for this one night so we could sneak out to share a smoke. But since neither of us *is* drunk, there's no justification for being outside on this particularly brutal December night, the kind where it's too cold to snow. People think that's a myth, but it's not.

"What?" Ally asks, offended by my knit eyebrows and pursed lips.

"But…?" I prompt her.

"But what?" She has one arm across her body, one hand in the crook of her opposite elbow, one forearm raised, as if we were indeed outside sharing that smoke. I half expect her to flick the butt, scattering ashes to the wind. I remember the way she was always able to ash out the window at the precise angle that prevented any ash from flying back into the car. I never possessed this skill, and Blue suffered from frequent burns in her upholstery as a result of stray embers.

Ally's face turns to a pout. "I swore to you I wouldn't tell anyone about your secret, and I didn't. How could you think I would lie about something like that?"

"Al, I love you, and you know I would understand if you told everyone what you know. Especially if Aaron's told anyone…" And by anyone, of course I mean Murphy. "I can't expect you to take that hit for me. If you let it slip that Danny switched your secret for someone else's… I mean, I *am* the only other crew member with a uterus."

Ally's face hardens as I speak. "First of all, I would like to think the people I'm closest to in this world believe me when I tell them the truth. That goes for you"—she jabs a finger in my direction—"and for all the assholes out there." She jabs her finger toward the living room. "If they heard some rumor that I had an abortion and chose to believe it, then I don't really care. They can think what they want. And if *you* don't believe I can't keep a secret to protect one of my oldest"—her voice breaks— "friends, then I don't know what to tell you." She starts to move past me.

"I'm sorry," I say, catching her arm. And I mean it. I realize I'm treating Ally like a person she clearly isn't anymore. A person maybe she never was. She looks into my eyes and must know I am sincere, because she softens. I pull her into a hug. "I didn't mean to accuse you of anything," I say. "I'm acting crazy."

She lets me hug her for a moment before I feel her stiffen. When she pulls away, her face is quizzical. "Why *are* you acting so crazy?"

I freeze. In that instant, I know she's got me.

"Seriously," she continues, "if *I* don't care that much what people think of choices I made in high school, why would *you* care? You've never cared what anyone thought about you. Except"—her face goes to a faraway place, remembering, calculating, watching as my eyes widen—"Murphy," she finishes. "Oh…my…God. Hardy wasn't the father."

I stare into her eyes, my breath caught in my throat.

"It was Murphy. Wasn't it?" she asks.

I don't move.

"Ruby!"

Slowly, I nod my head. This isn't how this was supposed to go, but this is how it's going. I wait for her to scream at me, to scream for Murphy, but she doesn't. Her face wrinkles. She shudders. "Ewww!" she cries. She starts hopping around, flicking her hands as if trying to shake off the visual image. "You did it with Murphy Leblanc?" She shudders again and continues to jump.

I can't help myself. I break into giggles. She starts to laugh too, and before we know it, we're clutching our bellies—hers swollen, mine empty. It's not until she starts to loudly sing "Ruby and Murphy, sittin' in a tree, K-I-S-S-I-N-G" that I stop laughing.

"Ally, shhh. Shhh," I say, covering her mouth with my hand. Just like when we were kids, she licks my palm. "Jesus, Ally," I say, wiping my hand on the back of her dress. "Listen, you can't tell anyone."

She stops playing then. "Really, Ruby? More secrets?" She says it like she's disappointed in me.

"I'm going to. I decided today that I would. But not until after the wedding, okay? If he's mad, I don't want it to ruin the wedding. After I tell him, you can tell—"

"No one. Then I'll tell no one. It's a secret between you and Murphy. It's no one else's business."

I want to kiss her with relief. "Thank you, Ally." I think back to the night in the fields by her house, the flashlights we had brought for one last game of tag at our feet, our hands in a circle. Reeling from her parent's divorce, Ally's impossibly tortured face as she made us vow to fight for our friendships and to always be honest with each other. She had needed us to do what her parents could not. And we would have promised anything to make her happy. "I appreciate you understanding. I know how important honesty is to you."

I did not mean it sarcastically, but I realize after I say it that she is, of course, lying to us all too. She hasn't revealed the contents of her envelope, no matter what she says.

Something strange appears on her face. "Yeah, well," she says, "some things are better left in the past. Some *people* too." She looks beyond me, beyond the walls of the beautiful house her husband has built for her. *When it comes to things that really matter, you guys barely even know each other.*

Even without knowing what her secret is, I suddenly understand something about Ally that I never did before. Behind each of her backhanded whisperings, there is a little girl desperate to confirm her beliefs are right, her choices are beyond reproach. When Ally makes snide comments about New York, or looks at the bookcases of my apartment and asks me where my great American novel is, she's really looking for confirmation, if only from herself, that she was right to stay in Vermont, to marry young, to pursue the career she's in. She deals with the fear of judgment by going on the offensive so she never has to play defense. I, on the other hand, have chosen to sit out of the game entirely.

She turns back to me. "Is that why you didn't come clean and say the secret was yours? You knew he would figure it out, because obviously *he* would have known if Hardy had knocked you up?" There is so much pain in her eyes—the old pain that I always favored Murphy's company over hers, the pain that I lied to her again. The pain of knowing how little trust I've placed in the girl who always saved me a seat.

I nod. "I never even slept with Hardy. I mean, I did junior year...all that happened. But the night of that party, the one after we graduated? I was just trying to prove a point to Murphy, but when I got in the car, I realized I was taking a giant leap backward and asked Hardy to drive me home."

"And he did? Just like that? You're lucky he didn't—"

"He might have, but I was so drunk I threw up in his middle console. He dumped me at my house pretty soon after that."

We share a laugh, conspirators in the systematic destruction of a boy who treated us both badly.

"Let's get back to the party," Ally says, brightening in preparation for her audience. "It's time for the group photo. Maybe we should ask Krystal to take it. Would that cheer you up?"

I move to protest, but am ashamed to find myself nodding as I follow her back into the living room.

It ends up being a four-glass night.

I lie awake all night, every memory I have of Murphy running through my head. At seventeen, watching him hit home runs in his starched white baseball uniform, feeling a confusing secret thrill when he winks at me after crossing home plate. At ten, telling me my haircut makes me look like a mushroom, or a boy, and he's not sure which one is worse. At fourteen, confessing in a whispered late-night phone call that he's been having nightmares about Danny stabbing Roger in the chest. At twenty-eight, the pressure of his hands, now calloused from his work, on my bare skin.

I hate myself for what I've done. For what I am.

Now I remember Danny, the way he looked that first night he came to me for help. Roger had practically yanked his arm out of its socket, and he hobbled toward me in the dark like a wounded bird. If I had been smart enough then, or had trusted Nancy not to break under the stress, if I had called out for her instead of keeping Danny's secret, would everything be different? Would Roger have been sent to jail? Danny freed from his abuse?

Could Danny have had a better life? Gone to college with me, even? If Murphy and I hadn't shouldered the weight of Danny's secret together, would we ever have become best friends and then lovers? Would Danny still be alive? And what if things had gone differently when he came to New York? I could have saved him one last time. Or really, for the first time.

None of you bothered to try to help me when I was alive, when it counted.

21

RUBY
BACK THEN—FRESHMAN YEAR, NYU

IT IS WAY TOO EARLY FOR MY BUZZER TO BE GOING OFF. I GROAN awake, resentful that my roommate, Lisa, has undoubtedly left her keys and ID behind in some fellow pretentious drama major's dorm room—again. Security at NYU is strict; even if they know your face, they don't let you up without your ID. Then I remember Lisa requested a room transfer and moved out yesterday. She swears it's to be closer to the theater where all her classes are, but I have a sneaking suspicion it's because I've been crying for two weeks straight—pretty much since I got here. (I guess it's hard to soak in New York when you're already drowning in your roommate's used tissues.)

I don't really care. In fact, it's nice to be able to experience my sorrow without the pressure of trying to appear normal. Besides, I have enough drama to carry me through freshman year without a roommate who majors in it.

I drag myself up, glancing at my alarm clock on the way to the door. It's five thirty in the morning. I press the brass button. "You've got the wrong room." There's no other explanation for it. Who would be visiting me? I haven't made a single friend here, due in no small part to my complete lack of effort. I'm about to flop myself back into bed when a voice crackles through the speaker. "Ruby St. James? There's a young man here to see you. Are you expecting him?"

A young man? I haven't had a single interaction with a male since I've been here. I've barely left my dorm except to go to classes, and there I just sit silently in a cavernous lecture hall among hundreds of other students. But what if...? My heart stops. If it's not someone I've met here, there is only one young man who might be looking for me.

I press the button again. "Let him up."

Oh my God. The words echo in my head: *Are you expecting him?* No, not expecting. Fantasizing, yes, in my darkest and weakest moments, but not expecting. This is too much like a movie to be happening to me. Girl is homesick and alone, thinking the boy she loves doesn't care about her. But now that she's really left, and the reality of her being out of his life is too much to bear, he drives all night—and he must have driven; there are no flights this early from the Burlington airport—to rescue her from her heartache.

My heart is pounding so hard I have to sit down on the bed, but I pop back up almost immediately when I realize I cried myself to sleep last night and haven't showered since the day before yesterday. I hastily spritz perfume, tie my hair back in a ponytail, and pinch my cheeks like I really *am* a girl in a movie, before there's a knock on the door. I force myself to wait a few seconds before I open it.

My face falls.

"Try not to look so happy to see me, Tuesday," Danny says. I try to rearrange my face from obvious disappointment to pleasant surprise, but as with so many things, I fail.

"You look like shit," I blurt out. It's true. His eye is swollen, his nose looks broken, and there are flecks of dried blood in his goatee. I thought I was done with battered Danny showing up at my door in the middle of the night.

"Thanks," he says. "You too."

I laugh. It's the first time in weeks that I've laughed. And then I realize this is *Danny* in front of me. Danny, who knows me, who's known me for as long as we both remember. I don't ask him what happened to his face. Perhaps I should, but I've learned my lesson about asking questions I don't want to know the answer to.

"I'm really, really glad you're here," I whisper. My eyes water despite my best efforts. It's like they're defective or something; they're a goddamn faucet I can't turn off.

"Hey now," he says. He drops the backpack he'd slung over one shoulder and pulls me into a hug. "No tears. My face will heal, I promise."

I laugh again, and a fresh wave of tears comes after it. He squeezes me tightly, and I inhale his unique mixture of menthol cigarettes and Old Spice deodorant and home. He pulls back and puts his hands on either side of my face, wiping my tears away with calloused thumbs. "I was hoping to find you here with some trust-funded film major, smoking flavored tobacco from a hookah and wearing a beret."

I knit my eyebrows together. "Why would you hope that?"

We both laugh. "Okay, maybe not exactly that. I just mean I

was hoping to find you happy. I wanted to see Ruby St. James in her grand new life. The one you always dreamed about."

I pull away from him, under the guise of clearing a space on Lisa's old bed for him to sit. It's piled high with clothes I haven't had the energy to deposit into the hamper, let alone wash. "Yeah, well, I guess it takes more than two weeks to build a new life," I say.

"Especially when you're in love with someone from your old one." He says it softly, gently, but it's not a question.

I almost laugh. He, like Ally, thinks I am in this state because of Hardy Crane. That I am broken by such a sack of scum. It would be easier if I let him believe it, like I let Ally believe it. But it's Danny, and he's trusted me with much worse than this. "This isn't about Hardy, Dan. That night at the party…it wasn't what it looked like. Nothing happened."

"I wasn't talking about Hardy."

"Then who—"

"Same asshole who gave me this," he says, pointing to his black eye. "Murphy."

My mouth falls open, my tongue lying heavy as lead. I'm not sure which revelation is more shocking to me, that Murphy and Danny came to blows or that Danny knew something about me and Murphy. I decide to start with the less-selfish line of questioning. "*Murphy* did that to you?"

He nods, then waves me off, apparently deciding the same thing. "But I don't want to talk about it. Let's talk about what he did to *you*."

I wait a beat. Maybe if I don't speak, he will elaborate on his thing. No such luck. "What did he tell you?" I finally ask.

He shakes his head. "Not a thing, I swear."

The gratitude I feel toward Murphy for respecting my privacy is quickly replaced by disappointment he didn't find it so unbearable that he couldn't help but talk about it with someone.

"It was the Fourth of July," Danny continues, and my heart thuds into my stomach, remembering what happened that night. "You went MIA again after Luke's party, and yeah, I figured you were hanging out with Hardy again. But we always watched the fireworks from your roof so I thought I would take a chance and stop by. Murphy's truck was parked outside. I had asked him earlier if he was going to your house like always, but he said since no one could get ahold of you, he was going to go to Burlington with his brother. The fact that he lied about it, combined with how weird you guys have been with each other…" Danny holds up two fingers on his left hand and two fingers on his right and then connects them. He put two and two together.

"So if you knew about it since July…I mean, that's not what caused *that*, right?" I point at his eye, wondering if Lisa might have left her ice pack behind in my mini-fridge. Although it's probably too late for ice at this point, since he's been driving for six hours.

"Not exactly."

"Dan."

"I said I don't want to talk about it!" He turns away from me and picks up a book of short stories lying next to my bed. As he flips through, he says casually, "So you're in love with him?"

"It's not that simple."

"But you are." I don't confirm or deny, but he takes my silence as his answer. He whistles. "You're in love with Murphy Leblanc, and I never want to see him again. *This* calls for a smoke."

I start to panic. How to handle this?

"Come on," he says, elbowing me. "I finished my pack in the car. Can I bum one?"

"Nonsmoking dorm," I say. "Sorry."

"Well, we can go *outside*."

"I don't have any."

"You're out? Seriously? You always have some. Well, whatever. This is New York. We can just go out and buy some."

"I quit."

He looks at me for a long moment. Eerily long. "You quit smoking after moving to a new place where nothing is familiar, and your heart is clearly broken?" He waves his hand at the moat of wadded-up tissues surrounding my bed.

"I haven't been feeling well," I say, hastening to pick up some of the tissues and stuff them in the pockets of my robe. "I've had a cold. Trying to give my lungs a break, you know."

He cocks his head. "Never stopped you from smoking before."

"Well, I'm an adult now. Out on my own. Gotta grow up and learn how to take care of myself." I know I sound like a lunatic, particularly because my voice keeps cracking. Danny's not even listening to me. He moves toward my desk, his eyes fixed on something.

"Is that what these are about?" he asks, holding up the pamphlets that I picked up from Student Health but haven't been able to bring myself to read: *Unplanned Pregnancy: Your Choices, What to Expect When You're Unexpectedly Pregnant, Your Body, Your Baby*.

"Tuesday," he says, his voice a mixture of compassion and disappointment. "You're *pregnant*?"

Danny goes with me to Planned Parenthood for the initial appointment. They assume he's the father, and this doesn't seem to bother him. They ask a lot of questions about my mental health and ask me like four hundred times if I'm sure about my decision. They pull me into a room separate from Danny to confirm this is *my* choice and I'm not being coerced into it. I wonder if this is standard protocol, or if the state of Danny's face has something to do with it. Although, if they were taking *that* into account, they would probably assume that I am the one in charge.

I try to schedule my appointment—the big appointment, the one for "the procedure," or "the termination," as they kindly call it—for tomorrow. But I am ten weeks pregnant, and since I have two weeks before I *have* to make a decision, Danny thinks I should give it a few more days.

"You can't undo it, Tuesday. I'll support whatever you want to do. I just want you to be *sure*."

I tell him I already am, that after two weeks of crying about it on my own and a few days talking it over with him, I'm finally sure this is the right decision. But I take his advice and schedule the procedure for early next week. The truth is, I'm *not* sure. I change my mind every other day. But when I strip away the hormones, and the voices, and the feelings I still have for Murphy, and the logistical questions about how this should be handled, all I have left is a screaming, pulsing fear. I am one large, exposed nerve. Everything hurts. Every single moment.

Meanwhile, Danny is a good distraction. I order takeout or sneak food from the dining hall to feed him. The dorm is so big that even his massacred face doesn't stand out as a nonstudent's when he uses the men's bathrooms. He sleeps in Lisa's old bed. While I'm at class, he spends his time wandering around the city or critiquing my writing assignments while he hangs out the window smoking cigarettes. I tell him he can't smoke (cigarettes or otherwise) in my dorm, but every time I come back from class, the windows are open and it smells like air freshener. He can't enter the building without an ID, which means he can't really pop out for a smoke unless it's timed with my return from class, so I let it slide. A smoking Danny is preferable to a nonsmoking Danny, and what difference does secondhand smoke make, really, at this point?

It's surreal to have someone here from the life I've been mourning. We don't talk about Chatwick, or any of its residents, but having him here is a connection to the place I am disgusted with myself for missing. All I ever wanted was to get out of Chatwick, and here I am in the most exciting city in the world but still every bit as stuck there as I always was. Danny is too, I think. He seems to be heartbroken but refuses to talk about it, and I still don't know what caused the bruises that have transitioned from blue and purple to yellow and brown.

I'm not sure what his plan is. I've dragged him to some of my classes, and because he's read my assignments, he raises his hand and gets in debates with my professors and the other students. I don't know why Danny isn't in college himself; he's so smart. I tell him I think he should enroll, to which he scoffs or rolls his eyes. I'm not sure if I'm thinking in his best interest or mine. It's not like working at Borbeau's and selling weed is some great five-year plan, and as he pulls me out the door to explore New York with him, I notice a boundless energy I've never attributed to him before.

It's his first time in New York, but he's better at it than I am. While the areas I've come to know through my father are shiny and safe, Danny leads me to Chinatown, where we're not sure exactly what we're ordering (and my insatiable appetite keeps me from asking too many questions); to the second act of an off-Broadway show by sneaking in with the smokers; to Coney Island, where I load up on chili dogs since I can't ride the rides. (It's like once he left Chatwick, he found reasons to get up in the morning. Perhaps this is the Danny he was meant to be.).

Despite the cloud of anxiety that radiates from every pore, I'm falling in love with this city. It's everything Chatwick isn't—loud, anonymous, and full of diverse strangers and new experiences. And if Danny is falling in love with it too, is it so crazy for him to stay? Maybe it's his chance to get out of Chatwick. And maybe it's mine to have someone to cling to when all this is over. Would it be so bad? Isn't it my turn to lean on someone?

Tonight, our plan is to see a movie, at my request. I am, after all, for however short a time, pregnant, and I'm exhausted from all the walking we've been doing. But on my way home from class, someone hands me a flyer for a new underground jazz club, and I smile because I know this is just the type of thing Danny will want to try, and I will get to be the one to suggest it.

He's been introducing the crew to new things since our ages were in the single digits. Granted, most of them have been drugs, but not all of them. When we were little, he always found the secret hideouts in the trails behind Ally's house, and he was always the one to get us to cliff jump at the granite quarry—offering gentle encouragement to Ally and me, bullying to Emmett and Murphy. Even since he's been here, in "my" new city, he's the one pushing me toward adventure rather than allowing me to drown in my crisis. Perhaps there could be something more between us, if I could just get him to stay.

Despite my feet, I practically skip back to the dorm, giddy at the thought of finally being the one to introduce something new to him. This has been happening since Danny's been here, these waves of normalcy, even happiness. Small, merciful moments when I know everything will be okay. Maybe not now, but eventually.

But the thing about hormones, and the thing about Danny, is that in an instant, everything can change.

When I get to my dorm room, Danny isn't alone. A guy I've seen in the dining hall is sitting on my bed, holding a small bag of white powder and watching Danny thumb through a stack of money. The only sound in the room is the *thwap, thwap, thwap* of each bill as he shuffles it from the uncounted to counted stack. Danny's buying drugs—bad drugs, not just a little harmless herb. But no... The visitor hastily clenches his fist around the bag and hightails it out the door, and Danny folds the money and tucks it into his cargo pocket. It's worse, somehow. He wasn't just *buying* bad drugs. He was selling them.

I slam my bag down on my desk; the flyer for the club flutters to the linoleum floor.

"How was class?" he asks as if nothing happened.

"What the hell was that, Danny?" I know the answer, but I just don't see how it can be true.

"I'm sorry. You usually don't get back from class before five."

"The professor let us out early. That doesn't answer my question!"

He picks up the flyer from the floor. "Hey, did you want to go to this? Looks cool."

"You're *selling drugs* out of my dorm room?"

"Ruby, don't play dumb. I've been selling drugs since tenth grade, and you know it."

"Yeah, *weed*, Danny. Not...not... I don't even know what that was, but I know white powder is not weed!"

"It's just a little blow. It's not a big deal!"

"Just a little *blow?*" My voice is approaching the screech Nancy makes when she finds her spices out of alphabetical order. "Do you know how much trouble I could get in? I could get kicked out of housing just for *having* you here for so long. If they found out you were selling drugs? Jesus, I could get kicked out of school!"

He's quiet, but his face reddens.

"And are you actually *doing* this shit now? How long has *that* being going on?"

He speaks evenly, pointedly. "Well, I see you have your priorities straight. Your first concern is for how much trouble you could get in. Your second is for me."

I'm so mad I can't even see his face anymore. Ten minutes ago, this boy was my life raft.

"But that's always been the problem, hasn't it?" he continues, mistaking my silence for guilt and taking the opportunity to get in one more jab. "I always come second. With you, with my mom, with everyone!"

"Oh, spare me the song from the world's tiniest violin, Danny. You have *never* taken responsibility for anything in your life, and look what good it's done you! You're not in school. The only job you seem to devote any energy to is *this*." I wave my arm at the door his "client" just exited. Suddenly, it comes to me...the real reason no one's reported seeing a beat-up stranger lurking the halls: they're all depending on him for their study and party aids.

His face goes blank, and I know my Danny has left the building. "Are you actually throwing *Roger* back in my face right now?"

"I wasn't talking about—"

"I killed Roger. Just go ahead and say it. I'm a murderer. Well, congratulations. Now you're part of the club!"

"*Excuse* me?" I narrow my eyes at him, giving him a *tread lightly* warning. But he's too far gone.

"How are we any different, Tuesday? By next week, *both* of us will have taken a life that has caused us pain. We *both* made the choice to do the wrong thing to make our own lives better."

Tears sting my eyes. I never realized he was capable of wounding me this deeply. All this time, supporting me, is this what he really thinks of the choice I'm making? "I don't give a shit what you've been through in your life, Danny; you have no right to say that to me. You have *no idea* what this is like for me. It's always been about what's happened to *you*. Nothing is ever worse, no one's pain ever compares. You're going to waste your life feeling sorry for yourself and justifying your habits by blaming everyone else for your life. That's what little boys do."

He takes a step toward me, his fist raised, but before he gets too close, he spins around and puts his fist through the drywall. My hands fly to my mouth, but I don't scream or make a sound. The moment of impact echoes between us loudly enough. Danny's breathing is heavy and panicked. So is mine. Blood drips from his hand. My reflex is to go to him, to patch him up and hug him and tell him it's all going to be okay. I want to take back the last ten minutes. I want to come in just a moment after the deal had been made, so I don't have to know about this. I don't want to lose another person. My last person. But I can't do the codependent thing again.

I pick up Danny's backpack, shove the pile of clothes he has strewn at the foot of "his" bed into it, and hand it to him. "Goodbye, Danny."

He doesn't say anything, just looks at me as he steps backward toward the door. The hurt in his bright-blue eyes makes my throat close. Absurdly, I think of the number of parking tickets he'll have on his car—it's been parked in the same spot for weeks—and I briefly consider offering him money. Then I remember there's no need. He's got a fistful of it in his pocket, and I felt more stashed away in the socks I just packed for him.

"Take care of yourself," I mumble, the lone nicety I allow myself to give. He slams the door behind him. The vibration from the impact tingles painfully in my fingers and toes long after he leaves.

I move my poster of the Chrysler Building to cover up the hole he's punched in the wall, then sit on my bed and shake, the adrenaline coursing through me. I want so badly to pick up the phone and pour out everything that just happened to Murphy, the one person who knows both me and Danny better than anyone. But I can't do that anymore. My ties to Chatwick, and everyone I've ever thought to be important, are now severed.

22

RUBY
NOW

It's December 24. Christmas Eve, and Danny's birthday to boot. It's going to be a rough one.

I pull Blue through the open cast-iron gates and onto the gravel path, having abandoned the rental Sentra in favor of my trusty steed. I turn the radio down and slow to a respectful speed, listening to the sound of my tires rolling over gravel, pebbles pinging off the wheel wells. I pull to the side of the path, exactly where I parked for Danny's burial, and brace myself against the ten-degree air. Without the sea of black suits and skirts and the smell of Aqua Net guiding me, I have to wander through a few rows before I find Danny's gravestone.

Nice to see you can show up for a person once he's dead.

Tracks in the snow lead up to and away from the stone, and a bouquet of red roses, already brown at the edges, is carefully balanced at the base, still in the plastic with the Martin's Grocery price sticker on it. I guess the etiquette of hiding how much you spend on gifts ends when the receiver can no longer read the tag. *Happy Birthday, Danny. Have some flowers you're allergic to for $12.99. They'll rot into the ground, just like you.*

I wonder who left them. It wouldn't be Charlene. She would know Danny well enough not to bother with something Danny wouldn't appreciate. Maybe it was some girl Danny had shot up with, or some tragic nineteen-year-old cashier who worshipped him silently when he came in to buy his Newports. Perhaps it was even a girlfriend, someone we had been completely unaware of sitting behind us at the funeral, as if our grief was all that counted. Someone who had been foolish enough to love him and to think he would get better for her. Maybe it was even someone he had gotten to do his bidding—Miss or Mr. AnonChat@yahoo.com.

I stand with my hands in my coat pockets, looking down at the granite slab that marks the life of my friend. His name and the bookend dates of his existence are the only words etched into the stone. I'm grateful for the absence of any bullshit quip about the Lord and his infinite wisdom, or some quote Danny was known for. What would Danny choose if he had planned his death even more elaborately? "Beer is good, but heroin is quicker," perhaps? I catch a laugh trying to escape at the thought, and then I remember that Danny is actually decomposing under my feet, and I choke on it.

None of you bothered to try to help me when I was alive...

My eyes are already puffy and raw from last night's wine and the sleeplessness that followed as memories of Danny and Murphy and Ally and Emmett flooded over me in the twin bed of my childhood. The tears that come now hurt as much physically as they do emotionally. But they are persistent, and I wipe them away with my gloved hand to make room for more. I want to sit on the ground, to pull my knees up to my chest and talk to my friend, but it's covered in snow. Even if it wasn't, all I know to say is *I'm sorry*, so I whisper it to him now. I'm sorry for so many things that I don't know where to start.

I feel a hand on my shoulder, and a scream escapes my throat as I spin around in defense mode, arms swinging.

"Hey, hey, hey, it's me. Jesus fuck!" Emmett cries, forearms raised to protect his face. "Careful…I'm forking out about a million dollars for a wedding photographer; I don't need a black eye to be captured on film for all eternity."

"Damn it, Emmett!" I cry, trying to catch my breath. "You scared me half to—" I stop before I say *death*. I look over his shoulder. "What are you doing sneaking up on me like that? Where's your car?"

He crooks a thumb westward. "I live a block away. I walked."

It takes some effort to catch my breath and slow the hammering in my chest, the dehydration from the wine working against me. Emmett couldn't have known I was here, which means he came to visit Danny on his own. "What are *you* doing here?" I ask, a bit more coolly than necessary.

He blinks at me. "It's Dan's birthday," he says, like it's the most obvious thing in the world, like I should be ashamed for not knowing he would visit him today. But there's a twitch in his lip. I know he's lying, but I can't imagine what other reason he would have to visit Danny's grave. I guess it's sweet that he remembered the occasion, although I can't say I'm happy to see him. True to form, he never apologized for harassing me about the *Times* piece.

He must sense my leftover annoyance, because his normally

perfect posture slumps slightly. "I'm sorry about, you know, the article thing."

"Whatever... It's fine," I say.

"I guess I'm just a little on edge about the issue."

"Yeah, well, it's not easy to see the place you live portrayed negatively."

"You're doing that thing I hate."

"Doing what?" I spin on him.

"Being too nice. Too forgiving. It's not like you, at least not with me. Take last night... Before you found out about my heart, you would have gone up one side of me and down the other when I confronted you about that article. You keep treating me like I'm dying, just like everyone else!"

I think about this for a moment. "Maybe. Or maybe we've just grown up." I can't resist adding, "Some of us anyway."

He laughs. "There she is."

We stare at the stone in silence for what feels like an eternity before I speak. "You know, I of all people was not naive about Danny. I knew...everything. And it's doesn't take a giant stretch of my imagination to believe he turned to heroin. Especially considering the last time I saw him." I wince, trying to clear the image of his face, snarling with rage, and the raised fist that switched direction mid-swing to land in my dorm room wall. "I just..."

I don't know how to finish without sounding foolish, especially to Emmett. But there were other things that made Danny who he was. Other memories I can't shake. How he always bought three of those hideous dyed carnations they sold at school fund-raisers— one for me, one for Ally, and one to bring home for Charlene—even though he was allergic. He would store Charlene's in his locker, and by the end of the day, he was sneezing, his eyes swollen and red. How he made up little raps at the lunch table to diffuse the tension of my and Emmett's latest debate. How he wrote poems on napkins for Ally when one of her dogs died. (This happened many times, because I was only one of the sick strays Ally's mother had a habit of adopting, particularly after Ally's father left.)

After the last day I saw him, whenever I found myself worrying about him, I invented a life I felt he could have realistically led, had that moment in my dorm room woken him up. Sessions with a counselor, classes at a community college, maybe a nice girl to marry and have children with. It used to make me feel better about never finding my way back to being his protector. Now it just feels sad, like an alternate ending on a depressing movie's special features. It doesn't erase the pain of the real ending, where the hero dies.

Emmett appears to be waiting for me to finish my sentence until he realizes I have no intention of doing so. "You always saw the best in him," he says, his smile tight.

"Someone had to." I look at him sharply.

"Yeah. I mean, look how much good it did him."

He knocks the breath out of me with these words, like he bowled a strike right into my intestines. I turn my back to him and cover my tears with a little laugh. "Of course you would pick a fight with me *now*," I say. "Here."

"Hey, I'm sorry," he says. "I didn't mean…" He puts his hand on my shoulder again, but quickly releases it. We are not an affectionate pair. In fact, the first time we ever hugged was at Danny's funeral. But like the rest of the group, Emmett and I are family. We're the brother and sister who swear they can't stand each other but ultimately miss the challenge at any gathering where the other is not present.

"What are you even doing here?" I ask again, not ready to forgive him.

Emmett ducks his head and nods. Fair play. "Things changed between Danny and me, you know, toward the end," he says, reading between the lines. "We kinda reached an understanding."

I stifle a giggle. "An understanding that he would sell you weed?"

He tucks his lips in defeat and rolls his eyes up to the sky as if he's having a silent conversation with someone up there. He nods decidedly and reaches into his coat pocket to pull out not one but two envelopes, both of them with his name on them, scrawled in Danny's handwriting.

He hands me one of them. "This was under my car windshield yesterday morning."

I hold it in my hands, looking from it to him until he nods his confirmation that I should open it. I have a feeling I know what it says. I pull out the slip of paper.

"'All things done in the dark have a way of coming to light,'" I read. I look back at Emmett. The words are right there on the tip of my tongue—"I got this message too"—but I don't say them. If I do, he'll know that Murphy lied and that we *both* have secrets left to tell. And I can't share the truth with Emmett before I share it with Murphy.

"I think I got it because I made up my secret," Emmett says like a scolded little boy. "Well, Steph made it up."

I'm stunned, momentarily unable to respond except for the opening and closing of my mouth and the occasional pathetic squeak. "You mean, your heart…is fine?"

His eyes widen, and he waves his hands. "No. No, no, no. That part is true. I do have HCM. I did have a defibrillator put in. All that's true. Oh God, no, she would *never* make something like that up. I would never let her get away with it if she did. It just wasn't the secret Danny wrote down."

Again, I am in the position of desperately wanting to demand the dirt on my friend but not being able to without being a complete hypocrite. But I don't have to. Emmett hands over his second envelope, this one slightly more worn around the edges, the envelope he received after Danny's funeral. He opens it and slides out the little slip of paper with Danny's handwriting on it, looks at it a moment, nods again—another decision—and hands it to me. I take it without removing my eyes from his. I want to give him every chance to take it back before I read it.

"Go ahead," he says. "Maybe you being here when I really came to yell at Danny's headstone was some kind of sign. Maybe if I tell you the truth, all this nonsense will stop."

So I read it.

I am a drug dealer.

And I burst out laughing.

His face falls.

"Emmett, what is this?"

"It's not funny. It's true."

"Yeah, okay. It's one thing to think of you puffing a little cheebah, but now I'm supposed to believe that Nancy Reagan went from total abstinence to being some Chatwickian kingpin?"

"Not a kingpin. Not even a dealer, really. I was a runner."

I scoff at him, searching his face for the joke. "Emmett. Come on."

He inhales in preparation. "A few months after the operation, the bills started rolling in. The shitty insurance I have at the bank has a twenty percent coinsurance requirement, which came out to thousands of dollars we just didn't have. Even before that, we bit off a little more than we could chew on the house. Between the mortgage and PMI and property taxes and utilities, our paychecks and credit cards were completely maxed out. But our salaries were just high enough that we didn't qualify for any financial assistance through the hospital. I was still recovering from the surgery and could barely make it through a full day at the bank, so Steph took a second job *stocking shelves* at Martin's at night." He shudders, and I get a flash of him in his red smock from his cashier's job in high school. "It still wasn't enough. We had credit agencies calling. It was a nightmare.

"So Steph was partially telling the truth. I *did* go to Danny one night for pot because neither of us had been sleeping or eating particularly well. He, of course, was a total dick about it, and I ended up blowing up at him and telling him all about the surgery, the money problems, all of it."

I cross my arms, waiting for the giant leap from buying a little herb to transporting drugs.

"You know Danny always sold," he continues. "Once he got into the harder stuff, he sold it out of the back room of Borbeau's. That night he told me his runner had quit, and if I were willing to assume the risk and drive to and from Montreal once a week for a few months, it would pay. Big. Enough to get me and Steph out of debt."

"And you accepted, just like that?" Emmett, who found the answers to a final exam and turned them into the teacher without hesitation. Emmett, who graduated summa cum laude from UVM without once indulging in the Adderall booster used by his classmates. Emmett, who premeditatedly hid the flashlight before slapping the mushrooms out of Danny's hand.

"No. I told him to fuck off. But when I went home, I found Steph crying at the kitchen table in her red smock, our mountain of bills in front of her. I couldn't let that happen again. It's my job to make her life better, but because of me... Anyway, the next day I went back and accepted his offer."

"And Steph *let you?*" This is almost as hard to imagine, even knowing Steph for such a short time. I mean, she's a *librarian*, for Christ's sake.

"She didn't know about it right away, not until the envelopes full of cash started appearing in the mailbox. And she was *very* against it, but my mind was made up and there was nothing she could do to stop me. She wasn't about to turn me in; then we'd really lose everything. That's why she leaked the HCM and the pot. She thought it would be enough to throw off suspicion."

I shake my head, still not convinced. "Did she actually think one of us would turn you in if you told the truth? I mean, did she *hear* what Murphy and I kept secret for Danny?"

"Well, you two weren't the only ones in the room, remember?"

"Al?"

He nods. "I love her to death, Ruby, but the police have been hot to bust *anyone* they can connect to drugs, and that salon of hers is like the Chat's oxygen tank. One of her clients lost their cousin to that batch that was laced with fentanyl. Do you really think she could keep her mouth shut?"

My eyes narrow. "You were the one who brought that shit into this town, Em? The stuff that killed all those people?"

He nods. Swallows. "I don't know. I might have. It's the reason I stopped. After the first death. I couldn't take it."

I look from him to Danny's headstone and back, as if one of them (at this point, I wouldn't have been that shocked if it were Danny) was going to break into a smile and yell "Gotcha!" Finally, I shove Emmett's arm, again and again, and the words find me. "Jesus, Emmett! Are you insane? You were a fucking drug mule?"

"I know."

"You could have gotten caught! That's a fucking felony! How could you be so stupid?"

"I was desperate," he says miserably.

"How did you even pull it off?"

"I honestly don't really know. Danny told me to dress like I was going to work because it made me look more legit. He gave me a car that Borbeau's was working on—a different one each week—and the address of a mechanic shop up there. He told me he would give them my license plate number, and when I got there, all I had to do was ask for an oil change. They hid it somewhere in the car, I crossed the border, I brought it back to Borbeau's, and I went home. A few days later, an envelope of cash was in my mailbox. I assume I got a cut after they sold it all."

"To people who then repackaged it, cut it with who knows what, and then resold it to a bunch of addicts who need help, not something to shoot up their arm. A bunch of addicts like Danny."

"Ruby, don't you think I already feel disgusted with myself about that? But just remember, those overdoses happened *months* before Danny died. He knew what it was doing to people, and he saved some of it for himself, waiting until he was ready to write all those wonderful notes before he shot it into his bloodstream. He wasn't some helpless victim. He made his own choices. He made the choice to let Roger die in front of him, and yeah, maybe given the circumstances, I can't blame him. But he made the *decision* not to come forward. He made the *decision* to never get help. He made the decision to numb it out with drugs. And he made the decision to die. To quit. That's not on *you*, and that's not on *me*."

I bite my lip, tears rolling down my face. "Danny didn't have the kind of life that you had, Emmett. He didn't have parents who brought him up to believe in himself. It's easy to sit in judgment when you don't have to walk in a person's shoes."

"But that's what you're doing to me!" he says, throwing up his hands. "Judging. When you have no idea what it's like to be fighting not to lose what you've worked your whole life for. To have to send the woman you love off to earn more money to pay for *your* medical bills while you're sitting on the couch. You have no idea what that's like. Just like I don't know what it's like to grow up with a bipolar mother or to hide the fact that your friend is being abused."

He's right. I know he's right. Here I am, defending Danny's fucked-up choices and judging Emmett just because he made some of his own. And all that before we get to my own past. "I'm sorry," I say. "I guess I just got defensive. You know, now that he's not here to defend himself."

"You *always* defended him. Even when he *was* here to defend himself. And most of the time he was smirking behind your back like the little brother who just got away with something by telling Mommy that the other kids were mean to him."

There's a hurt in his voice, and in his eyes, I see a frightened teenager realizing he was on hallucinogens against his will. I see a humiliated, gangly preteen sprawled out on the auditorium floor because Danny had stuck his foot out to trip him in front of the whole school. I see a little boy, gazing up at Murphy and Danny swinging from their knees in a moment of fearlessness he wasn't capable of. What must that have felt like to a boy who was, at five, already set in his ways? Like the earth was shifting on its axis. Like he would never be good enough. Suddenly I see Danny grinning maliciously down at Emmett from the tree, raising his middle finger. Whether it happened or not, it certainly feels like it could have.

"Murphy didn't love him more than you, you know," I say, almost forgetting that I'm now speaking to Emmett the grown man, and not the little boy. "He loved you both the same."

A deep crimson spreads across his cheeks, already pink from the cold. I'm about to apologize for embarrassing him, when he says, "Everyone has their favorites though. Dan was everyone's favorite." He glances at me for just a second before tearing his gaze away again. I wonder for the first time if maybe Murphy's friendship wasn't the only thing he competed with Danny over. Maybe it was mine as well. And Ally's too. Danny needed us more than Emmett, and so he got us. And Emmett got left out. As much as he tried to make Danny feel like an outsider, Emmett felt like one too. I guess, for one reason or another, we all did.

I don't want to embarrass him any further, so I keep this thought to myself. Instead, I say the first thing that pops into my head. "I saw this movie a few years back about this guy who could travel back in time and fix all the mistakes he had made. Any little thing he changed made all his loved ones' lives change completely."

"I remember it. No matter what he did, everything still ended up shitty, so in the end he did everything exactly the same."

"I read some interviews after I watched it. Originally it was supposed to end with the main character going back to the womb and strangling himself with the umbilical cord."

The words hang in the air for an uncomfortable moment, and I wish I hadn't said them.

Graciously, Emmett clears his throat and changes the subject. "So you didn't write the article, but when are we going to see your name in print?"

I shake my head. "I don't think journalism is in the cards for me. I prefer fiction. It's…tidier." I remember something from the variety of conversations I had last night. "Ally thinks I should write about this," I say, waving my arm at the headstone, then at Emmett, and then sweeping it around to indicate Chatwick as a whole.

"Maybe you should. You'd have to be a *bit* of a journalist to figure out the rest of the secrets. Of course you know mine, Danny's, and obviously yours."

My heart begins to pound. The look in Emmett's eyes tells me he's not buying that my secret had anything to do with hiding Danny's.

"And I'm guessing you know Murphy's," he adds. "Don't think I can't tell when he's lying," he says.

All things done in the dark…

"I don't know what Murphy's secret is," I say, wishing I could erase the edge of desperation in my voice.

He gives me the same nod. *Yeah, right.*

"Really," I add. "And it's none of my business."

"Me and Danny weren't the only ones Murphy loved." He gives me a meaningful look. "Still does, I'd bet the house."

I force a laugh. "I think you're in enough trouble without making ridiculous bets like that."

He smiles sadly. "Ruby."

I hear all his disappointment in those two syllables. We were having an honest moment, as honest as I can be right now, anyway, and I pulled away. It's going to take some time to break this habit. I swallow the lump in my throat and shake my head. "He doesn't even know me. Not really. He hasn't for a long time."

"And whose fault is that?" He waits a moment for his point to resonate and then cuffs me on the shoulder. "See ya at the wedding." He turns to leave.

"Emmett!" I cry after he's walked a few paces toward the exit. Suddenly, I feel desperate for him to stay. I'm not ready to say goodbye. To him. To Danny. To Chatwick. Emmett turns back. "Aren't you going to talk to Danny?" I ask. "That's what you came here for, right? To yell at him?" If he does, it will reset my perception of Emmett, and that feels easier than watching him grow up and become a man.

He shakes his head. "Do you really think it will make a difference?" he asks, but he walks back anyway, passes me, and snatches up the bouquet. "Danny would have hated these." He starts to walk away again, but I grab his arm and pull him into a hug. Our second hug ever.

When we come apart, I turn to Danny's headstone and say, "Happy Birthday, Danny." I try to keep a smile on my face when I say it. Just in case he's watching.

"Yeah and Merry Christmas," Emmett says. We look at each other with sad, tucked-in smiles. "And I'm sorry."

I look at him, surprised. "What are you sorry for?"

"Everything," he says, and something in his eyes tells me he's talking about more than just giving Danny atomic wedgies and calling him a loser every chance he got. But he doesn't say more, and I think we've pressed each other enough today.

"Come on, I'll give you a ride home," I say.

He nods, slings his arm around my shoulder, and we walk back to my car. And for once, we don't debate, or bicker, or dig at each other. We just let the silence settle over us. I look back at Danny's stone, left behind alone and in the cold. I try to convince myself that it's not him. That he's moved on to that hideously clichéd better place. That he's been forgiven for what he's done, and that maybe he's even forgiven himself. And us.

Halfway to the car it starts to snow. I've never been a big believer in the afterlife, but something tells me it's Danny's doing.

23

STEPH
SIX MONTHS AGO

THE KNOCK ON THE DOOR COMES IN THE MIDDLE OF THE NIGHT, so sharp and insistent I snap awake in fear for my life. Somewhere between the dream world and the real world, a thought appears: *The British are coming! The British are coming!*

Emmett awakes at the same time, and we look at each other silently, the blankets pulled up to our noses like children afraid of the boogeyman. Last week, Emmett made his last run from Montreal, and yesterday he deposited the wad of cash we got in the mailbox a few days after. Then he paid off our creditors, made love to me, and we both had our first good night's sleep in months. I thought we might be done being up in the middle of the night, worrying the police were coming for him.

The knocking doesn't stop, so finally I throw back the covers. Emmett does the same. I follow him to our front door, and when he opens it, Danny is standing there.

"Dan, what the fuck? It's two o'clock in the morning!" Emmett says.

Danny stands there, looking back and forth between the two of us, his eyes as wide as they can be considering he's stoned out of his mind. He looks like a wild animal in a trap. I get the sense that he's as surprised to find himself here as we are to see him.

"Hey," Danny says as if Emmett hadn't spoken. "Hey, man. Hey…you," he says to me, clearly not remembering my name. We've only met in passing down at Margie's Pub, so it's not like we're such great friends, but he *is* at my doorstep in the middle of the night, for crying out loud.

"Do you want to come in?" I ask. Emmett shoots me a look, and I give him one right back that says, *Hey, I don't necessarily want this person in my house either, but can't we at the very least get this over with?*

"Thanks," he says. He steps into the living room but stays close to the door, unsure what to do next.

"Let's sit," I say.

"Take your shoes off," Emmett says sternly to Danny, who obeys.

Emmett and I sit on our couch, and Danny takes a chair on the opposite side of the room. He fidgets a lot, rubbing the scruff that lines his jaw, running his hands through hair that hasn't been washed in at least a few days, scratching at his arm through his long-sleeved thermal T-shirt. Early summer has been unexpectedly brutal, the humidity suffocating. We've run our window AC unit twice already, and it's only the second week of June. But Danny wears a long-sleeved shirt because he has a lot to cover up.

I sit in silence, still so groggy I wonder for a moment if this might just be a dream.

"So…what's up, Dan?" Emmett prompts Danny.

"Listen, man," Danny says. "I've been thinkin'. I think it's time I get clean."

"That's great, man," Emmett says, but his tone is cautious. "What brought this on?"

"Steve's dead, and Chris is in the hospital," Danny says. He sniffs and wipes at his nose.

I look at Emmett, asking *Who are Steve and Chris?* with my eyes.

"Who are Steve and Chris?" Emmett asks.

"Customers," Dan says. "I think that last batch I sold them… There's something wrong with it."

My hand flies to my chest. Emmett's mouth opens and closes. We look at each other. The last "batch" Danny sold must have been the last batch Emmett brought in. Just a few days ago.

"How many people did you sell to already?" Emmett asks, his voice panicked.

"I don't know, man. A lot." Danny leans forward in the chair, both hands running back and forth through his hair.

I feel like I might vomit. I don't know any details about this arrangement Emmett has with Danny. Emmett doesn't even know how much "product" he brings in each week. There could be dozens or hundreds or even thousands of doses stuffed in the bowels of those cars he brings back.

"Do you need my help to…you know…get it all back?"

Danny looks at Emmett in surprise. I may even see a hint of a smile in his eyes. He shakes his head. "No, Emmett. I've started to spread the word, but that's not exactly how this works."

"What do you mean?" I ask.

"Junkies don't generally make a habit of giving their drugs *back*," he says. "All I can do is tell them it's a dangerous batch and hope they're smart enough to tide themselves over some other way."

I shudder, thinking about what other ways these people will find to "tide themselves over."

"So what do you want from me?" Emmett asks. His face is red to the tips of his ears again, and I squeeze his arm.

"I was hoping I could crash here for a few days."

"Here?" Emmett asks.

"Yeah, um, I know it's a lot to ask, but everyone knows where to find me at Mom's. If I'm going to get off this stuff, I can't be around... customers."

"But...here?" Emmett repeats. "What about Murphy's?"

"You know he and I haven't talked in years, Emmett. You practically threw a parade for it when we had our falling-out."

"But I'm sure if he knew you needed help..."

"No," Danny says.

"What about Ally and Aaron's? They live up on the hill, farther away from the tracks than us even and have all that extra room."

Danny starts laughing. He laughs until tears come out of his eyes. Emmett and I exchange a look. What kind of drugs is this kid *on*? It takes a long time for Danny to catch his breath. "Trust me, man, that's not an option," he finally says.

"What about—"

"Listen, we've never been best buds. I know what you think of me. Do you think I would be here if I had anywhere else to go?"

Emmett and Danny look at each other for a really long time. I want to interrupt, to say that Danny is welcome to stay with us for a few days. But that's not what I really want. This kid scares me. It doesn't feel safe even having him sitting in this living room, for more reasons than one.

"Do you need a place to hide from your junkie buddies, or do you need a place to hide from the cops?" Emmett finally asks.

In the three seconds that Danny hesitates, we get our answer.

"Get out of here," Emmett says, standing up.

Danny stands up too. "It's both!" he says, but too late.

"Yeah, right," Emmett says. He grabs Danny by the arm, leads him to the door, and opens it. "You manipulative piece of shit."

Danny reaches out to clutch Emmett's T-shirt. "You've gotta believe me, Emmett. Yeah, I need to lay low, but I also really want to get clean, man. I swear to God. I don't want to end up like Steve!"

"Don't come back here," Emmett says, giving him one last push outside and slamming the door in Danny's face.

"I helped you when you needed it!" Danny shouts through the door. "You fucking prick!"

24

ALLY
NOW

I should have said no when Steph first asked me about red satin for the bridesmaid's dresses. She probably would have listened to me. But no, I kept my trap shut so Steph could have everything she wanted. Now I'm standing here seven months pregnant, my belly looking like a giant tomato with a button at the center. Spanx engineered by NASA couldn't cover up this belly button in satin—the bitchiest of fabrics, if you ask me. I can only imagine how many times it will be pressed at the reception.

At least I'm not the only one who doesn't look her best. I finally wrestled Ruby into my chair to give her some highlights, insisting the dress would clash with her hair and make her look sick, which it does because she wouldn't let me do more than a partial, always so cautious ever since I made that one *tiny* mistake in high school. You couldn't even *see* the parts that turned black; I don't know why she had to be so dramatic about it. Anyway, her hair is still too strawberry. I did my best to give her a good updo and makeup, but it just doesn't look right together.

Emmett and Steph say their vows, the traditional churchy ones. Aaron is straight across from me, where the groomsmen stand. He catches my eye and winks. I swear, when he does that, it gets to me just like it did when we were kids. And here we are about to have a kid of our own. Someday *she* will get winked at and feel that skip in her heart that makes you stupid. What a scary thought.

Of course, I don't know *for sure* it's a girl. My sister-in-law told me not knowing the sex gave her that extra motivation to push no matter how tired she was, and I thought that sounded as sensible as anything so we decided to be surprised too. But I think it's a girl. I just have a feeling. Ruby said she had a dream it was a boy, but I think that's just wishful thinking on her part. She's always been more comfortable around boys.

I try to pay attention to the service, but they're doing a full mass, and honestly, it's enough to concentrate just on keeping upright. Finally, they get to the part where the bridesmaids and groomsmen get to sit down, and I collapse into the front pew and fan myself with the program that was on my seat. They really crank up the heat in churches (on account of all the old people), so it's hot as Halley's Comet in here. Ruby sits next to me. She notices a trickle of sweat on my forehead and wipes it away. Every time she does something tender like that, something I picture her mother doing when Ruby was little, I worry about Ruby inheriting Nancy's dark side too.

I remember researching bipolar in the Chatwick High library, wanting to understand why Ruby's mom was the way she was, and I read that it can be passed down to your kids but sometimes it doesn't show up until your midtwenties. Aaron tells me I'm just a worrywart. Well, he better get used to it. As much as I love Ruby, can you imagine what I'll be like with my own kid?

I watch Emmett closely, looking for signs he's not taking it seriously, but he doesn't take his eyes off Steph for even one second. Good. I don't blame him; Steph *does* look beautiful, angelic almost. Her dress… Well, I won't get into it because her family kept going on about how unique it is, but let's just say she could have saved herself the money by taking mine out of storage and tying a sash around the middle. It could have been her something borrowed!

But besides the dress and the hair and the makeup—all beautiful on their own—she has that look to her. I've been to a lot of weddings over the years, and you can tell the brides that just want to get married from the brides that are truly in love with their husbands, and she is one of the second kind.

She'll need it, being married to Emmett McDowell. I do not envy her. I love Emmett the same way Ruby does, in that we both want to kill him most of the time. He's become a little more thoughtful though, a little softer, since his secret came out. Seems to me his heart condition is making him more aware he *has* a heart. Or maybe I'm just not taking everything he says as hard.

I hate to say it, but I'm glad we're at the finish line, that tomorrow this wedding business will be over. And it's fitting they're getting married on New Year's Eve. Today will be the last day of this insane year, and tomorrow we get to start fresh. The last few months have been exhausting, what with the wedding planning and the bridesmaid bickering and the pregnancy. And then there's the fact that this all started with Danny in a coffin, which I haven't really even had time to process because I've spent so much of my energy being mad at him.

I tell myself I'm only mad because he's calling us all out on our private business, because he lied about my secret, because he caused so much trouble between Aaron and me and wouldn't let it fucking drop, having someone leave that creepy note in my mailbox. Danny didn't know I was pregnant, but I wonder if he did know if he would have given any thought to what that kind of stress could do to the baby.

All that is enough reason to be mad, but that's not really what pisses me off. I'm mad because he killed himself in the first place. I'm mad he became a heroin addict. I'm mad he never told me he was abused. You better believe *I* would have done something about it. I know people think of me as a big mouth, but don't you think that might have been a *good thing* in this situation? Really, what good did keeping secrets do him in the end?

And maybe that's the point he was trying to make with his little suicide project. Maybe. I'm still too mad at him to think like that, and the hormones don't help. Plus, it's hard to forgive someone when you're looking over your shoulder all the time, waiting for whatever booby trap he's set up to reveal what you've *really* been hiding.

I know what you're thinking. I'm a hypocrite. I'm the one who made us promise we would always be honest with each other. That stupid pact is what started all this in the first place. But hey, give me a break! When we made that pact, the worst thing we could think of to share once I had told about my parents' divorce was our middle names. (Mine is Dorothy. Emmett's is *Herbert*, if you can believe it.) Besides, obviously I'm not the only one who broke it. So back off!

Charlene gets up to do her reading, and Ruby and I clasp hands and wait for Danny's words to hit us. My heart stops when I see her walk to the podium with an envelope in her hand. Ruby must see it too, because she tenses beside me, her grip on my hand getting so tight my fingers turn red. Was Charlene the one Danny pegged to do his evil deeds? Is this the moment he chose for all our secrets to be revealed? I assumed it was some junkie friend of his, but seeing that envelope…

She pulls two sheets of paper out of the envelope and looks at each of them, like Alice in Wonderland when she's trying to decide whether to eat the mushroom that makes her giant or the one that makes her small.

I take a deep breath, like the doctor taught me to when I'm feeling stressed, and try to talk myself out of my panic. It wouldn't make sense for Charlene to be the one, or for this to be the time. When she read us Danny's letter, it was the first time she'd read it herself, and she was upset by it. No one is that good of an actor. Not on the day they bury their son. And Steph and Emmett weren't engaged when Danny died, so he couldn't have asked her to do it today. I must just be traumatized by those goddamn envelopes.

Charlene abandons one of the sheets of paper to the podium and holds the other in her shaking hands, looking at it for a long time as if she's trying to decide whether to really read it. Sensible or not, I hold my breath until she starts to read:

"Near to you,
I am safe and full.
My brain allows itself to slow,

and I fall into your comfort.

I sleep and dream of your face.

I wake and trace it with my fingertips.

How lucky I am

to feel this love.

This warmth.

If only for a moment.

To know this home

that exists where you are.

No words.

No need.

Just an effortless reach

for my hand,

and I know I am loved by you.

Wherever you are,

I am home

Near to you."

I hear Ruby sniff beside me, and I bite my lip to stop myself from bursting into tears. It's a beautiful poem. One I've heard before. And it's about me.

When Charlene finishes, she looks directly into my eyes.

At the reception, I look around for Charlene but don't see her. I want to catch her before the speeches are made, just in case she has some other kind of speech planned. Aaron notices the panicked look on my face and asks if I'm feeling okay. I tell him yes, that I'm just a little worn out from being on my feet all morning doing all our hair and makeup. It's not exactly a lie; I am exhausted.

Steph's mom hurries us to our seats at the head table. I look around again and still don't see Charlene. I allow myself to think she went home after the ceremony, and breathe a little easier. I was just being paranoid. She probably had two poems that she wanted to read and was deciding at the last minute which one felt right. She probably looked at me because I was a familiar face, the easiest one in the crowd to spot because I look like a giant tomato.

"Josh, do you think you could move down a seat? I would like to sit next to Murphy. You know, my *date*," Krystal says to Emmett's brother, louder than seems necessary.

I roll my eyes at Aaron. Honestly, I don't see why Krystal goes to the trouble of embarrassing herself over Murphy. He certainly wouldn't do it for her. After her bizarro behavior on the NYC trip, she went right back to swearing up and down that she and Murphy are not in a relationship and she's fine with that. She's still getting over What's-His-Name who she dated since high school, and she's not ready for anything real and blah, blah, blah. But then there's times like these when it's obvious she wants everyone to *treat* her like she's part of a legitimate couple. Weddings make people a little desperate, I think.

I'm glad I've never had to go to one of these things alone, with everyone else coupled off. Poor Ruby, the only one in the wedding party without a date. She's always been the independent one, trying to make it seem like it doesn't bother her that she's always single. Aaron thinks maybe it doesn't, but how could it not? I mean there's gotta be a reason she still keeps Jamie on her hook. Everyone gets lonely.

Ruby's parents are here, and so are my mom and Murphy's parents. Ruby hugs Murphy's mom, and Murphy hugs Ruby's in opposite corners of the reception hall, both mothers shouting about how the kids are so grown up and how they turned out so well. In high school, a lot of people thought that Ruby and *Danny* would make a perfect couple—both of them were so dark and brooding and intellectual—but I wasn't that surprised when I found out something went on between her and Murphy instead.

It was always Murphy I thought she belonged with back then. Murphy was funny and easy, and he never let her take herself too seriously. He shone some light into her darkness. And somehow, even though you would think she would bring him down, she lit him up too. Still does. I mean, just look at the way he's looking at her now! I think it's because she challenges him in a way the other girls he dates never have. He always opts for easy, but it's the hard that brings out the best in him.

I allow myself to get carried away and pretend for a minute that this is Ruby and Murphy's wedding and they're mingling with their own guests. Then I shudder. What a disaster that would be. Murphy's a Chatwick boy through and through, and if the last few years have taught us anything, he would sooner jump off a bridge than settle down. And Ruby. Well, now that I've seen her in New York, I can't help but notice how jittery and unsure of herself she is here, in the place where she grew up. Ruby's not comfortable in Chatwick, and Murphy's not comfortable a mile outside it. They would have to be married over Skype. Plus, in my experience, dark and light might be drawn to each other (as Paula Abdul herself says, opposites attract), but that doesn't mean they'll work out in the long term.

Still though, it's my fantasy, and if I want to picture her bucking her big-city life and settling down in Chatwick, I'm going to go right on ahead. I know Ruby did the right thing by not having that baby at eighteen, but that doesn't mean she couldn't pop out a brood of Murphy's hellion babies *now* that could be friends with my kids. It would be like the crew 2.0!

Ruby sits next to me and Aaron at the head table, and I notice her refilling her champagne twice over dinner. Either she's loosened up over the years, realizing that just because her mother's an alcoholic doesn't mean she is, or else she is starting to show signs... When I make eyes at Aaron, he mouths "worrywart" at me.

Murphy gives his speech. His hands shake as he reads from his piece of lined paper, and his voice is a little wobbly at first, but he does good anyway. He makes a joke about Emmett making all the wedding plans because he's too particular to leave them to Steph. He says how beautiful Steph is and how lucky she and Emmett are to have found each other. It's one of those moments when it hits home that we're all grown up. I'm sitting here pregnant, Emmett is getting married, and Murphy is giving a toast that doesn't have any burps or swear words in it. It's good and bad. Good because we're independent; we're choosing the lives we want to live. Bad because it's a slippery slope until we're old, and the first one of us has already died.

Krystal is up next, and to my surprise she gives a beautiful toast, talking about how Steph was the first one to tell her she should go to college, and how Steph's support is what got her through some really hard times with her, Krystal's, family. This is the first I'm hearing of it, but Krystal even lived at Steph's for a while when her family was down on their luck. People—including me, damn hormones!—are actually crying, wiping their eyes with the special red napkins I helped Steph pick out. I look at Ruby, who looks back at me. How strange... Krystal is Steph's Ruby. It makes sense to me now why they are so close. It even makes me like Krystal a little more.

We eat dinner, and then it's time for dancing. The only fun thing about being at a Chatwick wedding and not drinking is watching how stupid everybody looks the more *they* drink. The dance floor is full of fools, and even though I'm dead tired and my feet ache more than after a full day at the salon, I dance too. Your friends only get married once. Hopefully.

At one point, Aaron and I are dancing in the middle of the floor, and Emmett and Steph are next to us. Ruby and Murphy see us from their separate corners of the dance floor and hip bump their way through fourteen million of Steph's cousins to join us. It's like no one else is there, just our little crew, like always. I mean, Steph is new...and Danny's not here. But right now, all that matters is that the rest of us are together. My heart swells with the love I have for these people. My chosen family, who understand each other better than any outsider ever could, secrets or no.

And then Krystal is there. She swoops in from whatever corner she's been sulking in, and she's got that look in her eye like she's had about enough and is about to make a stand, ruining everyone else's time in the process. I shoot her a warning look, and she relaxes a little bit and pretends she just came over to dance. She shakes her way in between Ruby and Murphy, who, in Krystal's defense, *are* a bit glued together.

Ruby arches an eyebrow at me but tries to pretend getting boxed out doesn't bother her. She dances with Aaron and me instead, taking deep swigs from Aaron's beer. When Krystal leaves to request a song, there Ruby goes, back to Murphy, both of them throwing their heads back and laughing like they've never had a better time in their lives. If she's trying to butter him up before she tells him what she's hiding, I think it's working. The music changes to a slow song, and I see a moment of hesitation before they clamp together, swaying back and forth.

I stop paying attention to them and look into my husband's eyes. It's not our song, but I remember dancing to it at our wedding, and even though my swollen tummy makes it hard to be near to each other, I know we're even closer now than we were the day we got married.

I hear a stomping of heels, and suddenly Krystal is back. She puts her hand on Ruby's shoulder and gives her one firm push. "I'll take it from here, Ruby," she says, stepping into Ruby's place.

Ruby takes one step backward from the force but doesn't say anything. She looks stunned.

"Uh-oh," Aaron says to me under his breath.

"Krys, I was dancing with Ruby," Murphy says, standing motionless.

"Oh, trust me, *I know* you were dancing with Ruby," Krystal slurs, trying unsuccessfully to get Murphy to sway with her to the music. "The little slut's been all over you all night."

"Excuse me?" Ruby yells.

"*Uh-oh* is right," I say to Aaron, leaving him so I can try to stop this inevitable scene. Krystal clings to Murphy's arms, like she's hoping he will start dancing with her and then the fight will be over, and she wins. If you ask me, the prize isn't worth it. Obviously, I love Murphy, but he has got to be the most selfish person I've ever met in my life. He never does anything he doesn't want to do, and if he's doing you a favor, it's probably because either he owes you one or he's looking for you to owe him one. But these girls, it's like they think it's charming or something, his complete lack of thought for anyone else. Case in point, he doesn't defend either Krystal or Ruby. He just stands there and waits for me to clean up his mess. I'm a mother already, and I haven't even given birth yet.

I put one hand on Krystal's shoulders and one on Ruby's and lead them away from the crowd. They don't fight me. What are they going to do? Hit a pregnant lady? Aaron, Emmett, Steph, and Murphy all follow us off the floor and into the lobby of the reception hall. I might not be able to put out this fire, but I can at least try to quarantine it before it spreads across the whole damn reception. On the way out of the room, I catch sight of Charlene, who is propping up the bar and cackling to Nancy, who's thankfully sipping bottled water. So that's where Charlene's been all night. She looks at us curiously but I look away quickly. One problem at a time.

"What is your *problem?*" Ruby explodes once we're through the doors of the hall and in the lobby. "We were just dancing! We've been friends since we were little kids. I can't dance with someone I've known my whole life at our friend's wedding?" Ruby is Fired *Up*. I almost have to laugh, because it's just like the halls of Chatwick High—Ruby fuming because one of Murphy's girlfriends was rude to her. Is it the alcohol that's aging her down ten years, or is she just under the influence of Murphy?

"I'm getting a little tired of this lifelong-friend BS," Krystal says, arms crossed. "I barely even heard of you until Danny offed himself—"

"Watch it, Krystal," I cut in.

"Sure, Ally, stick up for your *best friend* Ruby because I mentioned your *best friend* Danny. Did you know your *best friend* Ruby was *sleeping* with your *best friend* Murphy?"

I pause. How would Krystal know about that? I glance at my friends, who all look confused except for Murphy and Ruby. Ruby shakes her head just enough so I can see. But the cat's out of the bag now, so we might as well declaw the damn thing. "That was a long time ago, Krystal. What business is it of yours?"

Krystal holds one finger about an inch away from my face and slurs, "One week after Danny's funeral, after I'd given Murphy the space *he said he needed*, I went to spend the night at his house. *Resuming our normal routine*." She directs this last sentence to Ruby, who is biting her cheek, her arms crossed now. "I smell perfume on my pillow that is *definitely* not mine. I ask Murphy about it, and he tells me I'm crazy. Then we go to New York, I hug Ruby when we get there, and for the rest of the day her *stench* is on my clothes and I know. I know it was *her*." She points at Ruby, who is no longer shaking her head.

Oh.

Like I said, when Ruby finally admitted Murphy was the father of her baby, it wasn't a *total* shock. But it never occurred to me they *still* had something going on, after all this time. And what business does Ruby have *sleeping* with a man when she hasn't even told him he knocked her up?

Aaron—my good old peacemaking, tension-breaking husband—slugs Murphy on the arm. "Jesus, Murph, change your sheets much?"

I can't help it. I laugh.

Krystal narrows her eyes at me. "Oh, is that funny, Ally? It's so *funny* that your perfect little Ruby *screwed* Murphy, even knowing I was in the picture? Oh, but that's right! I remember, you don't place too high a value on fidelity, do you?"

I feel like I've been slapped. And what's worse, Krystal is looking at me like Charlene has been—like she knows something about me.

Aaron's face hardens. "All right, I've heard about enough of this. Let's go." He puts his arm around Krystal, gripping her shoulder and trying to guide her outside, even farther away from the reception. At this point, I hope he dumps her in a snowbank.

"Don't put so much effort into defending your wife, Aaron," she says, practically spitting as she talks now. "She probably wouldn't even *be* your wife if you knew she slept with Danny Deuso!"

He drops his grip.

"That's right," Krystal says, marching back to me, breathing her cheap beer breath straight into my nose. "That's right, Ally. I heard the two of you talking about how Danny switched your secret with Ruby's. I wasn't eavesdropping; it's pretty hard *not* to hear everything in that shoe box she lives in."

Ruby holds up both hands. "Hold on, Krystal. That still doesn't explain how you know this. Ally didn't tell me her secret that night. Who's to say you're not just making shit up to cause trouble?"

Krystal sneers at Ruby. "I found it in her purse. That secret compartment Aaron told us about at Steph and Emmett's engagement brunch. It's not my fault she wasn't smart enough to throw it out."

And there it is. My secret is out. About a half second later, Ruby lunges for Krystal. Emmett catches her just one inch before her fist makes contact with Krystal's face. I can tell he didn't want to stop her, and I wish he had hesitated just one second longer. As he drags her away, Ruby shouts so many swear words that I haven't even heard some of them before. She must have picked them up on the subway.

Emmett puts his hand over her mouth. "Ruby, shut up. Jesus, the whole hall can hear you!" he scolds her quietly. She continues to struggle as Krystal stands there smugly even as she inches her way back over to Murphy, who keeps stepping farther away.

"Tell me this isn't true, Ally," Aaron pleads. I say nothing. I can't. He looks at me, his eyes starting to glaze over with tears. His hands go to his head, his fists clench around clumps of the hair I took fifteen minutes to style.

"Was it his?" he asks hoarsely.

I blink. "Was what whose?"

"Was it Danny's baby? The one you aborted?"

Oh my God, in all the confusion and all the beer, he's thinking that *both* the secrets are mine.

Emmett, Steph, Krystal, and Murphy have eyes as wide as saucers. If they didn't overhear Aaron shouting the word *abortion* at me on the street, they'll certainly figure out what was in my envelope now. But I don't care about them right now. I care about my husband. I shake my head, "No, Aaron, you've got it wrong—"

"Oh, *spare* me!" he yells, his arms flying up into the air.

"Aaron, let's just go outside and talk about this."

"I don't want to talk to you! Every time we talk, I get a different story. Speaking of which, real genius move getting Ruby involved. What did you hold over her head to get her to lie for you?"

Suddenly I feel like a caged animal. My eyes search desperately until they land on Ruby. She is still struggling against Emmett's grip, his hand still clamped firmly over her mouth. She is shouting through it and, judging by Emmett's winces, trying to bite her way out.

Aaron turns to leave, and suddenly I know if he walks out that door without knowing the truth, I will lose him forever. But even if I tell the truth, if I throw my friend under the bus in front of everyone, in front of Murphy, who shouldn't have to find out like this, it won't make a difference. He won't believe me.

"Aaron, stop," says Murphy, stepping out from the corner to block my husband's exit. We all whip our heads around to him. What could he possibly contribute to this situation?

"I don't know about Ally and Danny, not for sure anyway…and if something did happen, it was a long time ago. But I do know this. She didn't have an abortion. Ruby did. Danny put Ruby's secret in Ally's envelope."

Our mouths hang open like we're trying to catch flies.

"How do you know that?" Aaron demands. "Did they tell you to say that?"

"No," Murphy says. "I know because I'm the one who got her pregnant. I knew about it and never said anything. That was my secret."

―――――

"It was when we weren't together!" I yell after Aaron, who is walking away from me. We are in the parking lot, and neither of us have coats on to protect us from the December–almost January air. My teeth chatter, and in the back of my mind I'm worried about what a lowered body temperature will do to the baby. In the front of my mind is desperation at the thought of my husband leaving me. Even after he seemed to believe what Murphy said—by the way, what the fuck *Murphy*, right?—Aaron still walked out. Because my real secret, that I slept with Danny, is upsetting enough without bringing a secret pregnancy into it.

Aaron stops in his tracks. Turns. "So what, Al, you guys did it when you were like fourteen? You're telling me I wasn't your first? Where do the lies end?"

"No," I say, waving my hands. "No, it was that month when you first went away to college. *You* were the one who wanted to break up, remember? I was devastated! I loved you, and I wanted to make it work, but you thought it would be better for us to have some time apart, to figure out if being together was what we really wanted. You can't be mad I slept with someone when we weren't together! *You* slept with Christie Bedard during that time, if you remember."

"Yeah, but I came clean about it, Ally! And as I remember, I had to work for *months* to regain your trust after that, and *still* you've held it over my head for a decade. Always bragging that I'm the only man you've ever slept with, like you're some saint. And all the while, you slept with one of our friends? Danny, no less?"

"I was hurt! I thought we would be together forever, and then you dumped me! I just needed… I needed someone to make me feel less hopeless. And there was Danny, telling me he always had a thing for me…"

I can hardly remember the night. The first night, anyway. It was late. I had drank a good amount of wine, had a good cry over a chick flick, and then Danny called to tell me he had heard Aaron and I had split. He wanted to see if I was okay. I was drunk, and alone. Ruby was MIA, and my mom would have just told me that all men are shit, which isn't very helpful. I was still pissed at Emmett for the way he dumped Nicki, and Murphy would have taken Aaron's side. So I asked Danny to come over.

He was there in minutes. He told me he was sorry, that Aaron was an idiot, that if he had me, he never would have let me go. And then he told me he had feelings for me, that he'd had a crush on me since we were kids. I basically mauled him, I was so hungry to feel wanted, and besides, I had always thought Danny was cute in a below-the-tracks kind of way. I told myself it would just be the one time, but he kept showing up, never letting me feel down, never letting me be alone.

It was addicting. He was so fun and spontaneous, and he read me poems that he had secretly written about me and just *hid* for, like, *years*. I loved Aaron, but the closest I got to poetry with him was when he burped the alphabet. After a week, Danny told me he was in love with me, that he wanted to be with me. Instead, I got back together with Aaron.

"Always had a thing for you?" Aaron says. "Are you fucking kidding me right now, Ally? We hung out with that kid every day. You're telling me he looked straight into my eyes acting like we were all just such good friends, and the whole time he was trying to get you for himself?"

"No! I never knew anything about it until the night…it happened. I swear, he never said anything. He always respected our relationship. But then…we didn't have one, and…"

"And he took advantage of you," Aaron says. It's more a challenge than a question.

The countdown from inside the hall interrupts us. "Four… three…two…one…Happy New Year!" and Aaron and I just stand there, staring at each other, my heart in my hands. Aaron waits for reassurance I'm not sure I can give.

Danny didn't take advantage of me any more than I wanted to be taken advantage of. I may not have loved Danny the way he loved me, but I wanted him that night, and the night after that, and the week after that. The time he and I spent together was one of the most painful and beautiful times in my life—the only time in my life I imagined myself with anyone other than Aaron, imagined myself living an entirely different kind of life, running away and joining the circus, not giving a damn what anyone else thought—and when Aaron and I decided to get back together, I was sad to have to let Danny go.

No relationship is perfect, and when things get rough with Aaron, I always have the memory of my time with Danny to get me through. And when things get *really* rough—like last spring when the strain of trying unsuccessfully to have a baby for two years made us fight so much that Aaron went to stay with Murphy for a few weeks, Danny was there that night when I was drunk by myself at Margie's Pub. And in the morning, when I woke up next to him, it certainly didn't *feel* like he had taken advantage of me. It felt more like I had taken advantage of him, of the feelings I knew he still had. When I explained to him that Aaron was my husband, and that the night before had been a mistake and could we please never talk about it again, he had been crushed but not surprised. After all, it was déjà view for him.

Clearly, he hadn't been as understanding about that night as I thought. But if there's someone out there who knows the whole story, let the asshole just try and prove it. All Danny wrote was that

I cheated on Aaron, and I told him about the first time, and that's enough. I don't really care what Danny wanted anymore. I've spent the last four months torturing myself over Danny's suicide, worried that rejecting him again was what led him to kill himself. Maybe it was, maybe it wasn't. I will never know. The last thing I want to do is smear shit over the wonderful memories the two of us shared, the tender moments when he held me in his arms, when I saw in his eyes the person I always wanted everyone to think I am.

But I can't say any of that to Aaron. It would kill him, and for no reason, because Danny was never going to split the two of us up. I loved him, but not the way I love my husband, and I have to put him before Danny's memory. So I just shrug and let Aaron think that Danny was some jerk who preyed on my weakened state to get me into bed. I decide it's okay to keep my real feelings for Danny to myself, to keep this one thing hidden inside my heart. No slip of paper is going to destroy my marriage.

Oh, and before you all buy your ticket for the runaway rumor train, just chill. The baby is Aaron's. I'm not about to sleep with a drug addict without using a condom. I'm not that dumb.

25

STEPH
NOW

ALLY CHASES AARON INTO THE PARKING LOT; MURPHY DRAGS Ruby off before she can storm away; Krystal, happy with the mess she's created, practically skips back into my reception, looking over her shoulder to make sure Ruby isn't behind her. It's not like I *wanted* my best friend to get hit, and I know tomorrow I will spend at least an hour with her on the phone reassuring her that I understand why she would be angry at Murphy and that she had had too much to drink, and no, she didn't ruin the *entire* wedding reception.

But just for a *second*, I thought maybe Krystal could have used a pop in the face. Just for a second. And seeing Ruby so scrappy and ready to fight was also kind of thrilling. She's been so reserved since I've met her. Friendly, but like she was holding back. Can't take the Chatwick out of the girl, I guess.

It's just me and Emmett left in the lobby. "Welcome to the family, baby," he says to me with a wink. He pulls me into a hug, kisses my forehead, and rests his chin on my skull. I love it when he does that. I hate to sound old-fashioned, but it's nice to feel tiny and protected. I should probably be upset, both by the fact that this drama is currently gobbling up all the attention and by the subject matter itself, but I can't seem to stop smiling. I'm married. I'm Emmett's wife. I'm sorry for what Ruby had to go through, but other than that, the fact that his friends—my friends—have all humped each other doesn't seem like such an insurmountable crisis, considering the things we've been through this year.

Furthermore, it seems my strategy to reveal *just enough* about Emmett worked. Looks like everyone lied about their secrets, but we're the only ones who got away with it. I know he told Ruby the truth, so hopefully that will satisfy Danny's requirement and we are taken care of, karmically speaking. I'm not too concerned about Ruby knowing. Out of all of them, *that* girl, apparently, can keep one hell of a secret.

As for the bad karma we racked up from bringing that poison into town, well, let's just say our New Year's resolution is to start volunteering down at the drop-in treatment clinic. We'll never know if Danny was serious about getting sober when he asked us for a place to stay, but I (and I know Emmett too) will always be haunted by the notion that maybe we could have saved him. It was why I reacted so dramatically at Danny's funeral. At the time, I was entirely convinced that his death was on our shoulders. Maybe by helping out at the clinic, even if it's just bringing in food and helping check people in, we can make sure it keeps running so that people who *are* serious about saving themselves will always have a place to go.

I hear the countdown and kiss Emmett at the stroke of midnight. I can only hope this is the first of decades of New Year's kisses we will share. I sigh and bury my head in my new husband's chest, breathing him in. I don't ever want to leave his side.

I wish it could be just the two of us for just a little longer, but the door to the hall opens and Charlene pokes her head out into the lobby. "Everything okay out here?" she asks, the strap of her dress falling down from her shoulder. Judging by the droopiness of her eyes and the emptiness of the glass in her head, I don't think she notices.

"Yes, Charlene, everything is fine," Emmett says.

I cross to hug her and thank her for her beautiful reading. "Danny's poem was beautiful," I say.

She doesn't seem to register what I'm saying, keeping her eyes on Emmett's. "Are the secrets all out now?"

Emmett and I look at each other, confused. "Yes," he says cautiously.

"Oh Jesus, thank God!" she says. She reaches into her dress and pulls out a folded envelope from the depths of her bra, shoving it into Emmett's hands. The front of it reads, in Danny's handwriting:

Mom: Read this after everyone leaves.

Emmett looks from me to Charlene to the envelope. Charlene nods at him. "Open it."

Emmett does as he's told, pulling out two sheets of paper. The top one is the poem she read at the ceremony. The bottom is a letter. A new one that we haven't seen. Emmett reads aloud:

Dear Mom,

If you followed my instructions, you know about the dirt I had on each of my "friends." I'm sure you were disappointed in me for using you to gather them together when you didn't know what it was for. But I had to mislead you because I was afraid if you knew my plan, you wouldn't go through with it. I know I was a fuck-up, but I want my "friends" to remember that none of us is perfect. I want them to remember that I wasn't just some punching bag, some depository for all their crap.

So please, consider this my first and final request I make of you. Keep on top of them. Make sure they tell the truth. I've included a few reminders here for you to put pressure on them if they're not 'fessing up. And if they still don't tell each other the truth, it will be your job to expose them to the world. Don't think of it as mean, think of it as freeing them. After all, we're only as sick as our secrets. If I hadn't had to keep that secret about what happened to Roger, well, who knows how my life would have turned out.

Emmett stops reading then and just looks at Charlene. At the bottom of the page, all the secrets are listed:

Ruby had an abortion.
Murphy knew Ruby was pregnant and never told anyone.
Ally cheated on Aaron. With me. (Suck it, Aaron.)
Emmett is a drug dealer.

There are so many things I want to say but don't. I'll say it all later to Emmett, like how he was right about Danny being a manipulative piece of *you know what*. Playing on Charlene's guilt about Roger's death to get her to carry out this ridiculous mission? If that kid had just laid off the dope, he probably could have run the world.

"I cheated and read it before you all left, when I ran out while you all were fightin' about what happened to Roger. I thought maybe it would say something nice that would bring me some comfort but…" She waves her hand at the letter in Emmett's hand.

I think back to that horrible day, the strange look on Charlene's face when she returned, the way she looked when we all lied about our secrets. She had known we were lying.

"I'm sorry," Charlene says, biting her lip. Big, fat tears begin to slide down her cheeks. "I shouldn't have put those notes in your mailboxes. I thought about burnin' 'em, but every time I went to do it, I just felt like Danny was watchin' me, yellin' at me to do what he asked. It was the last thing he asked of me… How could I not…?" She shakes her head.

"I shouldn't have even *thought* about readin' those out at your wedding… I brought that because I knew Danny wanted me to embarrass all of you, but I just couldn't bring myself to do it once I was up there… So I thought I would wait and let you have your reception, and then maybe I could call you all over again tomorrow and do it there… At least then you could keep it between you guys… I don't know what I was thinkin'." She bursts into tears now, and I hug her again, shooting a look at Emmett over her shoulder to indicate that he should say something comforting.

He steps forward and puts a hand on Charlene's shoulder. "It's okay, Charlene. Really. I know how much you loved your son."

Charlene cries even harder, and I hug her and tell her that it's okay. Eventually, Emmett takes her from me and hugs her himself.

I'm surprised he's able to remain so calm, considering our wedding was almost ruined by this drama. Well, much earlier than it actually happened, anyway.

Emmett suggests I take Charlene to the bathroom to splash some cold water on her face, but I shake my head. "I should go check on Ally," I tell him. "Make sure she's okay." He nods and smiles, leading Charlene to the restrooms himself. I get the sense I've passed some kind of test by not throwing a fit about all this. I feel more like I've been hazed, and now I'm just relieved that it's over. Emmett has that letter tucked tightly in the pocket of his tuxedo, and I imagine while Charlene fixes her makeup, Emmett will be flushing it down the toilet in the men's room next door.

I sigh and grab my coat from the hanger, and Emmett helps me put it on. I grab Ally's too. If Aaron ran off, she could be outside alone and need to talk, and Lord knows how long that's going to take. As acclimated to the cold as any native Vermonter, I'm still in a strapless wedding dress, for Pete's sake.

I push open the door of the reception hall and peer out into the darkness. "Al?" I call. No response. The parking lot is empty of people and silent except for... What is that creaking? I scan the rows of cars and find Aaron's truck rocking back and forth, the windows all fogged up. I giggle to myself. Those two. I hope Emmett and I have as active a sex life as them when we've been married for five years and/or I'm pregnant with our first kid. The latter of which should happen any day now, if all goes well. I know Emmett's going to be okay. I know it. But I'm not taking any chances.

I turn and walk back into the hall, ready to return to the festivities. I decide to go to the bathroom first, and on the way, I hear voices in the stairwell. I know I shouldn't listen, but it could be Krystal and Ruby about to resume where they left off, and bloodshed is not exactly how I want this night to end.

"...this *whole* time?" It's Ruby.

"I'm sorry, Ruby. I—" And Murphy.

"*How* did you know?"

"Danny."

"But *he* didn't even know until *after* you guys fought. I thought you never spoke after that."

"We spoke once. He called me after he took you to your first appointment at Planned Parenthood to tell me what was happening. He convinced you to put the abortion off a few days to give me time to get down there."

"He *said* that?"

"He said he didn't care whether I stopped you or not; he just thought I should know and that I should be there."

"But you didn't agree? What? Too busy with your *perfect, pure* little girlfriend?"

"That's not fair."

"Don't talk to me about what's fair, Murphy Leblanc. Jesus, did you ever love me at all?"

Whoa. Now I *really* shouldn't be listening.

"Of course I—"

"Because I don't see how you could say you love somebody, how you could even claim to be my best friend, when you knew I was going through that and didn't even... You didn't even..." Her voice breaks, and I can tell she's crying. Or struggling not to cry.

"You weren't exactly innocent, Ruby. You made Danny swear *not* to tell the father of your child that you were even pregnant. Your *best friend*. I've been waiting for you to tell me yourself for ten goddamn years! How do you think it made me feel to be cut out of a decision like that? How do you think it made me feel that you wanted so little to do with me that you would do *that* to a life we made together, without even talking to me about it?"

"If you were so *hurt* by it, why did you sleep with me the day after the funeral? Why did you maul me at Ally's Christmas party? You didn't seem too hurt then."

"You didn't let me finish. I *was* hurt. But in the end, I knew you were making the only decision you could, given our…circumstances. I stayed away because I respected your decision to keep me out of it. I left you alone so you could do what you wanted and move on."

"Yeah, that sounds like you, Murph. So *selfless*. I'm sure it had nothing to do with the fact that you got off scot-free and didn't have to give up your little backup girlfriend," she spits back. "I lost everything, Murphy. And what I didn't lose, I gave away. Not just for me. It was so that *you* could be free to do what *you* wanted. I didn't want you to be forced to stay with me if I decided to keep it, and I didn't want you to have to go through the pain if…"

"If you decided to have an abortion."

"Right. Only those weren't the only two options, Murphy."

They're both quiet for a beat. Oh God, I think I know what's coming, and I only wish I could see Murphy's face. "What are you saying to me?" he asks.

"I didn't get the abortion, Murphy." She pauses, her voice lowering and the angry tone turning humble. "I had the baby, and I gave it up for adoption."

Just when I thought it was over, I find out Murphy Leblanc is a *father*. Just as I think I'm about to pass out, the lobby door swings open, and my mother tells me it's the last dance. My feet are heavy as lead as I walk away from the stairwell, where a bomb the size of Canada has just dropped on Emmett's best man. I let Mom lead me to my husband, whose tie is now wrapped around his head, and join him to enjoy the last few minutes of our wedding.

26

RUBY
BACK THEN—FRESHMAN YEAR; NYU

"That's it, honey, you can do it. Push! Push!"

The nurse props me up, her small frame almost completely wedged between myself and the inclined bed. A vague worry that I will crush this nice woman floats around somewhere in a distant part of my brain that can still think about things other than my own pain. She was assigned to me when I came in without the standard-issue clueless male to hold my hand and curse at for doing this to me in the first place. She wipes the hair off my forehead, slick with sweat from eight hard hours of labor. The epidural wore off around hour four.

I don't know the nurse's name. I'm sure she told me, but I blocked it out, along with the million other details of this day. Less to try to erase from my memory later. I allow her to wipe my brow, rub my shoulders, feed me ice chips. I allow her to take care of me like I haven't been taken care of in a long time. Every time she touches me, I stifle a cry until the pain comes again, so I have an excuse to let it out. It's not just the baby ripping through my body; it's my heart.

When at last the baby is born, the doctor, whose name I also pointedly ignore, asks me if I'm sure I don't want to know the sex, if I'm sure I don't want to hold the baby. I shake my head, tears rolling down my cheeks like the rain that streaks the windowpane I have now rolled over to face. I squeeze my eyes shut so I don't see anything. The baby cries, and a pain like I've never felt before rips through my body. I want nothing *more* than to know the sex of the life I've carried inside me for the better part of a year. I want nothing *more* than to hold that life in my arms.

"Get it out of here," I whisper instead. They move quickly and exit the room, but I continue to whimper, "Get it out of here."

The nurse stays behind. I want her to leave so I can cry the way I need to. Loudly, ferociously. But I don't want her to leave me either. I can't be alone so suddenly after having a little partner attached to me for nine months. She stays and "cleans me up," as she says. No matter what she does, I still feel inhuman. I can't believe billions of women have gone through this voluntarily, most of them more than once.

"You must think I'm a monster," I say to the ceiling, afraid to meet her kind eyes. "I just couldn't—"

"Oh, honey, no." She walks up next to the bed and lays a reassuring hand on my arm. "Some people want to hold them for closure's sake. Some people think it will just make it harder. Nobody's judging you, because either way, what you've done says more about the kind of person you are than anything that comes after."

I try to smile, to show her that what she says has helped me. But it hasn't, and I can't.

"Are you sure there isn't anyone I can call for you?" she asks.

"The adoptive parents..."

"They're already here," she says. "Do you want to see them?"

I shake my head. I chose them from a binder full of desperate barren couples, all smiling at me, their blurbs all trying to convince me they would be the perfect family for my child. Lucy and Michelle run a bookstore in Delaware. They found each other later in life and opted to adopt rather than shoot themselves up with hormones and sperm. I liked the idea of my child hiding in bookstacks and living in a small state. I made sure the adoption agency told them about the history of mental illness in my family. They were okay with it, so I was okay with them.

But I was very specific when we set up the terms for the adoption. I allowed them to pay my medical expenses so I wouldn't have to go through my parents' insurance. I allowed them to come to some of the doctor's appointments. But once I had the baby, I didn't want any contact. They asked for an amendment. They would have to tell the kid that he or she was adopted. (With two moms, he would be asked questions, and they didn't want to outright lie.)

They agreed to keep my identity private, but if he decides at any point that he wants a relationship, they'll contact the agency and the agency will contact me. If I change my mind and want to have (limited) contact, all I have to do is reach out to the agency myself. Ultimately, it's my decision whether to open the adoption back up. I'm already dreading the day when I will have to make that decision. Or worse, if I don't have to make it because he doesn't want to know me. Neither scenario feels right, and yet I know underneath all the pain that I'm making the right decision.

"Anyone else I can call for you? Your family?"

I shake my head again. There's no one. No one even knows I'm here except for Lucy and Michelle. Well, and my resident assistant. After I threw Danny out, I confided in my RA so she would appeal to the university on my behalf to keep the other half of the room unoccupied due to my "special circumstances." I figured she was a safe bet since she's bound by confidentiality and could be an emergency contact should anything bad happen.

But tonight when I woke up in a puddle of embryonic fluid, I slipped a note under her door rather than waking her up. I was perfectly capable of taking a cab myself, and I didn't know her well enough to obligate her to share this experience with me. About every five minutes during labor, I thought about calling Ally. Even after all this time with no contact, she would drive here like a bat out of hell if I picked up the phone.

My parents were easier to keep in the dark than I thought. I saw them once, at Parents' Weekend, when I was still not far along enough to show. After that, I made stuff up—I was skiing with my roommate in Aspen for Christmas, partying in Cancun for spring break. All the things I should have been doing my freshman year of college. After my second trimester (when I could no longer throw on an oversize sweater and claim the freshman fifteen), I begged out of every dinner request by my father, citing homework or a date.

I lived in fear he would get frustrated at my excuses and show up at my dorm one day, but my worry was for nothing. He isn't that kind of dad. I'm sure the people in my dorm and my classes have figured it out, but I made it a point to keep them strangers. They didn't say anything about it; they just waited until I passed to whisper. In that way, college wasn't much different than Chatwick.

"The father?" the nurse asks. "You left that blank on the birth certificate."

I tell her the same lie I told the adoption agency. "I don't know who he is." I had to say this; otherwise, Murphy would have had to sign off on the adoption. I was too scared, either that he wouldn't sign or that he would without a fight. I seesaw about which would be worse.

"Are you sure you don't want to see him?"

A current of panic shoots through me. Does she mean the baby or the father? Is my baby—Lucy and Michelle's baby—a boy? Even though I've thought of the baby as a he, I don't want to know that for sure. I can't. So I don't ask her to clarify. I just nod. Either way, I'm sure.

The nurse turns to leave, but I stop her.

"How long until the pain goes away?" I ask.

"Well, you'll be sore for a few—"

"That's not what I mean."

I knew when I made this decision that it would be hard. Even before my fight with Danny, the one where he basically called me a murderer, I had already been waffling. The judgment of my drug-dealing, stepfather-killing friend was not what put me over the edge. I still went to my appointment, but after I had been prepped and was lying there with my shaking legs in the stirrups, I sat up and told them to stop, that I couldn't go through with it. I knew I couldn't keep it, but I also knew that, without me and Murphy for parents, it might have a chance at a good life. A chance to make two other people's lives whole.

The nurse looks at me, pity filling her eyes. Normally I would find it condescending, but right now I can accept it.

She sits on my bed. "I've never given a baby up for adoption, but my first child was born early, much too early. Stillborn." Her eyes moisten. "I would imagine that, even though your baby is alive and well, it feels something like that."

I nod. Perhaps.

"I can't say you'll ever be completely free of it, honey. The first few weeks will be the hardest, because your body will be telling you it's time to feed the baby and your hormones will be all out of whack. It will get easier after that. Every day will get a little easier, and then one day, you'll wake up and you'll feel almost normal. And soon after that, you'll be grateful."

"Grateful?"

"I know it sounds crazy, but one day you will heal, and you'll be grateful you got through it. And you will be grateful for the choice you made, because it means a better life for four people. You, the new parents, *and* the baby."

Five people, I think. *Murphy.*

I worry that she is about to call Jesus into the conversation, belittling the women who did keep their feet in those stirrups and make the choice that was right for them. I don't have the strength to defend them, but I don't think they're any less brave than I am. They'll never be the same, either.

But she doesn't launch into a pro-life sermon. "I know I've only known you for a day, Ruby, but it's the hardest day you will probably ever have. And if it means anything to you, I think you're the bravest young woman I've ever met."

"I don't feel brave," I murmur. How can I? Right now, I feel like marching down that hallway and yanking my baby out of Lucy's and

Michelle's proud and loving arms. Right now, I feel like everything I've done to protect this secret was completely insane. It was crazy to think I could pull this off and walk away unscathed. I thought it would be the best thing for everyone. For Nancy, who once let it slip that her bipolar worsened after the stress and hormone changes that came with having children. For Murphy, who was in no way prepared to handle this. For the baby, who deserved a chance at a family who wanted it. And for me, who just wants to have the big life I always dreamed of. But right now, my life seems very small. Seven pounds, nine ounces small.

I cry into the nurse's arms until she administers a sedative and I drift off to sleep.

The next morning, I wake up, check out of the hospital, and try to pretend it was all a dream.

27

RUBY
NOW

THE STREETS ARE QUIET. THE CITIZENS OF CHATWICK—MANY of which were at Emmett and Steph's wedding last night—are cozy in their beds, sleeping off their New Year's Eve hangovers as the snow falls silently but steadily outside their windows. I am jealous of them as I pull up to the curb and step out of the car directly into a pile of slush.

I tug on the brass handle of Charlene's—her deli, not her house—pleased to find the door is no easier to open than it was ten years ago. Muscle memory kicks in, and I perform a combination of deftly aimed kicks and yanks before the door swings violently open. The patrons inside do not so much as glance up from their newspapers or tear their eyes from the chalkboard menu above the deli counter, familiar with this "secret knock" required to enter the deli.

The people in line study the chalkboard as if they don't have it memorized, as if they won't be ordering the same thing they did yesterday and the day before that. On the first day of this new year, already they are breaking their resolutions to eat healthier, to try new things. I'm sticking with mine: to be honest. With others, but most of all with myself.

A man in line is wearing a blue jumpsuit with the word *Borbeau's* in block letters on the chest pocket. I don't recognize the man, but part of me feels like I should approach him, tell him I knew Danny, tell him I'm sorry he lost his coworker. But upon closer inspection, I see it's not a man at all. It's a boy. About the age Danny was when he *started* working at Borbeau's, way back in high school.

This boy is Danny's replacement. Working on New Year's Day even though the shop is closed, either because he needs the money or because he's picked up where Danny's side business left off and there are lots of people just itching to break their promise that this year will be different. He even has sandy hair like Danny's, but his eyes aren't nearly as blue. And his presence isn't half as magnetic.

Murphy sits in one of the red-pleather upholstered booths that Charlene removed an aisle of liquor to make room for back when she became the owner. (Chatwick near rioted over the change.) He's in the booth farthest from the door, as if we're likely to have any privacy anywhere in this town. But he rightly suggested we finish the conversation from last night here, rather than his apartment, exactly *because* it's public. Even considering how we're both feeling right now, it would be too easy to get off topic at his place, to not talk about what we need to talk about. To not *talk* at all.

They're both really good at ignoring problems.

I'm a bundle of nerves as I slide into the padded bench opposite him. We make small talk about the weather for a few minutes—how unusual it is for the temperature to be above thirty-five degrees at the beginning of January, how this snowfall is nothing compared to the Nor'easter of '93 and should stop in plenty of time so that my flight home shouldn't be affected. I've never felt more awkward making small talk in my life, because I'm sitting with Murphy Leblanc and we're supposed to be past all this. An observer might think we're on our first date, rather than our last.

A waitress who can't be more than sixteen comes over. Plump white rolls of skin spill over the sides of her low-rise jeans, a lacy hot-pink bra strap peeking out from a black tank top. I want to ask her how she's not freezing, and that makes me feel old. I ask if Charlene is here, but the girl tells us with a smirk that she is home "recovering." I'm not surprised; as I climbed into Murphy's truck after the reception, I saw my parents piling her into their car to give her a ride home. Charlene's car remained in the lot for the hours that he and I stayed there talking. I know now that she was drunk on more than just the gin and tonics she was sucking down; she was drunk on relief, on freedom from her part in Danny's little game.

Emmett came to find us when the reception was through to invite us to the after-party at Margie's. When Murphy assured him we would "be along in a bit," Emmett knew he wasn't going to see us, so he filled us in on the second letter Danny wrote to Charlene, and her confession that she was the one who sent us those sweet little follow-up notes. All of us had thought it was some girlfriend or junkie customer Danny had guilted or bribed into doing his bidding.

All of us except Murphy, who received his note the day after the funeral and suspected *me* of threatening him, which explains his demanding my presence at his house and the carefully orchestrated conversation down by the bay about Danny's promised arrangement. He was trying to draw me out, to get me to confess that I was behind it. I guess I should be offended, but at this point, what does it really matter?

Once our order is in, we twirl straws and rearrange cutlery. Murphy is the one who called to invite me to lunch. Let him speak first.

"Quite the drama last night, huh?" he starts. He hopes I will take over from here, but I just smile and nod, take a sip of my drink. I'm too afraid to say anything. He has every right to be furious with me, and yet he seems…normal. I'm just waiting for the other shoe to drop.

He continues. "Mom says it's not a wedding without drama." I wonder if he's already told Cecile what we talked about last night but decide he couldn't have. If Cecile suddenly became aware there was a grandchild who had been kept from her, I would have heard from her already. It's part of the reason I did not tell Murphy I was pregnant. I was afraid I wouldn't be strong enough to stand up to her and the decision would be out of my hands.

"It was nice to see Cecile," I say.

"She misses you. You know she still has our prom picture on her mantel, still in the little cardboard thingy it came in?"

A breath of laughter escapes my nose. "Really?"

"Kept it up the entire time me and Taylor were together too. Used to drive her crazy."

The victorious little thrill that goes through me at this is embarrassing, but hearing Taylor's name reminds me of last night's conversation. I had demanded to know who he told about the pregnancy right after he found out. He said he didn't tell anyone, not even Taylor.

He thought it might be the reason they had so many problems, why he had a hard time staying faithful to her. (She finally broke up with him after two cheats in two years; Murphy didn't mention if I was included in that count or not.)

It was like part of him fractured off by not telling her the truth, by holding it inside and hating himself for what he'd done to me, to her, and he went looking for forgiveness in all the wrong places. It made me angry at first, that he reacted so selfishly to an act already so selfish, but in the end, I kind of understood. Maybe he didn't deal with it in the right way, but the choice he made left him feeling alone. Just like mine did.

"Listen, about—" Murphy starts.

I hold up a hand to stop him. "Do we have to go through it all again?" I ask. Last night, I told him everything: when I found out I was pregnant, all the thoughts that went through my head, what happened when Danny showed up, what happened after, and how I kept it a secret from everyone. Murphy defended his choice to stay out of it—he was hurt, he was scared, he didn't feel he had a right to interfere. I justified why I didn't tell him myself—I was hurt, I was scared, and I didn't want him to interfere. We didn't accomplish much beyond draining his gas tank from the blasting heat while we talked circles around each other, not even realizing we were saying the same thing.

He looks at me and swallows. "I think you know there's more to be said. I think you know that's why we're here." I realize he's nervous too, his eyes unable to focus on mine for too long before darting around. "I just stared at my ceiling all night, thinking of questions I should have asked, things I should have said differently."

I don't tell him that after we parted, I had the best night's sleep

I've had in ten years. But not before sitting at the kitchen table with Nancy, who was waiting up for me when I got home. We shared a kettle of hot cocoa and a plate of blueberry pancakes she had whipped up after the wedding and placed in the oven to keep warm.

After having several days to digest the news that I had hid an entire pregnancy from her (Charlene, thankfully, had not told Nancy even about the false secret), she told me only how sorry she was that I had gone through that alone. She thinks I made "the most beautiful decision" she could think of, and that she's never been prouder of me. I was still nurturing the anger from learning Murphy abandoned me, and I told her about it. "You have to remember, baby girl," she said. "Not everyone is as strong as you."

After Mom went to bed, I called Jamie, who was just waking up in London. I told him everything too. He wasn't angry that I kept it from him, or even hurt. It was my secret to keep, he said, and he was honored that I chose to share it. He also said it explained so much about me, in both good and bad ways.

"Okay," I concede, agreeing to Murphy's request to reopen the conversation. We both received new information last night, but when we weigh our secrets pound for pound, even I have to admit Murphy's *new* burden is more significant. "Where do you want to start?"

"I was so mad last night, but when I got home, all I could think about is how you went through all that alone. I'm sorry."

I stay silent. My instinct is to tell him that it wasn't his fault because he didn't know, but now I know that's not entirely true.

"What was it like? Did you have anyone there with you?"

I blink at him, realizing he could only be talking about one thing. "I don't want to talk about the birth," I say.

"But—"

"Murphy. It's off-limits. I'm sorry if that's not fair, but no." I can't go there. I will never stop crying if I do. The memory is mine, and no matter how descriptive I am, there's no way he can share it.

As the waitress delivers our sandwiches in red plastic baskets lined with checkered wax paper, Murphy grinds the ice in his cup with his straw, his jaw set. "Can you at least tell me if it was a girl or a boy?" he asks when she leaves. Neither of us touches our food.

I swallow. If only we could have started with a softball question. Perhaps: *Why didn't I see any stretch marks the day after Danny's funeral?* (Answer: You weren't looking for them.) "I don't know," I say. "I asked them to take the baby away right after. I didn't hold it." His face falls again. I feel like I have to give him something. So I say what I've never said out loud. "But I feel like it was a boy."

He gets a little sparkle in his eye. I know he's picturing tossing a baseball around with a hyperactive little boy with a mop of black hair. The sparkle vanishes as the daydream does, the anger from the impossibility settling in.

"Doesn't it *bother* you that a piece of you, a piece of *us* is walking around in the world not knowing us? And we don't know if he's happy, or safe, or feeling abandoned?"

"Of course it does. It bothers me every day. Every single day I worry about that. And I'm really sorry to say it, but now you will too." Even as I say it, I wonder if it's true. All these years, I've envied Murphy for not knowing. I even resented him for it, even though it was my doing. But now, knowing that he knew I was pregnant, I wonder. Will it be the same for him? Will it stay with him, crashing into him at random times with varying degrees of strength? Or will he be able to shrug it off, like getting hit by a pitch? Take his base and forget about it by the time he gets his next at bat?

The silence after this stretches on and on until finally Murphy asks. "He would be, what, ten years old?"

An alarm sounds in my head, and I stiffen. "Nine," I say.

"Do you know where he lives?"

I take a deep breath, hesitant to give him this one last piece of the story. It could change everything for so many people. "I do," I say. "The adoption is technically closed. I haven't had any contact with him or the adoptive parents whatsoever. It was my decision to close it, because I thought it would be best for the baby...less confusing...and it didn't feel right for me to have contact without you knowing anything about it." I bite on the inside of my cheek to stop from crying. "And I guess, if I'm honest, I thought it would be easier for me. I was stupid and young and thought if I didn't have regular contact that it would be easier for me to pretend like it never happened, like he didn't exist."

Murphy stares down at the table, shredding the paper wrapper from his straw into bits. His jaw is tense. He's angry at me, and justifiably so.

"But," I say, taking another deep breath, "Lucy and Michelle— the adoptive parents—insisted on adding a clause that should the child wish to meet me"—at this, Murphy looks up sharply—"meet *us*, they can contact the adoption agency and they will contact me to let me know and I would then have the choice. To meet him or not."

"But he—or she—hasn't?"

I shake my head. "There's more though. The clause goes both ways. If at any point I...we...decide we want to meet him...or her, we can also reach out through the adoption agency. Lucy and Michelle promised that they would leave the decision up to him, provided he was old enough to make the choice."

Murphy just stares at me for a moment. The anger has been replaced with something more frightening: hope.

"Murphy," I say, reaching to put one hand over his. "I can't imagine how you must be feeling about this, and I'm sure you're having some crazy biological paternal surge right now. I just want you to take some time, let some of this drama die down, before we make any decisions."

"Ruby," he starts.

"Your gut might be telling you to march into that house and get your kid or force your way into his life, but you can't just think about you anymore. You have to think about this kid, who has parents and a whole life that is most likely going just fine without us, and us coming into the picture would turn it all upside down. And if we're going to get involved, it's going to be hard, you know, for us to be on the periphery, and if you're still angry with me, then there's that whole drama that's unfair to heap on the kid, and—"

"Ruby!" he interrupts me, his hands raised in surrender. "Wow," he adds.

"What?"

"Look at you. You're a mother. You've been one this whole time."

When a tear slides down my cheek, he puts one of his hands over mine. With the other, he pulls a napkin from the dispenser and gives it to me.

"I agree with you," he says. "Right now is not the right time to make any decisions. We'll leave it alone, for now."

I feel a rush of relief like I've never felt before, and my sobs gain intensity until they feel like bullets from a machine gun. He holds my hand until I stop. If only the two of us had been strong enough, brave enough, mature enough ten years ago to have this conversation. What might have been.

When I recover myself, I tell him, "If he ever tries to find me—us—I promise I will include you in the decision to meet him or not."

He looks at me skeptically, then does the goofy face as he tries to raise one eyebrow. I laugh, wipe my hand on the napkin, and reach across the table to do it for him. "I swear, Murph," I say as my finger makes contact. "We're in this together now."

"My turn to ask questions," I say after I see that he believes me. I pull my hand back and use it to swat away the remaining tears. What I want to know is relatively unimportant, but it will change the subject. "This might seem stupid after all this," I say. "But I have to know why you and Danny fought before he came to see me in New York."

"Ah," he says. "I can finally tell you. It was about Ally."

"*Ally?*"

"I figured out that something happened between the two of them. Or at least, I suspected. It was right after Ally and Aaron got back together, and we were all at Danny's for poker night. The two of them kept exchanging this *look*, like they had a secret together. So when Ally and Aaron stepped outside for a smoke, I just lost it on Danny."

"Why? What did you care?"

"I don't care about this 'who knew who first' bullshit," he says. "'Original crew member or not,' Aaron wasn't just some guy Ally was dating. He was our friend. I didn't like the way Danny slid in and took over the minute Aaron's back was turned."

I knit my brow. After all the three of us had been through together, it doesn't quite compute.

"It seemed like he was doing a lot of that that summer," he adds.

Ah. "You thought there was something going on with me and Dan?"

He nods. "After what happened with us, you shut everyone out except for him."

I have to smile. How wonderfully *high school*, with all the seriousness of what we've been through, that Danny Deuso and Murphy Leblanc fought over a couple of girls. "Nothing happened, Murph. Danny and I were never more than friends."

He shakes his head. "That night he called me, to tell me you were pregnant, and that you were going to… That was the last time we ever spoke, and I didn't even say anything. He just told me what was going on and where I could find you and then hung up. I think he and I probably could have gotten over the fight eventually, if I had shown up for you. But I didn't, and when I tried to reach out when he got back into town, he didn't want anything to do with me. I don't blame him."

I reach across the table to hold both his hands in mine. There's nothing I can say that will make him feel better about this. If there's one thing I've known since I was a little kid, it's that sometimes things suck and you can't do anything about it. It will never be okay that Danny and Murphy wasted that time, that any of us wasted that time with him. It will never be okay that Danny is gone. It will never be okay, truly okay, that I gave away my baby, and it will never be okay that I didn't tell Murphy about it.

"I love you, Ruby. You know that, right?" He says it without looking into my eyes, just like the night he first said it.

I sniff back the fresh wave of tears and nod, but I still don't know what he means by it. There are all kinds of ways of loving someone, and it seems we've run through all of them. "I love you too. But where does that leave us?"

He shakes his head, and in that gesture, he is saying what we both know. There is not enough love to compensate for what we've done to each other, and there was never quite enough to compensate for our differences. Even if I moved back to Vermont, I could never live in Chatwick again. And unless it's Chatwick, for Murphy it might as well be the moon. I can't ask him to meet me halfway, or even a third of the way. He belongs here every bit as much as I don't.

"I could never say never," he says. "Not to you. But right now…"

"It's just so unfair," I say. The words escape me, and I know they are from the most childish part of me that used to believe in the fairy tales I read by flashlight, before the days when Danny threw rocks at my window. I have long since known that love doesn't conquer all. "It's just—" I hasten to cover.

"I know," he says. "We never got to be together."

I nod. My heart soars. Finally knowing that this is something he also regrets is a gift. A painful one, but a gift all the same.

The waitress comes back, and Murphy hands her a credit card without looking at the bill. "Maybe things can change a little now," he says after she leaves. "I mean, I miss talking to you. Maybe we can start there."

Damn it, Murphy. Here we are, an inch from finally closing this thing up, and he's got to crack that door open a millimeter. I nod, say of course, we'll keep in touch this time. But we won't. Not unless we decide to meet our child. It's too hard. And as much as eighteen-year-old Ruby would have clung to that crack in the doorway, I just can't.

"You know, I think he had the right idea," Murphy says. "Dan, I mean." The doubt must show on my face, because he explains further. "Maybe he wasn't just trying to get back at us for the way his life turned out. Maybe what he really wanted was to bring us all back together."

I have to laugh. "And Emmett thinks *I* saw the best in him."

"Really though, don't you feel better now that the truth is out on the table?"

I think back to my peaceful night's sleep, to the lightness of my shoulders, to the pictures of my friends we took on my phone last night before everything spun out of control. Maybe that *was* Danny's intention. Or maybe he was just stirring the pot. Either way, I can't regret coming home. I can't regret reconnecting with people who were once my family. And I can't deny that the burden on my shoulders feels a little lighter.

Speaking of which… "You can tell them, if you want," I say. He knows I mean tell our friends about the baby.

"No," he says. "It's your secret to tell or not tell."

I shake my head back. "It's not just mine anymore. That's how this works."

He thinks for a moment. "Okay. Then it should just be ours." He grins wickedly as he shrugs his Carhartt jacket on. It seems that he and I will always have secrets that no one else knows. No matter what Dan may have wanted.

We stand to leave, and Murphy pulls me into a hug. "I think you did the right thing, giving the baby up," he says into my hair. "And I'm really proud of you, the woman you've become, despite everything." I hold him tighter, refusing to let go until I can blink the tears back into my eyelids. "Just...get back to writing now, okay?" he adds.

I pull back, laugh. Nod. "I think I have some good material to work with." As we make for the exit, a familiar face passes through the door.

"Hey there, Miss Ruby," Shawna says, as if it were hours since my last shift at the Exchange instead of years. The Chat must have kept her informed of my return to town. I do not keep as cool. Seeing Shawna after such a nerve-racking and awkward conversation is like a glass of water after a marathon, and I thrust myself into her ample bosom for a hug. Murphy stands awkwardly to the side, and I wave him off.

You can go, I think.

Our eyes connect as he hesitates. *Are you sure?*

He still looks hesitant, and I know he's thinking the same thing as me—will this be the last time we see each other? Probably not. The last time I thought we'd never see each other again I wound up pregnant, tied to him forever.

Go. I think, pointing at the door with my chin. *You can go now. I'm okay.*

He turns, opens the door, and walks through it. The air outside is so cold the latch is frozen, and the door refuses to close all the way even when the waitress tugs and tugs on it. Finally she gives up and leaves it open just a crack.

———

"What are you doing in town?" Shawna asks. While she collects the takeout order she will bring home to her family, I tell her I was a bridesmaid in Emmett McDowell's wedding, which makes her laugh. She remembers Emmett as the pain-in-the-ass kid who would come in and point out the racks that weren't perfectly straight, never offering to rectify the situation. I tell her he hasn't changed much, but as soon as the words are out of my mouth, I realize that I'm wrong.

We grab an empty booth, cooling food be damned, and catch up. She tells me she has her own bookkeeping business, a dream she was too afraid to pursue until the Exchange went out of business and she had no choice. Her daughter, Ashley, who in my mind is seven, is getting ready to graduate from high school. She will go to prom this year, and Shawna's business is doing so well they were able to purchase her a car when she got her license last spring.

She asks me how I am and what became of me, and I can tell she is yet another person who is hurt I lost touch. I tell her I live in New York, that I think I'm finally ready to start writing.

"Donna always did say you were going to set the world on fire," she says with a sad smile.

A surprised laugh escapes me. "Most of the time I don't even have the energy to search for the matches."

"I hear that, sister," she says. "Speaking of fire..." She points her chin at the door, where moments ago Murphy made his anticlimactic exit from my life. "What's going on there?"

I shrug. "Nothing."

She cocks her head, surveying me, looking for clues. I fear it's beating on my sleeve—my heart, as broken as it was when I was eighteen but without the same concentration of grief and hormones rushing through it. "Old flames take the longest to burn out," she says.

"Maybe," I say, "but I think we've damn near stomped it out. Now—"

"It's all over but the crying," we say in unison, quoting from one of the songs we used to sing while closing up the shop at night. When our laughter dies down, she shakes her head. "I just have a feeling about you two. Maybe now isn't your time, but I'll be doing your makeup for your wedding someday. I just know it."

I don't argue; there's no point with her. I just smile and shake my head in amusement. "Maybe a little less glitter than for prom, yeah?"

EPILOGUE

DANNY
NOW

I watch them gather one by one. Emmett is first, perpetually punctual, and he hoists several camp chairs from his trunk, staging them and restaging them around the fire pit. Next to his own chair he places a full twelve-pack cooler on a pile of grass clippings left behind by some stoned teenage employee of the Chatwick Parks and Rec department. Earlier today, Emmett exchanged the key to the park's gate for fifty dollars, palming the money and sliding it into the kid's outstretched hand like he's seen in movies.

Before long, the others start to arrive, these people I watch over. The same people I was charged with watching my entire life, even though I didn't know it at the time. It was a while after my death before I stopped being angry with them. Before I died, I put it all on them. I blamed Ruby for throwing me out of her dorm and never reaching out again; Murphy for hitting me the way my stepfather hit me and then abandoning Ruby, proving to me he wasn't the friend I thought he was; Ally for breaking my heart, for choosing Aaron over and over and making me feel worthless; and Emmett for always giving me such a hard time, for not helping me when I really needed it.

In a way, I expected all of them to save me, but once I got here, I realized that wasn't their job. The living have this Hollywood notion that friends are meant to save each other, but really we're all just there to exist alongside each other, occasionally holding someone else's pain in our own hearts to grant them a moment of respite. When I got here, I had to forgive them, because now I understand that they are just human. Like I was.

Ally comes next, the only one accompanied by a guest. She bounces constantly now, in part to comfort the baby swaddled tightly to her chest in a kangaroo pouch contraption, in part to comfort herself. This is the first time she's left the house in weeks, and she feels a sliver of the insecurity Ruby wrestles with when she's in Chatwick—unsure of her place now that she has a new role. Isabelle is less than a month old, and it shows in the bags under Ally's eyes, the hair free of its usual careful coloring and styling, the pooch that remains from her stretched belly.

She is still every bit as beautiful as the girl I quietly lusted after for most of my adolescent years. More, perhaps. She loves Isabelle fiercely, but motherhood has been surprisingly hard for her to adjust to. Breastfeeding didn't work out no matter what she tried, which has made her feel like a failure, and while her heart is fully charged, she is exhausted and overwhelmed by the demanding little life she holds.

Aaron pretty quickly forgave her for her tryst with me, under the condition that she never again invoke the name Christie Bedard.

She hasn't since, but she will. And he will throw my name back in her face. That's marriage, from what I've seen. Regardless, she asked her husband to stay at home for this gathering. She wanted to say goodbye to me without Aaron looking for some sign of residual feelings. Fearing a hormonal surge, he didn't argue. Besides, I'm already dead; I'm not exactly a threat to him anymore. Not that I ever really was.

Murphy comes next, his nerves dampening the ferocity of his usually confident swagger. He hasn't seen or spoken to Ruby since their lunch on New Year's Day. He's picked up the phone to call, especially when he wakes from one of his nightmares, but he always hangs up before pressing Send.

Not long after the wedding, he told Krystal it was over. He was never going to commit to her, and he didn't want to waste her time. He did her a favor, but she doesn't exactly see it that way. Poor Krystal.

Murphy has been a suspiciously good "uncle" to Isabelle, constantly dropping by with new toys she's too young to play with, picking her up and making a fuss over her. Ally is confused by it, but grateful for the few minutes she can duck out of the room to take a shower.

Ruby is the last to arrive, her anxiety surrounding her in a fog no one but I can see. She hasn't been home since the wedding, but she's talked to Emmett several times, and she and Ally talk every Thursday evening. When Izzy was born, they Skyped, giggling as Ally held the baby up to the webcam as if she were Simba from *The Lion King*. Because of all the time Ruby has already taken away from work, and her rigid new self-imposed writing schedule, she wasn't able to come home for Ally's baby shower *and* for this gathering. Ally chose this. She had plenty of women at her baby shower, but no other woman in the world could understand *this*.

The crew greets each other warmly. Ruby and Murphy are the last two to embrace. Neither of them knows what Steph overheard in the stairwell. She's never told anyone, including her husband, proving further that she is too good for our Emmett.

They speak, one by one, about me and about the slip of paper they each hold in their hands. A secret of theirs I scribbled angrily before ending my life. A game I *thought* I was creating just to mess with them, to shake them out of their monotonous existences.

I feel like an asshole for putting Mom in the position that I did. I watched as she struggled over those hateful words I wrote, crying in her car after putting a follow-up threat in a mailbox or under a car windshield, or after hours of trying to figure out how to set up an anonymous email account. (Okay, I had a *bit* of a chuckle over that one, but I immediately felt bad about it.)

I thought what I wanted was to embarrass them, but when she brought that letter up to the podium at the wedding, I could have died all over again. Reading it at Emmett's wedding? It would have been a bit more soap opera than I intended, but just imagine Emmett's face as Mom announced—*in church*—that he was a drug dealer! And that's not to mention all the others. The scene *alone* following that would have fed the Chat for the entire next year!

I wish I could tell Charlene now that it all served a much higher purpose in the end, that what she's tortured herself over actually turned out okay. If I hadn't outed my friends, if she hadn't kept on top of them, they would have drifted back apart the minute I was in the ground. And worse, their secrets would have remained as buried as my body, never to be dealt with. I can't really blame them for not sharing the whole truth. They don't want to shine a light on the darkest parts of their souls, the weakest parts. They were sure, like all of us are sure, that no one could possibly love us if they knew who we truly are.

What they don't understand—what I didn't understand myself, until now—is that those dark, weak parts are not ugly. They are not unlovable. They are what make us beautiful. Resilient. Strong. They turn us into who we were meant to be. The way to be sure that happens, and to be sure we won't be crushed by the burden, is to redistribute the weight a little so someone else can come along, wedge their shoulder under it, and help us carry it.

Emmett starts off the ceremony, reading the same fake secret Steph did months before. He is happy to report his condition remains stable, and he is adjusting to "life at a lower intensity." (After this, he will pitch this phrase to Ruby for her next writing project, to which she will reply, "Write your own damn book.") He apologizes to the crew for hiding his illness from them, but they wave him away. Who are they not to forgive him?

When he's done talking, he tosses the slip of paper into the fire, and everyone cheers. Ruby shows no sign that she knows his real secret. Murphy doesn't either, although he was in on the scam. The garage Emmett went to? In Montreal? I had no connection to it. When Murphy's brother came for his weekly weed purchase, I made sure to tell him all about the big joke, including the dates of Emmett's "drug runs." Just as I suspected, the little puppet ran straight to Murphy, who took over from there, leaving envelopes of cash in Emmett's mailbox in the middle of the night.

Murphy never said a word to anyone, and I wish I had thanked him. And now that Emmett is out of the woods, I *really* wish I could tell him what we did, just to see the look on his face. God help me, I still get a chuckle out of it. I *do* feel a little bad that Emmett feels responsible for those people who died, but the work he and Steph are doing at the clinic has changed him, made him more compassionate, made him understand me better. And those people really do need help. It's that whole higher-purpose thing again.

Ally goes next. She talks about our time together, and how as much as she loves Aaron, she misses the way I used to let her be the worst version of herself, the weakest and the meanest, because with everyone else she felt like she had to be perfect. She's learning to let go of the mean, but share the weak. The sick thing? I preferred her at her worst because that's when she needed me. In the end, I was made of some of the same stuff as Roger. Ruby knows that from that awful fight in her dorm room. I'm not proud of it. (When she's done talking, she tosses her slip of paper into the fire, and everyone cheers.)

Murphy relays my phone call telling him Ruby was going to have an abortion. He says how much he regrets letting her go through it alone. He tells them he's been trying to change, to grow up, to get ready for a family. Nobody but Ally notices the look he shoots at Ruby when he says it. When Murphy's done talking, he tosses his slip of paper into the fire, and everyone cheers.

Ruby apologizes for hiding her pregnancy from Murphy, careful not to use the word *abortion*. A lot of questions came after their secrets were revealed, and piece by piece, the truth about what happened between them the year leading up to the pregnancy came out. Depending on who you ask, it is either a love story that has yet to find its true end (Ally), or a simple tale of a horny teenage boy who would do or say *anything* and everything to keep having sex after losing his virginity (Emmett). Only I know the truth.

Ruby talks about how my death has made her deal with things she hadn't gotten over, flicking her eyes to Murphy. She says she's finally truly moving on, and perhaps she finally is. Jamie, her old boyfriend, is coming to New York this summer to spend time with her, even scope out some "flats" if all goes as well as it has been on the phone. They've even talked about weekend getaways to some snowy, rustic cabin in Vermont—somewhere outside Chatwick but close enough to visit "the family." A change of pace from the city, where they can pour prose into their notebooks by a roaring fire. When Ruby's done talking, she tosses the slip of paper into the fire, and everyone cheers.

Ruby pulls out another slip of paper, mine, which she saved because it was one of the last things I ever wrote. During this visit home, she will visit my mother and collect the notebooks I filled up with poems and heroin-induced rants. She doesn't know it yet, but she will use them in her second novel, which will be about me. About all of us.

She hands the slip of paper to Murphy, her partner in my crime, and Murphy reads it to the crew. He and Ruby remember aloud the night Roger died, and all the nights leading up to it. The stones against Ruby's window. The bruises and cuts. The first of their late-night phone calls. Everybody cries, but when Isabelle joins them, they start to laugh. Then Murphy tosses my secret into the fire, and everyone cheers.

They have forgiven me my sins, and now I can move on, but I stay to watch for a while longer. I watch them as they hold hands—a little too Kumbaya for my taste, but okay. I watch the fire take their slips of paper, five pages of grief and love and shame igniting, pieces of them breaking away, little orange embers escaping into the black, cloudless sky.

They sniffle and watch, hypnotized, until the sound of a police siren jars them. They scramble to collect their chairs and the remainders of their bottles of beer. They run away, laughing, huddled together like a pack of wolves. They separate only when it comes time to jump into their cars and peel away from trouble, only to end up back together at Margie's Pub.

Look at them.

READING GROUP GUIDE

1. Imagine you are one of the crew listening to Danny's threatening letter. What do you do? Do you immediately tell the group your secret, or do you try to keep it hidden?

2. Secrets, and the many ways keeping secrets affect our lives, plays a major role throughout the book. How did keeping secrets affect the lives of each of the characters, as well as their friendships? How do you think their lives were changed when their secrets were revealed? How do the secrets we keep play a role in our own lives? Which member of the crew do you relate to the most: Ruby, Murphy, Ally, Emmett, or Danny? Why? Do you think you would've been able to keep their secrets? Whose perspective was most enjoyable to read? Who would you like to have heard more from?

3. Why do you think Danny set up this game? Was it because he wanted to bring his friends back together, or was something

more malevolent driving him forward? How do you think he would feel about the fact that none of them, at first, revealed their true secret?

4. Ruby St. James is the girl who got out of Chatwick. Do you think she is better off in New York City, or is she happier after returning to her hometown and confronting her past? Have you ever lived away from your hometown? How does it feel to return?

5. What do you make of the relationship between Ruby and her parents, particularly her mother? How do you think their relationship will change through Ruby's experience coming back to Chatwick?

6. Ally referred to Ruby and Murphy as darkness and light, respectively. How did this theme emerge throughout the story between them and other characters? Did it make sense to you that they did not end up together, or do you feel that their journey is incomplete?

7. We get the sense that Chatwick is the quintessential small-town America. What are the pros of living there? What are the cons? If you could move there, would you?

8. Describe Murphy and Ruby's friendship. Do you think it is a strong one? What do you think of Murphy when he chooses Taylor over Ruby after telling Ruby that he loved her? Do you think Ruby should forgive him?

9. Imagine yourself in Krystal's shoes. How would you react to Ruby returning to town? What if you were Ruby and you see that Krystal and Murphy have some sort of relationship? Do you think Krystal is justified to spill Ally's secret?

10. Who do you think has the biggest secret? What are the repercussions on the group?

11. Where do you think Danny's troubles began? Do you think his friends are partially responsible for his dark past or the way things ended for him? What could they have done differently?

12. How do you think Danny's letters affect each member of the crew? What do you think happens to each of them after the book ends?

13. Think of your closest or hometown friends. Do Ruby, Murphy, Ally, Emmett, or Danny remind you of any of them? In what ways? Do you think growing up with a group of friends makes them different from friends you meet later on in life? What is that bond like?

A CONVERSATION WITH
THE AUTHOR

What was your inspiration for Chatwick? Is it at all like where you grew up?

I did grow up in a small town in Vermont, which Chatwick was inspired by. Like Ruby, I moved away for a time but drifted in and out over the years. It's a special place that has gone through many phases, including a recent major revitalization to the downtown area, and I've always considered myself lucky to have grown up there. My husband and I actually plan to move there soon!

Which character do you relate to the most?

I actually relate to all of the characters. It's hard not to when you write through their perspectives!

I perhaps relate the most to Ruby because we share some similar experiences. When I was a teenager, I was desperate to get out of my hometown, and now that I've done that, I'm desperate to go back and be a part of that community. Ruby also has this dichotomy between belonging to her group and feeling outside of it. She feels different and dark and worries that if people really knew her, she wouldn't be loved or accepted. Who doesn't feel like that when they're in high school?

Which character was the most challenging to write?

Danny, for sure. Especially in the prologue, because I had to make him so mean to all the characters I love so dearly. But I had to show how angry he was at the people he used to count as friends in order to justify his behavior and the game he devised. A lot of people feel sorry for Danny—and, of course, he *was* a tragic character—but I was also frustrated with him because he consistently blamed others for his problems, many of which were of his own creation. And because he committed suicide, he didn't get to have that growth that the other characters got to experience throughout the book. I took tremendous creative license by having him experience this posthumously, but I just *had* to show that he had seen the error of his ways and became more loving and forgiving of the characters.

On the other hand, the most *fun* to write was definitely Ally. She is loosely based on a real person, but I amped her up about ten notches to be more of a Queen Bee type, and it was so fun to write through her perspective. When I read her back, she still cracks me up!

Your novel centers on the, at times, fragile but overall unshakable bond between these five childhood friends. While writing, did your own friendships serve as inspiration for these characters?

Yes. Like the town, the characters are also inspired by a group of friends I grew up with. As with Ally, I amplified everyone to create a more dramatic story, and I mixed and matched some qualities to create common themes. What I really wanted to capture was the unique relationships we had between each other and as a group. It's very cool how our friendship has changed and evolved but always kept the same solid foundation. I gave them each a copy of the book before it was published, and thankfully, they were all supportive and still like me!

Do you think there is a difference between the friendships we make when we are young versus the friendships we discover later in life?

Absolutely. The friendships we form when we're young—particularly ones that endure through adolescence and beyond—are so much more intense than the ones we develop as adults. Our very identity in youth is often wrapped up in who we're friends with. We're dependent on our friends for acceptance and belonging in school and outside our family structure. Childhood friends have such an influence on you and who you become even later in life. That's not to knock the friendships we form as adults—those help shape us and get us through the hard times as well. But when we grow up, partner off, and have children and busy careers, our priorities tend to change, and we're not as dependent on them in our daily lives.

I dedicated my book to "my crew, for the family kind of friendship that endures through all the drama, that feels the same no matter the time or distance between meetings, and that loves even when it doesn't like." I think that sums it up. I'm lucky to have the kind of friends who would drop anything to help and support each other, who have each other's backs, no questions asked.

Do you think Ruby gets a happily ever after once the story ends? Is it with Murphy or Jamie, or by herself?

Well, I certainly don't think I'm done with Ruby or any of these characters yet. I'm hoping I will get a chance to revisit them down the road, so we'll have to wait and see how Ruby's story continues... but I will say that I think Ruby is better off for having returned to Chatwick and unburdening herself of her secret to the people who really needed to know it. Murphy, of course, but also her mother, who she's had such a troubled relationship with. I think this revelation will help repair some of that damage and move them into the next phase of the parent/child relationship.

What do you think made Ruby and Murphy's relationship so complicated? Was it simply their youth or something more?

Oh goodness, what *wasn't* complicated about their relationship? I think they were originally bonded together by their shared secret with Danny about his stepfather's death, which is a lot for a couple of preteens to wrap their heads around. It was a somewhat tumultuous path to being best friends. Then, of course, whenever you introduce sex into a friendship, things get infinitely more complex. Murphy was Ruby's first love, which we all know is very powerful because it's the first time we experience such intense emotions, but it is compounded by the tie between Murphy and the baby she gave up (which she never allowed herself to process and move on from). They both have resentment toward each other—Ruby for being rejected and then later when she finds out Murphy knew she was pregnant and didn't reach out to her, and Murphy because Ruby didn't tell him about the pregnancy and because she took her friendship away as punishment for him choosing another girl. We also can't be sure what Murphy's feelings are (or ever were) for Ruby, but clearly, there is still a strong connection and attraction. They attempt to unpack all this in their last scene alone together. But as in life, we don't always get a tidy resolution or closure with the people from our past.

What do you like to do when you're not writing?

Ha! That's a funny question, because lately I feel like all I do is write. I also have a full-time job and do career coaching on the side, so I am one busy woman! But when I do have time, I like to veg out with my husband and my dog. We just started golfing together (my husband and I, not my dog and I), and my husband is very patient while I swear and beat my clubs into the ground. And I like to spend time with friends and family. I have three nieces and three nephews who I adore.

It's very easy to relate to Chatwick and this friend group. In some ways, it feels like the universal hometown and high school experience. How did you craft such a realistic portrayal?

Well, as I said, the town and friend group are heavily grounded in my experiences, so you can't get more realistic than that! But I think it's probably so easy to relate to because we all have those friendships, those traumatic events, those heartbreaks, those feelings of being trapped but also afraid to move on. No matter where we go in life, no matter how successful we become, everyone still has that traumatized little high schooler inside of them that they either try to live up to or overcome (or sometimes both).

If you could go back to your senior year and give high school Kaela some advice, what would it be?

Oh my God—SO much advice that high school Kaela probably wouldn't have listened to. I think I would have told her: Don't be afraid to share things with the people who love you (even, or especially, the ugly bits). Don't be afraid to be vulnerable and ask for help when you're going through something major. Don't push everyone away just because one person hurt you. Don't go to Boston—you'll hate it. Study psychology and writing in college instead of PR—you'll hate that too, once you start working in it. And for God's sake, your hair is curly; ditch the hair dryer and get some gel!

ACKNOWLEDGMENTS

First of all, I have to thank my agent, Stephanie Kip Rostan, and my editors, Shana Drehs and Sara O'Keefe, for championing this little piece of my heart. Your knowledge, guidance, and cheerleading have been much appreciated by this newbie.

Next, to my friends and family, thank you for the years and years and *years* you listened to me bitch about how hard it is to get published, without once outright saying that I should give up on the dream.

So many thanks to the wonderful people who read this book in its early phases: Randy Coble, Shayla Ruland, Cathy Wille, Meredith Tate Servello, Kathryn Saris, Loren Bowley Dow, and my mom, Deborah Plant (who, reverting to her schoolteacher days, put a checkmark at the top of every page that didn't contain a spelling or grammatical error), and to Louise Walters, my mentor through the WoMentoring Project. Without question, your honest feedback and relentless encouragement are what made this manuscript worth publishing in the first place.

I would be remiss if I didn't mention the beta readers for my first novel: Rebecca Nichol, Brian Holmes, Jaci Mills, and Veronica Grenier. Even though that book was not published, you gave your time and patience as you slogged through my early drafts and offered constructive criticism and ideas. Perhaps almost as important, you helped me get used to receiving feedback without inhaling a Costco-size chocolate cake in response.

To Meredith Tate Servello and Kristin Fields, thank you for all the advice and support you've offered me in the process of trying to get published. Thank goodness for Twitter, or I would never have met you! And to Amy Burrell Cormier, my writer friend, for understanding the trials and tribulations of being a writer. May we one day (tomorrow?) be sitting with a pitcher of margaritas, laughing about our naïveté.

The most meaningful compliment I received, and will ever receive, about this novel came from my sister, Stina Booth, who said she teared up at the end, sad that the story was over. If you knew her, you would know this is the highest praise conceivable.

And finally, I must acknowledge the most patient man in the world: my husband, Randy Coble, for dutifully playing video games or watching ESPN (anything I'm not interested in), so I can zone in on my writing, for cooking dinner on the nights I need more time to write, for making me take a break when he knows I'm burned out, and for holding my hand when I doubted the ability to make this dream come true. Abubus.

ABOUT THE AUTHOR

Kaela Coble is a member of the League of Vermont Writers and the Women's Fiction Writers Association, a voracious reader, and a hopeless addict to bad television and good chocolate. She lives with her husband in Burlington, Vermont, and is a devoted mother to their rescued chuggle, Gus.